THE SKIPTON HAUNTING

TALE OF THE RED RIBBON WITCH

ANDREW JOHN BELL

(SECOND EDITION)

COPYRIGHT AND DISCLAIMERS NOTICE

This book is based on true events, although names and places have been amended to protect individual identities by the author. There have been some scenes included which are fictional and are purely intended for entertainment purposes only. Any unwitting resemblance to persons alive or dead, events or places are categorically coincidental (in these fictional cases).

Warning: This book contains scenes of a sexual nature, violence, paranormal activity, and use of explicit language that some readers may find disturbing and/or offensive. Use of the South Durham accent is also prevalent, which some readers may find difficult to understand. This book is not intended for readers below the age of 18.

Advisory: Do not read out aloud any Latin verses... who knows what the consequences may be?

DEDICATION

To Helen, Lilly and Sophie (my light in the darkness).
To my uncle, Stuart.

I also dedicate this second edition to those who continue to support me with my writing progress. Thank you.

Table of Contents

THE BRIDGE LEADING TO 'SKIPTON ROAD'

Chapter One

The need to move home had been plaguing John Davidson's thoughts for some considerable time now. He was steadily sinking into debt, and his minimum wage job as a care assistant would certainly not get him out of it. Making matters worse, John's landlord had recently increased the cost of his rent, thus leaving him with no other option but to search through countless websites for a new place to live. It was by no means an easy task to undertake, but thankfully John's wife, Hannah, stood by his side through thick and thin, granting him some much-needed love and support.

'That house is near Lucy's school,' said Hannah in reference to their four-year-old daughter. 'It's a bit pricey though, isn't it?'

'Yeah. We could never afford that. I'll keep looking,' replied John solemnly, whilst toying with his St. Christopher pendant. 'This is a nightmare.'

'Don't worry,' assured Hannah. 'We'll find a house soon enough. Speaking of Lucy, I'll need to pick her up from school in a little while. I don't want to be late.'

'How about this one?' asked John, as he eagerly pointed out a three-bedroomed terrace house to Hannah. 'It's bigger than where we are now... and cheaper. What do you think?' Hannah grunted back, shrugging her shoulders in a dismissive manner. She was increasingly nervous about relocating, seeing as their present home was situated right in the centre of town, and what neighbours they had were quiet - perfect. The part of Newton Escomb in County Durham, which John presently fixated his attention on, had gained a notoriety for drug dealing and anti-social behaviour – hardly an area fit to be raising a young child in.

'Looks nice,' muttered Hannah under her breath. However, she found an instant disdain for the aged architecture and obvious small garden space. 'How much is it a month?'

'Let's see. Where's the rent price at on this webpage?' John immediately peered through the endless small print in search of the elusive figures. Eventually, he found them and gleamed back at Hannah with an enthusiastic smirk. 'Three-fifty a month. That's not bad... not bad at all! Just think of what we could do with the extra cash we'll save!' John's tremoring fingertips moved his laptop's cursor over the 'submit application' icon, preparing to activate it at any given second. Hannah nodded back slowly in agreement to her husband, though with a subtle hint of reluctance present within her hazel eyes.

'It seems too good to be true. Are you *really* sure about this, John?' whispered Hannah anxiously. 'I know it's expensive living here but we're happy, aren't we?' John's premature ecstasy quickly fell into despair. He and Hannah had talked about this move for over a month now, so why the sudden change of heart?

'Of course, I'm sure!' countered John with a look of frustration. 'We're doing this for Lucy. I'm sick of having to buy her cheap and nasty clothes. I want to treat our princess.' John then swiped the cursor away from the 'submit' button, confused beyond any reasoning as to where he and Hannah now stood on this fickle subject. 'We've already gone over this, Han. Are you not wanting to move now?'

Hannah gave out a remorseful sigh in response. It was more the fact that she had grown accustomed to their current lifestyle, albeit one stricken with borderline poverty. Without further word, Hannah repositioned the cursor herself and smiled back to her despairing husband.

'I do as well, John. I want a better life for our Lucy,' she implored. 'I'm just a little scared, that's all. We've lived here for six years now. This has been a good home to us. I'm worried about how Lucy will adapt, too - it's such a big change for her."

'I know,' replied John, slowly exhaling in a sympathetic manner. It was undoubtedly apparent to Hannah, though it unsettled her more, that this concern also lingered in John's thoughts. 'She's only a bairn... kids adapt well to change. I know I did after Mam and Dad divorced, back when I was little. At least we're not forcing that bombshell on her.'

'Never!' snapped Hannah lovingly in response, as she leant into John for a wantful kiss. 'I love you, John. I know you're doing this for our benefit... but it's just so much to take in.' John kissed Hannah again before returning to his laptop. An overwhelming sense of pleasure now coursed through his veins.

'Here goes nothing.' John playfully tapped to initiate the cursor onscreen. Within minutes their housing application had been accepted, and the harsh reality soon hit both Hannah and John that they were going to leave the settled, albeit impoverished, life they knew behind.

'That wasn't so bad, was it?' quipped John with a casual wink. 'I'd best phone Dad to see if he has one of his vans free sometime next week. You know how busy he gets this time of year - delivering eBay parcels and all those unwanted Christmas presents.' Hannah grunted back in detest once again. Moving just after the festive period, in her mind, was ridiculous and so ill-thought.

'You've only been speaking to one another for a few months now. Are you sure Dennis will help us move?' she seethed, knowing all-too-well that John had not yet even mentioned involving his biological father in the move.

'Dad's alright, Han. We've gotten over things now,' mumbled John bitterly. He hated talking about this period in his life, where he and his father went for two years without saying a word to one another. 'I know that he'll help us out. I've already messaged him about us wanting to move.' John deliberately kept his eyes from meeting with Hannah's; she had a keen ability to sense when he was not telling the truth. 'Seriously, we're cool now – chill_out.'

'Aye, for sure,' chuckled Hannah, whilst giving to John a contemptuous glare. 'Don't leave it until the last minute to phone him. Dennis' memory is just as bad as yours, John.' She formed a satisfied grin, tightly folding her arms together. 'You *know* I'm right.'

'Pardon?' sneered John, his mouth opened wide in shock. 'There's nothing wrong with my memory, and *you* needn't talk. Your memory's just as bad as mine.'

'Whatever,' said Hannah dismissively, with a flail of her arms. 'Anyway, I'll pick Lucy up from school today. At least where we're moving to is closer. Where is it again?'

'Seventy-One, Skipton Road, Newton Escomb, DL5 6G6,' explained John in an instructive tone. 'You'll need to tell your work about our move and the new address. I'll sort out the Council Tax and other bills, so don't you worry about them, okay?'

'Fine,' retorted Hannah. 'You go on like I'm an idiot, John. You can be such a tool at times.' John released a barrage of dirty laughter in response to this insult. *You can do better than that, Han*, he thought. Hannah switched off the Kindle she was reading and then left to collect their daughter from school, without any further word given to John.

'Give Lucy a big kiss from me when you see her!' emphasized John, as he ardently watching his wife walk away from their home. 'Love you!' He left it a few more tense seconds before moving his laptop's cursor onto a hidden tab. 'That should give me half an hour or so.' John formed a widened smile and began rubbing his hands together eagerly. 'Now for a bit of 'Me' time.' Suddenly, John's cell phone burst into song. 'For God's sake, man.' His chosen ringtone was *Streams of Whiskey* by 'The Pogues', only because he smiled inside every time it rang. However, it didn't this time. '01388 - who the fuck?' John swiped the answer button across on his smartphone to accept, trying not to reveal any anger as he responded. 'Hello?'

'Hello and Good Afternoon, Mr. Davidson,' replied the nuisance caller. Their voice was over-exaggerated in pronunciation, just how the old BBC reporters sounded during the 1950's and 60's. 'My name is Christopher. I am calling on behalf of your new landlord, who themselves wish to remain anonymous.' John slowly licked at his parched lips. The disappointment of not having any 'alone' time then swiftly left from him.

'Yes, speaking,' answered John, and in his politest "phone voice". 'Are you calling about the house on Skipton Road... number seventy-one?' The caller coughed in an awkward fashion; it seemed they were strangely apprehensive for some reason. 'Hello?'

'Yes, Mr. Davidson. This call is just to let you know that your bid has been successful. You will need to call into our offices at some point to sign the necessary documents.'

'That's great!' John declared. His fingers were trembling more now though not from his usual anxiety, but from anticipation. 'When can I get the keys, then?' The caller hesitated for a few more seconds. The irritating sound of typing then resounded through John's ears, his thinning patience almost at boiling point now. 'I want this to be a quick move.'

'Whenever you are ready, Mr. Davidson.' The caller seemed surprised himself to be saying this. 'The landlord has noted that they want new tenants in as soon as possible.'

'By, that's quick!' John gasped. 'I work twelve-hour shifts in a care home, so the next chance I'll get will be in a few days. Is that okay?' The static white noise crackling between them irritated John further, and why was the caller so reluctant to answer?

'This address has been unoccupied for some time, Mr. Davidson. The present landlord seems desperate himself for anyone to move in. No credit checks are required. Is next Wednesday okay?' whispered the caller, his reason for speaking in this coy way still remaining unclear to John. 'They're even willing to waver the usual administrative costs in order to speed up this agreement between yourselves. It's your lucky day!' John licked at his lips hungrily. More money to be saved.

'Sounds fine to me,' said John in an assuring tone. 'I'll need to speak with my wife, but I can't see there being a problem.'

'Fantastic, Mr. Davidson.' The caller sounded far-too overjoyed at John's willingness and naivety. 'On second thoughts, I will send out the documents and keys to you - don't worry about coming to see me. Congratulations!' The line then abruptly fell dead.

Everything was happening so fast now for John. After a few deep breaths to calm himself, he carefully placed his laptop back into its previous position, praying that he could now use it and without being bothered again.

'What a pleb,' chuntered John, as he initiated the laptop again. Despite him having a close and adventurous relationship with Hannah, John found that old habits die hard. He loved playing on his retro video games whenever such a free moment arose, and of which was very rare these days. 'I only have fifteen minutes now... bollocks.' John's eyes scoured across his laptop's screen toward a secretive tab that he always had in waiting for such moments of personal enjoyment. The internet page in question housed an emulator which allowed you to play 'Super Mario 64' – John's favourite and most-nostalgic game. 'You... beauty!'

'John?!' shouted the familiar voice of his neighbour, as she peered through the living room's window - yet another, unwanted disturbance. 'Let me in! I've just seen Hannah!' It was Janice. Any other time, John would have been glad to share in a black coffee and cigarette with his friendly neighbour, though not right this second. 'Howay, man. Let me in!'

'Won't be a moment, Jan!' replied John, his face moulding into one of a disappointment. 'I'm coming!' John hurriedly ushered Janice inside his humble abode. She already had a cigarette held in hand, aiming it towards his mouth with a lighter in the other.

'Alright, John? Have you stopped smoking yet?' questioned Janice, with a judgemental stare. 'I've just bought a sleeve off a friend for thirty-quid. You can have some if you like?'

'I haven't got much chance in stopping with you around, have I?' laughed John, though he still took the cigarette from Janice anyway. 'Not when you're making offers like that to me.'

'There's worse habits, hun.' Janice flickered her lighter under his tremoring lips igniting the pungent tobacco between them, somewhat calming the anxious tensions that had risen from making such a huge change in his life. 'At least you're not smoking wacky-backy.' John shrugged his shoulders in response, whilst taking in the first draw from a strong cigarette in over three weeks. A cocktail of guilt and self-satisfaction now coursed through him.

'Too expensive that stuff, plus it stinks of dog shit,' he chortled, trying not to cough on the painful wave of tar-laden smoke. 'I had a space cake in Amsterdam a few years back... never again.' Janice cackled at this apparent confession. 'What? Do you not believe me, like?'

'Bollocks!' boasted Janice, as she swiped her cigarette through the air. 'You're a light-weight, John, and always have been.' John laughed back politely. 'You know I'm right.'

'I'm guessing that Hannah told you about us moving?' John had to question this in being desperate to break the ice, his guilt-ridden conscience now increasing with every passing second. Janice took in a few more draws herself before hugging into John tightly.

'Ya daft sod! Why are you moving away?' Janice's voice crackled with a distant melancholy. 'Bernie and I don't want you to go.' John frowned and tightened his own grip around Janice's torso. 'We've grown to like you.'

'We're doing it for Lucy... to give her a better chance in life.' John tried to explain his reasons calmly, though it was difficult. 'The rent's cheaper, plus we'll be closer to our family at Skipton Road.' Janice's face instantly fell into a fearful expression. 'What?'

'*Skipton Road*? That's where you're moving to?' Janice took in several more draws from her cigarette. 'Jesus, John - *really*?" John inhaled a lengthy and agonising wave of tobacco smoke himself, unsure as to why Janice had reacted in this way. 'Bloody Hell.'

'Aye, Skipton Road. What's wrong with that?' John eagerly accepted another cigarette from Janice's never-ending supply. 'It's no-worse than any other street in England.'

'John, love...' Janice exhaled slowly before continuing. Her hands then began to shake in an uncontrollable manner. She tried to contain the falling ashes from her cigarette with John's stale coffee mug, which he had neglected to consume prior to her visit. 'Skipton Road is a fucking drug's den. How is that a better life for Lucy?'

'No, it's not, Jan. That's a crock of shit,' said John, visibly bemused. 'It might have been that way in the eighties. Nowhere is perfect these days,' he sighed. 'There was a stabbing in this street only a couple of months ago, can you not remember?'

'That doesn't count,' countered Janice, with a staccato-like precision. 'Emily stabbed that bloke because he tried to mug her - it was self-defence! What would you have done?'

'He *cheated* on her, Jan. That's why Emily stabbed him. He was her boyfriend, not to mention a dirty-bastard-creep.' John detested how these violent acts were becoming more frequent. It was like living on a talk show, with drama present around every corner. 'We're moving next week, by the way. I just need to sign the papers when they arrive.'

'Have you not heard any of the horror stories about Skipton Road?' Janice's eyes flared with a hopeful glint. 'It's a bad area, John.' She took in another lengthy draw. 'Seriously.'

'Like I said: we're moving there, maybe next week... whether you like it or not, Jan. There's horror stories for every road on this town, for God's sake,' he sneered. John then moved his window's blinds further aside, desperate to see Lucy's smiling face as an escape from this present inquisition. 'Hannah is happy to move there as well. I'm sorry, Jan. It's nothing personal, like, we'll stay in touch with you. I promise.' Janice motioned back towards the doorway, her entire body language shifting to suggest how dismayed she was with John and his stubbornness.

'You'll regret it, Love,' she whispered tenderly, like a mother scolding their child. 'But, if it's what you want, then go right ahead. You better stay in touch with us.'

'Of course, we will,' responded John in a stern tone. 'It goes without saying that you'll be the first invited to our house-warming party.' Janice intensified her maternal stare.

'If it's at Skipton Road, I'd rather pass on the offer, hun. No offense.' Janice's voice wavered again in dread. 'Take care, John. See you around, maybe?' She quickly took it upon herself to leave and, to John's further annoyance, forgot to grant him any spare cigarettes, as she would do normally.

Now finally alone again, John glared towards his laptop in want of reliving his childhood days. However, the resurging desire to satiate his need for nicotine had grown stronger than ever.

'Great! What I wouldn't do for another tab,' lamented John. A familiar shooting pain in the temples, associated with his lack of nicotine, soon rose to torment him. 'She could have left me even just one tab. For fuck's sake, man.'

Suddenly, John's cell phone blared out 'The Pogues' once again. It was rapidly losing its past, humorous appeal. 'Now, what?' The displayed number was instantly recognisable to him: it was Barbara, John's mother-in-law. 'Hi, Barb. How are you doing?'

'Hi, John!' Barbara seemed overly happy with her opening line. 'I hear that you're finally going to move home?'

'Aye,' said John frankly, while checking through the blinds for his elusive family. 'Hannah's been on the phone to you *already*?'

'Yes, pet. Hannah called me a few minutes ago with the good news.' Barbara gave out a gleeful squeak, deafening John momentarily. 'I'm so glad you're moving closer to us. It'll be so much better for Lucy.' John edged his way into the kitchen towards the fridge, in dire aim of retrieving a cold can of lager from within it. The beer would hardly replace his renewed lust for nicotine, but it was better than nothing.

'News travels faster through your Hannah than it does with the British tabloids,' jested John. He then tried to discreetly open his can out of earshot from Barbara. 'What's Hannah told you?'

'She just said that you're moving closer to us.' Barbara's voice had a hint of curiosity in it that John had now accustomed himself to. 'Which street *is* your new house in? Hannah didn't say.' John took a few sips from his frothy beverage and immediately choked. It was super-strength, at least nine percent, and ran down his throat more like treacle than lager, a gift he had willingly accepted from Hannah's father, Ivan.

'Skipton Road. It's just down from the 'Tin Donkey' pub.' An eerie silence followed from Barbara, though John used this to his advantage by taking in a few more gulps of rancid alcohol (without spluttering this time).

'Oh, that will be change from where you are in Bourbon Close,' stammered Barbara. John instantly knew that his mother-in-law disproved of where he was relocating her youngest offspring. 'Isn't it quite rough around there?'

'It's no different from any other street on this town, Barb.' John's voice hinted at some irritation. The beer, to his dismay, was having little effect on calming his shaken nerves. 'We might be moving in next week. I was just about to call Dad to arrange for one of his vans.'

'Sorry, sweetheart,' responded Barbara, her tone still noticeably unsettled. 'I'll let you crack on. You'll have so much to sort out. Send my love to Hannah and Lucy. I'll pop over later.'

'Cheers, Barb. I just want Hannah and Lucy to be happy, that's all,' assured John, and with little effect. 'I'll let you know what's happening. Please, don't worry about us.'

'Okay, Love. I'll see you tonight.' Barbara swiftly ended the call, something she had never done with John before.

'Bloody Hell. I didn't think I'd be getting this much grief!' John was becoming steadily enraged. After releasing a few angry grunts, he poured the remaining beer into his kitchen's sink. 'The last thing I need is to be getting hooked on this shit again. Fucking gut-rot.' John then sat himself upon his worn, leather sofa. The daunting prospect of moving home now firmly cemented in his troubled mind. 'Maybe I am rushing into this?'

Hannah and Lucy were unusually late. Instead of looking out the window like a gawking, peeping-tom for them, John used this time to type in his father's phone number, activating an awkward call between them. Thankfully, it didn't take long for a response.

'Alright, Son?' John's father was barely audible on answering; he was using his hands-free kit. All that John could hear were the whooshing noises of passing cars and nineties trance music booming in the background. More irritation. 'I'm...driving...A1...'

'Dad, can you hear me?' shouted John at his phone's shaking screen. 'Turn your music down!' Gradually, all that remained was the sound of speeding cars and his father's occasional gear change.

'Sorry about that, Son. I can hear you fine,' bellowed Dennis, and more understandable now. 'I'm on my way to London at the minute. The traffic down here is radge! It's going to be a long haul in getting home.'

'Nightmare, Dad,' humoured John, though with a hidden and dire concern for his father's safety. Dennis had recently suffered from a horrific stroke, although he had managed to make a "full" recovery. 'Be careful, and don't get caught out by the congestion charge again.'

'Oh, Aye!' responded Dennis, amongst some guttural laughter. 'The bastards caught me out big-time, didn't they? How's Hannah and Lucy doing?'

'Well, Dad, that's why I'm calling you,' moaned John, almost apologetically. 'We're moving to Skipton Road next week. Is there any chance of borrowing one of your vans?' The line went quiet for a few seconds. John prepared himself for yet another lecture.

'It's a bit short notice, Son,' whined Dennis, with reluctance streaming through his drawn-out words. 'I'll do my best to keep a van free, alright? And I'll ask one of my lads to help you as well. If it's Ronnie just give him fifty-quid and a few cans of cider - that should square him up.'

'Thanks, Dad.; John gasped in relief. It was one less thing to worry about. Dennis turned his trance music back up, a familiar signal that their conversation was coming to its end. 'I know that you're busy, Dad, so I'll text you sometime during the week to arrange things.'

'No bother. Take care, Son.' John's phone fell silent again. It was almost four o'clock, an hour after his family should have returned. Only the worst, however unlikely, scenarios now trickled through John's comprehension: they could have been knocked down by a car or, even worse, chosen not to return at all. *Moving home can be so stressful*, he contemplated.

'Where *are* they?' John peeked through his blinds again. He could smell the stale alcohol on his breath, but there was so little time to hide this now. 'It shouldn't have taken this long.' Just down the road, two small figures eventually emerged - they were Hannah and Lucy. Hannah was difficult for John to distinguish at first as she was wearing a thick winter coat, with only her long, mousey hair creeping out from under its furry hood to serve as a clarifying feature. Lucy was wearing her school uniform. With her curly, blonde hair, traipsing down the full breadth of her own thick coat, she looked so tiny – far too young to be away from her parents' side. John could hear Hannah and Lucy singing nursery rhymes to one another, each so blissfully unaware of the distress their lapse in punctuality had caused to him. 'It's about *bloody* time.'

'Daddy!' screeched Lucy on seeing her father. 'We have a new house!' she kept repeating, ardently. For a four-year-old child, Lucy was extremely intelligent, although still very naïve in many other aspects. How his daughter would react, after leaving the comfort of her only home so far, was John's greatest worry at this present moment. He reached down for his coffee mug, stupidly forgetting that Janice had stubbed her cigarette out in it, hoping to somehow freshen his putrid breath with its curdling contents. John immediately spat the cold remnants of ash and caffeine back into his cup, disgusted and ashamed by his need to rely on such a destructive substance – the same one that had already caused so much upset between himself and Hannah.

'Hi, sweetheart!' shouted John from the doorway, whilst opening his arms to invite Lucy's welcomed embrace. 'I've missed you, babe. How was school today?' Lucy gently placed a finger over her mouth, as if suggesting it was a huge secret, and rolled her eyes up sideways. John imagined her doing various fun activities but doubted his daughter would reply likewise. 'Have you been a good girl today?'

'Yes, Daddy,' sang Lucy, her expression bashful and filled with joy. 'Mummy said that we have a new house. Where is it?' John discreetly laughed to himself, recounting each reprimand he had just received for mentioning the infamous 'Skipton Road'.

'I'll show you after dinner, alright?' John leant down to kiss Lucy on her brow. As he looked up towards Hannah it was plain to see that she had a grave look on her face. 'What's wrong now?'

'I'm just a little nervous still.' Hannah swiftly brushed by John to get inside their home, omitting the kiss that he had anticipated from her. 'We haven't even seen it yet. Those pictures you showed me, they can't tell you what the neighbours and house are going to be like. I'm not sure if this is a good idea now.'

'Don't listen to what others say about the estate,' said John tenderly. He didn't want to make matters any worse by causing an argument – he never won them anyway. 'We'll have a look later on for ourselves. Until today, I hadn't heard one bad thing about that street.' John's attempt to calm Hannah's reserve sadly lacked the effect he wanted. She removed Lucy's coat and ordered for her to go upstairs and play, leaving both herself and John to stand in an uncomfortable silence for a few more seconds.

'Dad's sorting out a van for us next week,' assured John, with a pitiful squeal, hoping to break the current stalemate. 'He's down London today, making a big delivery.'

'Good for him!' snapped Hannah, showing little interest in Dennis' endeavours. 'Did you remind Den about the congestion charges? He's been caught out twice now.' She folded her arms and gave John a look to say: *like father, like son.* John even accepted the harsh fact himself that his memory was uncommonly terrible.

'Yeah...he knows,' sniggered John. 'I'll make us some fajitas for dinner, so don't be too long in getting changed.' He could just make out a few choice words coming from Hannah as she stormed upstairs, and they weren't endearing. 'Doesn't matter, Darlin'. Take as long as you need...' John looked down at his phone again, surprised that he had not received any more calls. He then checked his Facebook account – no messages; then his emails – nothing there, either. After rubbing at his tired eyes, John then swiped through a personal playlist he had recently made on YouTube.

'What a day,' sighed John with a lengthy yawn, as he scrolled down the endless stream of artist names and hashtags. 'Some 'Joy Division' should do the trick.' He inadvertently chose the song: *She's lost control* - not the greatest decision he could have made, since Hannah mistook it to be a personal jibe from her husband.

'John, turn that crap off – it's so depressing!' commanded Hannah, now from Lucy's bedroom. John grumbled in objection to his wife's apparent lack of musical taste, which he had hoped would have worn off on her by now. John continued to scroll through his never-ending playlist in a pleasant daze.

'How about this one, then?' he called out, enthusiastically. Within seconds, the first few chords from *Don't dictate* by 'Penetration' started to play. 'They're from 'round here, this band. *Proper* music!'

'Stop taking the mick, John!' Hannah's voice had risen and became more frustrated, signalling to her husband that his own tastes were not being appreciated. 'Put something we all like on!'

'Fine.' John subjected himself to Hannah's overpowering will. He swiped across his phone's screen with a furious precision. 'There you go!' The song he now chose, to suppress Hannah's fury, was *Hazard* by 'Richard Marx'. This decision seemed to go down well with Hannah, seeing as she aimed no further insults at her husband afterwards. *'She used to love the sun go down...'* hummed John in tune, as he started to delicately slice away at some red onions. Tears began to form in his eyes, and he was unsure as to whether they were caused by the acidic fumes or mounting pressure presently building up inside. 'Get a grip of yourself, John,' he thought to himself. 'You need to be strong for Hannah and Lucy. *Tears don't solve anything* – that's what Dad always says.'

21

'Is dinner ready, Daddy?' whined Lucy in a high-pitched squeal. 'I'm *so* hungry!' she emphasised, successfully forcing John into an unwilling guilt-trip with little exertion needed. 'My tummy hurts!'

'Nearly ready, babe!' John shouted back over the crackling sounds of sizzling chicken and shrivelling vegetables. 'Come down and set the table for Mummy and Daddy, please!' Tiny footsteps soon bounded down the staircase, which itself lay just above where John now stood. 'Like a herd of elephants, you two!' he joked. 'Come on, you're not the only ones who are hungry!' John and his family then sat down for their evening meal, with his playlist set onto shuffle mode (much to Hannah's further annoyance).

'You listen to some weird music, John,' laughed Hannah, as she took in a few painful mouthfuls of spicy fajita sauce. 'That's why I love you, though - you're so random.'

'Thanks!' spluttered John, with a mouthful of burning sauce himself. 'Hurry up and finish. We'll go see the new house when you do.'

'Yes!' exclaimed Lucy. 'I want to see it now! I want to see my new house!' Hannah playfully scrubbed at her daughter's hair, then looked to John with raised eyebrows.

'At least *someone* is looking forward to moving,' chuntered John, easing some of his fermented frustration. Hannah raised her eyebrows even higher with a glaring stare to follow. 'I'm just saying, Han. I've had nothing but grief from people about moving to Skipton Road. It's doing my head in.'

'If you're moving us to a shit hole, John, I'm leaving you.... and I'm *not* kidding.' Hannah said this as a joke, but John failed to see the funny side of it. 'Lighten up a little, hun. I'm only messing with you.'

'Aye,' whispered John anxiously. His meal seemed to take on a bitter taste now. 'There's *nothing* wrong with that area,' he snapped, taking both Hannah and Lucy by surprise. 'I don't want another word said against it, alright? I'm doing my best.' Hannah lowered her eyes away from John, secretly angered by his attempt to silence what concerns she had. Her husband did suffer from chronic anxiety and depression, but this didn't justify the way he was talking to her. 'I don't mean to take it out on you.'

During the remainder of their meal, Hannah and John ate without speaking, both reluctant to fall further out of favour with the other. Lucy whistled away to herself quite happily, innocent to what troubles lingered in the surrounding and tense atmosphere.

'Howay, you two – finish up!' implored John. He was being cautious with his tone now as he, Hannah and Lucy placed their cutlery upon the empty plates in front of them. 'Let's go take a look at our new house. The suspense is killing me.'

'I swear to God, John,' growled Hannah through gritted teeth, deliberately trying not to attract her daughter's attention. 'If it's a dive, we are not living there. I'd rather stay put here.'

'Give it chance, *please*, Han. Don't you be giving me grief as well,' begged John, with pathetic-looking puppy-dog eyes. 'It can't be all that bad...can it?'

'From what I've heard today – yeah,' replied Hannah, ominously. 'Mum says—'

'Just give it a chance, man.' John slid himself away from the table, his patience growing fouler by the second. 'We'll see for ourselves soon enough, won't we?'

'I guess so?' Hannah begrudgingly accepted John's lack of empathy. She and Lucy then made their way towards the exterior door, where they spent five minutes cladding themselves with numerous layers of clothing – it was February, after-all. 'Are *you* coming, John?'

'I'm sick of all the crap I've been getting today. I'm absolutely fed up with it!' despaired John, whilst fighting with his hoodie's zip to close it. 'It's like...I can't do anything right. It's doing my head in.'

'I *know*, John. I understand.' Hannah's response was forced and, somewhat, resentful. 'At least it's not too far away. Come on, Lucy. Outside, please.' Lucy reached out for her favourite Barbie doll; it was stripped naked and had borne the brunt of her artistic crayon skills, looking more like a figure from the TV show 'Hammer House of Horrors' than anything else. Lucy quickly sped past her parents, jumped out from the open doorway, and proceeded to skip down the street – luckily in the right direction.

'Don't run off, Lucy! We won't be able to keep up with you!' pleaded John (being overweight certainly made it a struggle to match his daughter's agile pace). 'She takes after you, Han,' he sniggered to his wife, who herself was now keeping a comfortable distance away from him. 'Please don't be cross with me. I've got enough stress going on at the minute, for God's sake.' John held out a wanting hand to Hannah which shook tremendously through the desperation being fed into it. 'Look, I'm sorry for being such a dick.' Hannah couldn't help but smile at this affirmation. 'I... sorry.'

'I so wish I recorded you saying that,' snorted Hannah, whilst slowly wrapping her fingers around John's. 'Anyway, I'm starting to feel more excited about this move. It'll be a fresh start for us.'

'It will, hun.' John placed a firm kiss upon Hannah's hand and face. 'One door closes - another one opens, they say.'

Skipton Road was a mere ten-minute walk away from Bourbon Close; although, it actually took John and his family twenty minutes, due to Lucy slowly skipping for most of the way. A small, make-shift bridge separated Skipton Road from Newton Escomb's town centre. Beneath the dainty causeway, a thin stream ran across the whole length of Skipton Road's housing estate. It was murky and clouded by sediment from the recent rainfall, and also smelled heavily of rat urine.

'Don't lean over the bridge, Lucy! You'll fall in!' screamed
Hannah, as her child clasped onto its rusty railings. 'Be careful, for
goodness sake!'

'I'm looking for fish, Mammy. I want to find Nemo,' replied
Lucy in a stern manner, much like her mother would when
disappointed with her, even down to the forced frown and raised
eyebrows. 'I can't see any. They must have all swam away. Poor
Nemo.' John investigated the stream himself, trying desperately
not to gag on the sickening stench of wet rodents that lay nearby.
'Can you see any fishes, Daddy?'

'There's no fish, sweetheart - but plenty of pennies!' replied
John, in an exaggerated voice. 'Should *we* make a wish? It looks
like a lot of other people have.' Hannah faintly laughed to herself,
her eyes rolling in disapproval to John's innocent gesture. 'What?
Do you not believe in magic, Han?' mocked John, whimsically.
'You'll upset the river faeries thinking that way. I believe in
magic... so should you.'

'If it helps get rid of all the bad luck we've been having, I'm all
for it,' whined Hannah. She gently released her tightened hold
from Lucy, just so that the child had enough space to move her
arms. 'Be careful...'

'Come on, Daddy!' bleated Lucy excitedly, with her hands held
out in anticipation. 'Can I have some pennies to throw into the
magic river? pretty-please!'

'Here...' John fed a hand into his jean pockets, brushing aside his
phone, his half-empty lighter and an old toffee wrapper (which he
couldn't remember placing there), eventually finding a single
pound coin which he then quickly gave to Lucy. 'Don't tell anyone
what you're wishing for; otherwise, the spell won't work!' he
murmured, hoping to highlight the mystery. 'Make it count!'

'I wish... I wish...' whispered Lucy, with her hands placed
together as if in prayer. 'Oh, I wish...'

'Please just throw the coin in, Lucy,' pleaded Hannah, her lips shivering from the passing cold breeze. 'It's bloody freezing out here.' Lucy threw her golden coin into the murky depths without further thought. It gradually sank to join countless other wishes, many of which were likely unanswered. 'There's a good girl. Now, hold onto Daddy's hands and *don't* wander off, okay?' Lucy nodded her head and clasped onto John's arms lovingly, his hands being too cold to touch.

A dense haze eerily lingered in the surrounding air as John and his family moved closer towards Skipton Road. Newton Escomb had been founded on foggy marshland, which during the Second World War was ideal to hide a secret ammunition factory there. It was nothing more than a frequent nuisance now.

'Nearly there,' said John through his chattering teeth. 'It's just around the corner.' Lucy suddenly gasped and pointed through the growing mist. 'What's the matter, sweetheart?'

'Look, Daddy! There's a park!' Lucy pulled at her father's arms with an astonishing level of strength, dragging both over to the nearby play area. "Can we go play there? Please?"

'I don't think we have any time to...' John instinctively looked across to Hannah. He hated not giving Lucy what she wanted, but also knew how much his wife despised being out in the cold for longer than was necessary. 'Maybe another day, Lucy? It's too cold at the moment.' John kept his eyes firmly upon Hannah's. 'It looks like a nice area so far, Han. There's a nice park for Lucy to play in, and it's not too far from the town centre.'

'John, I'm freezing my tits off out here... hurry up!' snapped Hannah, her face momentarily flushing with a scarlet hue. 'You can play there tomorrow after school, Lucy. I promise,' she said in a gentler tone to her daughter. 'It's nearly dark now. There'll be naughty boys and girls hanging around there.'

'Okay, Mummy.' Lucy clasped onto John's arms again, then together they carried on along a narrow, tarmacked path. The pathway itself led up a muggy embankment, and at its end lay a small row of black-bricked terrace houses.

'So, this is the notorious Skipton Road? Spooky!" taunted John, whilst wavering his fingertips manically like a demented pianist. 'What do you think, Han?' He looked again to his doting wife for her reluctant verdict. 'It looks alright to me.'

'Why are they... black?' questioned Hannah, as she sunk her face further into her coat's furry hood. 'That's so... strange.'

'It just adds to the character, doesn't it?' replied John, his resolve stubborn and absolute. 'I bet that they're nice and warm inside - better than where we are now,' he said, while Lucy rubbed their hands together to form some wanted heat. The fog at this point had become thicker, steadily unbearable, and made the houses in front appear like towering shadows within the haunting midst.

'The house number is Seventy-One, isn't it?' chuntered Hannah, whilst moving over to stand closer beside John, yearning for his comforting touch. The trio then stared at Skipton Road's foreboding structures like lost children; they were curious in amazement, yet also greatly confounded. 'I think it's that one over there.' John glanced to where Hannah fixated her glare. A glimmering, golden sign faintly displayed the mentioned numbers.

'Aye, that's the one,' confirmed John, with a child-like grin. 'I have a good feeling about this street. Just think, this time next week we'll be moved in and all our worries will be in the past. It'll be a new era in our lives.'

'That's easy for you to say,' Hannah sneered, dismissively. 'Let's go back home. It's getting colder by the minute.'

'Do you not want a closer look?' John tilted his head in dismay and quickly sighed like a disenchanted teenager. 'I'm back at work tomorrow, Han. This'll be my only chance before the weekend to see what we're throwing our money into.'

'It's freezing out here, and the fog's getting worse too. No.' Hannah growled; despite the fact she could barely motion her rigid lips. 'You can stay, John, but we're going. Lucy, come here with Mummy.' She hastily grabbed onto Lucy's hands, tearing them both away from John's despairing presence. 'Bye, John,' she declared, from over her left shoulder. 'See you later.'

'I'm coming, I'm coming,' whimpered John, his face grimacing with disappointment. He looked once more at the blurry, black houses. John could swear that someone was watching them in the distance, though he didn't want to increase his wife's risen temper by investigating (for someone so quiet, Hannah could have a vicious tongue when she wanted to). 'This time next week...' John nodded to himself assuredly. 'This time next week.'

'Look what I've found, Mummy!' Lucy yanked at her mother's arms, aiming them towards the muddy embankment beside their pathway. 'It's so pretty - I want it!'

Amongst the dirty shards of grass, and under one of the dimly lit streetlamps, lay a single strand of tattered, crimson cloth. A very peculiar find.

'Don't touch it, Lucy!" Hannah's whole face contorted at the very sight of the tattered cloth. 'Who knows where that's been? A dog could have peed on it. Come on, sweetheart, before you catch a cold.' The crimson cloth sank further into its shallow grave. What past beauty the ribbon had was now corrupted by filth, neglect and time. 'Howay, John! I want to go home!' John caught a fleeting glimpse of the tattered ribbon as he walked by it. He wondered whether it had fallen from a baby's stroller, or maybe some kid dropped it on their walk home from school. It seemed so out of place. 'Please, John. This street is starting to give me the creeps.'

'Honestly, I'm going as quick as I can,' mumbled John to himself angrily. 'I can't see anything wrong with this street. You should never judge a book by its cover...'

CHAPTER TWO

The weather forecast for John's moving date had predicted a lengthy dry spell with occasional cloud. However, this could not have been any further from the truth.

'Sunny - my arse!' roared John at the T.V screen, his head held lowly within his hands. 'It *would* piss down with snow on the exact same day we're moving home, wouldn't it?'

'Calm down, John. It's not the end of the world,' pleaded Hannah, with rolling eyes. 'There's not that much to take over. We'll be fine.' She quickly ushered for Lucy to go and play out in the garden, away at least from her father's increasing despair. 'I'll put some old newspapers in the boxes to stop our stuff from getting wet. Stop worrying.'

'Thanks, Han,' replied John in a guilty tone. 'I'm sorry for getting so wound up.' He then nestled himself into Hannah's side and, to his relief, she kindly accepted the companionship being offered. 'Dad's van should have been here by now. I hope he hasn't forgotten about us moving today?'

'Dennis won't let us down, hun. You said so, yourself.' Hannah stroked at her husband's hands tenderly. She found that this would usually calm John's unpredictable bouts of anxiety. 'What time did your dad say he was coming over?'

'I-I can't remember. Oh, shit!' John reached down for his phone, which, to his greater frustration, had slid in-between the sofa's heavy cushions. 'Three missed calls. Bollocks.' He frantically swiped across the phone's greasy screen to retrieve his father's contact details. 'I'll try phoning him.'

'You're as bad as each other!' chuckled Hannah, increasing John's annoyance further. 'I don't see why he didn't just turn up. You're terrible for answering calls.'

'Shhh, it's ringing.' John raised a tremoring finger to rest upon his lips. 'Come on, Dad... answer!' A few tense seconds passed before the monotonous ringing tone burst into Dennis's familiar voice. 'Dad, can you hear me?' John tutted towards Hannah. His father was using a hands-free kit and, as usual, could barely be heard. 'I'm sorry that I missed your call. Are you alright?'

'It's okay, Son – no worries,' replied Dennis, with a sporadic outburst of laughter. 'I was about to send a carrier pigeon...would have heard back from you sooner!'

'The cheeky git,' whispered John to Hannah, his mouth opened wide aghast. He was about to correct his father but thought it unwise, given the desperate circumstances they were in. 'I'm really sorry, Dad. I've been busy sorting things out for the move.' No response. 'Can you hear me? Are you on your way now?'

'Aye!' Dennis' response was sharp and hinted to John that his father was not impressed. 'It's a good job that one of us is on the ball, isn't it? I'm outside now, Son.' John slowly moved his eyes away from Hannah towards their living room window; it was badly clouded with condensation, though John could still make out that his father was not where he said he was.

'I can't see you, Dad,' grumbled John, whilst scratching at his shaven head in confusion. 'Are you sure?'

'I'm in the Sprinter van - how the hell can you not see it?' laughed Dennis again, but with a mocking undertone this time. 'The big, silver one. Howay, Son, pull yourself together!'

'Hold on,' interjected Hannah, with a knowing smirk. 'Is Dennis saying that he's outside?" John nodded silently in agreement. 'Ask him which street...'

'Dad, what street are you in?' stammered John, his voice burdened with apprehension. 'Are you in Bourbon Close, because we can't see the van anywhere.'

'*Bourbon Close*?!' Dennis's arrogant streak swiftly diminished. "No, I'm in Ladybrown Street, and I've been sat here for over half an hour! My cock's shrivelling away to nothing now in this icy weather! I hope you're happy?' John reacted with an instant face-palm, much to Hannah's amusement. 'Bloody freezation!'

'Dad, we haven't lived there for ages, man!' John would have normally humoured over his father's lapsed memory, though today had already driven him towards breaking point. 'We're at Eleven Bourbon Close now. I'll see you in a bit, yeah?' John lifted his phone to cut the call, hoping this would hasten Dennis's arrival.

'Ta-ra, Son.' Dennis cut the conversation between himself and John before his son even had chance to. Ten more minutes followed with no sign of John's dad, or his elusive van.

'Is everything ready just to go, Han?' questioned John, as he paced back-and-forth along their living room. 'Where's my guitar at?'

'Your guitar is still in our bedroom, exactly where *you* left it after playing on it this morning,' responded Hannah, softly. 'Please, stop worrying so much. Everything's going to be alright. Lucy is really excited. Why don't you go and spend some time with her before Dennis arrives?'

'Yeah, that's a good plan.' John then smiled for the first time that morning. 'Lucy always knows how to cheer me up.' He turned to observe his daughter playing happily outside in the snow. 'Can you keep an eye out for Dad?' Hannah took in a deep breath and then grunted something indecipherable to John, as she moved away from him towards their window. 'Keep an eye out for dad's van, Han.'

'Why don't you play on the swing with her? We can't exactly take it to Skipton Road, can we?" uttered Hannah, almost sorrowfully. 'The gardens there are all paved over or concreted, from what Mum said. It's such a shame. Lucy loves that swing.'

'Oh, I forgot about that,' sighed John. 'It *is* a shame. Poor Lucy's barely had chance to use it.' He continued to watch his daughter skip around the large lawn they had, endeared beyond words by

31

how her wellingtons left small imprints in the falling snow. A great sense of regret now entered John's thoughts, then went away after being replaced by his lust to provide Lucy with a 'better life'. 'Give me a shout when Dad turns up, Han.'

'I will,' Hannah responded forcefully, ushering John outside into the cold winter's air. 'Go and spend some time with Lucy. Today is a big deal for her... she needs her daddy.'

John slowly slid open his patio doors. The freezing breeze instantly hit hard at his face, forcing him to clench his eyelids together to shield them from it. The snow had also begun to lay heavier now and was at least four inches thick. Moving in this weather was going to be a nightmare.

'Lucy!' shouted John, from the fading warmth of his living room. 'Should we build a snowman, before Grandad Dennis comes?' Lucy clapped her woollen mittens together excitedly in response.

'I love the snow, Daddy!' screamed the child in ecstasy. 'I want to build a snowman! A big one!' John slipped on his old work boots and prepared himself for the arctic conditions lain ahead.

'We can only make a small one, sweetheart,' explained John, glumly. He placed his feet into the crumpling snow and then sighed. 'Grandad won't be long.' In response, Lucy playfully clasped a ball of snow together within her petite hands to throw right into her father's face. 'Lucy, man!' berated John, on swiping the remnants of Lucy's snowball away from his reddened cheeks. 'Less of that, now. We don't have long to build our snowman.' Lucy chuckled to herself, before grabbing some more snow into her shivering palms. Together, John and his daughter rolled a small bundle of snow around the lawn to form a boulder that was no bigger than a soccer ball. It was a perfect match to their petite size.

'Looks great,' said John, smirking proudly. 'Now, make a little one for the head, then we're done.' Lucy gladly followed her father's instructions. She placed another bundle of snow upon the figure's torso to form a disturbing, humanoid creature. 'It's a bit wonky, but it'll do.' John then used a finger to create two eye sockets and a crude-looking mouth. 'We've made worse.'

'Daddy, why have you made our snowman look sad?' frowned Lucy, as she tried to correct her father's lacking skill with a pristine thumb swipe. 'I wish I had that pretty ribbon to put on it...'

'What pretty ribbon?' questioned John, with an instant look of confusion. 'That one you found last week in the mud?'

'Yeah,' whimpered Lucy. 'It was so pretty.' Before John had any time to react, Hannah called out to him from behind the patio doors.

'John, your dad's here!' The patio doors briskly opened again. 'Come on, Lucy! You're coming with me to Nanna's house, while Daddy and Grandad Dennis move our things.'

'Tell Dad that I won't be long, Han.' John lifted Lucy into the air, brushing the snow from her wellingtons as he did so. 'Go on, sweetheart. I'll see you soon, okay?' Lucy tightly clasped onto John with both arms, before leaving him to follow Hannah into the passageway. 'I'll phone you when we finish.'

'Be quick about it, John,' emphasized Hannah, before leaning into him for a parting kiss. 'I don't want you catching a cold, either.'

'I won't,' said John in dismissal. 'I'll be sweating my tits off from lifting – if anything. Send my love to Barb and Ivan.' Hannah granted John another kiss and then left with Lucy, without saying any word to Dennis as she walked by him.

'Alright, Dad?' asked John, shuddering, whilst his father came forward to greet him. The air outside seemed to be getting colder now, although perhaps this was only in John's weakened mind. 'Sorry about the mix-up. I've had such a busy morning, sorting things out. My head's bouncing, man.'

'You're telling me, Son. Fucking nightmare!' snorted Dennis as he gestured back aggressively towards his overheating van. 'It's been a struggle to get through the snow in this old thing. Having no load in the back of it hasn't helped. At least Skipton Road isn't too far from here, and your fat arse might help keep some traction on the tyres.'

'Ha-ha-ha,' remarked John, sarcastically. 'Howay, Dad. I'm bloody frozen, plus I want to be finished by lunchtime.' Dennis rolled his eyes and quickly reached down to place a nearby cardboard box into John's hands. 'We'll be finished in no-time, Son. We're on a mission – let's get cracking!'

After loading John's meagre belongings into Dennis' van, the drive to Skipton Road was expectedly precarious due to the worsening road conditions. The lightweight van swerved in an uncontrolled manner along the whole journey, and John could swear that he heard a few fragile items clash against one another in the back of it.

'Of all the days you choose to move, Son!' sniggered Dennis. He quickly turned the radio up, only to blare out some retro trance tunes, most of which were from the late nineties. 'Ah, I remember this one from Ibiza... fuckin' class sketch that was!' John's eyes glared in fear, seeing as his father's attention was swiftly falling away from the snow-laden road. 'I was dancing to this one when my mate, Titchy-Tom, got sucked off by some lass from Barnsley next to me – a proper mong, she was. She stunk of fish...'

'Jesus! Dad!' squealed John. 'Can you watch where you're driving? We nearly clipped the curb there!' Dennis rubbed at his eyes and tutted back. 'Bloody Hell, Dad.'

'Calm down, Son, I know what I'm doing.' The van swerved again to miss some fallen branches. Every yard taken was having a great impact on John's faltering nerves. 'You worry too much, Son. Be like your old Dad here!' Dennis slammed a fist several times into his chest like an Alpha Gorilla, supposedly to signify his masculine prowess. 'Don't give a shit and live each day as it comes – Carpe Diet.'

34

'It's *Carpe Diem,* Dad, and I'd like to see Hannah and Lucy again... that's all,' mumbled John, in utter dread. 'We're nearly there now, thank the Lord.' Dennis turned up the music to a deafening volume, quenching his son's persistent whines. John strangely welcomed this, as the pain being inflicted on his ears was somehow distracting him away from Dennis's casual, albeit dangerous, driving abilities.

'Here we are!' Dennis gleamed. He suddenly slid up the hand brake and turned sideways towards a row of black houses nearby. 'Skipton Road. Home-sweet-home!' Without the lurking fog, Skipton Road seemed far-more inviting (from a certain point of view). On what would be the grassy area in better weather conditions, and laying just before John's new house, a group of children were out playing. They had made a large snowman together, impressive in comparison to John's earlier attempt. 'Looks like a nice area, Son. You've done well getting a house here.' John smiled and laughed to himself at the same time. It was such a relief to have someone commend him for choosing Skipton Road as his new abode, given all the grief he had previously received from countless others. 'It's a canny little street.'

'Thanks, Dad. Apparently, it has a bad reputation. I don't see why, though.' John leapt from Dennis's van and immediately reached for a set of keys stored within his back pocket. 'It'll be the first time I've had an in-depth look around inside today... should be interesting,' he chuntered.

'You what? You haven't had a look around yet?' gasped Dennis in total disbelief. 'Has Hannah not had a look, either?' John angrily kicked at the thick layer of snow beneath his feet. 'Seems a bit daft, doesn't it?'

'No, Dad. I did go to a little viewing with the letting agent, but I was in a rush and it was dark. I didn't have a chance to take a good look around. Besides, it was part of the deal: we had to move in asap,' he said in a pitiful tone. 'We saw some pictures on the letting agent's website... it looks canny enough inside.'

'Look, Son, you go ahead and have a look around. I'll start unloading the small things. Don't take all day, though.' Dennis clambered towards the back of his van with a vacant expression of joy. He was proud of his son, though he didn't really know how to show it.

'Thanks again, Dad. I'll be back in a minute.' John slowly walked up to his new address, his heart beating fast, his lips parched further from the draining anxiety inside. 'I hope Hannah and Lucy like it,' he pondered, with a worrisome frown. 'Here goes nothing.'

John gradually unlatched the lock on his new home's gate, savouring this anticipated moment. The garden had noticeably been neglected for some time and was strewn with a varying array of weeds that peaked through the lain snow. The first door John came to stood before a kitchen area that had been painted with a hideous, lime-green colour.

'It's definitely going to take a few coats to cover this,' sighed John. 'What's that... smell? I didn't notice that during the viewing.' A distinctive stench of rotten meat lingered within the stale air; it was an aroma that John instantly recognised from working in the care home – death. 'Phwoar! I'll have to get rid of that before Hannah comes in.' The lower passageway proved no better, especially in better light. Its wallpaper looked to be from the early sixties and stunk of foist and stale tobacco smoke. 'It just gets better,' whined John, performing another face-palm. 'For God's sake, man. What have I gotten myself into?'

Things only deteriorated thereafter: the living room was a nauseating orange colour; upstairs was a blinding yellow shade, and the room which should have been Lucy's was covered in black mould. 'Bollocks! Hannah's gonna kill me.' John succumbed to his disbelief, sitting on the staircase with his phone ready in hand to inform Hannah of the disappointing news. 'Yep. She's definitely gonna kill me, and I wouldn't blame her.'

'John?' cried out Dennis from his van. 'Are you helping me or what, Son?'

'Coming, Dad!' replied John, his tone one of defeat. 'It stinks in there, mind. I'll have to sort it out before Hannah and Lucy come.'

'New homes always have teething problems,' replied Dennis whimsically. 'You'll be alright. Just keep your chin up and everything will be okay.' Dennis hastily threw a small box into John's waiting arms. 'Now, shift some of this crap before I freeze to death. I've got a date tonight and need a certain extremity to work... get what I mean?' He nudged into John's arms, though his son gave no response in return. 'Cheer up, Son. It could be worse."

'Really, Dad?'

It took two hours for John and Dennis to complete the move. During this time, Hannah had sent numerous messages to John on his phone, most asking how long it would take, and also if the house was as great as he had recently deemed it. John responded each time with a smiling emoji and several kisses, all a ruse to hide his hidden shame and growing guilt.

'Right, John, we're done,' concluded Dennis, rubbing his cold hands together in satisfaction. 'I'll catch up with you soon for a few pints. The Tin Donkey pub is just around the corner, isn't it?'

'Aye,' replied John, wearily. 'I'll give you a text when I'm free. I've got a lot on this week.' Dennis rolled his eyes again. John's promises were not always well-kept, especially to him.

'No worries, Son. Send my love to the girls.' Within moments, John was left alone to dwell on his hasty decision. A deep sense of regret soon set in. He couldn't face the putrid stench inside, not without visiting the local corner shop first for some super-strength bleach (and a few cans of nine-percent lager to ease the present headache).

'Hannah's going to hate it, I just know she will.' John's nervous disposition worsened greatly on contemplating his wife's predictable reaction. 'What a mess I've landed myself in now.' He took the short walk to Skipton Road's local corner shop, the whole time thinking about what excuses he could make up for the dilapidated state of his and Hannah's new home. Once at the shop, John purchased some strong bleach, four cans of stomach-rendering lager, and a packet of cigarettes (which he believed would not be detectable within the nicotine-soaked household). On his journey back, John tried to think positively, despite the unnerving revelations encountered. 'I'd best phone Hannah. She'll be getting pissed off with me now, no doubt.' John lit up and then took in a quick draw from his cigarette, just before activating the phone in his other hand. 'What should I say? What *can* I say?'

'Hi, John,' said Hannah apprehensively, on answering her husband's long-awaited call. 'What's it like, then?' John took in another discreet draw, pretending that as he exhaled all his worries left with it. 'Is it... nice inside?'

'It's like a palace, Han - absolutely gorgeous!' John could barely believe his own words and was deeply ashamed at having to lie in such a way. 'You'll love it, babe. We'll need to do some decorating. That's about it.' A couple of silent moments passed. 'Han?'

'That's fine.' Hannah didn't seem at all phased. 'Mum and Dad said that they would help us decorate, anyway.' Her mother's laughter was now evident in the background. 'We'll come over now, if that's okay with you?'

'Yeah, sure, that's not a problem.' John gulped in a nervous fashion. 'Come over in about an hour, though. I want to clean up first.' He could hear Hannah's enthusiasm dwindle through her audible grunts. 'Honestly, it's lovely.'

'Aye, it better be!' shouted Ivan, Hannah's stepfather, down his daughter's phone. 'If it's a shit hole...'

'Tell Ivan that it's great and send him my love, Han,' stuttered John. He instinctively reached for his syrupy lager, hoping that it would cease his increasing nerves. 'I'm definitely gonna need an hour or so to sort things out. That's all I'm asking for.'

'One hour, and then we're coming over.' Hannah ended the call abruptly. John slurped away again at his can and drew several more puffs from his cigarette along the way home to Skipton Road. As he re-entered, the smell within his house had deteriorated further. John frantically sprayed the contents of his bleach bottle around the many rooms and passageways, praying this would shield any harrowing smells before Hannah and Lucy arrived.

'For fuck's sake!' John used the last drops of bleach in his kitchen, where the strongest stench of death lingered. His attempts were in vain, however, as the bleach only intensified the pungent fumes of rotten carcasses. 'Why me? Why can't something just go right for me... just for once.'

'John?' Several knocks rattled against the kitchen window – it was Hannah. 'Are you finished?'

'Come in!' commanded John, reluctantly. 'I'll be in the living room!' The steady sound of increasing footsteps moved closer towards him like a predator ready to pounce on their prey. To his surprise, Hannah had a radiant smile on her face, and on seeing him lunged forward with a forcible kiss. "Alright, Han?"

'I love it, John!' declared Hannah, with a widened smirk. "It's not as bad as I thought it would be.'

'Can you not smell anything funny?' asked John, with a fearful frown. 'Especially in the kitchen?'

'Nope. All I can smell is bleach... have you farted or something?' asked Hannah with a jubilant grin. 'I can't believe that you've actually done some cleaning - that's the biggest shock.'

'Cheeky bitch,' laughed John, slightly annoyed. 'I'm well-domesticated me, you know.' Lucy's expression, however, was not showing any similar appeal to her new surroundings. 'Do you like our new home, sweetheart?'

'It's stinky, Daddy.' Lucy's expression grimaced in the same way John's had, on first entering their new home. 'Where's *my* room at, Daddy?'

'It's the one next to the bathroom,' John replied. 'Why don't you go and take a look?' Lucy quickly left her father's company to wander upstairs by herself. Hannah inspected the hideous colours, scowling all the while as she did so to John.

'We've got a lot of painting to do,' she muttered. 'It's like being on a bloody acid trip. What kind of person would choose these shitty colours?' John couldn't help but laugh at his wife's keen observations. 'They're vile! It'll certainly take a few coats to cover. You told me that you viewed the house, so why keep this bombshell so quiet?'

'I know. We'll sort it out in no-time, hun.' John glanced across lovingly to Hannah; her smile always managed to rekindle his hope. 'Why don't you choose what colours you want, then I can go into town and get some paint?' Hannah winked back in turn, accepting this offer. 'Will that make up for things?'

'Sounds good to me. How about we go for black and white; they're neutral and modern, aren't they?" John scratched at his head, though reasoned that it would be unwise to unsettle Hannah anymore by disagreeing with her.

'Okay, and on that note, I'll go into town and get some paint.' Before John had a chance to leave, Hannah shouted upstairs for their daughter's attention. 'Lucy! You're going into town with Daddy to get some paint!'

'I want some Barbie dolls!' screeched Lucy, reaching the capacity of her small lungs. 'Can I get two, for me and my new friend?" John and Hannah looked to one another with a confounded expression.

'Which 'new friend' are you on about, sweetheart?' questioned John. Hannah was still distracted by the abhorrent colours surrounding her and stayed silent. 'You've only been here a few minutes...'

'The little girl who lives upstairs,' said Lucy in an innocent voice, as she tumbled down the staircase. 'She likes playing with dollies – just like me!'

'Okay...' replied Hannah, in a drawn-out breath. 'If you're a good girl, Daddy will buy you a new doll.' Lucy nodded back enthusiastically. 'What is your friend's name?'

'It's a secret!' Lucy's reply was both disturbing and mysterious. 'She wants to be my friend and wants to play with me, but her name is a big, big secret!'

'Lucy's at a funny age,' assured John to Hannah. 'It'll be strange for her to move home. I'll get her some dolls to keep her happy.'

'Don't go spoiling her, John – just one,' countered Hannah, in a stern and bitter manner. 'I know it's a huge change, but don't go mad. Just get Lucy one doll...we don't have much money left, anyway.'

'No worries.'

John quietly sauntered up the staircase to meet up with Lucy. With each step taken, he could hear his daughter singing her favourite song: 'The family fingers'. Lucy's voice was truly angelic, and her words perfectly formed, yet a peculiar undertone ran alongside that sounded more like an elderly woman than that of a young child.

"Lucy, who's up there with you?" enquired John, fearfully. He turned towards his daughter's room, reasoning that perhaps his ears were playing tricks on him. 'Lucy?'

'Daddy finger, Daddy finger, where are you?'

'Howay, Lucy!' roared John, his patience wearing thin. 'We're going into town now, just me and you. I'm going to buy you a new dolly!'

The haunting chorus continued:

'Mummy finger, Mummy finger, where are you?'

"Lucy!" John shouted, held within a deep level of frustration. 'Come and get ready, NOW! Do as you are told!'

'There you are, there you are... now I'll kill you!'

John instantly froze, his body fully paralysed with terror. It wasn't Lucy's voice singing, and the feeling of being watched quickly surrounded him within the darkening atmosphere. 'Lucy, who *are* you playing with?' he questioned, in safety from the upper passageway.

'I'm playing with my new friend. Her mammy doesn't like you, Daddy,' responded Lucy in a frank manner. 'She doesn't like you... not-at-all.'

'Get your tiny buns out here right now, missy!' commanded John, still not daring to venture into Lucy's room in fear of what he may find. 'I don't care what your *friend's* mammy says... hurry up!'

'Okay, Daddy.' Lucy suddenly appeared before John, and in her hands rested a small, red ribbon. From where she had retrieved the thin piece of cloth, John could only ponder. '*She* gave me a present - see?'

'That is going straight in the bin.' John snatched the worn garment from Lucy's hands and, with tremoring hands, placed it into his back pocket – away from sight. 'This new friend of yours isn't very nice, Lucy. I don't think you should play with her anymore.' Lucy wailed with a piercing shriek at her father's judgment.

'That's not fair! I like her, and she likes me,' whimpered the child pitifully. 'That ribbon is *mine* – not yours, Daddy!'

'Now listen here, young lady,' scorned John, though gently as not to upset his 'perfect princess'. 'You *do not* talk to Daddy like that – ever. You haven't before and won't do again – understood?' Lucy slowly nodded in agreement to her father's wishes.

'Yes, Daddy.'

"Good girl. Now, go downstairs and get your wellies on.'

'What's going on up there?' shouted Hannah from the kitchen. 'John?!'

'We're alright, hun. Lucy's just mucking about.' The silent response from Hannah spoke louder than any words could have. 'Can you put Lucy's coat and wellies on for her, please? I'm just going to check around the rooms again... for damp.'

'Don't take long!' Hannah snapped. 'It's going to snow again later this afternoon. All I need is for you and Lucy to catch a fever.' John slapped at his forehead; he had to vent his frustration somehow.

'I'll only be a minute...' John peered back into Lucy's room, at first with is eyes closed. 'Whoever you are, you're not welcome,' he muttered cautiously, into the empty space. 'My Lucy is a good girl, and I'm not having her play with some... *freak*!' John chuckled to himself despondently. He was a keen sceptic of anything supernatural; the sheer fact he was speaking to some disembodied presence now felt so foreign to him, yet somehow necessary. 'I'm throwing away this ribbon and that'll be the end of it.'

'Daddy finger, Daddy finger...'

'Fuck...off!' spat John, in defence against the ethereal voice now lingering within his head. It should be noted that this voice wasn't child-like, nor did it sound human in any other way; it was guttural, hoarse and truly menacing – wholly unnatural. 'Whatever you are, leave this house and my family alone.'

'There you are, there you are...'

'John! Lucy is ready now! What are you doing up there?' cried out Hannah again, in an emphasised plea for her husband's appearance.

'I'm coming, hun. I've just been checking how bad the mould is in Lucy's room.' John latched an ear against the neighbouring wall, reasoning that perhaps it could be someone from next-door he was hearing. 'Strange...' Only a strong silence greeted him.

'Get some paint remover when you go into town as well,' groaned Hannah, her own patience wavering greater than John's. 'The snow is getting worse.'

'Ego...Sabina.'

'The fuck?!' John pondered to himself in utter terror as to how the ghoulish woman somehow managed to keep communicating with him. The whispering voice in his head was becoming louder and clearer; it was more like a beast's roar than human. 'What kind of language is that?' A malicious cackle echoed in his ears, and no matter how hard he tried, John could not find a way to deafen himself from it.

'Ego... Pythonissam.'

'JOHN!' roared Hannah, her patience with him now totally spent. 'Stop messing about and get down here!'

'I'm coming, Han.' John struggled to catch his breath. The voice that resounded without any physical presence seemed to be that of an elderly woman; their voice was gravelly, though still powerful and foreboding. John knew in his heart that he had not imagined this strange encounter, yet he chose to dismiss it as merely being a side-effect of the intense stress he was presently under. 'All's well, Han. I won't be sec,' he stuttered.

'Daddy took away my present,' grieved Lucy to her mother. 'Can I have it back please, Mummy?'

'What present?' Hannah looked down to her daughter with a confused glance, then peered up the narrow staircase in search of John. 'What on earth are you on about, Lucy?'

'The pretty ribbon. My friend gave me it,' whispered the child, in not wanting for her father to overhear. 'It's mine - not Daddy's!' Hannah looked down towards her daughter again initially disturbed, although her frustration with John had grown far stronger. 'John, get your arse down here – RIGHT NOW!'

'I'm coming, man!' John stumbled down the stairs in a cocktail of fear and disbelief. 'I'm losing the plot, me...'

'Too right you are,' Hannah jibed. 'Did you take something from Lucy?' John halted his steps, looking back up the stairs once more to ensure that he wasn't being followed (because it certainly felt that way). 'She's rambling on about some... *ribbon.*'

'Aye, the last tenants must have left it,' said John, his eyes glazed as if lost in a vacant stare. He carefully removed the crimson cloth from his back pocket to inspect it closer. 'I'm getting you a new doll today, Lucy. Isn't that better than some old piece of manky ribbon?'

'No, Daddy!' screeched Lucy, stomping her feet. 'It is *very* special. I want it back!' Hannah gasped at her daughter's unusual behaviour. 'It's mine - MINE!'

'Who do you think you are talking to, missy?' Hannah placed her hands upon her hips, just like the headmaster at her junior school used to do when annoyed. 'You *never* talk to Mummy or Daddy like that. We love you... show some respect.'

Lucy latched onto her mother's side, sobbing at this apparent loss. As John entered the kitchen he was met with an icy reception from both his wife and child; neither one showed any endearment, only a rising hint of detest.

'This is what all the fuss is about,' remarked John, with a snide smirk. He quickly reached into his pocket to retrieve the secretive ribbon; it felt like a greater burden to bear than any other now. 'It's going in the bin, okay?' Silence ensued. 'I don't know what has gotten into you, Lucy, but I am *not* very happy at all with how you're talking to me. I'm your daddy and I love you.'

'It's mine - MINE!' wailed the disheartened child. 'Give it back to me, Daddy!' John bundled the crimson cloth into a dense ball and then, without further thought or guilty conscience, threw it into the nearby trash can. 'No!!'

'It's gone now. Gone.' John's delivery was cold and littered with dread. 'We're going into town now, and you're never going to mention that ribbon or your new *friend* again. Understood?' Lucy nestled herself more firmly into Hannah's side, her only comfort. It was as if John had torn the child apart from something truly beloved. Lucy's genuine tears proved to confirm this. 'Howay, sweetheart.' John tried to be more sympathetic, seeing the reaction given from Lucy. 'I'll make it up to you,' he assured. 'I promise. Daddy doesn't break his promises.'

'Mam and Dad are coming over soon to help decorate, so don't be long in town,' smiled Hannah, herself relieved by not having to decorate herself. John reached out his arms in response for Lucy's embrace, though was only to be met with a look of scorn from the grief-stricken child.

'I can't do anything right, can I?' mourned John to Hannah. 'I'll be as quick as I can. God forbid I piss anyone else off today.'

46

'I'm not angry with you, John.' Hannah leant into kiss John again on his lips. 'Moving home is stressful. It's bound to take some getting used to.' John kissed Hannah back in the same way, softly and long enough to satisfy both their needs. 'Try to relax.'

'See you in a bit, babe.' John then clasped onto Lucy's petite hands and braced himself for the freezing conditions outside. 'Should I just get some white emulsion, you know, so we can white-wash the whole place?'

'Yeah,' agreed Hannah, through gritted teeth. 'Anything to get rid of the nicotine stains and mingin' colours in here. I don't care what colour you choose,' she chuckled.

The short distance into town involved having to walk back through Bourbon Close. Lucy and John stared upon their previous home together as they passed by it, both sharing in a moment of silent reflection at the familiar comfort which had now been lost to both.

'We don't live there anymore, darling,' said John with a remorseful undertone. 'Someone else probably lives there now.'

'I know, Daddy,' responded Lucy, her saddened smile instantly struck a heavy guilt in John's heart. 'I don't miss that house anymore. I have a new friend now.' John took in a deep and laboured breath. He had hoped that Lucy's new imaginary friend had been just a passing phase.

'Your 'new' friend... what is her name?' questioned John, his voice wavering with reluctance. 'By the way, why is she such a *big* secret?'

'You're a man, so you're not allowed to know her name.' Lucy's remark was firm and hardly coincidental. 'Men are nasty, and they should *all be punished*, that's what my friend's mammy said.' John froze, unable to physically take another step. His chest tightened, a sickening convulsion then lifted from his stomach, and the regular pain of anxiety swiftly coursed throughout him; it was an infliction which John had fought against for many years.

'You don't need to keep secrets from me, Lucy,' stammered John, during his struggle to calm each passing breath. 'I'm your daddy. No matter what happens, or how old you get, you can always talk to me.' Lucy swayed her arms quite playfully, totally innocent to what dark power was having its influence on her young mind. 'I mean it. Don't ever keep secrets from me.'

'I love you, Daddy.' Lucy smiled, her pale-blue eyes shining even brighter now against the fallen snow's reflection. 'But my friend's mummy said that men are nasty, horrible people. I'm not allowed to talk to you about them.' Despite the freezing climate, John stilled his and Lucy's progress for a few moments longer, wishing to divulge into her disturbing claims.

'Is that right?' seethed John. He was on the brink of a severe panic attack, though he thankfully managed to keep this at bay – but only just. 'I think that you've been watching too many YouTube videos, especially when me and Mummy aren't around. Never-mind what your friend says to you. I'm your Daddy, and *I* say that you are not allowed to talk to them anymore. Okay?'

'No!!' cried out the child, despairingly. 'They were hurt by nasty men - *you're* a nasty man, and *she* wants to hurt you!'

'That's enough, Lucy!' commanded John, even taking himself by surprise. He'd never had to shout at his daughter like this before.

Just then, an elderly couple walking by shook their heads in a unified disgust at John's parenting skills. John grinned back coyly to them and rolled his eyes in a dismissive way. 'You have to be firm sometimes with bairns these days,' he attempted to reason, yet the couple only continued to shake their heads disapprovingly as they passed by. 'Says a generation that used the cane against kids...' thought John to himself, angrily. 'Whatever.'

'I *want* to play with my new friend, Daddy,' pleaded Lucy in a sorrowful whimper. 'If you stop me playing with her, then the nasty lady will hurt you.' John rubbed at his face coarsely, almost drawing blood from his blistered lips.

'I'm telling you, Lucy—' John tried to be more diplomatic this time in his tone with the impressionable child. He couldn't bear to attract anymore unwanted attention to neither himself nor his daughter. 'You do *not* talk to them again in any shape, way or form. *They* are nasty... not me.'

Lucy kept her eyes fixed upon the ground as she and John continued their journey into town. Along the way, John (to his relief) came across a familiar and close friend – Donnie.

'Alright, Donnie-lad? How's tricks?' John grinned wildly, showing no sign of his previous anger. 'We've finally moved, mate.' Donnie winked to Lucy and then smiled back to his oldest friend.

'That was quick, pal,' commented Donnie, smirking. 'You only got the keys a few days ago, didn't you?'

'Aye. No fuss – straight in,' replied John, proud in his stance. 'It stinks of smoke, and the walls look like something Picasso himself mastered. Easy sorted, though.' A unified burst of laugher followed between both friends. 'You couldn't help me and Hannah out with some decorating, could you?'

'I can't, mate,' Donnie sighed. 'I need to learn a few songs for this weekend... got a gig up the Tin Donkey pub on Saturday.'

'No worries,' said John with a sympathetic shrug. 'Anything I'd recognise?' Donnie swayed to-and-throe, signalling without any words that the set list was not to his liking. 'Is it that bad?'

'Just some cheesy cock-rock from the eighties... nothin' special. It's for a workmate's wedding reception – I barely know the guy.'

'Money is money, mate. Beggars can't be choosers,' sniggered John. Lucy continued to stare down at the ground. 'Anyway, when you get chance, have a look over to our new house. It's Seventy-One Skipton Road.' Donnie's jovial expression instantly fell.

'My Mam lived at Skipton Road when I was little,' whispered Donnie, his evident mannerism filled with one of dread. 'It's haunted that street. You're mental, you are, moving into that road.'

'Load of shite, and don't *you* start!' laughed John, in attempt to hide his feeling of nuisance. 'This town's full of ghost stories. I've not seen anything... yet.' Donnie persisted to stare at John anxiously, though he tried not to show this fear towards Lucy. 'Don't tell me that you're into all that mumbo-jumbo?'

'Mam swore that she used to see an old man sitting at the end of her bed - a monk, or something like that. Just ask her,' said Donnie, almost pleading in his words to John. 'If I were you, I'd Google a good exorcist, mate.'

'Nah,' jeered John with a dismissive swipe of his free hand, the other still firmly attached to Lucy's. 'A good painter is what I need, not a priest. Anyhow, I'll catch up with you next week, if you're free? I could do with a laugh.'

'Sure thing, bud,' said Donnie, grinning. He tickled at Lucy's chin and then, whilst walking away, gave to John a knowing wink. 'Take care of yourselves, and don't let the demons get ya!'

'*Demons*,' tutted John, again held in dismissal. 'Have fun at your gig. Don't get snatched up by any cougars who are after some young meat, hey?' Donnie rose a sly middle finger to John on parting from him. The journey into town had suddenly grown sourer. 'Is there not *one* person happy for us moving into that street?'

'My friend is happy, but *you* won't let me play with her,' scowled Lucy. John knelt to directly face his daughter. He slowly licked again at his dry lips and glanced to the penetrating sun rays now falling through the dense snow clouds above.

'I don't want us to fall out, sweetheart.' John gently placed his hands upon Lucy's, much to her disapproval at this time. 'There's no harm in having imaginary friends, but when you're telling me that they want to hurt us... it makes me very worried.'

'They don't want to hurt me or Mummy,' explained Lucy, reservedly. The clarity in her response concerned John, so much so that he fell into a silent stupor. 'Just *you*, Daddy. That is, if you won't let me play with her.' John exhaled into his chest and clenched at it with Lucy's hands.

'Guess I don't have a choice, do I?' John rose his arms into the air, accepting this humiliating defeat. 'Howay, Lucy. Let's get this paint before Mummy wanders where we've gotten to.'

'Mummy is okay, Daddy. *They're* looking after her.' Lucy whispered again, enduring the secretive nature of her new-founded friendship. John diverted any further talk of Lucy's phantom protectors on their journey back home. He kept glancing down to his unusually quiet daughter, desperate to laugh with her as they always did (prior to the recent move).

'How about some Pizza tonight?' asked John to Lucy, as she skipped ahead of him. 'I'll order your favourite...'

'Yes, please, Daddy,' Lucy chuckled. Any tensions between herself and John had seemingly vanished, or so John hoped. 'I want *lots* of cheese!'

'Aye, alright,' sniggered John. 'Not too much though, or you'll have nightmares!' Lucy carried on with her skipping, and then started to sing to herself on nearing Skipton Road.

'*Daddy finger, Daddy finger, where are you?*' blared the child, happily. John's anxiety quickly began to rise again. '*There you are, there you are...*' The words echoed relentlessly in John's mind. However, it was not his daughter's voice performing the innocent nursery rhyme.

'Fucking ghosts and demons,' thought John, whilst his heart paced frantically with each step taken towards Skipton Road. 'That's all I need.'

'Ego... Sabina.'

CHAPTER THREE

Three, non-eventful, days passed by and John had made every excuse possible not to start painting his new home. Without any doubt, he was emotionally and physically drained, and it also hadn't helped with him having to work four shifts off the belt.

'You have the whole day off, don't you?' mumbled Hannah from behind her Kindle to John, as they both lay together upon their sofa. 'Any chance of you painting the house today?' she asked, pleadingly. 'It proper stinks of old smoke, which can't be good for our Lucy's health.'

'Aye. Put me on a guilt-trip, Han, why don't you?" mused John. He gradually turned his head to look at the two-litre emulsion tin, which itself was still held, untouched, within a shopping bag in the living room's farthest corner. 'I'll make a start on it today, hun. I promise.'

'I'll help, if you want me to?' replied Hannah. She momentarily lowered her Kindle to look directly into John's eyes. 'Mam and Dad said that they'd help, too. Don't put them off this time.' John yawned loudly, struggling to stay awake, despite the decent sleep he had the night before. 'I don't expect you to paint the entire house alone.'

'No worries, Han' John smiled back to her, sincerely. He then turned back towards his TV and the television show playing, which Hannah had chosen to watch (regardless of the fact that she was reading from her Kindle) was 'Loose Women'; a program that John could not stand, especially as its presenters were now discussing the topic of vaginal dryness. 'It'll be better than watching this load of bollocks. I think I'll make a start on it now.'

'Don't get any paint on the carpets.' Hannah lifted her eyes again. 'You ruined the ones at Bourbon Close,' she chuckled, then quickly returned to her Kindle.

'You do it, then!' snapped John, in a humorous tone. He then clumsily rolled from the sofa, landing upon his cold mug of coffee. 'Shit! Oh, well. I've ruined the carpet anyway,' he humoured, though Hannah was not as amused in comparison.

'Nice one, John. We can't have anything nice, can we?' Hannah briskly stood herself to inspect the damage John had caused. 'It'll come out. You're lucky, this time.' Hannah gently tickled at John's sides whilst he tried to right himself. He (wrongfully) took this as a hint for some intimate fun. John was, however and disappointingly, mistaken. 'No, no, no!' Hannah chortled with a sly wink. She swiped away John's wandering hands, just as they neared her upper thighs. 'You need to preserve your energy for all the painting you'll be doing.'

'You always have some daft excuse,' said John, his frustration clearly evident to witness. 'I'm going to do the kitchen first...it bloody honks in there.' Hannah frowned at first, then quickly returned to her vampire novella. 'Honestly, can you not smell anything in the kitchen at all?'

'I can't smell anything, John, just your B-O,' countered Hannah, with a dismissive shrug. 'You're losing the plot you are, babe.'

Suddenly, a quick succession of taps rattled along the living room's window. Outside stood Hannah's parents – Barbara and Ivan. Both were shuddering from the morning's icy air, despite the snow melting around them (that should have otherwise signified a warmer climate).

'Won't be a minute,' assured John in a stammering voice. He was still suffering from a rising anxiety, and the loud bangs from Barbara's ring finger upon the glass pane did nothing to alleviate this. 'It's a good job we didn't start getting frisky. I don't think your mam could have coped with seeing that.'

'Shut up, you dirty git!' sneered Hannah, as she reached into her jeans to retrieve the living room's door key. 'You're sick in the head, you are.' John chuckled with a perverse grin on his face. He swiftly fell into a silence on Barbara and Ivan's arrival inside, performing the 'good' son-in-law role. 'Hi, Mam. Hi, Dad. Are you both alright?' whispered Hannah, as she embraced the two.

'Yes, sweetheart, just a little cold,' replied Barbara. Nestled within her hands was a large supermarket carrier bag. "I've brought some spare brushes and turps. Are you looking forward to doing some painting today, John?'

'Aye, ready as always,' replied John, with an overexaggerated smirk. In truth, all he wanted to do was go back to sleep. 'If I start in the kitchen, could you and Ivan work your magic in here, please?' Ivan clasped his hands together, rubbing them briskly.

'No worries, my lad,' said Ivan, grinning widely. 'It might take a few coats to cover up the nicotine stains - disgusting habit... smoking.' He looked directly at John whilst saying this. 'How long have you been stopped for now?' John shrugged, not daring to look at Hannah or her parents through his guilty conscience.

'A few months or weeks, maybe?' stammered John, stoically. He was an adult, after-all. If he wanted to riddle his body with chemicals, then that was his choice. That's how John justified to himself, anyway. 'I haven't really been keeping track. I'm thinking about getting a vape pen to help me quit.' Panic quickly set in, as John realised that he had left one of his lighters and a secret packet of cigarettes in with the painting equipment upstairs. 'I'll go get things ready... won't be sec.'

'He's a canny lad, is John.' Ivan then smiled to Hannah; she was his world, despite only being a part of it from the tender age of three. 'How are you both coping with the move?' Hannah slowly switched off her Kindle and ran her fingers across Barbara's hands. 'Is everything alright, Love?'

'I know that he's been smoking again, and he's started drinking that horrible stuff you like, Dad,' whimpered Hannah, moving herself against Barbara's waiting arms. 'I just wish that he would talk to me, instead of relying on that crap.'

54

'It's just a phase, darling,' implored Barbara. 'He's under a lot of stress. Once we've finished decorating, it will feel more like your own home, and then you can all get back to living normal lives again.' Hannah sighed and nodded back politely to her mother. 'Everything will be okay in the end, sweetheart.'

'I hope so, Mam,' said Hannah, bluntly. 'We can't go on living like this.' She paused for a moment to look at Lucy's recent school photograph, which itself was lying upon a sealed cardboard box nearby. 'What's worse is our Lucy has started acting really strange. She's become obsessed with a red ribbon she found on our first day here, and I haven't a clue where she got it from.'

'She's only a bairn, Hannah,' sniggered Ivan. 'Kids are like magpies: they latch onto anything shiny or new. Don't worry.'

'You haven't seen it, Dad.' Hannah abruptly left her parents company to see where John had disappeared to. 'John! What are you doing?'

'I'm coming, man!' scowled John, as he stashed the half-empty packet of cigarettes and lighter into his underwear draw upstairs. 'Why don't you go into town and get some food for dinner tonight? We'll be done by the time you get back.'

'What do you mean by that like, John?' fumed Hannah, her fingertips clenching tightly on the stair rail's bannister. 'It won't take me that long! I tell you what, why don't *you* make your own dinner tonight, and I'll take Lucy to her Nanna's?' John instantly regretted his ill-timed humour.

'Okay, Han.' John exhaled wearily. 'That's probably a good idea, to be fair. The paint fumes might be too strong for Lucy. Come back for supper, though, okay?' A tense silence followed. Hannah then left without further word, leaving John to be comforted by his parents-in-law. 'Me and my big mouth...'

'Are you alright, John?' asked Barbara from the passageway downstairs. 'Don't take any notice of Hannah. Both of you are very stressed, though it'll come to pass.'

'Cheers, Barb,' replied John, as he carefully walked downstairs with a handful of various paintbrushes and a more burdened mindset. 'I'll make it up to her... somehow. I've never seen Hannah this vexed before. It's like everything I do just pisses her off.' Barbara gently nodded her head and forged a pleasant smile. 'Howay, let's get this painting out the way.' The distinct sound from a can being opened echoed from John's kitchen.

'I've brought some liquid courage along for us, John. Wink-wink, nudge-nudge,' gleamed Ivan. In his hands were two opened cans of frothy, super strength lager. John shrugged awkwardly at first, but soon accepted his father-in-law's generous offer. 'It won't hurt having a couple of these to make the day go quicker, will it?' Barbara growled under her breath and swiftly replaced Ivan's lager with a large paintbrush.

'Don't worry, Barb. We'll take our time supping these down,' assured John, whilst ingesting a small quantity from his favourite beverage. 'It's a little early to start partying, anyhow.' He laughed, nervously. 'On second thought, I'll put mine in the fridge for now.' Barbara winked approvingly to him, signalling her praise.

A quick succession of heavy thumps then rang from John's kitchen door, taking both himself and Hannah's parents by surprise. Behind the clouded glass window, John could make out a wavering figure; it was a man no taller than himself, though drastically thinner.

'Hello?' John called out to the mysterious stranger. 'If you're selling anything, we're not interested, mate.' The man continued to hammer at John's door. 'Oy! We're not interested! Go and do one!'

'Surely, they're not a Jehovah's Witness?' snorted Ivan, after taking a larger slurp from his warming lager. 'Listen, pal. We're not interested, so... fuck off!' The man slumped himself against the door, then slowly dragged his torso down it – enraging John to a whole new level.

'The cheeky bastard!' roared John aghast. He frantically unlocked the door and as he did the man slumped into a heap within the kitchen's entranceway, all the while laughing to the three unsuspecting witnesses as he did so. 'Who the fuck are you?'

'Hi! It's nice to meet ya! I don't think much of yer manners, though... callin' me a fuckin' bastard, like,' stuttered the man in a dishevelled, Yorkshire accent. He was obviously drunk: his trousers were stained with what appeared to be old urine; his eyes rolled side-to-side as they tried to focus on John; his hair was laden with grease, and skin mottled from not being bathed for at least a week or two. A total, vomit-inducing, mess. 'My name's Sid.' he stated, in-between several hiccups and the odd belch. 'I live next door to ya, neighbour!'

'(Nice one) My name's John. Would you mind getting out of my kitchen, *mate*?' he snarled, trying to hold back his raised fist. 'No offense, but I think you need to go and have a lie down... in a bath.' Sid cackled in response, exposing what few rotten teeth remained within his mouth.

'No offense taken,' said Sid, his tone pitiful and pathetic. 'I understand why ya feel that way about me.' It took a few painful attempts, but Sid eventually manged to stand himself upright. 'I'm trying to come off the drink, ya know. It's not, fuckin', easy. When did ya move in, anyhow?'

'A few days ago. Did you not see the van?' questioned John, with a harsh mannerism. He turned around to Barbara and Ivan, rolling his eyes in suggestion as to how disheartened he was in having Sid live so close by. 'I'm surprised you haven't heard my little girl singing in her bedroom. She's got a good set of lungs, has our Lucy.'

'Nah, not a thing,' replied Sid, staring manically. 'So, there's just you, yer lass and one bairn, is there?' John froze in reluctance to answer Sid's questioning; it was bad enough having the alcoholic linger in his doorway, he didn't want him to have any more to do

57

with Hannah or Lucy. 'I'm alright me, ya know? Don't judge a book by its cover.' Barbara cautiously stood herself between John and Sid, glaring at the latter as if he were some insect that was about to be crushed under her own will. 'Fine bit of 'totty' you are, darlin'...'

'It's been lovely meeting you, Sid.' Barbara forced herself to remain civil when, in reality, all she wanted to do was slap the smirk away from Sid's tremoring face and kick him so hard that he could never reproduce. 'We're busy decorating today, so if you'll kindly excuse us...' Sid raised his palms up defensively and then placed them together in a begging fashion. 'It's lovely meeting you but—'

'I'm sorry. I'm *truly* sorry, missus.' Sid sounded like he was about to cry, leaving John greatly confused. He didn't know whether to feel sorry for the poor soul or to be disgusted by him. 'I'll leave ya's to it. Cheerio, peeps!' Sid stumbled back into the garden, lifting up a half-empty bottle of white cider which was lain against the bin outside as he left.

'Hannah's going to kill me... when she sees Sid,' spoke John out aloud (he hadn't meant to). He soon swallowed heavily in dread on turning to face Barbara again. 'If I didn't have bad luck, I wouldn't have any luck at all.' Ivan quietly retrieved John's can of lager from the fridge and then handed it to him. 'Cheers, mate. That's the medicine I need.'

'Don't worry about that piss-head,' chortled Ivan, sensing John's sorrow. 'You haven't met your other neighbours yet. Just take things easy, Son.' John willingly accepted the cold can from Ivan, despite only hours before telling himself that he would cut down on his alcohol consumption. Within seconds John downed the can's contents, finding himself to be slightly less stressed as he took the final few slurps. 'Feeling better now?'

'Aye – too right!' replied John in a more jovial tone, as he wiped a line of froth away from his upper lip. 'Let's get cracking. I want to be done before Hannah and Lucy come back tonight. It'll be a nice surprise for them.

'That's the spirit,' said Barbara, smiling. 'We'll do upstairs if you do down here - that way we'll be finished in no time.'

John set to work on layering the first coat of paint along his kitchen walls. Each stroke he made with the paint brush thankfully managed to lift his depressive outlook. Within a mere matter of hours, John had transformed the lower rooms in his house into a whitewashed masterpiece; yet, the harrowing stench of death continued to dwell throughout his kitchen, despite him plastering an additional two coats of paint over it.

'For Fuck's sake,' growled John angrily to himself. 'Where *is* that smell coming from?' He slid out his washing machine to inspect for any leaking water or evidence of damp; however, there was nothing to suggest this was the case. He then searched through each of his kitchen cupboards for any food left behind by the home's previous occupants – nothing in them either. 'What the...'

'Is everything alright down there, John?' shouted Barbara enthusiastically, from Lucy's bedroom. 'We're nearly done up here!'

'Yeah, Barb! responded John, more calmly in his tone now. 'I just can't get rid of this awful smell... that's all.' A thundering chorus of footsteps hastily bounded down the staircase. Barbara and Ivan entered John's kitchen, both with a look of perplexment and concern. 'Can you guys smell it as well?' Ivan shrugged, whilst Barbara sniffed around the air like a highly trained hound.

'All I can smell is paint, darling,' assured Barbara. 'New homes always have their own unique smells. Once you're settled in properly, your own smells will take over.'

'Aye. Just have a few beers and a curry... that'll kill off any other smell in here,' jested Ivan, as he winked suggestively to John. 'Know what I mean, pal?' John gave Ivan the thumbs-up sign and then sniffed around the kitchen in unison with Barbara.

'It's like rotten meat,' whispered John fearfully, as he scoured the kitchen space. 'Hannah said that she can't smell it, either.'

'Stop worrying, sweetheart.' Barbara suddenly wrapped her arms around John for a lengthy embrace. 'You've worked very hard today - we all have. Get some rest before the girls come back. Ivan and I need to go now, anyway; we're playing Bingo tonight at the Tin Donkey pub.' Ivan rolled his eyes slowly behind Barbara's back.

'Oh, aye. I can't wait to play Bingo for three hours in a room full of pensioners,' sniggered Ivan. 'Have a power nap, John. It'll do you the world of good.'

John hugged both Barbara and Ivan, then graciously allowed for them to leave his presence. Once alone, the atmosphere within the house drastically began to change. John started to feel extremely nauseous. He reasoned that it was likely caused by his consumption of super strength lager, whilst eating little less than a slice of toast and a chocolate bar from Hannah's private collection during his tedious manual work.

'Well, I've got no Wi-Fi... so there goes having a sly retro-gaming session,' John despaired. 'Hannah and Lucy won't be back for a few more hours. I'll have that last can and listen to some music - that'll cheer me up.'

John searched through several cardboard boxes until he came across one of his favourite CD's. It was the album *Closer* by 'Joy Division'. Despite the depressing lyrics and melodies, John found listening to this band made him feel happier (in a serene sort of way). The track 'Isolation' certainly felt fitting in his current surroundings.

'I'd better text Hannah... let her know we're finished decorating.' John quickly grabbed his phone from the sofa and began to type in a message – keeping it as short as possible, given the level of intoxication he was now under.

Hi, babe. Finished painting now. When U coming home?

John waited ten minutes for a reply, which soon turned to twenty and without any response at all. After gulping down the last few drops of lager left in his remaining can, he lay down upon his sofa and started to fall asleep. While the ambient tracks playing from his CD faded, John slowly slipped into a deep and needful slumber.

In his dream, John found himself standing within the familiar setting of Bourbon Close. It was late at night, though no stars shone in the sky above, nor were any street lamps lit. John glanced into the neighbouring houses; there were no signs of any activity going on within them, so he began to walk along the darkened street like a lost child.

'What's happening to me?' thought John anxiously to himself. Each step taken now seemed heavier, as if his feet were being weighed down by some unseen force. 'Where the fuck is everyone?' A startling cackle resounded in the air behind him. He didn't dare look, though something forced him to regardless. 'Who's there?' he screamed out in terror. 'Who's laughing at me?'

The innocent laughter quickly shifted to sound more demonic in nature. It was a mixture of an elderly woman giggling, blended with a series of deep animalistic noises. 'Wake up, John - wake up!' he kept repeating to himself. The need to flee greatly overpowered John now. He attempted to sprint, though found his legs were now firmly cemented into the ground beneath. 'Let me go!' he commanded against the invisible force. 'Get off me!'

'Daddy finger, Daddy finger, where are you?' taunted the gravelly voice of this wicked creature. *'There you are, there you are...'*

'Stop it!' screeched John with all his might. He clasped his eyelids together tightly, yearning that this inane torment would soon come to its end. 'Wake up, John! Wake up!' A piercing shock then ran throughout John's body from his lower back. As he turned, he was then met with a sea of recognisable faces: friends, family, and even a few old enemies stood behind him. In each of their hands they held a weapon of some sort: knives, hammers, axes – anything that could cause some serious damage. John tried to smile at them, believing this would ease the risen tension. He was sorely mistaken. 'What are you all doing here?' questioned John, apprehensively. Every face had a vacant stare upon it. 'Stop messing with me, guys.' The sharp pain returned in John's lower back, and from it ran a small trickle of fresh blood. He had clearly been stabbed.

'Permitte mihi te occidere'

John tried to ignore the disembodied woman's voice. He frantically ran his fingers across where a pool of blood now formed on the back of his t-shirt. The pain felt so real. An agonising, electrical surge coursed from the wound across John's entire body.

'The...fuck?!' cried out John to the zombie-like creatures stood before him. 'Which one of you fuckers stabbed me?'

'Ego sum non innocentes.'

'Stop talking in that dumb language! I don't understand a word of it!" whimpered John, pitifully, within a harrowing scream. 'Who...*are* you?'

'Ego... Sabina.'

'Sabina?' John tried to think of anyone he had ever met with that name. 'I don't know anyone called "Sabina". Why do you talk like that?' He instantly regretted asking such a question, given the threatening ordeal that currently surrounded him. 'It doesn't matter... I don't want to know!'

'Baal est meus...'

The gravelly, demonic voice rose in temperament, instantly sending John's aggressors into a frenzied riot. John's friends and family charged violently against him, despite his pleas for their mercy. A succession of multiple slashes and stab wounds followed that inflicted every inch of John's body, while he lay powerless on the freezing tar mac to contemplate the meaning behind all of this.

'Why would you hurt me?' stammered John, through a gurgling spew of blood in his mouth. 'I'd never hurt any of you...'

'There you are... There you are...'

Though his vision grew blurry from exhaustion and blood loss, John could faintly make out a youthful-looking woman, someone of whom he had truly never met before. She sauntered between the attacking mob, staring back at John all the time with a satisfied grin.

'Sabina?' John concentrated on the woman as she passed by. She had wavy, brunette hair that fell freely to her waist, and was wearing a long, white dress that ran down to her bare feet. Centred around the woman's slim waistline was a piece of red cloth (possibly a ribbon), that looked to be soaked in congealed blood – the only colour present within this haunting atmosphere, as all else turned dark and grey. 'Go away! leave me alone!'

'Ego... Pythonissam.'

Sabina slowly edged towards John, casting aside his friends and family without even lifting a finger. She then straddled herself upon his upper legs, squirming as if trying to entice him, making orgasmic sounds that echoed loudly within the narrow street. John fought against the natural urges flowing into his groin and, just as he thought this ordeal was to be over, Sabina lowered her head, only to then suddenly raise it.

'Ego sum Rubrum Uitta Pythonissam!'

John howled in terror, his voice breaking instantly from the ferocity of his heart-wrenching cry. Sabina's beautiful features had instantly transformed into a haggard, old woman's (almost corpse-like). The temptress' auburn eyes had sunk back far into their sockets, leaving only two black pits that looked scorched and agonizing to behold. Sabina's hair appeared damp and littered with mud, smelling strongly of death. Her white dress was now noticeably saturated by filthy water and stunk of foist. John continued to scream, pathetically, as Sabina laughed in a malicious tone back at him. Finally, after a few more moments of torment, the nightmare came to its end... or so it seemed.

'Fuck me!' John gasped aloud, as he awoke within the quiet surrounding of his living room. What the hell was all that about?' He inhaled three lengthy draws of humid air and then collapsed back into a foetal position on the sofa. 'That's the last time I drink that super-strength shite!'

John's CD player suddenly kicked back into life. He welcomed the droning tones of Ian Curtis, as they were far more pleasant to listen to than the screams he had just unleashed inside of Sabina's nightmare. Another hour had passed by and John still hadn't left the safety of his sofa. He flicked through some Facebook and Twitter feeds on his phone, laughing slightly at the mundane posts that appeared along with other pointless video links (mostly involving cats or people acting dumb). A rattling sound eventually came from the kitchen door. 'Hannah? Lucy?'

'We're back!' shouted Hannah, with a hint of joy in her voice. 'You've done a good job with the kitchen, John.' Lucy appeared first and quickly ran to her father for a quick embrace.

'Daddy!' giggled Lucy to John. 'Is my room pink? I wanted pink!' John gladly lifted his daughter into the air for a tighter hug.

'Yes, sweetheart. Nanna and Grandad painted your bedroom; I did downstairs.' John smiled in satisfaction, although he was still greatly disturbed by the horrific dream encountered earlier. 'Go and have a look, but don't touch the wet paint.' Lucy squirmed from John's clasping arms and sprinted away, barging past Hannah as she moved by the kitchen area.

'I'm pleasantly surprised,' murmured Hannah, in a teasing voice. 'You didn't get any paint on the skirting boards or carpet.' She planted a sharp kiss on John's cheek and then left to inspect upstairs. 'You're quiet,' were her parting words. Hannah lingered around the lower steps, waiting for John's reply.

'Aye,' snapped John, whilst shrugging his shoulders remorsefully. 'I had a proper bad nightmare. I'm not having any more power naps.' Hannah frowned to herself for a second or two, then returned to John with a forced expression of concern.

'What happened in it, like?' Hannah gestured for John to sit back on their sofa, then joined him. 'Have you been eating that dodgy blue cheese again?' she asked, sniggering.

'No,' whined John. 'It was...different. It was like the ones I used to have years ago, before Mam and Dad divorced.' A sickening sensation began to overwhelm him again. 'I can't remember if I've told you about them...'

'You've told me bits.' Hannah sighed anxiously. 'Did you see the goat-headed man again?' John's eyes glared open wide and his fingers started to tremor uncontrollably. 'It's all in your head, John. Don't overthink it.'

'The demon-guy wasn't there...' John hesitated, held in doubt. 'But I saw a woman with a white dress and red ribbon around her waist. At the end of the dream, she transformed into some evil, wicked—'

'Witch?' interjected Hannah, with a dismissive grin. 'Seriously, John. I think that it's *you*, not Lucy, who has been watching too many YouTube videos.'

'It was terrifying and REAL!' roared John fearfully. He could barely contain his anger at Hannah's passive response. 'She said her name is... Sabina. Do you know anyone called that?' By this point, Hannah had already left John's company.

'No, I don't,' dismissed Hannah, from the passageway. 'Stop drinking that horse piss and eating crap – then maybe you'll get some decent sleep?'

John thought it would be wise to allow Hannah some time to cool off from his unexpected outburst. He reached for his phone again, swiping this time onto Google in search of anyone called Sabina within the local area.

'None of these people look like her,' grimaced John at the blank screen. 'Sabina's dress looked medieval. That might also explain the weird language she was speaking?' He filtered through the endless search pages, now wanting to learn of Newton Escomb's farthest history. Not much turned up, only a couple of pages discussing the ammunition factory and old marshland that was there prior to World War Two. 'Bollocks...'

'John?' Hannah's voice seemed both vexed and worrisome as she called out his name. 'Can you come upstairs, please?' John flung down his phone and quickly made for Lucy's room, where he presumed his family would be. 'Do you know anything about this?'

'Here, your Mam and Dad painted upstairs,' countered John. "I've not been up here at all!' Distant shuffling sounds came from the walls, while John took his first few steps up the stairwell. 'These walls must be made from bloody breeze blocks!'

'John, please come here – quick!' demanded Hannah, in a more desperate tone. 'Can you please explain...this?' John turned into Lucy's room, finding his daughter knelt with a small, red ribbon nestled within her tiny palms. 'Didn't you throw that out?'

'Aye, I did,' said John, his heart racing faster. 'Lucy, where did you find that?'

'My *friend* gave it to me,' replied the child, begrudgingly. 'You can't have it!' Before John had chance to, Hannah tore the ribbon from Lucy's clenched fingertips. 'That's going back in the bin... and it's staying there.'

'But, Daddy!' Lucy sobbed. 'It's special! It's MINE!' Her voice eerily sounded older, agonised and unnatural. '*She'll* get very cross with you!'

'Who will?' asked John, with a fixated glare. His eyes, for some reason, then looked to the farthest corner of Lucy's room 'Go on... tell me and Mammy.'

'The lady in the pretty white dress...' Lucy froze, as did John, into a petrified state. It was Hannah's turn now to become agitated.

'Whatever stunt you two are trying to pull on me, it isn't funny,' snarled Hannah to John. 'Keep your ghost stories to yourself. Don't get our Lucy involved.' John spread his arms out wide in dismay, then clamped them firmly upon his scalp.

'Honestly, you think I would get Lucy to say something like that?' John snatched the red ribbon from his wife's hands, though reluctantly. 'I don't find it funny either, you know.' He side-stepped hastily from Lucy's room, dragging Hannah along with him. 'There's something not right about this place. Me and Lucy can sense it, so why can't you?'

'If you're thinking about moving again so soon, you've got another thing coming,' stressed Hannah, with tears now forming in her eyes. 'Why don't you and Lucy go and see Gran and Grandpa Murray - get out the house for a bit?'

'I... don't know,' shuddered John, as not to attract Lucy's keen hearing ability. 'Grandad's getting worse with his dementia, and it's getting late.'

'Can we see Granny and Grandpa?' piped up Lucy, now sounding more like her usual self. *'Please?'* John rolled his head to Hannah; he was too late in diverting Lucy's interest.

'Grandpa might be asleep now, Lucy. We'll go and visit them tomorrow, okay?' John prepared himself for the expected guilt-trip.

'Aww, Daddy!' Lucy whinged. 'I want to see them now.' She immediately appeared before John and Hannah, her head tilted, and eyes opened like a pleading beggar. 'I love them so much...'

'Friggin' nice one, Han,' groaned John, under his breath. 'I'll call Granny now to let her know we'll be coming over tomorrow, after I finish work, alright?'

'Thank you, Daddy,' said Lucy, her smile sincere and satisfied. 'I love them *so* very much! I miss them.' John reached for his phone, all the while staring at Hannah in frustration. He looked at the time, seeing it was 19:30pm. This meant that Coronation Street would have already started, no doubt making it difficult to contact his grandmother.

'Corrie would have started. I bet that I can't get through,' sighed John to Hannah. 'You and your big gob...' John swiped across his grandmother's contact details. The phone rang for a number of seconds, causing John to believe that he was correct with his rational. 'Gran won't like me disturbing her while she's watching the soaps.' John's grandmother, Marie, answered, and as he suspected wasn't too happy on having her TV schedule interrupted.

'Hello, John,' replied Marie, in a tired voice. She was Grandpa Murray's main carer and was understandably exhausted by this commitment. 'Corrie's just come on, pet,' she sighed. 'Are you and the girls alright? Are you settled in nicely now?'

'Yes, thanks,' replied John, sheepishly. 'Sorry to bother you, Gran. I was just wondering if it will be okay to come visit you and Grandad tomorrow, after I finish work at two o'clock?'

'Of course, pettle,' said Marie, with an instant joy arisen in her tone. 'It'll be lovely to see you and the girls. Grandpa's not been too well over the past couple of days, but we understand why you haven't visited – with the move an all.' John rubbed at his tired eyes in shame. Grandpa Murray had always been such a strong father figure to him; to see how his once muscular body had wasted away through the effects of dementia was becoming too difficult for John to willingly comprehend.

'Aye. I'm really sorry I've not been over yet,' said John, his guilt increasing with each passing second. 'We'll be over by two-thirty at the latest.' The line fell silent for a couple of seconds. 'Look, Gran. I'll let you get on with your soaps. You must be shattered?'

'I am a little, to be honest. Grandpa has another infection – in his lungs this time.' Marie was evidently crying as she said this. 'Give Lucy a big kiss and cuddle from me. I'll see you tomorrow, pet.'

'See you, Gran. Love you.' John swiftly ended the call. Lucy continued to stare at him and his phone with her puppy-dog eyes.

'Can I speak to Granny?' pleaded Lucy. John slowly shrugged his head from side-to-side, trying not to show his concern for Grandpa Murray's wellbeing to the innocent and ever-watchful child. 'Aww! That's not fair!'

'Granny's going to bed, sweetheart,' implored John, whilst quickly placing his phone out of view. 'I'll pick you up from school tomorrow and then we'll go straight around to see them.'

'How's Grandpa doing?' enquired Hannah, cautiously. She could tell from John's face that the news wasn't good. 'I don't know how Gran copes...' Without warning, a loud bang came from next door, followed by several rattling noises that scraped along Lucy's walls.

'For goodness sake, Sid,' muttered John. This instantly caught Hannah's attention.

'Have you met our neighbour yet, John?' Hannah questioned bluntly. 'What are they like?' John gently rocked back-and-forth to calm his growing anxiety. How could he possibly tell Hannah the truth?

'He seems... canny,' said John, as he cautiously paced away from Hannah to go downstairs. 'I'm gonna chill on the couch for a bit, if you don't mind settling Lucy down?'

'Sure,' Hannah replied. 'Don't have a late night, though. You need to be up early for work – remember?'

'I know... I know,' grumbled John. He looked in the fridge for a can of lager and then proceeded to slump himself upon the sofa again with it. 'You better not visit me again... Sabina. I've got enough on my mind at the minute,' he stated, fearfully. 'Go and pay Sid a visit... like he'd even notice.'

'John Davidson...'

'For Christ's sake, leave me alone!' growled John, gutturally. He took a few more sips of lager to help ease his nerves, but nothing could stop the voice in his head from speaking now. 'What have I done to deserve this?' Without warning, the living room door suddenly opened and then slam shut again. 'Jesus!' John gasped, his body immediately convulsing from a stronger wave of dread. 'What was all that about?' The door opened by itself again, then slammed shut. 'Shit...'

'We shall enchant thee, John Davidson. Bid us discourse.'

CHAPTER FOUR

John had thankfully slept well, suffering no further encounter with the demonic witch from the previous night. He had to be at work for seven-thirty, and his shift lasted until two o'clock - a mere six hours, although they would feel much longer (given his disturbed sleep pattern).

'I'm going to be late – again,' John chuntered. He quietly snuck around his and Hannah's room in search of his uniform, unwittingly banging his feet upon a set of dumbbells. 'Shhh...'

'Too late,' stammered Hannah, in her half-awake state. 'Don't disturb Lucy, though. She had a really unsettled night.'

John placed a finger upon his lips and winked back to Hannah. He eventually found his uniform, albeit crumpled in a corner of the wardrobe. 'I forgot to iron it... bollocks.' Despite this, John quickly zipped up his tunic and located his fob key. 'I'll see you this afternoon, babe. Love you.'

'Love you, too,' said Hannah yawning, as she readjusted her flattened pillow. 'Don't forget that you're taking Lucy to see Gran and Grandpa.' How could John possibly forget? He still couldn't remove his grandmother's sorrowful voice out of his head from the call last night.

'I won't forget,' said John, his voice fell deep and monotonous. 'Bye, hun.' He had just enough time left to kiss Lucy goodbye. John slowly opened the door to Lucy's room, ensuring it didn't creak to awaken her. Sunlight was only just starting to creep through Lucy's cotton curtains, something which John was truly grateful of, as he despised the dark winter mornings. 'Love you, sweetheart,' he said, on gently planting a kiss upon the sleeping child's brow. 'See you in a bit, darling.'

The snow outside was starting to melt, making the journey to John's workplace even more precarious. He carefully slid his leather shoes across the slushy ground, trying to make a game of it instead of succumbing to a painful fall.

'I'm *definitely* going to be late now,' John despaired. Luckily, he made it to the care home just in time, as not to be docked any wages – his biggest concern. 'Champion!' remarked John, whilst slipping his fob-key across its clocking-in sensor. 'Two minutes to spare an'all...'

'Good morning, John,' said an enthusiastic voice from the manager's office. It was Sally Macintosh – John's boss. 'Cutting it short there, John. You were nearly late.' She turned to look at a clock on the wall behind, while John grimaced with a remorseful smile in response.

'Sorry. It's a nightmare walking through the snow in these shoes - they're like bloody ice skates.' John chortled, coyly. 'How are things going?'

'Not too bad.' Sally looked to her night nurse despondently. 'One of our residents passed away a few hours ago.'

John glanced aside to his colleagues with a genuine display of melancholy. 'That's awful. I hope they died peacefully?' He shuffled to remove his hoodie; inside the care home was like being stuck in the tropics. 'They didn't die alone, did they?'

'No, thank goodness,' interjected the night nurse, in a sharp tone. She was surprisingly awake, despite the lengthy shift. 'We sat by their side most of the night. None of her family turned up though, even after I left them several messages.'

"They'll be at the funeral though, won't they?" chuckled John, knowingly. "They all appear out the woodwork then."

'Her only next of kin, believe it or not, lives next door to you, John,' said Sally, with raised eyebrows. She then quickly began to fill out numerous documents for the CQC lain out before her. 'A chap called 'Sid'. Have you met him yet? He's never visited here, as far as I know.' John shuffled his feet awkwardly. 'You shouldn't judge a book by its cover. Who knows what goes on behind closed doors?'

'Aye,' remarked John. He was soon lost within his own thoughts, recounting the strange experience with Sid from the day before. 'Everyone has their own cross to bear, they say.'

'It's such a shame,' spoke another voice from behind John. 'We look after these poor souls and some barely get any visitors. It makes me so...mad!' It was Millie talking, John's closest friend at work. 'Doesn't it boil your piss as well, John?'

'Aye...' John continued to stare at Sally's fast writing skills and was gradually becoming hypnotised by her shifting pen strokes. 'It's a funny old world we live in, and one full of heartless gits.'

'Language, please! Anyway, can we get handover started?' Sally's tone was even graver now. 'It's not our place to judge any of the relatives... even if they do live so close, like in John's case.'

'Sorry, Sally,' whimpered John, like a bashful child. 'We'll shut up now.'

The remainder of this shift passed like a blur. Before he had even realised it, John was clocking out and had left the warmth and safety of his workplace. Outside, regardless of the melting snow, the temperature felt like it had plummeted dramatically. A dreary fog began to lift along the journey back to Skipton Road, intensifying once John reached it.

'Hey! Here comes my new pal!' screeched Sid. He was leaning over his fence with a cigarette in one hand and a can of rancid cider in the other. He didn't show of any signs of grief, despite the horrific fact his mother had only just passed away. 'Busy mornin' at work, ey?'

'Yeah. I'm always on the go, me,' said John with a forced smirk. 'Had an eventful one yourself, Sid?' he laughed to himself, though felt guilty in a way for being so snobbish.

'Too right I have. A fuckin' belter! A nasty old cow who I know just died – happy days!' Sid gleamed. 'Time to *party*! Ha-haaah!'

Now it all made sense to John. Sid proceeded to throw his can onto the path ahead of where he was walking, splashing some of its contents onto his newly polished shoes. 'Sorry 'bout that.'

'No worries, Sid. I'll just have to polish them... again.' John sped up his steps, deliberately keeping any eye contact away from Sid whilst walking by him. 'What were all those bangs last night?'

'What bangs?' countered Sid, his expression sincere and studious. 'I passed out around six-thirty last night and can't remember much after that.' Something made John believe that Sid was telling the truth, making him even more anxious to delve any further into this subject. 'The last lot said they kept hearing funny noises from my house... fuckin' called the cops on me three times... the twats.'

'Nah, I believe you, mate,' assured John, as he quickly reached for his keys to leave his neighbour's company. 'My ears must be playing up. Catch you later.'

'See ya around, kiddo.' Sid smirked sadistically. John then heard the faint sound of a heavy object landing on the bin next door, no doubt his neighbour misplacing his foothold upon the fence. 'I'm alright!'

'Aye...' chuckled John to himself, only after locking his door securely. 'It'll be a cold day in Hell when *he's* alright.'

'John?' Hannah gasped as she entered the kitchen. 'I forgot that you finish early today.'

'Bloody Hell, Han,' laughed John out aloud. 'You say *my* memory is bad! I'm going to see Gran and Grandad Murray this afternoon with Lucy – remember?' Hannah playfully punched at John's nearest shoulder. 'Oww....'

'Yes, I remember.' she grinned, her smile cute and forgiving. 'Who exactly were you talking to, just a minute ago?'

'Sid... the bloke from next door,' replied John hesitantly. 'I wouldn't bother making friends with him, though. He can barely string a sentence together.' Hannah folded her arms and glared to John with a raised eyebrow.

'Nice estate, you said.'

'Come on, Han,' John sighed. 'We're talking about one fella in an estate that holds hundreds of people.' He peered into his fridge, hoping for any sign of alcohol to numb his growing anxiety. Nothing. 'Sid's okay. He's just a character, that's all. After I've been to Gran's, I'll need to get some shopping in. The fridge is bare.'

'You mean, you're missing a few cans of lager?' Hannah sneered to John as she too inspected the empty contents of their fridge. 'Don't get into the habit of drinking every night - it's not good for your health, and Lucy is starting to pick up on things.'

'I know, hun.' John leant into Hannah, nestling his head upon her chest like a scared infant. 'I only have the odd one. There's worse habits—'

'Well, if you want to end up like our friend 'Sid' next door...' Hannah pointed John into the direction of Sid's rotten fence. 'Go right ahead. I didn't get married to a pisshead, and you can stop going on about your weird dreams in front of Lucy, too. You're freaking her out – and me.'

'Thanks for being so understanding, Han,' grumbled John, as he looked in panic to the time on his phone's screen - 14.55 p.m. 'Shit! I need to pick Lucy up from school!'

'Mr. Punctual,' said Hannah, frowning. 'Give her a big kiss from me, and send my love to Gran and Grandpa Murray,' she mumbled with a regretful whimper. 'I'm not feeling too well today, babe. It's probably best that I don't pass whatever I've got onto your grandparents.'

'No worries, hun. I'll send them your love,' spluttered John frantically, on leaving.

Once alone, Hannah held onto her stomach with both hands, rubbing at it softly with her trembling fingertips. She hadn't said

75

anything to John yet, but it had been a few weeks now from her last menstrual cycle.

'Oh God.' Hannah wiped away a solitary tear, then after taking a couple of deep breaths lay upon her sofa. 'I better not be...' She reached for her Kindle, hoping that the raunchy stories of vampires and werewolves might take her mind off things. 'How are we going to afford another bairn?' She started to cry fully now. 'Oh God...'

Soon, Hannah drifted off into a vagrant daydream and this quickly turned into a deeper sleep. She found herself, strangely enough, within an ancient marshland setting that was completely unfamiliar. Hannah could feel her bare feet sinking into the murky bog beneath. Sharp strands of long grass scratched along her tender legs, as she tried desperately to free them. It was terrifying.

'Where on earth am I?' Just across from where Hannah stood was, what appeared to be, a medieval settlement, which itself was surrounded by an alluring fog. Crude wooden structures littered the peculiar dwelling space, with a small well held at their centre. Hannah trudged through the grimy landscape towards the nearest 'house', struggling to reason whether this was really a dream or not – it felt far too real.

'What *is* this place?' Hannah peered into the home through a tiny opening. Inside, she could make out a woman and child; both were clearly malnourished and related to one another through their identical features. 'Aww...' Hannah smiled at the child, who herself was combing the mother figure's long, brunette hair. This reminded Hannah so much of how she would play with Lucy, yet something didn't feel right.

'Gentle, my child,' said the angelic woman, her voice riddled with apparent angst. As of yet, Hannah couldn't reason why this should be the case; there didn't seem to be any nearby threats. 'Steady. Gentle. Practice thy verses: Lux in tenebris...' Suddenly, several cries could be heard from within the centre of this ethereal settlement. 'Hide, Eliza! Make haste my child!' Hannah gasped herself in unison with the woman and young girl. She carefully slid against the wooden shack, trying to hide herself behind a bale of hay close by. 'Satan hast sent forth his demons!'

'What's happening?' Hannah began to weep softly. She feared for own safety, though also for the wellbeing of those now out of her reach. 'What... demons?' Three loud crashes struck against the wooden shack, startling Hannah and sending the woman hiding inside into an absolute frenzy.

'Bid us entry!' decreed a cruel-sounding man, as he struck at the home again with a violent fist. Hannah slowly moved her head to look at the imposing menace. 'Our Lord commands it of thee!'

'Thou art unwelcome in my home. Evil, be gone!' screamed the mother with a harrowing roar. 'God hast forsaken thee!' The whole structure shook from another aggressive strike. Hannah could make out the figures of three men; each clad in course-looking, brown robes - monks, perhaps?

'What...the...hell...is...going...on?' Hannah tried to silence her increasing breaths, dreading what would happen if she were caught. 'Monsters...' Hannah could genuinely sympathise with the mother's maternal instinct to protect her child. She writhed in guilt and torment at not being able to intervene. 'Animals. *Fucking, animals!*'

A proceeding shriek echoed throughout Hannah's ears, rising with the heavy fog that now lingered. The cloaked figures easily managed to smash through the shack's rotten door, tearing apart the dwelling within seconds for their wanted prize. Hannah peered around again and saw, to her dismay, the wicked men whom were now dragging a small child across the sodden plain towards a wooden cart nearby.

'I curse thee, foul beasts!' screamed the mother, as she dragged herself from within her ruined home, her aura now purely surrounded with malice. 'Return my child!!' Hannah lost any sense of self-preservation to release a sorrowful cry. The men tossed the dainty girl between one another's arms, each taking it in turns to lift her dress to perversely leer up it.

'The child is of age,' cackled one of the men, maliciously. 'Our Holy Father hast decreed...' The following words became indecipherable to Hannah, for a deafening rage now built itself up inside of her.

'Cowards!' Hannah sprinted towards the men with a renewed sense of urgency. However, as she approached them, something held her back. 'Leave her alone!'

'Crudelia fatem.'

'What?' Hannah froze in terror; an understandable response, given the nature of this demonic voice now talking to her. The surrounding fog thickened to a point where Hannah could no longer see the men and child, although, there was still a feeling that she was not alone. 'Who... are you?'

'Ego est mater...'

'I'll kill John when I wake up! This is *his* fault!' Hannah whined. A burning sensation quickly saturated her skin from the imposing fog, rendering Hannah's want and need to intervene on behalf of the stricken child. 'Wake up, Hannah... wake up.'

'Somnum. Ego... Sabina.'

'Seriously, John! Just wait until I get a hold of you!' cried out Hannah, to whom though still remained a mystery. The boggy marshland beneath started to draw her in again, though this time more viciously and without any sign of relenting. 'Wake up! Wake up... for God's sake!'

78

'Ego sum Rubrum Uitta Pythonissam!'

Hannah now felt the murky waters below reach her throat. She could also feel herself being drawn towards a darkened shadow that lurked just to the side of where she now drowned. A feminine outline began to form within the emerging darkness. Hannah tried to scream at it, but to no avail. Then, a blinding burst of light lit the surrounding area, dispersing the sickening fog, leaving a trail of Hellfire in its wake.

'Pati mecum apud...'

A mouthful of distilled, slimy water surged into Hannah's mouth. She struggled for her last few breaths, eventually accepting her painful death to be coming soon.

'Lucy...' Hannah focused on her daughter, her 'light in the darkness'. 'I'll never see my baby again.' Just as Hannah gave up all hope the fire vanished, along with the painful drowning sensation. She found herself stood before the mother figure, whom she had been watching only moments before. The difference now was that Hannah could see the mother's features more closely, and they were beautiful. Her skin was golden like the risen sun, her eyes the colour of mahogany, her smile sincere and loving – yet mournful, too.

'Sabina?' asked Hannah, apprehensively. The woman tilted her head in agreement and then directed Hannah's attention towards her waist, where a scarlet cloth encircled it. 'I'm... not scared of you.' Sabina laughed faintly in response, feeling no threat to herself at all. 'You're a... witch?'

'Thou art foolish to dwell upon such false love,' said Sabina, sighing wearily. Despite her sympathetic smile, she still held an air of ancient evil. Suddenly, the witch morphed into her demonic appearance, terrifying Hannah. 'Tis men that should fear my presence,' she cackled wildly, still holding onto her womb and the ribbon that encased it. 'Thou shalt fear only my master...'

Hannah tensed her neck muscles to turn away from Sabina, though with each movement the witch only reappeared and became stronger in her malice. Sabina edged closer towards Hannah, staring upon her stomach with a sordid glare.

'Stay away from me, BITCH!' Hannah roared. She flared her eyes in both an act of fear and contempt. 'You're not real! You're NOT real!' Sabina cackled louder, now merely inches away from Hannah's forlorn face.

'Pray for thy husband's redemption... for all men shalt fall under my just curse!' Sabina's face began to decay, her voice now beast-like and haunting. Hannah cried out once more, a wasted effort in defeating Sabina's malignant presence. 'Awaken and rejoice, for I shalt grant for thee to live...' grinned the witch, menacingly. 'Sanctum Spiritus!'

Hannah clenched her eyelids shut. She could not bear to look upon Sabina for a second longer. The witch's eyeless glare was just too much to take in, to bear witness to. A putrid stench of death and rotten decay filtered through Hannah's nostrils, only leaving them as she awoke from her horrifying ordeal.

'I'll bloody kill him!' said Hannah wheezing, whilst accustoming herself to her more familiar surroundings. 'What a weird dream. John has a lot to answer for – dickhead.'

***

John and Lucy had already arrived at their grandparents' home. It was a harrowing experience for John on entering his grandfather's garden, which was once strewn with various flowers and vegetables, though now was bare of them, all replaced by cobbled flagstones.

'It's such a shame,' thought John, sorrowfully. He took a moment to look at Grandpa Murray's yellow rose bush – the only remnant of his handywork left. 'I wish I paid attention to Grandad's gardening lessons; I could have looked after his garden for him and Gran then.'

'Hurry up, Daddy!' pleaded Lucy, as she latched onto her father's arms in frustration. 'I want to see Granny and Grandpa!'

'Alright, sweetheart – chillout,' replied John, still riddled with sentiment. 'Just remember: Grandpa Murray isn't very well, so be a good girl, okay?' Lucy nodded back with a pleasant grin. 'That's my girl. Go on, give Granny a big hug when you see her.'

John ushered Lucy inside. His grandmother always left the door unlocked for his grandfather's carers to come in more easily. John's heart sank further on entering his grandparent's home, for a doctor lay in wait for him within the kitchen space.

'Good afternoon,' said the doctor, in a polite and calm manner. 'I'm presuming you're Henry's grandson?' John nodded his head slightly in agreement. 'Ah, it's probably best your grandmother gives you the news. Data protection laws are so strict these days.'

'Aye,' growled John, with a detesting smirk. 'Red-tape is such a nightmare, isn't it?' The doctor silently moved aside from John's company, leaving space for his grandmother to enter. 'Hi, Gran,' said John, with a risen smile. 'What's this 'news' Doctor Morran is talking about?' John's grandmother instantly removed her smile in response.

'It's your Grandad...' Grandma Marie immediately turned to Lucy in want of her embrace, a tactical manoeuvre harnessed in order to divert the present conversation. 'Hello, pet. Have you been a good girl for Mammy and Daddy?' Lucy screeched excitedly in response. 'What a daft question to ask - you're always a good girl, and so very clever!'

'Gran,' John snapped, though as calmly as possibly. 'What's the matter?' Marie clenched onto Lucy with all her might. It was obvious to John just how distraught she had become from the doctor's visit. 'Just... tell me.'

'Your Grandad's really sick,' whispered Marie, her expression dire and forlorn. 'It's bad this time. His PEG feed is infected, and so are his lungs – again.'

'Aww, Gran.' John reached his arms lovingly around Marie. It made him so angry to be so helpless. 'Has the doctor given him any antibiotics?'

'She refused,' explained Marie, again with a vacant expression. 'I understand though, John. It's in your Grandad's best interest.'

Best interest. John had heard those two words often at his place of work, though this was personal and certainly harder to cope with.

'Doctor Morran is one of the best GP's at Grandad's surgery,' sullied John. 'She knows what she's doing. Poor Grandad, though.' He forced himself into the living room where Grandpa Murray rested in his nursing bed. John's grandfather was once the same as him: broad built and stocky. Now he was almost skeletal, totally paralysed from dementia, and hadn't spoken nor opened his eyes in many months. John held back his tears, for Grandma Marie and Lucy's sake. Lucy took it upon herself to lie upon Grandpa Murray's nursing bed, which itself was situated where the dining table had previously been downstairs. 'Don't wake Grandpa up if he is asleep, Lucy.'

'Shhh, Daddy,' implored Lucy, with a firm finger raised upon her lips. 'You're noisy – not me.' John released a single burst of laughter, as did Marie. 'Hello, Grandpa,' sang the child, affectionately. '*Daddy finger, Daddy finger...*'

'Not that song please, Lucy,' emphasised John, taking Marie by utter surprise. 'Sorry, Gran. That song creeps me out.'

'You're a funny lad, John,' commented Marie, now smiling. 'Let Lucy sing what she wants to. You're Grandpa used to love hearing you and your sister perform songs like that.'

'I'm not sure if Grandpa would appreciate that now, Gran,' grieved John. He slowly moved into the dining room. It was littered with catheter paraphernalia and various topical creams. *It's just like being back at work*, thought John resentfully. 'Has the doctor prescribed any anticipatory drugs yet, Gran?' Marie's responding expression proved otherwise. 'For goodness sake. If they won't prescribe antibiotics, surely they could have prepared some decent pain relief for him?'

'No, pet. I just have the paracetamol suspension,' whimpered Marie, with a helpless sigh. 'Will that not help him?'

'Wey, I'm not a doctor,' John groaned, 'but surely they should have given Grandad something a wee-bit stronger?'

'Why don't you speak with Doctor Morran the next time they come over?' said Marie, with a hopeful glint in her eyes. 'You know more about medicines than I do.' John rolled his eyes, the only means of venting his growing frustration. 'That's if, you don't mind?'

'Of course, not. I don't mind at all, Gran,' replied John, as he nestled himself into Marie's side. 'It shouldn't take us begging for help to get anything sorted, though. Poor Grandad. It's not fair.'

'Grandpa Murray! Grandpa Murray!' Lucy screeched, ecstatically. 'Play with me!' John snapped out of his sorrowful state to remove Lucy from his grandfather's lap.

'Don't climb over your Grandpa like that, Lucy. He's not well,' commanded John, sympathetically. 'Get off the bed NOW, young lady.'

'Aww,' moaned Lucy with a disappointed frown. 'I want to sing with Grandpa.' This was too much for Marie to take. Grandpa Murray's dementia was worsening with each passing day. John accompanied his grandmother into the kitchen area, holding onto her as both a physical and emotional support.

'I'm sorry, Gran,' simpered John, to keep his words from reaching Lucy. 'The bairn just doesn't understand Grandad's illness. She believes that he's just sleeping.' Marie wrapped her arthritic fingers around John's more plump digits. She then reached out for some kitchen roll nearby, wiping her tears away as quickly as they appeared.

'It's not Lucy's fault, John. Don't scold her like that,' said Marie, with a judgemental stare. 'The poor bairn is too young to understand anything. How can we explain dementia to her?' John shrugged in response, as he didn't know how to react otherwise.

'Beats me, Gran. Some adults still don't understand it, so we've got no hope in explaining the symptoms to a four-year-old, do we?' Marie rested her head tenderly against John's chest. 'You're amazing, you know, Gran. The fact Grandad has lived this long is all down to the love and care you give him.'

'Well, I get a lot of help from you and the rest of the family,' replied Marie, affectionately as ever. 'I couldn't bear putting him into a care home...' She froze for a moment, hoping that this comment didn't offend John in any way.

'I agree with you, Gran,' assured John, in a frank tone. 'He's getting well looked after, and that's all that matters.' Marie waved her hands in front of John's face, her usual signal to change the conversation.

'Are you settling in alright, in your new home?' asked Marie. 'If you need a hand with anything, just let me know.'

'You've got enough on your plate, Gran,' dejected John. 'It's a lovely area. The house needs a good face-lift; otherwise, it's great.' Marie patted playfully on John's shoulders, as a wider smile now arose on her face. 'Honestly, don't worry about us.'

'I do though, John. You'll always be our *Son of Gold*.' Marie leant into her trouser pockets to retrieve a twenty-pound note. John loved how his grandmother would always refer to both herself *and* Grandpa Murray in conversations, as if his grandfather was still his usual self. 'Take this and put it towards getting something nice for your new home.'

'Gran, you don't need to give me any money.' John held out his hand anyway in receipt, knowing that Marie would not relent unless this offer was accepted. 'I'll get Lucy some new clothes with it.'

'I don't care what you do with the money, John. All I want is for my family to be happy – that itself is priceless.' John clenched the note in his hands and then embraced Marie once again.

'I love you, Gran,' he whispered softly into her ears. 'Just... take things easy. We don't want you to get ill as well.' Marie snatched herself away from John's embrace as politely as possible.

'There's nothing wrong with me, pet. I might have arthritis and the odd bout of gout, but that's it. I'm all there in the brain department.' *Thank God*, thought John. He was finding each visit harder now, especially with his grandfather's worsening state.

'We won't stay too long. I've left Hannah alone, and she hates that.' John discreetly looked to his phone in expecting at least one message from Hannah, most likely asking how long he would be. 'You know what she's like...' Marie gave to John a maternal look which he could only dream of replicating.

'You better be treating Hannah right, my lad,' said Marie, as she waved a finger against John's nose. 'She's a rose between thorns, that girl. You're lucky to have her.'

'I know!' laughed John, awkwardly. 'She just doesn't like being left alone for too long, that's all, Gran.'

'If I find out you're not treating her right, John, you'll get a smacked bottom!' chuckled Marie. Seeing his grandmother smile was such a great relief to John. 'I know you're a good boy, though. Look, why don't you and Lucy just go home? I don't want to be keeping you.'

'Don't be daft, Gran,' said John, with a dismissive shrug. 'Hannah will be fine - she understands.' A distant groan suddenly came from the dining room, and it wasn't Lucy.

'Henry!' screeched Marie.

John and Marie quickly returned to Grandpa Murray's side. He was coughing with a death-like rattle now. John grew instantly bitter at the fact that there were no drugs to give his Grandpa for his struggling breaths; each agonized cough only enhanced this growing anger.

'I'd get back onto the doctor's surgery, Gran,' suggested John, quite forcefully. 'Tell them to pull their finger out and prescribe some Hyoscine, for Pete's sake.'

'Can you do it, John?' pleaded Marie, tearfully. 'You know what you're talking about...'

'No worries, Gran. I'll sort this out.' John swiftly made for his grandmother's landline. He then dialled in the number for Grandpa Murray's surgery. Number sixty-two in the queue. *Bollocks*, simpered John within his thoughts, with an increasing resentment. 'The surgery closes soon, Gran. I-I've got to go. Our Lucy needs her dinner. If Grandpa Murray's breathing gets any worse, call for an ambulance.' John couldn't get his words out fast enough, despite the stuttering.

'I do *not* want him going into hospital again!' scorned Marie, from the dining room. 'They'll just let him rot in some cold corridor!'

'I'm sorry, Gran. Really... I am.' John reached for Lucy's shoes and then hunted the child down just as quick. 'Come on, sweetheart. We need to go home.'

'Aww, Daddy! I want to sing with Grandpa Murray!' despaired the child. 'He hasn't woken up yet!'

'He won't...' John tore at himself for saying such a cold remark, especially right in front of his grandmother. 'Howay, Lucy. Mammy's waiting for us.'

'Be a good girl, Lucy,' said Marie in a broken and fragile voice. 'Do as Daddy says: get your shoes back on, pet-lamb.' John could hear his own heart pace faster; it ran with a guilt-ridden force through his veins and conscience.

'We love you, Gran. I'll come back around in a few days or so,' said John, as he swiftly tied his shoelaces together. 'I'll phone you before we come over.'

'Don't rush yourself for my benefit, pet,' sighed Marie, as she leant into John for a parting embrace. 'Give my love to Hannah when you see her.'

John looked up to the dreary clouds above as he left his grandparents' home. Lucy skipped on ahead, already knowing the way back to Skipton Road.

'Don't wander off, Lucy!' bleated John, cupping his hands together over his mouth. 'We need to cross a main road. I want you to hold onto my hand.' Lucy carried on regardless to her father's plea. 'Come back here, missy!'

After crossing the busy main road, John happened to notice something which he hadn't before. The grassy area leading to Skipton Road was extremely boggy; this was noticeable in comparison to the other areas around Newton Escomb. Pale and wiry grass lined the pathway back into John's street, a feature he had neglected to pay attention to prior.

'Marshland...' John gulped in dread, tightening his fists as a mean to vent his nervous disposition. 'Just like Sabina mentioned... fuck me.'

'Hurry up, Daddy!' Lucy squealed. 'I'm cold!' She then ran off ahead, taking John by surprise.

'I told you not to run off!' John followed his daughter in hot pursuit. He grimaced at the toll smoking all of those cigarettes had taken on his stamina, painfully wincing with each breath taken in. 'Just you wait until I catch up with you!' John turned the corner into Skipton Road and found, much to his immediate relief, that Lucy was sat patiently outside their garden's gate. 'Don't you ever do that to me again!' scorned John. 'You had me worried sick. Anything could have happened to you!'

'Now, now... there's no need to go on like that,' said an elderly woman, who had taken the liberty of standing watch over Lucy. 'The bairn's okay. There's no harm done.' The woman was at least in her late sixties, her bobbed hairstyle and false teeth making this evident to John. 'I'm Pat, your other, nicer neighbour.' She smiled, winking suggestively towards Sid's home. 'It's nice to finally meet you.'

'Aye, like-wise,' replied John, in-between catching his breaths from sprinting after Lucy. 'My name's John, and this is Lucy – my daughter.' Pat proceeded to stroke at Lucy's long, golden locks.

'Such a pretty bairn. I'm guessing that she takes after her mother?" cackled Pat, endearingly. *The cheeky bitch, what's that supposed to mean?* thought John, in his initial response.

'Oh, aye. Lucy takes her looks from my wife, and her temper from my me.' John's humour fell heavily on deaf ears. Pat merely continued to stare at Lucy with an innate sensation of love. 'Mind you, don't let her looks deceive you - she's a little tinker!'

'I highly doubt that,' replied Pat with rolling eyes. 'I don't know, parents these days just don't understand how lucky they are.' John gasped, in not really knowing how to react against such a remark.

'I'm only kidding. Lucy is good bairn,' chortled John, as he joined in with stroking his daughter's thick hair with Pat. 'It's nice to meet you, too.'

'Don't listen to what other people say about this estate. There's no bother here... apart from Sid,' said Pat, her expression swiftly dwindling into one a contempt. 'He put his mother through Hell, that is, until she was put into a care home.' John restrained himself from commenting on this. 'Poor Mary. The only family she had left wanted nothing to do with her.'

'Everyone has their cross to bear,' John said this without any thought. It was easier just to mimic his colleague's responses, rather than to willingly divulge into a tricky situation. 'I think it's a lovely estate. Do you actually get any trouble? Everyone else seems to think so.' Pat initially shrugged and then warmed herself to John's questioning.

'There's the odd ghost story,' said Pat, enthusiastically. 'They're a load of tripe, though... if you ask me.' John found no humour in this remark; instead, he found an urgent need to seek out answers.

'What ghost stories?' asked John. 'Do any involve a witch?' Pat's expression spoke louder than any words. 'One called... Sabina?'

'Erm... no, pet.' Pat's response was sharp and seemingly rehearsed. 'I've heard of an old man and little girl that wander between the houses...'

'A little girl?' John's curiosity instantly grew with Pat's attained knowledge. 'What does she look like?'

'Don't tell me that you believe such cod's-wallop?' asked Pat, with a swift swipe of her hands and judgemental glare aimed against John. 'It's a load of rubbish. This estate has been my home for over twenty years, and I've seen nothing – zilch!'

'Fair enough,' replied John. His attention turned again to Lucy. She was staring up at her bedroom window and smiling. 'Who are you smiling at, Lucy?'

'Eli - you're not allowed to know her name, Daddy!' Lucy quickly made for the kitchen door. 'Come on, Daddy. I'm so cold!'

'Let the bairn in,' remarked Pat, her humour seemingly returning. 'Send my regards to your wife... she seems lovely.' John nodded fervently in response, hoping to dismiss any risen tension between himself and his 'nicer' neighbour. 'Ta-ra for now.'

It was a strange feeling for John. He was scared to return home, given the ferocity of his nightmares experienced there, though was desperate to escape Pat's judgemental stance. John helped Lucy remove her shoes and coat, grimacing all the while at the stench of death still lingering within his kitchen.

'Bloody Hell, the stench is getting worse!' he mourned, whilst pinching at his nose. 'Another coat of paint might do the trick...'

'John?' cried out Hannah from their living room. 'Get your arse in here - right now!' John rubbed at his face wearily. What had he done now to upset Hannah?

'I'm coming, babe... won't be a minute.' John slipped off his converse trainers, hitting them against the nearby wall. He then noticed how a small, metallic bowl had been placed adjacent to the fridge; it was filled with water on one side, and cat food on the other. 'Hannah, I hope this isn't my dinner?' he humoured.

'No. We're looking after Katelyn's cat while she's on holiday, and then maybe for a few more weeks after... until she gets her new house sorted,' replied Hannah, through a filtered sea of laughter. 'She's asked us to look after Sox for a week or so...'

'Seriously?' moaned John, out of ear shot from Lucy. 'We've been landed with looking after that friggin' cat. It's backwards, man!' A few moments of silence followed, only broken by Hannah's distant bursts of laughter. 'It whines to be let out and then, when you do open the door, it whines to be let back in. Plus, it took a shit on my new work shoes the last time we watched her. I don't know, Han.'

'It's only for a little while, John!' Hannah sniggered away to herself. In truth, John liked cats, although Sox was an exception. 'Do you honestly have a problem with that?'

'No...' replied John, with a drawn-out gasp. 'That cat's mental, though. I can't believe we have to look after her again – she'll send me barmy!'

'Don't be such a knob, John,' Hannah sneered. 'Katelyn's helped us out plenty of times. Looking after Sox is the least we can do in return.'

'Aye.' John took in a deep breath before noticing Hannah's leering eyes. 'Oh, great - now what have I done?'

'I've just had a freaky dream, and I'm blaming you for it,' responded Hannah, sharply. 'I was stuck in some marshy field, and a witch attacked me... sound familiar?' John froze again. 'Aye, just you stand there like a numb arsehole, looking innocent. It's *your* fault I had such a crazy dream!'

'Don't blame me!' countered John, whilst also trying to act shocked. 'Any chance that the 'witch' spoke to you?' Hannah fell silent. 'Did she have a red ribbon around her waist?' Again, silence. 'Did she tell you that her name is 'Sabina'?'

'Go and do one, John!' commanded Hannah, as she aggressively swiped her Kindle into activation. 'You put that weird shit into my thoughts. It's all your fault.'

'Oh aye! It always is!' John hastily ushered Lucy upstairs to go and play, deeming it necessary to settle his and Hannah's dispute away from the child's innocent ears. 'Does *"Ego Sabina"* sound familiar?'

'Get lost, John. You're not funny,' snapped Hannah, eradicating any familiarity. 'You're starting to annoy me.' She then lifted her Kindle up to block John's present line of sight. 'The witch spoke in English to me, anyway.'

'Did she, now?' John threw himself upon the sofa, directly beside Hannah. 'I've worked out the language – it's Latin.' Hannah continued to blindly read through her Kindle's pages, desperate to avert John's current interest. 'I've Googled it and the phrase means: *I am Sabina.*' Hannah drew in her Kindle closer.

'Right, sod it, I'm off to bed,' grumbled Hannah, as she rolled herself away from the sofa. 'Goodnight, John.'

'Oh, c'mon!' John lowered himself to his knees in a begging fashion. 'Spend some time with me... I'm *so* scared.'

'You've got your left hand... that'll keep you company,' sneered Hannah. She left John without any parting kiss or other embrace, much to his disappointment.

'Love you, babe.' John cast himself upon the heated sofa, looking towards the blank TV while doing so. 'Here goes another sleepless night. Sabina, you better keep out of my head.' He lay there in solitude for a few hours, staring at the white-washed ceiling as an only form of escape, not daring at all to sleep.

Eventually, John closed his eyes and fell into a coma-like state. He abruptly awoke to the shrieking sound of Sox the cat, cowering and howling from the staircase nearby. 'That *bloody* cat...' John left the comfort of his sofa to inspect what was going on. As he turned into the lower passageway, he discovered Sox. The cat was trapped by its neck in the stairwell's railings and was seemingly being choked by some unseen force. 'What the fuck?! How'd you get in that state, Sox?' John managed to rescue the cat, though it took some considerable effort and force. 'What are you playing at?' Sox continued to howl in terror, its fur standing high-on-end, and its eyes widened as if she had been placed before a speeding car. 'Great! So, the witch is after you as well now, is she?'

'Daemon...'

'Here we go again,' was how John initially reacted to the disembodied, beast-like voice. It was a pitiful attempt to lighten his mood. 'Go and bother somebody else. I'm done with these games of yours, Sabina. Picking on innocent animals now, are we? Fucking coward! Who do you think you are?!"

'Ego sum Rubrum Uitta Pythonissam!'

CHAPTER FIVE

Although he had consumed four cups of strong coffee on rising, John could barely keep his eyes open. His tremors had also returned. They were an embarrassing symptom of his chronic anxiety, which plagued him on a daily basis. Along the whole ten-minute journey to Lucy's school, John struggled to contain his recurring yawns and need for sleep, and neither could he see any end to this present torment.

'Howay, Lucy,' groaned John to his daughter, whilst yawning again. 'You don't want to be late for school, do you?' Lucy skipped on ahead, singing happily to herself. 'There's a good girl...'

'*Daddy finger, Daddy finger, where are* you?' A sharp bellow from John quickly halted Lucy's performance. 'Daddy!'

'NOT that song, Lucy. Sing anything... but that one,' John commanded, with a sudden outburst of energy. 'Sing something else... something happy.'

'I don't want to,' replied Lucy. It was as if she could sense her father's growing anger. The small child ran further ahead, out of earshot (or so she thought) from John. '*Daddy finger, Daddy, finger...*'

'LUCY!' John suddenly felt a burning sensation enter his chest. He paused for a moment, clasping onto his ribcage, dreading if this was a sign having some sort of stroke or heart attack. 'For God's sake!' John's movements slowed down into a pained and sluggish walk. Lucy was almost out of sight now, which only made this agony worse. 'Wait for me, Lucy!'

'We'll be late, Daddy,' implored Lucy, with an innocent smirk. 'Hurry up!'

John couldn't even muster enough strength to speak. His breathing became more rapid and steadily uncontrollable. He was too young to die. He couldn't leave Hannah and Lucy... alone. 'Wait for me, darling!'

'No! I'm going to be late for school!' Lucy carried on, ignorant to John's current plight. John shrugged off the debilitating pain, eventually managing to jog in order to catch up with Lucy.

'Wait...' pleaded John. 'Bloody Hell, man.' He struggled to keep Lucy in view, her pace too agile for him. Finally, and much to John's relief, Lucy made it to school and just in the nick of time. After a swift kiss goodbye, John watched his daughter leave both his sight and protection. Now came the daunting walk back to Skipton Road.

'What a morning it's been,' sighed John to himself. 'A good lie-down should sort me out.' He felt a bulge in his coat's left-hand pocket – his secret carton of cigarettes. 'Err...maybe I shouldn't?' The pain in his chest was still there. Surely, smoking would make this worse. 'Ah, bollocks to it. One won't hurt me.' John's fastest movement that morning was to light the mouldy tobacco stashed within his pocket. 'That's better,' he said on exhaling a darkened plume of smoke into the air above him. It was a bittersweet relief, given the family history of smoking-related illnesses. 'There's worse habits... at least I'm not on Smack.'

'Good morning!' exclaimed John's more socially acceptable neighbour, Pat. She was walking her Yorkshire Terrier along the same route John took home. 'Isn't the weather lovely today?'

'Aye. It's beautiful... for a change,' said John, in half-awake daze. 'I might make the most of it, actually. The Tin Donkey pub has just opened up a new beer garden - that's my plan for this afternoon, since Hannah will be around her sister's.' Pat raised a judgemental eyebrow. 'Life's too short.'

'I don't know how you afford pub prices - they're bloomin' extortionate!' Laughed Pat, with a condescending undertone. 'Just think of your little girl, sonny. Don't come back home half-cut."

'I never do,' countered John, defensively. 'I can handle my drink... unlike some.' He then guided Pat's attention towards Sid, who had collapsed into a heap on the outer side of his fence. 'I kind of feel sorry for him, in a subtle way.'

'Looks can be deceiving,' replied Pat, with a contemptuous glare. 'He comes from a troubled family, from what I've heard. They're from a line of Romany Clairvoyants,' she whispered cautiously. Why this was such a huge secret was something John could not understand. 'Strange, strange people. He needs to sort his life out.'

'We live in a different world now, Pat,' countered John, taking himself by surprise at how defensive he had become on behalf of Sid. 'The Salem Witch trials are long-gone. People can believe in what they want now, can't they?' Pat shifted herself backwards awkwardly. It was evident just how embarrassed this comment from John made her feel. 'I'm not trying to be funny, just saying...'

"Yes, you're very right.' said Pat sheepishly, as she looked down at her dog's restless movements. 'Anyhow, I mustn't keep Suki here waiting. She's been wanting her walk since 06:00am this morning.' Pat shuffled away from John's company without uttering another word to him – not even a quick goodbye.

'Daft, old cow.' muttered John to himself. 'Pagans. She talks about them like they're some massive threat,' he chuckled. 'Let's see what state Sid's in today, then.' John then leered over Sid's lifeless body. His concern soon fell, however, as a lengthy fart noise left from the alcoholic's rigid carcass, depleting any worries that he had passed away. 'Charming...'

'Morning,' grumbled Sid, his hands still held firmly against his turbulent gut. 'How ya doin', John-boy?' John lit up another cigarette, then kindly handed one down to Sid, believing it may help sober him up in some way. 'Cheers, mate.'

'You'll freeze to death out here, Sid,' said John, as he ignited both cigarettes at once. 'Get yourself back inside, where it's warm, mate.'

'I don't feel the cold, me!' stated Sid, with a manic outburst of laughter. 'Hard as fucking nails, I am.' He then furiously beat his hands upon his bony chest, like a football hooligan about to strike out at their prey.

'Aye. I can believe that, Sid,' said John, dismissively. While he took in a few draws of thick smoke, all attention was still being paid to Sid's frantic breathing. 'I'm telling you, mate. Get your arse back inside before it freezes off.'

'Alright, Mam,' Sid whined, his voice similar to Lucy's when she was disheartened by her father's scorn. 'I need a shite, anyway. Can't do that out here.'

'Lovely,' said John, his face grimacing at the disgusting image now cemented in his mind. 'See you later, Sid.'

'Tattie-byes!' cackled Sid, fully aware and gladdened by the discomfort he had wrought upon John. 'You be careful, now.' John halted himself immediately, turning to face the pitiful creature behind once more.

'What do you mean by that?' John moved in closer; his fists tightened, his heart pacing. 'What did you say?'

'I'm just sayin'... be careful.' Sid inhaled a lengthy wave of smoke, then blew it towards John's position with a hateful stare. 'Your house is haunted... so, be fuckin' careful.' John's eyes flared in shock.

'How do you know that?' John waited for what felt like a lifetime in anticipation of Sid's response. He was to be disappointed, however, as the immense volume of alcohol circulating through Sid's body now took its toll on him. 'Fuck's sake, Sid.' John struggled to lift his neighbour's motionless body from off the ground. For a skinny man, Sid still held some weight on him, evidently. 'Let's get you back inside then, hey?' Just as

John made it to Sid's kitchen door, the alcoholic sprung back into life, swiping away like a feral cat at his saviour's face. 'Whoa, Sid! What the fuck's gotten into you, man? I'm trying to help you!'

'You're not comin' in!' Sid snarled, now foaming at the mouth. He contorted his body to look like Gollum, which made John laugh for split-second. 'Go on, fuck off back to your own, precious house!'

'Suit yourself,' replied John, nervously. 'You need help, mate - seriously.' Sid slammed the door in John's face; however, this didn't bother him in the slightest, as the smell of stale vodka and hand-rolled tobacco was too much for John to bear. 'What a fuckin' mong...' John quickly made his way back into the safety of his and Hannah's back garden.

'John,' said Hannah faintly from the living room, as he entered their home. 'How was Lucy when you took her to school?' John shuffled at his shaven head in perplexment. 'Was she nervous?'

'She was fine, Han.' John frowned at the deathly smell lingering in his kitchen, though tried to hide this from Hannah as best he could. 'Why ask? Lucy isn't fazed by anything.'

'It's...nothing.' Hannah's dubious body language suggested otherwise. 'I have a bone to pick with you, by the way. I had another weird nightmare that involved a witch... sound familiar?' John looked at his watch. The promise and respite of sitting in a beer garden was still too far away for comfort – especially now. 'You put those weird things in my head... knob.'

'Cheers for being so understanding, Han,' chortled John. 'Don't blame me for having freaky dreams. It has nowt to do with me.' He sat at the kitchen's small dining table, alone, whilst lifting his phone out to inspect it. 'Bloody Hell, man. It's not my fault that our house is haunted.' This was difficult for John to say, and even harder to accept. 'Sid can even back me up on that one.'

'Oh, aye?' muttered Hannah in a frustrated tone, her eyes fleeting over the screen on John's phone. 'Do you expect me to take the words of a pisshead seriously?' she folded her arms to comfort herself. 'What time are you going to the pub this afternoon?'

'I'll find out now,' said John, with a corresponding swipe across his phone to land its screen position upon what friends he still had. 'I'll text Donnie and Ryan to see when they're free.' Hannah tilted her head diligently. In truth, she wasn't happy about John leaving herself and Lucy alone, given the realistic nightmare she had encountered the night before. 'Are you still alright with us having a catch-up?'

'Yeah,' Hannah sighed. 'Just don't come rolling in again. You're back at work tomorrow, and the last thing your residents need is the smell of manky beer greeting them first thing in the morning.' John laughed, though did feel some guilt in his wantful actions.

'I'll behave myself... I always do.' John continued to tap away at his phone happily, his time at the Tin Donkey now growing closer. Hannah tutted in disagreement and was quickly becoming bored with this recurring subject.

'Anyway, how was Grandpa Murray when you saw him? You haven't said much about him,' whispered Hannah, fully aware of the distress this question could cause. 'Is he any better?' John paused his finger, leaving it to momentarily hover above his phone as if he were petrified.

'He's still bad - worse, actually.' John continued to text away again, a perfect distraction. 'He's picked up another infection or two. Poor Gran is beside herself. The doctor visited yesterday but did sweet fuck-all to help him.' John's face contorted, displaying his fermenting hatred, upsetting Hannah more. 'He's suffering, Han. The NHS has gone to shit.'

'No, it hasn't,' assured Hannah. She then rested her head against the back of John's. 'If the doctor gave Grandpa Murray more medicine it would only prolong his suffering, and none of us want that.' John lifted his head away from Hannah's, torn between agreeing with her and hating the fact that this statement was true.

'I know, Han. You're right.' A fickle apparition of fear started to form in John's eyes. He rarely showed such emotion, though the circumstances certainly warranted it. 'It's just not fair! Grandpa Murray is a decent bloke; he's never hurt anyone, yet he's stuck like a prisoner within his own body. It's so *fucked* up! It makes me so... mad!' Hannah leant in against John more firmly, hoping that her loving touch could ease his pain. 'Why is it always nice people who have to suffer in life? It's so unfair.'

'Life isn't fair, John. We just have to go on as best we can, babe.' Hannah gulped heavily, with tears of her own now forming. She had lost her own grandfather ten years prior, and in an equally distressing way. 'Stay strong... for Gran's sake, at least. That's all we can do. It is shit, but that's the way life works sometimes.' John punched a fingertip solidly against his phone's send icon. His friends were eager to meet up with him at the pub as soon as possible.

'What gets me,' growled John in a low voice, 'is that you have absolute fucking wasters, like Sid next door, who abuse their bodies and do nothing for society that live - yet, people like my Grandpa, who have done nothing wrong to anyone, suffer and have to die an undignified death. Where's the true justice in that?' Hannah slowly moved her head side-to-side. She totally agreed with what John said, though found it a depressing realisation. 'It boils my piss something rotten, it does. The injustice of it all.'

'Like I said, there's nothing we can do about it.' Hannah looked to her own phone, finding several missed calls from Barbara and two from Ivan. 'Mam's tried to call me. I won't be a sec, John.' Hannah left the kitchen to move into the hallway, where she found some respite in the solace this empty space offered her. She quickly activated a call between herself and Barbara, praying that her mother would answer.

'Hi, Mam,' said Hannah, her voice forcibly pleasant (as to not raise any suspicion). 'Sorry I missed your call. Is everything alright?' Barbara proceeded to inform Hannah of some local gossip; a notable mention was John's father, Dennis, who had landscaped a neighbour's garden next to Barbara and Ivan. 'Oh, you've seen Den, have you? Did he say anything?'

'He said that it was a nightmare moving you and John from Bourbon Close, with the bad weather and what not,' replied Barbara. 'Do you feel like you're settling in yet?' Hannah tried to not leave a noticeable silence in-between her responses. 'Are you... happy?'

'Yeah, we've settled in really well, Mam.' Hannah again forced a pleasant reply; her mother already had enough to deal with. 'John's off to the pub this afternoon, so can me and Lucy come over yours for tea?'

'Yes, of course!' It was obvious that Barbara was slurping away at something as she talked. 'Sorry, pet. I'm just having a drink with your dad. We're at the Tin Donkey.'

Hannah rolled her eyes. 'John's heading over there this afternoon – you might even see him.' A strange silence followed. 'Mam?'

'We'll be gone by the time John arrives. Is he coming over with his friends?'

'Yes,' said Hannah, coyly. 'Donnie and Ryan are meeting up with him. I've told John that he better not get drunk again.' Barbara laughed at first, then quickly realised how serious Hannah was in saying this. 'It's not funny, Mam. He snores like a bull when he's drunk.'

'Sorry, pet.' A muffled static noise then filtered through Hannah's ears. 'I've been trying some sloe gin. It's gone straight to my head.' More static noise came through, then a hiccup.

'You're breaking up, Mam. I'll call you again in a bit.' Hannah then abruptly ended the call before her mother could answer. She couldn't be bothered with John's current state of despair, so instead chose to go upstairs where her Kindle lay. 'I'm going for a little lie-down, John.'

'Okay, hun,' he replied. John's attention lay on something other than his wife at present. 'I'm just checking my emails. Ryan has text back. We're going to the pub for about two o'clock – is that okay?'

'Yeah,' said Hannah in a drawn-out breath. 'Make sure you don't leave your drinks lying about, either. I don't want you getting spiked.'

'Aye, I couldn't be doing with that.' John was reading through the BBC News' webpage. There had been another terrorist attack in London. A man in his late fifties had mown down several pedestrians on Westminster Bridge. 'Fucking animals...' John read through the remainder of this article meticulously. 'Nowhere is safe these days.' The next article mentioned a local steelworks plant going into liquidation. 'What kind of world have I brought our Lucy into? It's the mine closures all over again...'

'John?' Hannah cried out to him from the stairwell. 'Can you come here, please?' *What now,* John pondered.

'I'm coming. For crying out loud, I can't have a minute to myself, can I?' John trudged his way to where Hannah now stood, within Lucy's room. 'What's the matter?'

'Look...' Hannah pointed ominously towards some faint chalk marks that had been etched along Lucy's bedroom wall. 'Lucy's never done anything like this before.' The lines formed a definitive circle and had peculiar symbols scribbled within it. 'What...the hell...is that all about?'

'Before you say anything - I didn't do it,' implored John, his voice breaking evermore now with dread. 'They look...masonic.' He studied every fine detail. Surely, this couldn't be Lucy's work?

'Ma...what?' Hannah wrapped her arms tightly into herself again. 'Are they demonic?' John brushed a hand across his bristly hair; perplexed, just as Hannah was.

'You've seen *Ghost Adventures*, Han,' commented John, with a fleeting glance and involuntary shiver. 'Mind you, I've never seen *this* symbol before.' The chalked drawing displayed, what looked like, an iron railing with a centred heart, and smaller circle lain just above it. 'I think Google will have to help us out with this one,' he humoured, trying to diffuse the horrifying atmosphere.

'No!' Hannah cried out, her entire body trembling now. 'I'd rather not to know, John.' She stepped backwards out from Lucy's room, keeping her eyes to the ground as she did so. 'Just... get rid of it.'

'Okay, okay...' John removed the thick cardigan he was wearing, using it to wipe away any remnants of Lucy's masterpiece. 'There - it's gone.'

'Don't say anything about this to Lucy. I don't want her to be frightened.' Hannah edged further away, slowly moving into her and John's bedroom. 'And don't mention any more nightmares of yours in front of Lucy... or me.'

'I won't, hun.' Riddled with guilt, John frantically brushed the chalk dust away from his clothes before replacing them back upon his torso. 'She's just a bairn... don't take any notice, man.'

'I won't, as long as you do the same. I still don't think Lucy did this.' Hannah's tone had fallen serious, almost paranoid. 'We haven't been in this house for less than a month and we're already having issues!'

'Look, Han, there's little we can do to change things.' John glared at his phone; he still hadn't received a reply from Donnie yet. 'Try to chillout this afternoon. I know that I'll be.' Finally, a message came through from Donnie:

'I'm free today and heard from Ryan, mate. See you at the pub for 14:30pm. Get the first round in, lad.'

There were no lingering marks on Lucy's wall now. John felt satisfied that whatever evil had made its presence known, it didn't manage to affect him (as seemingly desired).

'Do you fancy something to eat, before I go?' asked John to Hannah, softly. 'I'm gonna make myself a cheese and onion toastie – fancy one?'

'I'm not hungry, John. Thanks anyway.' Hannah had already turned her Kindle on and was soon transfixed by it. Without even realising it, she had turned the light on in her bedroom – despite it being so early in the afternoon. This was a miniscule line of defence against the growing evil within her home, though this action somehow calmed Hannah's unease. 'Text me when you're coming home.'

'Will do.' John entered his bathroom. He hadn't showered yet and didn't fancy turning up at the pub smelling of B-O, seeing as this would only add fire to Donnie and Ryan's usual line of humour. 'I'm just gonna take a shower first, Han. Can you make that toastie for me, please?'

'No! You can make your own, ya lazy bastard,' she replied, in a distant voice. The need for sleep started to gradually overwhelm Hannah, but she didn't dare satisfy this growing impulse – fearful of the witch's return. Sabina's haunting vision and words still played heavily in Hannah's thoughts: the evil acts of those monks, the cruel nature of how Sabina was torn apart from her defenceless child – all so real.

'Lazy bastard?' grumbled John. He turned on his shower, ensuring that it was flowing at the hottest setting possible. 'Who's *she* calling me a "lazy bastard"?' John sang to himself as he bathed, despite forgetting most of the words. His anxiety was flaring up yet again; it was so debilitating, so overpowering, so... humiliating. Hannah must have slipped downstairs, as the CD player suddenly came into life. The song *This is not our farewell* by 'Within Temptation' then echoed throughout their home. John exhaled in relief, thankful that Hannah hadn't chosen one of her Norwegian Thrash Metal albums. Together, he and Hannah sang along to the mournful track in perfect unison.

'In my hands, a legacy of memories.
I can hear you say my name...'

BANG! After this horrifying noise, something stuck against the bathroom mirror, now opposite to where John showered. He almost slipped from the fright it caused, only just managing to keep his balance by latching onto the curtain rail.

'Fuck me!' John gasped. 'What was that?' He slowly released his grip away from the shower curtain, pulling it aside to inspect where the disturbance had come from. 'Hannah? Are you messing with me?' No response. 'Shit.' The high density of steam clouded John's mirror, but there was something clearly written upon it. 'Come...to...the...marshes?' John looked at it again in total disbelief. '*Come to the marshes*? Hannah, this isn't funny!' He knew, in truth, that it couldn't have been Hannah who wrote this. John's doting wife could be faintly heard pottering around in their kitchen, and the smell of toasted bread quickly entered his nostrils. 'Fuck this!' John reached down for his towel without further thought. He carefully motioned forwards to wipe the condensation away from his mirror, though now something else appeared on it – a dark and growing shadow. 'S-Sabina?'

'Ego Sabina! Ego sum Rubrum Uitta Pythonissam!'

'Did you say something, John?' asked Hannah, shouting from the stairwell. 'I'm making you that sandwich, only because I'm *such* a good wife!' John couldn't answer; he couldn't even move. The shadow lurking in his mirror now lost its blurry appearance, forming into the stature of a beautiful woman, who lovingly smiled back at him in return. 'John!'

'I'm coming...I'm coming!' he shrieked. John sped into the hallway, naked and not caring whether people could see him through the windows from outside. 'God help us...' He kept repeating, as he trundled down the narrow stairs, almost losing his footing.

'What *are* you doing, John?' Hannah instantly burst into laughter on seeing his naked rear-end pass by the kitchen. 'Where are you going like that?' John knelt himself, breathless and shaking in the corner of his living room. 'What's gotten into you?'

'I saw...' John stopped himself from speaking, instead turning towards the hallway with a furious stare. 'There's no point in telling you. You'll only just laugh and tell me that I've *lost the plot*, won't you?' Hannah slammed the knife in her hand upon the kitchen's worktop in response. She then slowly dragged her feet towards where John now cowered, with a small tea-towel held within one of her palms.

'Here!' Hannah threw the small towel at John's face with great accuracy. 'Cover yourself up! That'll be big enough for you...' She twitched her head sideways, also granting John a sarcastic wink aimed towards his private parts. 'I'm getting tired of these little games you're playing.'

'Han...' John reached out for his wife's attention with a shaking hand, though it was too late. Hannah had already returned to the kitchen area, where a plume of smoke now started to appear.

'Nice one!' Hannah seethed. John then entered the kitchen to find her stood upon one of their small stools, where she was waving another tea-towel under the fire alarm. I've burnt your toastie now!'

'It doesn't matter. I'm not hungry anyway,' John replied, content that omitting his lunch would only make the alcohol seep in faster through his bloodstream. 'I'll get some pork scratchings down the pub. Nothing too heavy.'

'Remember that you're at work tomorrow,' said Hannah, swiping away at the air like a frantic matador. 'You shouldn't be drinking before a shift...'

'Oh, I forgot to mention that I've managed to get my shift swapped. I sorted it out with Sally this morning.' John then made his way back upstairs, cupping his privates with both hands to protect what floundering dignity remained. 'I'll still behave myself. Don't you fret.' Hannah remained silent, consumed with anger and concern.

John looked down at his phone's screen to find that several missed calls from Donnie and Ryan were displayed upon it. 'I'm not late... why the rush?' He swiped at the screen to call Donnie. No answer. 'Shit.' John then swiped across Ryan's contact details – this time it answered. 'Thank God.'

'Alright, John?' Ryan sounded drunk already. 'When are you coming? There's a Karaoke competition on!'

'I'm in my birthday suit at the minute, mate,' John replied, albeit through some sporadic bursts of nervous laughter. 'Karaoke? We *have* hit a new low!'

'Bollocks! There's nothing wrong with our singing skills,' chuntered Ryan. Donnie's laughter could also be heard in the background. 'We've made a plan to win, John-lad. Me, you and Donnie... we're going to do *Bohemian Rhapsody* – we'll smash it!'

'Bloody Hell, Ryan,' moaned John. 'You can piss off if you think I'm doing the high notes!' More laughter fed itself through the phone's tiny speaker, and then, suddenly, Ryan's call came to an end. 'The cheeky bastards...'

'Are you going to the pub now, John?' enquired Hannah, in a stern tone. 'You may as well, we've got nothing else planned today.'

'Aye,' said John, nodding in agreement. 'I'll text you later. Love you, babe.' Displeased, Hannah moved her face away from John as he leant in to kiss her. 'So, that's how it is?'

'Have fun, John,' said Hannah, in a deeper and more frustrated tone now. 'Send my love to the lads. Watch your drinks.'

'Should I give them a big, sloppy kiss from you?' John laughed, although his humour immediately fell into an embarrassing stalemate with Hannah. 'See ya, then... I guess.'

John slammed the kitchen door shut on exiting. Within a single breath, he reached into his coat's inner pocket for the secret stash of cigarettes. 'Shit, only two left.' John lit one up, inhaling the burning fumes with a gladdened smile. 'That's better.' The exhaled smoke wafted within the rising fog outside, merging slowly into the dim light that somehow managed to prevail. 'I hope the lads have a pint ready for me. I'm gagging.' Before he knew it, John had spent his cigarette. He reached into the packet, mourning over how empty it now looked. 'I'll need to buy some more, but can I afford to?' John was halfway down his last cigarette as he made it to the Tin Donkey pub. Ryan was outside, shivering from the freezing winds, smoking his own cancer-inducing cigarette.

'It's about frigging time!' Ryan snorted. He quickly lit up another cigarette on John's approach. 'Fancy one, lad?'

'Cheers, mate.' John reached out for the cigarette, despite still having one in his mouth. 'I've ran out. How's tricks?'

'All's well, bud,' said Ryan, smirking. 'I've put our names down for the Karaoke competition.'

'You... twat.' John protested, subtly. 'I hate singing - plus, you and Donnie are shite at harmonies.' Ryan punched at John's arms playfully in return to this remark.

'You're hardly Frank Sinatra, John.' Ryan drew in a lengthy plume of smoke, only to release it directly into John's face. 'Life's too short, mate. Live a little.'

'Aye, you're right there.' John glanced into the pub, seeing to his surprise that Donnie was not there. 'Where the fuck's Donnie?'

'He'll be taking a piss, no doubt.' Ryan rolled his eyes as he said this. 'You know what he's like after one pint: like a fuckin' bairn needing the bog every five minutes.'

'I should have brought some incontinence pads from work, shouldn't I?' John sniggered. 'I might need one myself, depending on how heavy this session of ours gets.'

'I'm taking it well steady, mate,' said Ryan, his expression suddenly falling serious. 'I'm at my gran's funeral tomorrow. Can't say I'm looking forward to it.'

John squirmed awkwardly, not knowing how to respond. "Sorry, pal. I didn't realise that your gran had passed away,' he said in a sympathetic whisper. 'That's awful, mate. I'm so sorry.'

'It's fine. She hated me, anyhow.' Ryan took in an even lengthier draw from his cigarette. It was obvious that he was, in all truth, upset. At least John wasn't the only person to gain some comfort from wrecking his lungs in this destructive manner. Both took in another lengthy draw before continuing with their conversation. 'It's a free bar at the wake, so I'm gonna get bladdered.'

'Fair play, bud,' replied John in an awkward daze. 'Just keep off the whiskey chasers today then, hey?'

'Oh no! We'll be having a few of them bad-boys,' assured Ryan with pleading eyes. 'I'll see to that!'

'Oi, dickheads!' cried out a voice from the pub's entranceway – Donnie. 'Are you coming in or what?'

'Aye!' replied John and Ryan in unison.

"Never mind incontinence pads, that fucker could do with being catheterised!' humoured Ryan, his cackle reminiscent of a hyena's. 'Howay, let's get this session started!'

Inside the Tin Donkey, John was first greeted by the pub landlord's rottweiler, Percy - a huge, albeit soft natured, and imposing member of the pub's regular fleet.

'Bloody Hell!' John struggled to remove the heavy rottweiler away from his legs. 'Here, Gazza! Stop your dog from humping my leg, will ya?' Gazza, the pub's landlord, continued reading from his tabloid newspaper – completely ignorant towards John's present humiliation. 'I'm wearing black jeans, for fuck's sake! How am I going to explain dodgy, white stains to my wife?' Gazza now laughed, given he couldn't ignore John's squeals any longer. 'Gazza, man!'

'Howay, Percy! Here, boy!' Gazza whistled gently to tear the dog away from John's leg. 'He must like you, John. Percy likes 'em rough.'

'Balls to that!' John quickly planted himself upon one of the bar's stools, as far away from Percy as possible. 'What's on tap today, bar-keep?'

'Only the finest selection of British ales, my good sir.' Gazza replied, in a condescending tone. 'How about this one: nine percent ABV?' John rubbed his hands together hungrily. 'I'm guessing that's a yes?'

'Too bloody right!' implored John, now slavering like the barkeeper's dog. 'I'll have two pints, please. I need to catch up with these pillocks.' Donnie and Ryan looked to one another aghast.

'Nine percent? For this light-weight?' cackled Donnie. His laughter was reminiscent of a sea-lion's belch. 'Give him some smooth, three percent - at the most! At least he won't pass out on us that way.' Gazza pulled away at the nine percent pump, and a plume of gut-wrenching aromas swiftly followed suit. 'We have to carry this flabby bastard home, you know?'

'I only live around the corner now!' countered John, in-between a few slurps. 'I'll crawl the way back, if I have to. And for your information, I've lost weight – five kilos, to be precise.'

'Where are you living now, John-lad'" asked Gazza, in a politer tone. He actually didn't care in the slightest. 'Anywhere nice in particular?'

'Skipton Road,' murmured John, with a reserved smile. He couldn't be doing with anymore judgemental comments. 'It's a nice estate.'

'Whoa! It's fucking haunted, is that street!" interject Gazza, after initially gasping from shock. 'I used to live there. Nice neighbours, just the fuckin' spooks put me off.' He quickly handed the pint to John with trembling hands. 'You're braver than me, daft-lad.'

'Seriously?' John exclaimed, only after taking another slurp from his ulcer-inducing beverage. 'How's it haunted?'

'Well,' Gazza shifted his eyes away from John's, pretending to peer across the room at some other regulars nearby. 'Put it this way: we had some weird shit go down – poltergoose activity,' he whispered.

'You mean... *poltergeist*?' asked John in correction, with his eyes rolling back. 'A few bumps in the night, yeah?'

'Aye. More than fucking bumps, though,' frowned Gazza. 'My lass hired some so-called medium to come to our house, thinking they could 'cleanse it'. It turns out that there's some old monk who sits at the end of people's beds - and what's worse, there's a demon... which made the medium run off like a shot.'

'Fuckin' Hell.!' gasped Ryan in a drawn-out whine. 'It sounds pretty serious, Gazza.' John stared at his pint with a blank expression, trying not to let these revelations affect him. They did. 'A demonic presence, hey?'

'Aye! Of the worst fucking sort, an all,' confirmed Gazza, his expression both fearful and genuine. 'A 'proper' demon... with a witch added into the mix!'

'Right!' bleated John, suddenly. He slammed his pint down on the bar, then tried to shrug off his outburst with a pitiful grin. 'I'm ready for another pint – barkeep!' He slammed his fist against the bar again like an impatient child. 'Come on... round 'em up!'

'This one's on the house,' implored Gazza, as he hastily poured out another pint on John's behalf. 'You deserve it... for living on *that* street.'

'Load of old fairy tales and horse shite,' chuntered John, whilst swigging down half the pint in one sitting. 'Thanks though, Gazza. *Cheers*!'

The next half-hour involved John and his friends consuming several shots of Sambuca and whiskey – a lethal though satisfying combination. By the time Gazza's Karaoke competition came around, John was at the point where he was ready to go home and sleep. However, he fought against this impulse. 'Howay, lets show these amateurs how to sing, lads.'

'Too right!' cheered Ryan, as he inspected his watch. 'Hold on, we still have half-an-hour. I'll put some tunes on the jukebox.'

'None of that New Monkey crap!' piped up Donnie. 'Put something classic on like 'Oasis' or 'The Stone Roses'.'

'I'll choose what I fucking-well like!' declared Ryan as he approached the jukebox. He soon returned to his friends' company with a suspect smirk present. 'Good Jukebox in here, like.'

'What have you put on?' grumbled John, as his eyebrows raised in suspicion. 'It better not be any prog-rock... the Karaoke starts soon.'

'Nope,' assured Ryan. 'The first song is a 'Smiths' classic!' With perfect timing, 'The Smiths' *How soon is now* blared through Gazza's PA system.

'Ah! Good choice, my friend. I take it all back,' said John with a promising smile. He then nodded his head in time with the music, trying to show some interest in it. 'Can't go wrong with a bit of Morrissey!' His joyful expression soon fell, however, as the track played for a second time. 'Hold on! This track's already been on.'

111

'Eh?!' snapped Ryan, himself perplexed. He then looked to Gazza with a piercing glare. 'Your jukebox is gash, Gazza! It doesn't work right!'

'You're taste in music is what's gash, daft-lad!' responded the pub landlord sharply, only shifting his sight away from the tabloid paper lain before him to unleash his scorn. 'It's a touchscreen jukebox. How many times did you tap it?' Ryan shrugged dismissively, giving to John and Donnie a look to say: *I've really screwed up, this time.* 'Howay! How many times?'

'I don't know! Maybe a couple of times... maybe five?' Ryan shuddered apprehensively, awaiting his friends' despairing responses. 'I didn't know if it loaded or not.'

'FIVE times!' screeched Donnie and John in unison.

"Don't say that you've put this song on repeat five times, Ryan,' groaned Donnie, tilting his head back in disbelief. An awkward silence then ensued. 'You utter bell-end. It'll be on for hours!'

'It's not *my* fault!' Ryan lowered his head into his hands in attempt to muffle the laughter that now left from him. 'I've put some 'James Blunt' on after this...'

'No chance! On *that* note, let's start the Karaoke early, shall we?' Gazza's question was undeniably rhetorical. He threw his paper against Ryan's forehead, then reached over to turn off the pub's jukebox in the fastest manner he could. 'I'd rather listen to someone murder *Wonderwall*, than put up with half-an-hour of Morrisey singing.' Donnie and John both patted on their friend's back, for what sympathy they actually felt towards his humiliation. 'You three can go first – get the worst out of the way, before I get a migraine.'

'Ha-ha.' bleated John, in-between a few frothy slurps. His vision was starting to blur now (which wasn't necessarily a bad thing, given that there was a middle-aged biker dancing half-naked in the corner of his eye). 'Very funny...' John hastily finished off his drink, only so he could grab the one microphone that didn't give off the odd electrical shock first. 'Let's rock n' roll, boys!'

Half-way through their (horrendous) rendition of *Bohemian Rhapsody*, John and his two friends were duly booed off stage, much to their utter shock and disappointment. 'I thought we were doing well,' sighed Ryan in defeat, as he and John moved away from Donnie for another cigarette break. 'Get another round in. Don.'

'Nah, miss me out,' interjected John, trying not to vomit. 'I'm done in. Early night for me, lads.' Donnie and Ryan raised their arms in disbelief. 'I'm goosed, man.'

'No way! We're only just getting started!' Donnie protested. 'Howay, John. Just one more – then go.'

'No! No! No!!' It was a miracle that John even managed to say these three words. 'I'm knackered. I'm goin' home, mate.'

'Fine,' snapped Donnie, his expression one of dismay. 'I'll text you later, bud. Send my regards to Hannah and Lucy.'

'Will do.' John suddenly felt a greasy hand brush across his left forearm – it was Sid. 'Hello, Sid.' He tried to remain civil, though it was incredibly hard. 'How are you doing, pal?'

'All's well, my mate.' said Sid, staring back manically. John was surprised at how immaculate his neighbour looked. Perhaps it was the drink? 'I'm cutting down on the booze. It's pure orange juice for me now. I'm only here for the competition. World-class singer, I am!'

'I'm off home,' replied John, amidst a set of gurgling noises. 'It's an early night for me, I'm afraid.'

'I think you need it, my boy.' Sid stared harder at John, as if peering into his soul. 'Don't be having anymore nightmares...'

'I'll try not to.' John could feel his anxiety kicking in again. Sid unwittingly brought Sabina's presence back into thought, her evil smile permeating John's very being. The alcohol didn't help this either. 'How do you know about my nightmares?'

'Come on, mate. Let's get you home,' interjected Ryan, before Sid had a chance to respond. He supported John along the way back to Skipton Road, almost carrying him at one point. The evening fog had already set in, making their return all-the-more daunting and undesirable. 'Take care, pal. Come over mine when your free for a movie night. I'll get some cans in for us, okay?'

'Aye. Cheers, Ryan. John embraced his friend, almost struggling to let go of him. 'Take care. You're such a good mate...' Ryan tore himself away from John and left. 'Thanks for a great night!'

On entering his home, John found that Hannah and Lucy were nowhere to be seen, possibly still at Barbara or Katelyn's house? He flung himself onto his sofa in a drunken stupor and soon drifted off, the wicked marshland setting once again taking hold over his mind and soul. Little did John realise that in in the corner of his living room stood a tall and dark shadow, a menacing monstrosity. The creature lingered in wait for John to fully fall into a deep and meaningful slumber, yearning to torture his spirit again.

'Ego Sabina. Ego sum Rubrum Uitta Pythonissam!'

CHAPTER SIX

Hannah gently placed a blanket across John's sleeping body. His position hadn't moved at all from where he had passed out. A cold wave of sweat poured from John's skin and it reeked strongly of stale alcohol, combined with his usual, sweaty aromas.

'I'm guessing you had a good time, then?' Hannah leant down to kiss John upon his forehead, only for her to instantly recoil, wiping away a layer of salty grease from her lips, as she stood back from him in detest. 'Christ's sake, John,' she spluttered, nauseously. 'You couldn't have just had a couple of pints, could you? You always have to take it that one-step too far.'

John was oblivious to anything else going on around him. He had fallen into the deepest of sleeps, lost in a realm where demons and witches reigned-on-high. The setting that John now found himself in felt remarkably different than before. He was lost again within the ancient marshes, though he didn't feel threatened at all by them, this time. No fog lingered, nor did any foul smells. John sensed that something yearned for him to turn around, so he did.

'Sabina?' John whispered, with trembling lips. To his horror, he soon found the witch standing within their sinking environment. Sabina was in her 'fair' form: long brunette hair, silken to the touch; penetrating amber eyes that suggested a sorrowful soul within; her dress as white as purest snow, though torn to reveal her plump breasts - something John couldn't ignore, no matter how hard he tried. 'What do you want with me?'

'Thy body,' replied Sabina, within a set of orgasmic noises. 'Thy soul...' The witch then teased her fingertips along her exposed breasts, reaching them down to tear the thin dress even more. She then slowly began to reveal her pubic hair to John (to his reluctant pleasure), an act she herself seemed to take no joy from. 'I *shalt* enchant, thee...'

115

'No,' responded John in a sharp manner, his head motioning side-to-side. 'Leave me alone!' Beast-like whispers suddenly echoed around him, which were certainly not from Sabina. They spoke in Latin, with an underlying, deeper and demonic nature ringing throughout them.

'Anima Mea.'

'FUCK OFF!' screamed John, in several directions, but not at the witch. He didn't dare aim his anger at her. 'Leave...me...alone!'

'Thou forsaken, wretch!' growled Sabina. 'I SHALT enchant, thee!' John felt the ground beneath him shudder; its water shifted like there were thousands of small serpents swimming within. As he looked back up from his submerging feet, there was Sabina and now in her abhorrent form. The witch's eyes had sunk back into an endless void; her skin death-like; her hair mottled and filthy, and dress covered in a murky, watery moss. 'Thy sins...haunt thee.'

'Sabina...' gasped John, clasping at his chest. Panic began to take over him, his breaths erratic and agonizing. 'I don't know what you have against me – I don't want to.' The witch unleashed a horrific blood-curdling cry, only moments before she turned to chase John through the darkening marshes. 'Leave me alone!' John sprinted as best he could through the sodden landscape, and it felt like his legs were being constantly pulled at by unseen hands. He looked down, only for a split-second, finding to his dismay that there were ghastly arms reaching out from the waters below, each aimed against him. 'FUCK!' John kicked at them as he ran, but this only slowed him down more. 'Go to Hell!' Sabina cackled wildly, given how close she was to John now. 'Help! Anyone! Help me!'

'Our Father, who art in Heaven. Hallowed be thy name. Thy kingdom come...'

116

Sabina roared with disdain. This new phantom voice was not of her making, nor her master's; it was gentle and thankfully familiar to John – his Grandpa Murray. How John's grandfather, whom had not spoken a word in months, could commune with him now painfully tore away at him. The demonic voice instantly returned:

'Yahweh. Jehovah. Yeshua. HABENT NIHIL POTESTATEM!'

Despite his grandfather's apparent and divine intervention, Sabina quickly gained ground on John, now merely a few feet away from him. He sank further into the freezing marsh waters. In return, Sabina hungrily reached out to grasp onto her prey, only to be halted once more by Grandpa's Murray's soothing performance.

'Lead us not into temptation... but deliver us from evil.'

'NIHIL! YAHWEH!'

John felt as if he were trapped within a battle between archaic angels and demons. The two phantoms - one malicious, the other benevolent - proceeded to try in out-doing their enemy. All that remained, within the biblical atmosphere, was Sabina and John - their eyes fully locked against one another now.

'I'm not scared of you, Sabina,' whimpered John, as he cowered beneath the witch's baiting presence. 'Go away!' The witch tilted her head, appearing to show some false pity towards him. She then slowly motioned one of her arms into the air, performing a mock ritual of the Holy Trinity, before unleashing a blinding light that stunned John into a total silence.

'Thy, Heavenly Father...' whispered Sabina, whilst morphing back into her fairer form. John reluctantly opened his eyes to be met with an astounding and real vision. He was knelt inside, what looked to be, an old stone church. The welcome smell of incense and burning candle wax swiftly replaced the humid and putrid stenches encountered within Sabina's Hellish marshes. The witch herself was also knelt like John, also in a praying position, though she was placed just before the church's altar where a fat, elderly monk stood menacingly in front of her, towering over her.

'Thy body belongs to me,' whispered the witch to monk. 'Thy sins shalt haunt thee for all eternity...'

'Thy sins shalt burden *thee*, Sabina!' countered the monk, his mouth foaming with excitement. 'Confess that thou'st a witch... our Lord shalt forgive thee.' Sabina licked at her lips slowly, inducing a small movement to rise inside the monk's lower robes. 'Blessed be thy choice.'

'What...the fuck...am I watching?' groaned John, himself feeling strangely aroused by the witch's provocative motions. 'Sabina? What are you playing at?' Suddenly, after another blinding flash, John found that he had switched places with the monk. Sabina looked up to her 'prey' with wantful eyes and then, carefully, licked at his now-protruding phallus. 'What's going on?'

'Bid me discourse and I shalt enchant thy body,' replied Sabina softly, her mouth now filled by John's tremoring erection. 'Thy terrible sins shalt be no more.' John couldn't help himself. He allowed for Sabina to pleasure him, in only a way his wife should, then came a maelstrom of instant guilt as he pushed her away – screaming. 'Fuck you! Fuck you, whore!'

'Ego sum Bestia? Ego sum Rubrum Uitta Pythonissam!'

Another blinding flash followed, after yet another heart-wrenching cry from John's weary lungs. Only darkness lingered around him now. No light at all permeated, nor did any sounds or fragrance. The air fell icy cold to the point where John could feel his own breath freezing on exhalation. He could sense that someone, or something, was now stood behind him. John froze immediately in fear, a harrowing sensation of the likes he had never encountered before.

'I see you, Child of God - Sinner! I can feel your heart racing; its beats grow stronger in my presence. Fear consumes you! Bow before her! Bow before... Sabina!'

John thought of Hannah and Lucy, his only defence in attempting to defeat the risen malice now lurking behind him. 'So, you *can* speak in English?" questioned John to the demonic voice, reservedly. "I'm not scared of you, either. I won't bow down to you *or* Sabina!' he snapped furiously. 'Fuck you, too!'

'You are bold for a mortal man. Latin is my chosen tongue, but I speak in many languages, and in all dimensions. Your speech is crude, much like yourself.'

John still couldn't turn to face the demon. It was hard enough dealing with Sabina's evil, let alone another and especially one that was clearly far-more ancient than her. 'What do you and Sabina want from me? What the fuck have you been saying to me in Latin?'

'Vengeance! Sabina seeks revenge upon 'Man' for the rape and destruction of her only child! God's men committed this crime! God's sons shall be punished!'

'What happened to Sabina's child was horrific - barbaric.' John pitifully attempted to reason with the demon – what else *could* he do? 'But you can't punish other *innocent* people like this, and for a crime that was committed so long ago. It's not fair.'

'Infidel! You are cursed! Your fate – sealed! Sabina... the Red Ribbon Witch, her vengeance – purified and willed by my power – shall destroy you! I am Sabina's master! I am her... God! I am *your* God! Once connected, never can a bond be broken!'

'Our Father, who art in Heaven. Hallowed by thy name...'

'Grandad?' John didn't know how Grandpa Murray was talking to him, but he didn't care; his voice always brought a calm to any storm. The urge for John to join in with his grandfather's holy words overpowered any other natural impulse. 'Thy kingdom come...'

'DEUS EST MORTUSS!'

'You hold no power over me!' declared John, feeling braver somehow by his grandfather's loving presence. 'I am *not* scared of you! You can't hurt me!'

'Fool! Your curse shall increase ten-fold! Sabina WILL have her vengeance!'

Without warning, John felt an abrupt surge of agonising electricity course through his entire body. The malignant presence, which John realised to his horror, had now positioned itself directly before him. John slowly opened his eyes again, held in utter dread and fear for his life, then spoke into the deepening void of darkness. 'I'm... not scared. This is only a dream.' No demon met against him, only the flashing image of Sabina's 'wicked' form.

'I am Sabina. I am the Red Ribbon Witch.'

120

John finally awoke, soon finding that his face was covered by many shed tears and frigid sweat. He also had a full erection – surprisingly, given the severity of his nightmare. 'Bloody Hell...'

'Oh! Was it a fun dream you were having?' questioned Hannah sternly, from the armchair opposite John, as she stared at his bulging jeans. 'You better not have had a 'wet' one,' she jested.

'No chance!' snapped John, both embarrassed and still fearful from his ordeal. 'I had another nightmare.' Hannah's body language shifted to be more forgiving towards her husband. She could see that something had clearly upset John, though didn't know how to ask him about this, at least, without causing further upset. 'It was more vivid than before. I saw the 'Red Ribbon Witch' again.'

'*She* has a title now?' asked Hannah, almost resentful in her delivery. 'I think it's time that you went to see a doctor... seriously. You're starting to freak me out, John.' She shuffled herself beside him, deliberately catching John's erection to divert his attention away – a strange and ill-received tactic.

'What are you playing at?' winced John, as he cupped his hands over the tender region. 'That *really* hurt!'

'It better be over me and not that witch!' she chuckled, while John continued to writhe from the misplaced strike against his groin.

'Look, Han, I'm going to be honest with you...' When John said these words to his wife, it was never a good thing. This statement would usually proceed some sordid confession or pointless tirade. Hannah folded her arms in anticipation of where John's train of thought now lead, struggling to not just walk away from him. 'In this nightmare, Sabina was trying to suck me off, but...'

'You what?' Hannah roared in surprise. 'I'm booking you an appointment at the doctor's surgery - for this afternoon!' John held out his arms pleadingly, his eyes glistening still from the tears present within them.

'Please, Han. I'll go to the docs sometime this week – I promise. Just not today,' said John, in a begging tone. 'What we need is a look out somewhere. How about Whitby?' he shrugged suggestively, with a hopeful smile. 'You love it there.'

'Fine. But you better go to the doctors soon,' muttered Hannah coldly in response. 'I'm taking Lucy around my Mam's for tea after she finishes school. You just chill-out today and get some rest.' She turned away from John, attempting to hide her sorrowful expression. 'We'll be back for supper. Is that alright with you?'

'Yeah, no probs.' John's reply was vacant, given his thoughts had unwillingly returned to the horrific vision of Sabina in her malicious form. 'I'll just chill and listen to some music while you're gone. Don't worry about me.' Hannah sighed back heavily and then, without even a kiss goodbye, left John to his own company. 'Send my love to Barb and Ivan!' shouted John, as Hannah quickly slammed their kitchen door shut from outside. 'Please don't be angry with me...'

John tried to think of what music he should play, now that he had free reign over the CD player. However, his mind went completely blank, clouded with the evil words spoken to him by Sabina and her demonic "master". 'Howay, John! Pull yourself together – for Hannah and Lucy's sake!' He then moved into the kitchen to fill up his translucent kettle with fresh water, staring blankly at it as the liquid inside came to boiling point. 'I can't be arsed with this...' John pushed his kettle and empty coffee mug aside, instead choosing to sit upon one of the kitchen stools where he could stare outside into Skipton Road's dense fog. 'Looks like I'm in for an exciting day, then?' A shadow eerily moved within the fog outside, and it evidently wasn't Hannah by its larger scale. 'Now what?' pondered John, angrily. 'I can't have a minute to myself.'

'John-boy! Are you in?' It was Sid, although his voice sounded so much clearer and less slurred than before. 'John?'

'I'm coming (what does *he* want?).' Instinctively, John removed his frown to replace it with a fake smile as he opened the door for Sid's unwanted entrance. 'How are you doing, Sid?'

'Better than you, my boy, by the looks of it,' said Sid, with a feigned smirk. 'You were pretty worse-for-wear last night. Hangover?'

"I'm good, thanks." replied John, whilst carefully closing the door behind Sid. 'Do you fancy a cuppa?'

'That'd be grand, pal. I take black coffee – weak with no sugar! *I'm* sweet enough,' he jested, though with a serious expression. 'I've been off the drink for a few days now – never felt better!' John nodded his head politely in response. Sid must have been lying, he reasoned. 'Ever since you've moved in, I've lost the urge to drink myself into oblivion. Maybe I should be thanking you? Sid's grin widened more.

'There's no need for that, Sid,' John muttered. He poured out the strongest coffee possible for his neighbour, regardless of Sid's personal preference – why should he show such care anyway? 'I'm happy for you – really, I am.' Sid ran his eyes up and down John's tremoring body, inquisitive to what plight now plagued him.

'Do you suffer from anxiety or Parkinson's? Only, you're shaking like a shittin' dog.' questioned Sid in an abrupt fashion. 'You can be honest with me, you know. I suffer from anxiety and depression myself – fucking horrible, it is. What meds are you on? Ought flashy?'

'Nothing... yet,' shrugged John, as he struggled to make himself comfortable upon one of the hard kitchen stools. 'I'm going to the docs later in the week. I want a day out with the girls, first.'

Sid raised his eyebrows to show his genuine interest in John's words. 'Oh, Aye? Anywhere nice in particular?' He took his first sip from John's coffee, find it bitter and incredibly difficult to swallow. 'Fuck me, John. It's a wee-bit too strong for me, is this,' he laughed.

'You're joking, right?' blared John, without realising how aggressive his tone had become. 'You've been living off shit like over proof vodka until only a few days ago... how's my coffee any worse than that stuff?'

'Whoa, boy...whoa!' Sid implored, and in a surprisingly calm manner for him. 'What's stressing ya, lad? Not pokin' the fire enough with Hannah?'

'Leave it out, Sid,' snapped John. 'Me and Hannah are fine... in that department. It's just—' He hesitated, and then hesitated even more on realising that he was hesitating. Such a vicious circle. 'I'm having some trouble getting to sleep at night.'

'Oh, I see,' said Sid in a gravelly whisper. 'Is the witch plaguing you, by any chance?' John instantly froze and then rubbed at his eyes, wondering whether if he had misheard Sid. 'You know, the *Red Ribbon Witch*?'

'How do *you* know about her?' John gulped nervously. 'I must say, it's a huge relief to know that I'm not losing the plot.' Sid politely sipped again at his coffee, despite its horrendous taste. 'Seriously, mate.' John reiterated, but this time in a friendlier way. 'How do you know about... her?'

'I've got Romany blood, my lad!' exclaimed Sid, proudly. 'I'm a Medium on the side, an all – a fucking class act, an all.' He continued with an even wider smirk. However, John was more reserved in feeling any relief from Sid's apparent confession. 'Do you not believe me, cheeky fucker?' Sid's eyes flared wildly now. 'I'm the real fuckin' deal!'

'Hey, don't get me wrong, Sid...' John raised his palms up to suggest that an innocent misunderstanding had taken place. 'I believe you - I do! It's just...' John slowed down his breathing, also trying to ease the tension between himself and Sid. 'So, have *you* seen Sabina?'

Sid frantically lifted a finger against John's lips, his eyes now swarming with fear. 'Fuck me, boy,' he whispered, cautiously.

'Don't say her name out aloud! She can hear ya!' His tone fell into one of utter disbelief at John's naivety. John was none-the-wiser. 'I thought you were a clever lad. Don't *ever* call out a demon's name; it empowers them!'

'I'm not thick!' countered John, whilst removing Sid's greasy fingertip away from his mouth. 'It's not like I've had to deal with witches and demons before.'

Sid paused again, this time actually taking a full mouthful of John's rancid coffee. 'You're hexed, John. It's so fuckin' obvious.'

'Oh, cheers!' whined John, in amongst a set of sorrowful gasps. 'It's been a real pleasure having you around. You're a huge help!' John abruptly motioned for Sid to leave, though the 'supposed' Medium refused to budge a single inch. 'Some friend you are!'

'You need me, John-boy. Only *I* can help break your curse!' Sid pleaded, with tears now coursing down his emaciated face. 'Don't you want to know what this 'curse' is all about?' John sighed and then submitted himself to Sid's teachings; there was little else he could do, and the need to know more greatly overwhelmed him. 'Shall I tell you about the Tale of the Red Ribbon Witch?'

'Aye,' responded John, his motions and reasoning reluctant though also consumed by a thirst for further knowledge. 'I'd really appreciate if you could, mate.' Sid cracked his knuckles together like a pianist might before performing some lengthy composition. 'Please, Sid. I'm fucking desperate. She's starting to get to Lucy, too."

'Oh, she will,' Sid sneered. 'It's a sad story, John - terrifying... and true. Don't you be mistaken, my boy.' He leered into John's face with his murky-grey pupils. 'You better have some toilet paper ready, 'cos you're going to shit yourself.' He then laughed aloud randomly, breaking the grown tension for only a split second. 'I don't know the full ins-and-outs, but I *can* tell you why you're now a victim of this witch's curse. You have a right to know.'

'Cut to the chase, Sid,' pleaded John, now starting to feel the effects of a lengthy hangover. 'Just... get to the point. I can't bear the suspense.'

'It's not really a curse, more-so a calling.' Sid shuffled closer into John's personal space, somehow still reeking of alcohol and stale tobacco. 'I held a séance in here with the last tenants, before they kept calling the fucking cops on me... ungrateful bastards.'

'Howay, Sid!' implored John. 'What happened? Tell me!'

Sid moved in closer, whispering to John more discreetly. 'They didn't bless the circle before starting – big mistake. I told them to, but they wouldn't listen.' Sid rolled his eyes and shook his head. 'Anyway, we started our session. I asked if there were any spirits surrounding us, and, if there were, for them to turn the lights on and off as a way to communicate.' John licked at his lips eagerly, dreading what Sid was about to say next. 'More than that happened, my boy. The girl who used to live here had her hair pulled, and her partner got slashed three times across his back! What a fuckin' state they were in!' He laughed again. 'Fuckin' amateurs...'

"Was it...Sabina?' asked John, his expression vacant and pathetic. 'Was it her that harmed them?' To John's further frustration, Sid continued to merely laugh at him. 'Howay, Sid! I'm being fucking serious with you here!'

'Was it fuck, the witch.' Sid sniggered to himself, whilst wiping at his face wearily. '*She* wants revenge. A few scratches and some hair-pulling just aren't her style. I know this, because *she* told me herself.' He rubbed his hands together hungrily, yearning for John's reaction. 'The witch didn't attack them; it was her *master*, and you don't want to get on the wrong side of him.' Sid took a few more sips from his coffee, only to make John's suffering last a little longer, such was his sadistic nature. 'Don't ask me to tell you who *they* are, either. Not without a bail-full of sage and some holy water.'

'You're taking the piss, aren't you?' The agitation in John's voice increased with each passing word. 'I'm asking you for help and you're making an idiot out of me. Cheers.' John tore himself from the stool to lean over Sid, his fists raised in unison to his burning hatred. 'You're nought but SCUM! GET OUT!'

Sid remained calm – too calm. He downed the remnants of his coffee and then patted at John's shoulder's sympathetically. 'My lad, I'll do all I can to end this curse. You need to trust me. I tried to help my last neighbours, but they didn't let me. Now look what's happened: you're bearing the brunt of their fuckup.'

'Sorry, mate,' mumbled John sheepishly, as he sat himself back upon the uncomfortable stool. 'It's really getting to me.'

'I can see...I can see...' said Sid, like a mother would to soothe her child's woes. 'The Red Ribbon Witch got her name from the crimson cloth that adorns a part of her body on each visit – usually her waist. It's a symbol and metaphor of the blood bond she made with her master and followers...'

'Sabina had followers?' gasped John. 'There's more like her?'

Sid tutted back at this display of impatience. 'No. Not now at any rate. The witch lived in Newton Escomb during the Middle-Ages; a cruel, dangerous period in our region's history. The settlement where the witch and her young daughter lived was controlled by a group of holy men – but they were anything but.' Sid paused, as if lost in his own mournful thoughts. 'These holy men decreed that all women, particularly of child-bearing age, had to sell their bodies for them, ya know, to satisfy their ungodly lust.'

'Sick bastards,' replied John, with a nauseous groan. His thoughts intermittently turned back to what the demon had spoken of regarding Sabina's daughter, and the witch's terrifying vision. 'Fucking... paedos.'

'These were different, fouler, times. That was the norm, back then. The holy men had grown greedy for wealth. Selling their women's bodies and innocence was an easy way to gain power. However, their plan backfired – big time.'

John's phone suddenly began to vibrate – it was Hannah, but he still ignored it, consumed by Sid's twisted tale.

'Are you not going to take that?' questioned Sid, with a confounded glance towards the shifting phone. 'You're brave.'

'No. If it's important Hannah will text me back,' assured John, his voice and body now trance-like. 'Carry on with your story.'

'Fuck me, you *are* brave... in not answering your wife's call.' Sid cackled loudly, revealing what few teeth remained inside his rotten mouth. 'Anyway, the holy men had become bored with their middle-aged whores, most of which had contracted numerous sexual diseases – not good business. One-by-one, the young girls of ancient Newton Escomb were removed from their parents' possession... each sold off into prostitution or slavery. Very good business. The final straw came for Sabina when the witch's child was taken...' John's phone rang again. 'Just take the fucking call, John,' chuntered Sid impatiently. 'Don't leave your missus hanging. I can't stand the fucking 'Pogues'.'

'Alright, Han?' asked John, in a panicked and sharp response. He could barely hold his phone steady, something which Hannah could somehow tell. 'I'm fine, honestly. How's your mam and dad?'

'They're okay, just worried about you,' replied Hannah, sorrowfully 'We all are, John. Are you sure about being alone today? I'm not sure if it's such a good idea.' John chuckled and then silently rolled his eyes to Sid.

'I'm fine, Han. I'm looking forward to our day out at Whitby...' John fleeted his sight to the calendar positioned opposite. 'I've got some time off next week. We'll go there on Wednesday, yeah?'

'That'd be great!' Hannah's tone seemed a little-more jovial now. Whitby was a town she held so dearly in her heart from being young. 'I'll see you later on, hun. Love you.'

'Love you, too. Bye.' John ended the call there and then. He was desperate to learn more of Sabina's alleged past, if only to satisfy his need to be recognised as 'sane'. 'She's a good lass, is Hannah, just worries too much about daft things.'

'A diamond in the rough. I don't need a fuckin' woman in *my* life. They're nowt but a burden,' grunted Sid. It was crystal clear just how little he regarded the need for holding any affection towards his opposite sex. 'I'm my *own* master,' he sneered, jabbing at his bony ribcage.

'Hannah's great. I'm lucky to be with her.' John became increasingly defensive and regretful over allowing Sid into his home so freely. 'Carry on with your story, Sid.' An awkward stalemate followed, only broken by the need for something stronger in both men. John looked first to a half-empty bottle of scotch whiskey, itself situated on top of his fridge. Then, just as hungrily, Sid glanced to it. 'Fancy a wee dram, Sid?'

'No. I shouldn't, John,' whimpered the needful alcoholic. 'Fuck me, you'd make a great incubus... with temptation skills like that.' The pair laughed together, albeit forcefully. 'Go on... one won't hurt.' John reached for the bottle and felt some fleeting remorse on opening it. Sid by this point had found two clean glasses for the neat whiskey to be poured into. 'That's very kind of you, my boy. Cheers!'

'Carry on with the story, Sid,' commanded John, as both clinked their glasses together. He took in the first mouthful of 45% proof alcohol, choking on its fumes – unlike Sid. 'By, I forgot how strong that one is.'

'It's beautiful,' gleamed Sid, on his first mouthful. 'Now, where was I?' He then looked back out through the kitchen window. A thick fog had emerged, increasing the horror surrounding Sid's haunting tale. 'Ah, yes! The witch had her child taken from her, so she made a pact with the other women that remained in town... for revenge. It should be noted that the *Red Ribbon Witch* was once, until her dark pact, a Wiccan. She only used her magic for good, creating potions that healed and other things of the same sort. Anyone who wished to seek vengeance along with the witch wore a cloth soaked in her blood around one part of their body – a blood pact. Powerful magic... and incredibly evil.' Sid himself became nervous, taking John by surprise. 'It was to bond them with her and her master, you see. We're not talking of a dozy fella dressed in red tights with little red horns, here. The witch's master is fucking terrifying, John. You don't need to see 'It' to realise they're around.' Sid frantically stood himself and then poured the rest of his whiskey down John's sink. 'Fuck, I-I've said too much. The witch told me this in confidence.'

'Fuck her! I want to know more!' implored John, whilst holding out the whiskey bottle to Sid as a bribe. 'I *need* to no more!'

'I've said *way* too much.' Sid looked upon the empty glass in resentment, wishing to have taken just one more sip before disposing of its contents. 'I'll be going now, John. Take care and heed my warning: do not summon the *Red Ribbon Witch*.' John had no time to reply, as Sid left without uttering another word or granting any further 'advice'.

'Why would I want to summon her?' John pondered. He then woefully topped his glass of whiskey up again, pouring some back into its bottle. 'That's it!' he exclaimed, as all dread suddenly seemed to fade away. 'I need to cleanse the house... but how?' John pulled out one of the 'moving' boxes from a cupboard beneath the stairs that was labelled: Books and DVDs. 'Where is it? Where *is* it?' A line of cold sweat began to draw itself down his face. John was desperate, and melancholy soon set in. 'Where's my bible gone? I know that I packed it in here somewhere.' Finally, after a few more curse-words, and to his immediate relief, John found his copy of the King James' Bible.

'Right,' said John, affirmatively. Just holding the small holy book in his hands again, for the first time in many years, wrought with it a cocktail of emotions and deep-seated resentment. John laughed initially at how desperate he had become, at how desperate Sabina had now made him, to turn to such superstitious texts. '*She* and that demon-thing hated it when the Lord's Prayer was being spoken...' John carefully moved aside some of the silver-lined pages, licking at each of the corners as to not tear their thin pulp. 'I wonder if there might be a psalm or a special passage that could help me - why are there no indexes for exorcism?? John chuckled anxiously, hoping to calm his nerves. 'Here goes nothing...'

The first page John landed upon was within the book of Job:

Job 4:8 – As I have observed, those who plow iniquity and those who sow trouble, reap the same.

'What a great start,' frowned John, as he flicked through a few more pages. 'You reap, what you sow? What have I done to deserve this? I'm reading from the Bible, Sabina. Does that piss you off? I hope it does.' A cold surge of electricity instantly swam across his arms and neck. John slowly turned towards the stairwell, sensing that a presence was there, staring right back at him. 'How about one this, *Sabina*?'

Proverbs 4:16 – For they cannot rest until they do evil; they are robbed of sleep, until they make someone stumble.

'I can relate to that one!' grieved John. He clasped his holy book shut, lost as to how it could possibly help him against such a wicked and ethereal menace. 'I'll try something I saw on *Ghost Adventures* instead. Maybe that'll do the trick?' He inhaled a painfully extended breath, then released it into the icy air surrounding him. 'Spirits! You are not welcome here!' John raised his arms up like a Pastor blessing their congregation of willing listeners. 'Leave this home! Be gone! Your evil is not welcome here! You are not welcome here!'

Suddenly, a series of vicious whispers fell into John's ears and ever-fearful soul. He turned away from the stairwell, towards his living room, though the being only seemed to follow John's line of sight.

'Falsa... verba'

'Be gone, evil spirits!' continued John, his bravery now starting to falter somewhat. 'Leave my house! Leave my family alone!'

'Yeshua est MORTUUS!'

John felt driven, beyond any measure, to make a final statement against the demonic voice that now loitered within his mind. 'Our Father, who art in Heaven. Hallowed be thy name, thy kingdom come!'

'Infernum manet!'

'It's all in my head. This is ALL... in my head!' whimpered John, fighting greatly to hold back any tears now forming. The demonic whispers echoed from all sides against their prey in return, relentless in their tirade and hateful aim. 'Thy will be done, on Earth as it is in Heav—' Without warning, a fairer, more-feminine voice made itself known behind the demon's, acting just like a translator.

'Ego Sabina!'

'Her name... is Sabina.'

'Ego sum Rubrum Uitta PYTHONISSAM!'

'She is...the Red Ribbon Witch.'

'Iohannes... Iohannes!'

'John...John!'

'MORS VENIT!'

'She wishes death upon you. She wants... control.'

This was too much for John to bear. His body shuddered with the sensation of being drowned, forced into a realm which he had no knowledge of. The whispers finally ceased now, although their impact on him had been truly horrific and paralysing. In wake of his torturer's absence, John lay helplessly within the living room; his eyes blinded from fear and ears deafened to all noise other than that of his own racing heartbeat.

'Fuck you, Sabina. Fuck you... whatever you are!' Nothing replied to John. Nothing else seemed to exist for that matter, other than his contrived feeling of death, of his utter worthlessness. 'Hannah... Lucy...'

Time slipped from John's conscious self. He remained held in a foetal position for another two hours before Hannah and Lucy eventually returned home. The distinctive sound of metal grinding against metal reverberated through his mind. John understood, without any doubt, that this noise was Hannah turning the key in their door. Something had a control over every inch of his body now, compelling him from speaking, let alone muster enough strength to move.

'John?' cried out Hannah, her fragile voice suggesting that she was thinking of only the worst scenarios possible. 'John! Where are you? Why aren't you answering me?'

'I'm... here,' replied John, sounding as if he was being choked. 'Hannah! Hannah!' The words barely left his mouth before disappearing into an inaudible haze. 'Hannah... help me!'

'Daddy?' mumbled Lucy, her whole body frozen in fright, as she gradually entered the foreboding atmosphere of John's living room. 'What's wrong with you, Daddy? Are you poorly?' She started to cry, adding further agony to John's humiliation and despair. 'Mummy! Mummy!' screeched the child. 'Daddy's here! Daddy's poorly!'

'What the Hell?!' gasped Hannah, on being reunited with her small family again. 'John! Have you had a stroke or something?' She reached down to wrap her husband within her arms; this most-selfless action was also supported by Lucy. 'Oh, God! I'll call an ambulance! Lucy, get my phone – quick!'

'No!' implored John, his words now slightly clearer to fathom though still strained. 'I'm not having a stroke! Get me out of this room!'

'Okay...' Hannah whimpered, her eyes fleeting across John through sheer panic. 'I can't lift you, John! You're too heavy!' No matter how much strength and wilful force she used, Hannah barely moved John an inch from his incarcerated position. 'Shit! I'll call Mam and Dad! Maybe they can help?' John shook his head violently in response to this notion.

'No! Don't tell anyone!' John eventually began to move himself, appearing as if in slow-motion, away from Hannah and his watchful child. 'Open... the door! OPEN THE DOOR!'

Before Hannah had chance to form any instruction, Lucy intuitively bolted across the room to open its outer door. Mother and child then held on to one another, both lost in grief and confused as to what infliction John was suffering from.

'What's going on, John? What's wrong with you?' quivered Hannah, in-between some sporadic gasps of terror. 'What's happened? Oh God! Are you hurt?' John silently dragged his heavy torso across the rugged carpet beneath, aiming for the cold air outside. To him it seemed strangely warm, inviting - a place of solace. 'John! Talk to me!' Hannah fell into a trance of her own, whether she was attempting to pray or merely curse in dread could not be deciphered by neither herself nor John at this moment.

'Quick!' begged John, frantically. He was almost 'there'. He could feel the sharp blades of grass tear across his exposed forearm as he finally punched a fist into the sodden earth outside. 'Help! Get me out of this house!' Hannah and Lucy clambered to aid John, neither knowing how to end his current plight. They pushed at him, however, in total disregard of their doubts. 'I can't breathe! I can't... BREATHE! She's choking me!'

'John!' wept Hannah. 'If you're playing a prank on me, this *isn't* funny!" she scorned. 'What's gotten into you? You're scaring Lucy!'

'Ahhh...' sighed John aloud in utter relief, whilst allowing for his body to fully sink into the freezing, sludgy mud. 'Thank God!" He then exhaled as if it were his last breath. 'I'm not messing with you, Han. Honestly.' He gently shook his head, still weakened from his ordeal. 'Something - oh, FUCK IT! Sabina got to me, okay? I was dumb. I antagonised her!'

'What?' Hannah responded with a stern and judgemental glare, also shielding Lucy's ears with her hands to prevent the child from hearing John's foul language. 'You're going to the doctors' surgery tomorrow, John, or else... I'm leaving you. Don't you *dare* think for a moment that I'm not being serious.'

'Daddy! My poor, Daddy!' Lucy pushed Hannah aside to lay with John, not caring at all for how her mother would react. 'Daddy needs a doctor!' said the child, with an innocent smile. 'My poor, Daddy. Stop shouting at him, Mummy!' Lucy wrapped her small arms across John's shivering chest, hoping that her own warmth would add to his. 'Don't die, Daddy! I love you *so* much!'

'I'm okay now, sweetheart. Daddy's not going anywhere,' assured John, with what strength remained. He silently stroked at Lucy's hair to comfort her, as it was still so difficult for him to speak. 'Daddy will see his doctor tomorrow, alright?' Lucy nodded back in response, then wiped a tear away from her face. John slowly attempted to stand, though he received little assistance from Hannah – the rift between them now firmly setting in. 'Just... give me a sec. I'll explain everything.' John, to his further dismay, slipped upon the greasy soil, landing back beside a huge puddle of filthy, putrid water. 'Shit...' His eyes fleeted frantically around him, finding that everything was now a blur again... apart from the murky puddle. 'Pull yourself together, John.' A dim light gradually transpired within the murky water that swam freely, swirling itself into random spirals, forging into Sabina's haunting features. 'No! NO!!" growled John in utter anguish.

'Get back inside, for God's sake!' commanded Hannah, as she pulled Lucy and herself back into the warmer setting of their home. 'People will see you, John! They'll think you've gone mad!' He didn't care. Nothing else mattered. All that existed to John was himself and Sabina's growing apparition in the water lain before him. 'You can sleep on the couch - freak!' shouted Hannah from the living room's window, after slamming its door shut. 'Go and play upstairs, Lucy,' was all John heard. An eerie silence then ensued, not even the passing breeze seemed to create any faint sound. Sabina's entrancing features soon began to change into her demonic self and, as they did, a red ribbon appeared around John's neck in his reflection, tightening itself with each passing breath.

'Sabina...' said John, hypnotised and consumed by the witch's morphing face. 'Leave me and my family alone - please!'

'*Lowly worm. Thou art forsaken! I shalt enact my vengeance upon thee. Once connected, never can a bond be broken!*'

John clambered back inside, confused and terrified. Hannah and Lucy had already gone upstairs, leaving him alone to dwell on his peculiar actions. He sat on the sofa for a few moments, stewing over what had just taken place: his failed cleansing, his lack of power to repel the demons and their hatred... Sabina's ultimate possession over him. John's family, regardless of the strong love he felt for them, now seemingly moved to fall apart. John didn't want to fall asleep. At this moment, John didn't even want to be alive.

'There is no light in the dark... only revenge.'

CHAPTER SEVEN

Hannah and John hadn't slept apart for almost five years. Neither of them wanted this cold stalemate, though little could have been done to prevent it, in greater hindsight. After recovering from Sabina's possession over him, John spent the remainder of his evening alone and quickly succumbed to regret over his naïve cleansing attempt. Him reading excerpts from the Bible did not remove the Red Ribbon Witch and her demonic master as intended; in fact, his actions merely enticed their malice further. How could John have been so careless, so stubborn... so foolish?

'I'm such an idiot,' John chuntered to himself bitterly as he rocked back and forth upon his sofa, held within a seething level of frustration. 'What made you think *that* would have been a good idea? Absolute... idiot.' He glanced across the living room to where his small Bible lay, finding it was now strangely open upon *The New Testament's* first two pages. 'More fun and games, Sabina?' The pages lifted slightly as a mild draft passed over them, though were prevented from completely turning by some unseen force. 'Nothing is sacred to you, is it? I need a miracle... not a holy book.'

'Goodnight, John,' whispered Hannah from the stairwell. 'You can come up if you want? I'd rather you weren't left down here by yourself, especially after what's happened.' She clasped onto the railings, hoping that her husband would heed this plea. 'It's nearly half-one in the morning. You'll freeze down there, babe. Please come to bed.'

'I'm fine, Han,' snarled John, his expression vacant and emotions drained. 'I'm gonna listen to some music on my headphones – have a chillout session.' He ran a fingertip over his CD collection, eventually landing it upon his favourite 'Nick Cave' album: *Murder Ballads*. This music would be fitting for the mood he was currently in. 'You get yourself back to bed, hun. I promise... I'll go and see a doctor tomorrow.'

Hannah tightened her grip upon the bannister, riddled with a level of fear which she had never encountered before. 'I don't want us to fall out with each other, John. I love you."

'I Love you too, Han.'

'Really?'

'YES!' John's patience had finally broken, as did Hannah's guilt towards her husband's plight. 'I'll see you in the morning. Don't wake Lucy up.' Hannah silently ushered herself into the master bedroom - confused, saddened, and fearful at how this situation was seeming to only worsen. 'Goodnight.'

John moved his *Murder Ballads* CD away from its case slowly, like a heart surgeon manoeuvring their tools inside a vulnerable body, albeit with far less consequence involved.

'God, I wish I had some beers left.' John sighed glumly. He then slipped a finger over the play button, forgetting that he had previously set the player to its highest volume. 'Shit!' he gasped, deafened by the low droning noise now coming through his headphones. '*Song of Joy*, it is.'

'Have mercy on me sir, allow me to impose on you...'

'That's better,' thought John, with a satisfied smirk. 'I'll be asleep in no-time.' Suddenly, he jolted up in fright. 'But... do I *want* to fall asleep? Sabina and that demon of hers will only come back to haunt me... I know they will.'

'Let me tell you a story, about a man and his family and I swear that is it true...'

John fought hard against his heavy eyelids and drying mouth. He didn't dare fall asleep, for he knew what would await him. It was becoming a regular occurrence, these vivid nightmares and disturbing visions – Sabina's loving gift to her latest victim. Less than thirty minutes passed by, and all the while John continued to struggle against his natural urge to rest.

'I don't want to sleep - I can't!' John proceeded to gently weep, and then quickly muffled his mouth as not to awaken Hannah and Lucy with his pitiful whimpers. 'What did I do to deserve this? I've never hurt anyone. I'm not... a sinner.'

The disembodied woman - Sabina, whose voice resounded with a choking rasp, soon answered John's plight:

'Expecto...'

'Fuck off, Sabina!'

'Domiam et mundamini?'

'I said... FUCK-OFF!'

'SLEEP! Sleep and be cleansed.'

'No!' countered John, his whole body now trembling in fear. 'I don't want to. Just... leave me alone.'

'Dormiam et videre verum.'

'I won't give you the satisfaction. Go rot in HELL!'

'Sleep and see... the truth.'

As if under a powerful spell, John's eyes closed against his fighting will. The now-familiar stench of dense fog filtered through his nostrils, mixed with the horrifying sensation of no longer being alone. John opened his eyes and, to his instant dismay, found himself stood within Newton Escomb's ancient marshlands once again.

'What now, Sabina?' called out John. He tried to act brave, though his wavering voice signalled otherwise. 'How do you plan to torture me now? I know that you can hear me. I know that you can see me. Where are you?' Without warning, Sabina appeared beside John in her fair form. She displayed no malice in her auburn eyes, only a sorrow that John immediately pitied. 'Why won't you leave me alone, Witch?' he mumbled, under an anxious breath. 'Why don't you plague someone else—'

'Men!' roared Sabina, her response staccato-like - piercing and filled with hatred. 'Thou art a man, feeble and lowly. God hast forsaken thee.'

'I'm not the one who made a pact with the devil!' seethed John, as he forced a rigid fingertip against Sabina's exposed and frozen chest, resting it there to sense whether she was real or not. 'All men aren't monsters, Sabina. Some of us work hard for a living and care for our families. You would curse me for just being... a man?' The witch unleashed a sound from her throat similar to being choked once more. It was evident that, with talking to John so calmly, this conversation wrought an intense agony upon the begotten witch. 'You are no worse than those monks. Evil runs through you like a disease – it controls you, Sabina. I feel... sorry for you.'

'Audite nihil mali. Loquer nihil mali. Videre nihil mali.'

'What's *Master* saying to you now?' questioned John, as he shrugged his shoulders together firmly. 'What's *it* saying to me? I can't understand Latin!' Sabina's wicked grin widened in unison with her eyes opening to display a fiery hue. 'I'm not scared of either of you. Leave me alone,' he growled.

'*Master*?'' cackled the witch, wildly. 'My master saved me – he saved my soul,' she whispered. Sabina's settled manner then swiftly turned to one of pure hatred, whilst her features morphed again to display her inner demon. 'My master shalt cleanse thee of all sin. His will must be done.' She then held her palms out steadily to John, offering him a thin cloth soaked in blood within them. John shook his head against the sordid gift, disgusted by it, although he moved to retrieve the ribbon, nevertheless. An overwhelming urge compelled him to.

'No! I don't want to!' he screamed, directly into the witch's ageing face. 'Who do you think you are? You have no power over me!' A cold line of sweat ran down John's entire face now, saturating him. 'You're dead! *You're* cursed – not me!'

'I am Sabina!' declared the witch in retaliation, now appearing as her true fallen presence. 'I am the Red... Ribbon...WITCH! I am VENGEANCE!' A blinding flash instantly burned at John's eyes. He rubbed at them to ease the pain, though it did little to help. 'Suffer with me, John. Share in my burden!'

A new smell then swept through John's senses; a familiar one that both saddened and yet somehow brought comfort to him.

'Grandad?' Though John could not see clearly at this moment, he could hear his grandfather's laboured breaths and the sound of his ventilator plainly. 'Grandpa Murray?' John then found himself stood at the bottom of his grandfather's nursing bed, in the dark, in silence, and they were seemingly alone. 'I'm here, Grandad. It's me... John. Can you hear me?'

'All men aren't monsters...'

Sabina's cruel statement echoed around John as mocking whispers, but there was no sign of the witch. He carefully placed himself beside Grandpa Murray, holding onto his arthritic hands as a way of telling him that he was there. 'How are you feeling, Grandad?'

142

'J-John?'

'You spoke!' John gasped in disbelief, overwhelmed with shock at his grandfather's unexpected response. 'I can't believe you spoke to me. This is amazing!' His smile couldn't lift any higher. John saw his grandfather more as a father-figure, their relationship closer than any other male relative. 'I miss you so much.'

'She's coming,' muttered Grandpa Murray, his tone cautious and fearful, his eyes still firmly clamped shut. 'My *Son of Gold,* why has such an evil creature latched onto you? What have you done?'

'I don't know,' replied John, pitifully. He brushed along his grandfather's skeletal wrist, hoping to comfort him. 'I've done *nothing* wrong, Grandad. I should've never moved home. It's all my fault.' He thought back to his and Hannah's argument, their awkward silence, and their lingering doubts. 'I don't think that Sabina will ever leave us alone. It's not fair.'

'I wasn't talking about the 'witch', John.' Grandpa Murray gradually opened his eyes, looking to John through a seeping layer of pus that had formed over them. 'Evil comes in many forms. They are not always obvious, bonnie-lad. What have you done?'

'Sine Patre! Sine caelesti lumine!'

"Not now, Sabina.' John looked around the room again, glad that the witch still remained out of sight. 'I want to spend some time with my grandad... before—'

The house then tremored violently, as if besieged by an earthquake. John tried to throw himself in protection over his grandfather, but an unforeseen presence instead dragged the two further apart. 'Grandad!' screamed John, reaching out to him desperately with trembling arms. 'I won't let them hurt you!'

'Inferno... LUMINA!'

'Stay away from him!' John wailed, whilst frantically reaching out to grasp onto his helpless grandfather. 'Don't you dare go near him!'

'Inferno... EXPECTAT!'

John's attention was then drawn to the kitchen, which lay solely adjacent to Grandpa Murray's present place of incarceration. It seemed that one of his grandfather's carers had arrived, and unannounced. A young woman dressed in a purple tunic casually made her way towards Grandpa Murray, her face hidden from view by her long-flowing, black hair. In the stranger's youthful hands was a tray that contained numerous medical supplies, most notably a cut-throat razor blade.

'Hello, Henry,' said the woman, in a heartless tone. 'Look at you. Look at what you have become... filthy and pathetic. Let me *cleanse* you.'

'Keep the FUCK away from him!' ordered John, sensing something wasn't right about this visitor. 'Move away - NOW!'

'Pray, John,' implored Grandpa Murray. 'Pray, my boy. Look for the light in the dark...'

The carer teased her long and filthy fingernails across the blade's tip, laughing as she caught herself upon its thin edge.

'Red is such a noble colour, is it not, Mr. Murray?' taunted the carer, cruelly. Her long, brunette hair swayed apart slightly to reveal a corpse-like appearance. 'Red is the colour of a woman's womb – God's greatest creation,' she snarled, whilst slowly turning her head towards John's frozen position. 'Men are God's greatest folly. All men shall suffer! Let us begin.' A howling shriek then echoed throughout the room from her.

'Stay away from him!' pleaded John, scowling. 'You touch him - you dare touch him, and I'll fucking kill you.'

'Such is the foul mindset of man: violence, ignorance... arrogance!' scorned the carer, as she rose the thin blade in her hands across Grandpa Murray's throat. 'Suffer with me, John. SUFFER!'

'Get away from hi—' Suddenly, John's pleading cry was smothered, forcing him into an unwilling silence. A red ribbon slithered around his throat and mouth like a serpent; its origins, as yet, unknown.

'Men shall know my pain,' whimpered the woman. She then began to pierce Grandpa Murray's flesh with the crude blade, as well as releasing a set of orgasmic groans. 'MEN shall suffer as my daughter did!' John tried to pull the ribbon away with every ounce of strength that he could muster, but it was futile. The cloth merely tightened with a greater ferocity, clamping John's windpipe, forcing him to gurgle over the next few words.

'Why?' asked John, whilst fighting for every breath he could. 'Why must men suffer?'

'Silentium!'

The demon's words echoed in John's ears, taunting him, forcing his weakened resolve to fail even more. He now fought for his life; every breath was being robbed of him, and what made this worse was the fact he had to watch on helplessly as the unknown woman started to peel away Grandpa Murray's skin with her blade.

'Leave him alone!' cried John. His face was turning scarlet now, the very same colour as the ribbon constricting him. 'I'll hate you! I know it's you, Sabina - WHORE!'

The witch gasped as if taken back by John's comment, then allowed for her blade to fall freely upon Grandpa Murray's blood-soaked bed.

'A *whore*? Is that to be.my legacy?' Sabina wept momentarily, then wiped away some of the tears with her bloodied hands, licking at them with a sickening satisfaction. 'I shall show thee, John. I shall enchant thee... with my true purpose,'

'SABINA!' John instantly suffered from another blinding flash. He had been taken back to the ancient marshlands, to Sabina's home. 'I don't care what you'll show me... you're nothing but evil.' He scoured the foggy landscape in search of its dormant malice, yet John remained alone it seemed. 'Whatever happened to you - whatever made you the evil witch you are - must have been deserved...'

> *'Ego sum Rubrum Uitta Pythonissam.*
> *I am the Red Ribbon Witch... and a mother.'*

What dwindling sunlight remained in the marshes swiftly vanished, leaving John in total darkness. No starlight shone. He couldn't even see his own hands that were, at this point, swaying erratically before him. John closed his eyes, breathed in deep, and immediately thought of Lucy. What drove him to focus on his child felt cruel and corrupting.

'Go on – show me!' John reluctantly accepted his helpless position, regardless if he didn't want to. 'Show me, Sabina. Show me why you hate men so much.'

A more-innocent voice responded, youthful and feminine:

> *'Not all men are monsters.'*

'I know that I said that - and I still stand by it, Sabina!' snapped John, somewhat anxiously. The thought didn't even occur to him, due to his growing hatred, that this other voice was so child-like and unfamiliar to the witch's. It was the same voice which had acted as a translator before. Just show me what I need to see and then put an end to this torment!' A trickling sensation then steadily ran up John's throat and towards his eyes; they were cold fingers, wet and held a putrid stench of death. Then another peculiar feeling entered his body, although this felt pleasant and somehow calming. 'I *do* want to know. I want to know... the truth.'

'Ego et mater est...'

'confusione fini! End this confusion!'

'You're a mother?' John gulped with a confounded expression, astonished by what had just happened to him? 'Is that...right?'

'Yes...'

'What's going on?' For a moment John revelled in his new ability to understand the Latin words. However, it soon occurred to him that this was not necessarily a good thing. 'What does you being a mother have to do with my *supposed* curse?"

'Not YOUR curse! ALL men shall suffer!'

'Whatever.' John shrugged in defeat and would have done anything for a cigarette at this moment. 'What could *men* have possibly done to you... to make you into a witch?' A nauseous sensation then entered John's stomach, with a pain similar to a stab wound. 'Stop playing games with me – show me!'

'I will, John. I will show you what MEN did to me, to my... daughter.'

After another blinding flash, John found himself in the stony church again. Its candles were lit but only halfway down, and flickered as if they were about to extinguish. The pleasant aromas of incense and melting wax managed to lift John's spirit, but there also lingered a malicious presence somewhere nearby.

'A church? This is the last place I'd have thought you'd take me to,' pondered John, apprehensively. 'Why have you brought me here?'

'Silence!'

John obeyed the witch's command, feeling he had no over choice. A distant burst of muffled laughter then reverberated around the church, although no joy imprinted from it within the holy walls.

'Am I a... whore?'

John jolted upright aghast. One of the oak doors close by suddenly sprung open, its heavy hinges creaking with every movement. A fat, elderly monk entered first with his head held low. He was then closely followed by a young woman dressed in white, with a red ribbon wrapped around her waist – Sabina. The monk struggled to seat himself upon the church's altar, wheezing as he lifted the rolls of fat around his waist to steady his position. Sabina knelt herself, not even glancing once towards John, and began to lift the monk's robes up across his cellulite-inflicted thighs.

'Thy lowly child of God,' exhaled the monk, with a perverse grin and licking at his lips. 'Pleasure my needs - cleanse thy soul of all sin.' Sabina nodded back submissively, then glanced towards the monk's flaccid penis with a look of utter disappointment.

'Holy Father? Is my beauty not worthy of thyself?' asked Sabina to the increasingly embarrassed monk. He grunted back, his cheeks reddening further from a cocktail of anger and self-loathing.

'Make haste with thy tongue!' demanded the monk, furiously. He then tore at Sabina's hair with his plump fingers, pulling at her her closer towards him with a forcible clench and strong enough to remove several strands. 'Consume my seed... and be cleansed.'

'Thou shalt bear no shame,' assured the witch, sympathetically. 'Drink from this potion of my own making...' She slowly unravelled her dress to reveal a small vile which held a dark and thick substance inside of it, offering it to the monk. John shook his head in knowing that this could only be poison (the herbal fumes gave evidence to this). 'Thy seed shall flow this day - only if thee drinks from this.' A tense moment of silence followed between the witch and holy man. Finally, the monk tore Sabina's vile away from her steady hands, consuming it without any further thought. 'Good! Thy choice is wise...'

'Make haste with thy tongue!' commanded the monk, his breathing now becoming more rapid and strained by the second. 'Pleasure... me.' Sabina, once again, willingly obeyed. She lowered her mouth, wrapping her lips gently around the monk's stumpy phallus, initially gagging on its rotten taste, and then began to perform the 'necessary' duty of fellatio.

'So, you *are* a whore,' uttered John, cautiously. The witch merely ignored his taunt. 'I knew it.' To John's instant regret, Sabina turned an eye towards him and then to a window nearby. Within the dim candlelight, John could just make out the blurry features of another monk, who himself was partially hidden and peeping in from outside. It was plain to see that this voyeur was also pleasuring his own needs, though his sight was not lain on Sabina; it was fixated upon the empty vial beside her. 'What's he doing?'

'*Judas!*'

'Judas?' quipped John. 'You're saying... that he is a traitor?'

'He betrayed his Lord. He betrayed the balance between good and evil. He betrayed... me. He is no holier than Judas.'

'Really?' John kept his sight upon the monk outside, his appearance now blurring from a layer of condensation building up on the window. 'How? How did he betray you?' A blood-curdling suddenly cry left from the other monk's lungs as Sabina finished her sexual purpose. 'You poisoned him, didn't you?' The witch glared at her customer with a sadistic and satisfied smirk, whilst still holding his slimy seed inside her mouth. 'That's disgusting!'

'S-Sabina...' spluttered the monk, showing no sign of joy now from the witch's impressive performance. The veins on his neck began to pulsate, his face flaring with a scarlet colour like the cloth wrapped around Sabina's waist – which she swiftly removed at this terrifying point. 'Thou art... a WITCH!'

'What have you done to him?' questioned John, aggrieved by what he had witnessed. Sabina slowly turned to him; her mouth still full of the monk's putrid semen. 'You... murdered him, didn't you?' The witch smirked proudly and then held her ribbon out before John, then back towards her current victim. 'You *are* a monster!' John could see a few darker blots of red upon Sabina's ribbon emerging – her own blood perhaps? The witch opened her mouth just above the ribbon, allowing for the yellowish, stringy mucus to fall precisely onto it. 'What *are* you doing?'

'It is old magic – magic my master granted to me.'

A dark and shrouded mist then formed behind the flailing monk, easily towering over him. John didn't need to question Sabina as to what this foul presence could be, because he knew. He'd seen this monstrosity before - many years ago, and in another vivid nightmare. Two large, skeletal hands rose from within the black mist, which then slowly manoeuvred around Sabina's victim. The fat monk gasped helplessly, fearfully, knowing that his time upon this earthly plain would soon end.

Within seconds, fourteen razor-sharp talons quickly wrapped around the monk's pulsating throat, tearing away at it cruelly. Sabina laughed and then cackled louder, whilst she bowed before the demonic apparition. John could only make out the disfigured hands, seeing as no other features yet appeared. The talons gradually made their way up to slash a mocking image of a crucifix upon the monk's forehead, though strangely enough no blood ran from this. It seemed that the demon's attack had seared what flesh lingered thereafter.

'You made a pact with a demon – for what?' John whimpered. He felt a peculiar pity towards the monk's present plight, despite their malicious actions. 'You sold your soul, willingly, to the Devil?'

'Dominus!'

'Leave me alone!' replied John, sharply. 'This *can't* be real – none of this can be!' From the pitted darkness, a row of thorns emerged that slithered around the monk's brow to form an agonising crown. 'Animals! How could you do this to another human being?'

'He removed Sabina's light, so I removed his.'

An overwhelming impulse drew John's attention back to the monk outside – he'd gone, though their cries of *Witch!* and *Murder!* could be clearly heard over the distance. 'I get it now,' said John in assurance to Sabina, sorrowfully. 'That other monk told everyone else... about what you've done here. That's how he betrayed you.' The witch silently wiped away any remnants of stale semen left from her lips, and her facial features morphed once again into an

151

old, haggard wench's. The fallen monk's corpse was now completely consumed by many layers of blood-soaked thorns, with the demon's mist and talons continuing to linger over him – just like a puppet master. 'You turned to Satan, Sabina,' stated John, in a frank and judgemental tone. 'It is *you* that is cursed and condemned... not me... not all men.' Sabina cackled again in response. 'How can you laugh about this? What made you sell yourself in this way?' Before John could utter any other word, Sabina shrieked with a piercing howl – unleashing her hatred and scorn against him. 'You're only proving to me how evil you are, Sabina. You deserve to burn in Hell.'

The stone church instantly collapsed with a roar into a pile of festering dust, although, as if miraculously, no harm came to John. As the choking flakes of sandstone subsided, John found himself stood again within the foggy marshlands of ancient Newton Escomb. He looked around for any sign of Sabina, but she wasn't there - nobody was. A large pool of water nearby began to bubble as if it were boiling, calling out to John's curiosity, enticing him over towards it.

'Now what?' fretted John. He carefully stepped closer towards the bubbling pool, finding it looked more like tar the nearer he approached it. 'Whatever game she's playing now, I'm not biting. I'm not... afraid," he chuntered, anxiously. 'Show yourself, WITCH!'

Sporadic bursts of thick, black fluid shot into the air from the pool in response to John's defiance. Gradually, a humanoid figure rose from within the viscous substance; they were small enough to be a child – certainly not, Sabina.

'What the is that thing?' John leaned his body in to take a closer look. 'Who... are you?'

'You sought a reason... I grant it to thee, John Davidson.'

The child's head was held low, allowing for the black water to seep from it freely along their extending arms. John stood himself directly before the young figure to speak with them, but no words left from his mouth. He was too uncertain as to what might happen, should he do so.

'A light in the darkness... my light.'

Suddenly, a white light burst from the child's presence which then surrounded her. It was plain to see that the small girl was wearing a similar white dress to Sabina. The likeness was uncanny.

'Eliza.'

'Eliza?' questioned John, now aiming a pitied stare towards the little girl. 'Is that your name, sweetheart? Are you the little girl who plays with my daughter, Lucy?' The child raised her head with a bashful look and displayed a keen resemblance to Sabina, albeit with far less scorn. 'Is your mummy... Sabina?' The child whimpered sorrowfully and rubbed at her tiny fingers, not willing a single word to John in response. 'I'm not a bad man. You can talk to me...'

'Et lux in tenebris.'

'All men are bad, or so my mother believes, whispered the child, finally breaking her silence, whilst looking over John's left shoulder in a growing dread. 'Bad men hurt me.'
'*I'm* not bad,' assured John, desperate to get this message across both to the child *and* Sabina. 'I'd never hurt you. I would never hurt anyone.' To his shock and horror, a trail of blood began to trickle down the girl's legs, the light in her eyes faded, and several

large bruises began to appear across any revealed flesh upon her petite body. 'The bad men... they did *this* to you, Eliza?'

'STAY AWAY FROM HER!'

Sabina's demonic face now shot before John's own. He had no time to react, not even to lift his arms up in defence. Before he knew it, John awoke again, his brow saturated with cold sweat. He looked down to his phone – 06:30 a.m. He breathed in a thankful sigh, as it was his day off from work and would be the day he would once again return to his doctor about the recurring mental health issues which continued to plague him... along with Sabina.

'That was so weird,' thought John, as he strained to swallow. 'These nightmares are getting worse by the day. Christ, I daren't sleep – what am I going to do? This can't go on.' He lifted his arms up, instantly recoiling from the pungent aroma that left from them. ' I need a shower. I just hope I don't wake the girls up.'

'John?' Hannah's voice resounded from upstairs. 'Are you awake, babe?'

'Yeah,' John replied, his voice hoarse and still riddled with anxiety. 'I'm gonna take a shower.'

'Quick! Come upstairs!' ordered Hannah, though she didn't seem angry at all with John; any previous ill-feelings had evidently dissipated. 'I need to show you something.'

'I'm coming.' John jolted upstairs in the quietest manner possible, given his clumsy footwork. He found Hannah stood outside of Lucy's room with a grave expression on her face. In her hands she held a small, red ribbon. 'You have *got* to be kidding me?"

'I wish is was.' Hannah shook her head in dismay. On closer inspection, it was clear for John to see that she had tears welling up in her eyes. 'I don't know where Lucy found it. Look at her wall, John.' The same peculiar symbol had been etched again beside

Lucy's bed in red crayon. 'What's going on? What does this picture mean? How could a young bairn, like our Lucy, know how to draw something... like that?' So many questions, yet so few answers in return that John could deliver.

'Don't worry,' he whispered, trying not to wake his sleeping child. 'I'll look into this... after I've been to the Doc's. He glared at the masonic symbol once more, wishing for it to reveal what secrets surrounded its hidden meaning. 'There's *something* in this house, Hannah,' he mumbled, then clasped onto both of Hannah's hands. 'I'll sort it out though. I'm the man of this house, and it's my job to protect you and Lucy.'

'Forget it.' Hannah snapped her hands away from John's and then waved them at him dismissively. 'This is *our* home. Whatever's playing with us needs to realise that.'

'Shhh!' John's plea to Hannah to lower her tone was already too late, as the child awoke with a sudden gasp. 'Great...'

'Daddy? Mammy?' Lucy whined, as she gradually looked across them both. She then stretched out her arms and released a lengthy yawn, before looking to the haunting symbol for herself. 'Don't wipe it off!' she commanded, sternly. 'Please...DON'T!'

'We've already told you, Lucy, that you're not allowed to draw on the walls,' iterated Hannah, with flickering eyes. 'That's *naughty*.'

'It's not! My friend told me to do it!' implored Lucy, herself now becoming teary like her mother. 'She said—'

'What's your friend's name?' asked John, to an instant look of scorn from Hannah. 'Is it Sabina, by any chance?'

'No!' cried Lucy. 'That's the nasty lady! My friend is...' She clasped her hands over her mouth, silencing any further divulgence.

'Eliza?' interjected John, his breathing and heartbeat racing dramatically in unison. 'That's her name, isn't it?'

'Yes.' Lucy gave to John a look as to say: *how do you know?* 'You're not allowed to know her name, Daddy. It's a BIG secret.'

'That's enough – both of you!' screamed Hannah, as this was all too much for her to take in. '*Never* talk about them again. I'm freaked out enough as it is.'

'Eliza's a *good* witch,' said Lucy, her smile now risen and joyful. 'She's helping—'

'ENOUGH!' Hannah stormed out the bedroom, swiftly followed by John after he kissed his daughter upon her brow. 'I can't take this anymore, John. I just... can't,' she simpered to him. 'Promise me that you'll go to the doctor's – today. No ifs, no buts.'

'I will, hun,' replied John, sheepishly. He rubbed his hands gently up and down Hannah's arms, and then reached into her for a tender embrace. 'I'll get things sorted out. What we need is some time away from this house. How about, at the weekend, we go to Whitby – just me, you and Lucy? It'll be just like old times.' He smiled pitifully, hoping that this bargain could work in his favour. 'How about that? Does it sound like a good plan?'

'Yeah.' Hannah nodded in agreement. 'I'd love to go to Whitby again, and it'll be nice to get out of town – even if the weather's bad.'

'We'll make a day of it.' John's grin widened, and the sense of all things foul quickly left from him. 'Whitby's our favourite place, so let's make sure that Lucy likes it in the same way.'

'Daddy?' Lucy popped her head around the corner of the door slowly in search of her parents. 'Do *I* need to see a doctor?' She hugged tightly into her blanket, whilst looking to John and Hannah with a worrisome stare. 'Am I poorly, too?'

'No. You're not poorly, sweetheart,' said John, in a gentle and reassuring tone. 'You're going to school, young missy. Mammy will take you this morning, okay?'

'Phone the doc's first thing, John,' implored Hannah, with a sharp emphasis. 'I'm really worried about you.'

'Don't be.' John nestled his head against Hannah's. 'We'll be back to normal in no time - you'll see.'

An hour passed by. John managed to take a quick shower and had successfully booked an appointment with his own GP, whilst Hannah and Lucy made their way to school. Soon enough it was midday, the time when John made his way into town to see his doctor, to come face to face with his growing problems. It was lucky that he had remembered to set an alarm on his phone, since the town clock was still under repair and had been for many months.

'It's taking ages to get that bloody thing fixed. What are the council playing at?' chuntered John to himself, as he slurped on a carton of bitter and over-priced espresso from the local coffee shop. 'I better make my way to the Doc's. It'd be such a shame if I was to miss my appointment... not.'

'Good Afternoon,' said one of the doctor's receptionists to John, as he entered the surgery. 'Can I take your name, please?' John fumbled for a moment; he was trying to hide a packet of cigarettes which were poking out from his back pocket. 'Are you alright?'

'Aye. Sorry, I'm not with it today,' said John, with a flummoxed frown. 'My name's John Davidson. My date of birth is...' He slid the cigarettes discreetly into his larger coat pocket as he spoke, hoping that the receptionist would be too distracted to notice them. 'I live at Seventy-One, Skipton Road, Newton Escomb.'

'Lovely. Thank you,' gleamed the receptionist, with a sensual Scottish accent. She proceeded to type in John's details, and then pleasantly smiled back to him. 'Please take a seat in waiting room 'B', Mr. Davidson. Doctor Kain will be with you shortly. John could tell, from how she had emphasized the word 'shortly', that it was going to be a lengthy wait before he'd be seen. 'It's just down the corridor, to the right...'

'Cheers.' John responded with an immature shrug and then seated himself like an obedient dog beside an elderly gentleman, who had an apparent chest condition. 'Do you want some water, pal?' asked John, his 'carer' instincts kicking in. The old man was coughing profusely into a tattered handkerchief, which was without question beyond its capacity to hold anymore thick mucus. 'That's a nasty cough, mate.'

'Aye, it is,' replied the elderly man, within a set of sporadic wheezes. 'I'm here to see Doctor Kain about it. This cough'll be the death of me.'

'Nah, you'll be alright,' assured John, though in his mind he knew that the prognosis couldn't possibly be good. 'What time's your appointment?'

'In half-a-bloody hour! I'll be dead by then,' groaned the man, wearily. 'It's taken me two weeks just to get *this* appointment. I don't know...' John gently rubbed at the man's back, not even realising that he hadn't asked for any permission first; however, the gesture was warmly welcomed. 'Thanks, bonnie-lad.'

'You go in before me. I can wait,' said John. 'I can wait another half-hour or so. Honestly, I don't mind.'

'I wish there were more young'uns like you in this world,' responded the elderly gentleman with an endearing smile. John remained silent. 'There's too many of these *hoodies* and *yobbo's* about. I rarely leave the house now...'

In the corner of his eye, John noticed his name appear on a large TV screen nearby.

'Mr. J. Davidson – Doctor A. Kain – Room 2'

'Go on, pal. Just tell Doctor Kain that I've sent you in first... he shouldn't mind.' John briskly stood himself upright, assisting the elderly gentleman from his seat without any reservation. 'Take care, mate. Don't let him fob you off with paracetamol.'

'I won't, laddie,' assured the gentleman, his face wrinkled and emanating a beetroot complexion. 'The name's Henry Smith. Look out for me in next week's obituaries,' he chuckled, after a painful-sounding gasp. 'Ta-ra, sonny. Thanks for letting me go first.'

'See ya, and all the best.' John replied with a hopeful smile and it was false – how could he be honest, given how frail the elderly man appeared. 'The poor fella...'

John looked around the waiting room for any familiar faces. There was one, but it was a girl he'd dated in comprehensive school and things hadn't ended well. Not even ten minutes passed before the sound of a blue-light ambulance neared from outside. 'I hope it's not for poor Henry,' pondered John, as he looked down the corridor towards Doctor Kain's room. 'It better not be for him.' Sadly, it was. The next few moments passed by like a blur: paramedics flew into the surgery with a stretcher. One held a de-fib unit in hand, whilst another had what looked like some morphine which was already set up in an injection. 'The poor bloke,' John sighed, as he watched on helplessly. 'Take care, Henry. It was nice meeting you,' he murmured over to the elderly man, who was now being carried out on the stretcher. Henry slowly lifted a thumbs-up gesture back to John. 'You're in good hands, mate,' implored John gesturing his thumb back in the very same manner.

'Mr. Davidson?' A deep voice resonated from down the corridor. However, John was lost in a trance-like state, and oblivious to it. 'MR. DAVIDSON?'

'I'm here,' grumbled John. He still had his sights on Henry being lifted into the ambulance outside. 'That's what happens when you need to wait two weeks to be seen by a GP...'

'Ah! Mr. Davidson.' The deep voice turned out to be Doctor Kain. He was stood quite calmly outside of his room, holding onto a clipboard, and showing no distress at all from what had just transpired. 'Please, come in.' Doctor Kain towered over John – which wasn't a difficult feat, given that he was only five-foot, seven inches tall. Doctor Kain swiftly ushered John into a small, suffocating room. John was just grateful that he didn't suffer from claustrophobia. 'What ails you, my good sir?'

'Nothing as bad as what that poor fella's going through,' said John, now feeling totally embarrassed by how pathetic his ailment was in comparison to Henry's suffering. 'I'm having problems with my anxiety again.'

'I see,' said Doctor Kain, with an inquisitive glance at his computer screen. 'You've had problems with your mental health for some time now, Mr. Davidson.'

'Aye. Nothing like this, though.' John couldn't even look his doctor in the eye. He didn't want to be there, anyway. 'I keep hearing voices and having weird, vivid nightmares.'

'Uh-huh.' Doctor Kain didn't seem remotely interested. In fact, it appeared that he was already typing out a script for John. 'Audio and visual hallucinations? You've had these symptoms before... when you were about ten years old. They were a result of your parents' divorce, I gather?' John had forced those memories far back into his deepest level of consciousness. He didn't appreciate this unexpected reminder. 'Is that correct? Otherwise, I'll need to update your notes.'

'Yes, they're right. I try not to think about them though, Doc.' John was steadily becoming angry, feeling like his presence here was unwelcome – a hinderance. 'It's not the same. I'm dreaming about a witch and a demon. They're real, man. I've not gone mad - I don't need sectioning or ought.'

'They're only *real* to you, Mr. Davidson,' replied the doctor, in a condescending tone. 'These are common side-effects of extreme stress and fatigue. Have you been doing anything recently that has caused you more agitation or frustration?'

'I've moved home,' muttered John, through gritted teeth. 'It's not that, though. I know it isn't.'

'I believe... it *is*.' The sound of Doctor Kain's Dot Matrix printer sprung into life, readying itself for the pre-emptive prescription to arrive. 'I would like to ask you a series of questions, and please answer them truthfully – okay?'

'Okay,' snapped John. 'Go ahead and ask.'

'Very well. On a scale of one to ten, how anxious do you feel?"

'I'll go with a seven,' lied John. 'Or... maybe eight.'

'How many days out of seven do you feel uncommonly depressed?' asked Doctor Kain, with his eyes still fixated against the computer screen ahead.

'Every single one,' sighed John, glumly. 'It's been worse over the past few weeks,' he groaned louder. 'If I'm being honest, I feel like that all the time.'

'Would you consider yourself to be a danger to others?'

'Nope.'

'How many units of alcohol do you consume within a week?'

'Maybe, I don't know - two or three?' said John, lying again. 'I have a few pints with my mates... now and then.'

'Okay.' Doctor Kain saw right through John's dishonesty. 'And have you recently considered taking your own life?'

'Erm...' John paused, and his morale sunk to an even lower depth. 'If I'm being honest... yeah. But I'd never go ahead with it. I couldn't be without my wife and our little girl. I couldn't do *that* to them. I'd never want to hurt my family.'

'I am glad to hear that, Mr. Davidson.' Doctor Kain granted a false smile to john, his entire posture reeking of arrogance. 'I'm diagnosing you with severe anxiety and depression.' *NO SHIT!* thought John in disbelief. 'Therefore, a regime of Mirtazapine at a fifteen-milligram dose is what, I believe, will help you. DO NOT consume any alcohol whilst taking this medication. It is vital that you stay sober.' John lowered his eyes further away from the Doctor's glare. 'I *must* emphasize that you *cannot* consume any alcohol while you take this medication. It can be very dangerous.'

'Understood, Doc.' John responded with his own false smile. It was a difficult bargain to accept, for alcohol (up to now) had been his first port and call – his quickest route to solace. 'Let's hope they work.'

'I believe they will. Good Day, Mr. Davidson.'

And with that, John left the doctor's surgery with a handful of tablets he'd never considered taking before. Something then compelled him to visit his mother and stepfather. Was it guilt, or was it the innate love they shared for him which was so lacking from his own life at this horrific time? It was only a twenty-minute walk to his parents' home, plenty of time for John to consider his options.

'What am I going to tell Mam?' thought John, ominously. 'The last thing she needs is to be worrying about me... again.'

'A mother's love is endless...'

'Leave me alone, Sabina - Jesus!' bleated John. 'Now I'm hearing you outside of the house.'

'Once connected, never can a bond be broken.'

John reached into his back pocket for the secret stash of cigarettes. However, and to his disappointment, he found them to be soggy - as if soaked in mud. 'What the Hell?' After a disgruntled whine, John threw his damaged cigarettes into the nearest bin possible, and as he did the mud left from the packet on his hands seemingly vanished. 'I'm losing the plot. Maybe I should take those tablets?'

Along Ladybrown Street, where his mother and stepfather lived, John cane across his young nephew, Andrew, who was out playing with his sister – Katherine. The pair looked at John as if he were a ghost, being that it had been so long since he'd last visited them.

'Alright, Bro?' asked Katherine, with a genuine smile. 'It's been *ages* since we last saw you. Why haven't you called?' John reached down for his nephew to pick him up. 'Andrew's nearly one now. It's hard to believe, isn't it?'

'Yes! You're a big boy now, aren't you?' John grinned to his nephew, and Andrew was just as equally pleased to be in his uncle's company. 'He's strong, Sis - definitely takes after you.'

'No. I'd say that he takes after *you*,' replied Katherine, her expression bemused. 'He's certainly got your temper... even your little rabbit-arse.'

'Ha-ha,' sneered John. 'Very funny. It's nice to see you both...' He looked to his mother's home. The lights were on, but that didn't necessarily mean that anyone was in. 'Are Mam and Sean in?'

'Yeah. They're just on making dinner,' said Katherine, as she hastily removed Andrew from John's company. 'They'll be pleased to see you.'

'That's why I'm here, Sis.' John tried to hide his prescription bag from Katherine's sight, but it was too late. 'These are just some sleeping tablets. I've had a few issues with my sleeping pattern recently.' Katherine raised a single eyebrow, much like how Hannah would to John, as if in suspicion. She knew her brother too well. 'That's all they are - honest.'

'Whatever. As long as you're okay.' Katherine reached a single arm around John to tightly embrace him with it. 'I love you, Bro. I wouldn't want anything to happen to you or the girls.'

'I know. Hannah and Lucy are... fine.' John couldn't help but be hesitant in answering with this lie. 'Howay, let's get inside. It's bloody freezing out here.'

John wiped his muddy trainers before entering his mother's home; it was something she always emphasized, especially to him.

'John?' bellowed a voice from the living room – it was Sean, John's stepfather. 'How are you doing?' Sean, like many others, towered over John and easily picked him up into his arms. 'It's been ages since you last visited...'

'I've been doing a lot of over-time at work. Sorry,' winced John, as he gasped for breath. 'You're looking well, Sean. Where's Mam?'

'Toyah's on the phone to your Gran.' Sean's joyful smirk quickly turned sour. 'Your grandad has taken ill again. It's not looking good.' John didn't know how to react. His grandfather had a dementia and was in a constant state of being physically ill, so how could it be any different? In truth, John didn't want to ask. 'He's got another chest infection.'

'Has he?' stammered John, trying to hold back his sorrow over Grandpa Murray's declining health. 'I better go and see him...'

'John? John!' Toyah flew into the kitchen, throwing her phone aside into Sean's hands. 'Aww, Son.' She wrapped herself tightly around John's beating chest. 'I've missed you so much. I'm so glad you're here.'

'I've missed you too, Mam,' replied John, with an equal sense of melancholy. 'I do text you... every other day.'

'I know, but it's not the same,' whimpered Toyah, into her son's tremoring torso. 'You're still my baby.' John rubbed at his mother's hair, mimicking the way in which he would calm Lucy during her fleeting periods of sadness.

'I'm going to see Grandad and Gran tomorrow. I've got the day off from work,' said John, his words seemingly devoid of any emotion. 'I'd go over more, but—'

'But...what?' interjected Toyah, scowling. 'They only live around the corner from you now, John. I'm starting to get worried about your gran's health. She's Grandpa Murray's main carer, after-all - *and* she's eighty-five. She's making herself ill.'

'I *know*, Mam.' John couldn't have felt any guiltier if he tried. 'I'm going over tomorrow. It's hard, you know...' He paused for a second, doubting whether his next statement would make any sense to someone who didn't work in the care sector. 'I've looked after a lot of people with dementia. I know... what's coming.'

164

'Then you need to be there for Gran *and* Grandad,' implored Toyah. Sean and Katherine nodded in unison, backing up their loved one's plea. 'Please, John. We're your family as well...'

'I know!' snapped John. He'd never acted this before to his mother, taking all by surprise. 'Sorry. I haven't been sleeping right. My head's in the shed.' The bag of Mirtazapine suddenly slipped from his coat pocket, landing directly before Toyah's feet.

What are...these?" 'enquired Toyah, as she lifted the white bag before John's trembling eyes. 'Are they sleeping pills?'

'Sort of... they have a sedative effect. They're for my anxiety.' John's breathing became more rapid, despite his desperate attempt to calm himself. 'I've been under a lot of pressure.'

'Mirtazapine?' As Toyah read out the medication's name, John became more and more flummoxed. 'Are you depressed, John? Oh, my poor baby. Why haven't you said anything to me?'

'I don't want you to worry. You've got enough going on to be stressed over.' John tried to make light of the situation, though it was of little use. 'It's with the move and working overtime. I don't get much chance to chillout.'

'Listen here,' Sean stood himself between John and Toyah. 'I'm going to a Sex Pistols tribute band tonight. Do you want to come along with me?'

'Sounds great!' replied John, enthusiastically. 'I'm up for that. We haven't been to a gig together in ages.'

'Your medicine box says that you can't drink any alcohol. Don't be drinking, John,' said Toyah, in her sternest motherly voice. 'I don't want you getting ill.'

'I'll behave myself, and so will Sean,' chuckled John, whilst tapping at Sean's shoulders to cement their masculine bond. 'I could do with a break - especially if it's a 'Pistols' tribute.'

'Good. Make sure you let Hannah know though, John.' Toyah stared down at his back pocket, eyeing up the outline of his phone. 'Don't you go without telling her.'

'I wouldn't dare!' John obediently reached into his pocket for the phone, then dialled in Hannah's number. She immediately answered. 'Hi, Hannah. Sean's taking me to a Sex Pistols tribute band tonight... if that's okay with you?'

'I guess so,' she replied, quietly and despondent. 'It'll mean you leaving me and your daughter in a haunted house. But you don't care, do you?' Thankfully, Hannah's words couldn't be heard by anyone other than John. 'It's a bit short notice, isn't it?'

'I won't be late getting back, and I'll behave myself,' emphasized John in a serene tone; however, inside his guilt was steadily building up. 'I'll be back by midnight.'

'Too right you'll be back by midnight!' Hannah didn't seem scared, only angry at John unexpectedly going AWOL. 'You can sleep on the couch again. You'll only wake Lucy up if you come to bed.'

'No probs. Love you, babe.' John ended the call with a pathetic kiss down the phone to Hannah. 'She's fine with us going.'

'Nice one.' Sean rubbed his hands together hungrily. 'It's been a while since me and you have had a look out.'

'Aye. It's well overdue,' said John, whilst rubbing at his throbbing temples. 'I could do with a good session – blow off some stress.'

'NO ALCOHOL!' implored Katherine. Both she and Toyah stared at John until he answered.

'I'll have one pint – one, and that's it,' chortled John, nervously. 'Can a lad not have one night off without getting the Spanish Inquisition forced on him?'

'Show some respect, John... Andrew's present,' scorned Toyah, moving her eyes back and forth between John and his nephew, who was still standing beside him. 'You need to be a good role-model, for Andrew. You both look so alike. He copies everything you say and do.'

'I promise... one drink, Mam.' John could barely convince himself. 'One drink, and then we'll come home after the first set, okay?"

'Peccator!'

'I'm *not* a sinner,' screeched John within his thoughts, against Sabina's provocation. 'Leave me alone!'

'Sean,' said Toyah, as she looked towards her husband with a knowing glare. 'Please make sure that both you and John take things easy tonight. Don't go mad.'

'We won't, pet,' said Sean, nodding his head. 'Like John said: one drink and then we'll come home.'

'A sinner and a liar? Thou must be cleansed...'

CHAPTER EIGHT

Hannah stared at her kindle with a blank expression whilst lying alone in bed, which itself was becoming far too normal now. She was still angry with John, over how he had behaved the night before. It had taken Hannah ages to settle Lucy down, and all the while she had to contend with her own growing fears, regarding the nightmares she was encountering - nightmares which she continued to hide away from John's awareness.

'Let's see if "His Worship" is awake, yet.' Hannah flung her kindle upon the bed, and then quickly made the short journey downstairs towards John. 'He's got some explaining to do. Last night was ridiculous.'

John was lying face down upon the living room's carpet. His 'Joy Division' album was still playing quietly on repeat in the background, something which Hannah soon turned off with a disgruntled whine.

'John? JOHN!' bellowed Hannah, with a firm slap against his back.

'What the f—' John jolted upright, then wiped at his sweaty brow with a confused expression. His hangover was well under-way, its infliction excruciating. 'Sorry, Han...'

'Aye. And so, you should be.' Hannah kicked a crumbled and empty can of lager towards her inebriated husband, with a precise aim directed towards his groin. 'Arsehole! You came in here well after midnight, stinking of whiskey and rambling in some weird language!' John whimpered in agony from Hannah's keen strike. Slowly, he began to regain some of his sense and then looked around the room in even more confusion. 'What have you got to say for yourself?'

'I-I can't remember.' John rubbed at his sore groin, and then at his equally sore forehead. 'Sean got a few whiskeys in...'

'Don't go blaming Sean!' Hannah seethed. 'You poured that drink down your throat – not him!' She looked down to the battered box of Mirtazapine strewn beside her and John's TV set. 'Have you taken any of your medicine? Can you even remember a thing from yesterday?'

'Aye – Doctor's orders,' replied John, coyly. "They're the ones I got from Doctor Kain...' Hannah inspected the small box, then frowned even harsher. 'He thinks they'll work.'

'NO ALCOHOL!' Hannah threw the box at John, this time striking him upon his nose. 'You're not meant to drink and take this medicine at the same time! Bloody Hell, John... you'll kill yourself. What were you thinking?' She started to cry now, remorseful for her inflicting actions against John, as well as her understanding towards his obvious struggles. 'I'm *really* starting to worry about you. You've turned into someone else. I don't like it.'

'Got a funny way of showing you love me,' humoured John, as he cupped his throbbing testicles in both hands. 'I only took one tablet...'

'So, what?' Hannah gasped in dismay. 'It says: NO ALCOHOL. No means none at all, John... not six pints and a whiskey chaser.'

'Look, I'm sorry,' pleaded John, his eyes widening like a puppy's. 'The thing is: when I drink, I don't have any nightmares – I don't see... Sabina.'

'Not *her* again, John. You've made her up,' responded Hannah, her head tilting side-to-side. She didn't enjoy acknowledging the witch, even if she had encountered a different experience with her in comparison to John. 'Those tablets are meant to help you. I'd rather you take tablets than rely on booze - just think of our Lucy.' John's guilty conscience quickly came into play again. 'You need to think of our little girl – as well as me. Lucy won't want to grow up with a pisshead as a father. I know, I wouldn't.'

'Oh, shit!' John opened his mouth aghast. 'I'm taking Lucy to see Grandpa and Grandma Murray today. I almost forgot!'

Hannah rolled her eyes in response; an action John should have been getting used to at this point. 'I'll have a shower and then go over with her. Is our Lucy awake yet?'

'Yeah.' Hannah slowed down her breathing, hoping this would also calm the rising anger inside. 'She's playing upstairs and had her breakfast over an hour ago.'

'Champion. I'll get ready then.; John shrugged off the tingling pain in his groin and then made his way towards the bathroom upstairs, only after planting a kiss on Hannah's left cheek. 'I'm sorry, babe. I'm trying my best to sort things out.'

'It's okay, just get a shower... you reek of whiskey,' sniggered Hannah, despite the urge to scorn John further. 'Go on, I'll make you a coffee while you get washed.'

'Thanks, hun.' John peered into Lucy's room as he passed by it. The strange symbol was gone; Hannah must have wiped it off. 'Hi, Lucy.' He slowly stepped into his daughter's room. She was singing the 'family finger' song again. 'Are you alright, sweetheart? I'm sorry if I was noisy last night.'

'Hi, Daddy,' replied Lucy, revealing her teeth with a wide smile. 'I'm just playing with Eliza. I can call her that now. *She* said so.'

'Oh, aye?' John searched around the room, once again finding that no-one else was there. Even with closing his eyes, John couldn't sense another soul in the room, apart from himself and Lucy. 'What is Eliza up to?'

'She's teaching me magic spells.' Lucy lifted her palms up into the air, then proceeded to swipe them across it in several directions. 'She's a *good* witch. She wants to keep me safe.'

'Right!' John knelt himself directly before Lucy with a stern expression. 'I don't want you playing with Eliza anymore. Her mammy is a *very* nasty woman.'

'We know.' Lucy's response gave John an even greater cause for concern. 'Eliza's mammy and the Goat-Man want to hurt you, so

170

she's going to teach me some magic spells. They will stop you getting hurt.'

'I don't think so, madam!' John's train of thought and emotions flurried into an anxious and dangerous cocktail. His daughter was innocent – too young to be feeling threatened in this way. 'You're not playing with Eliza anymore, and that's the end of it! Go downstairs, please.' John pointed towards the stairwell outside of Lucy's room. The child obeyed her father's command, though only after a few disgruntled murmurs aimed against him. 'Less of your cheek as well, missy.'

'But, Eliza's a *good* witch!' pleaded the child. 'She wants to help you!'

'Do not mention Eliza to your mammy, understood?' implored John, his stare to Lucy both cold and fearful. 'Be a good girl and do as you're told.' Lucy grunted once more, then stormed downstairs like a well-rehearsed drama-queen. God help me when she's a teenager,' commented John, laughing to himself. He ensured this time that the shower was at a colder setting. *No more day-visits from Sabina*, he prayed.

'John! Are you gonna be in that shower all day?' shouted Hannah from the stairwell. Lucy soon joined in. 'Hurry up!'

'Come on, Daddy! I want to see Granny and Grandpa Murray!' John flicked the shower off and hastily made his way downstairs, with only a small white towel on to hide his delicate parts. 'Oh, Daddy!' sniggered Lucy, bashfully. 'You look so funny!'

'Bloody Hell, John,' snorted Hannah, almost dropping the mug of hot coffee in her hands. 'You could have gotten dressed first!'

'You said, *come down*, so I have.' John rolled his eyes sarcastically. 'I'm gagging for that coffee. Cheers, hun.'

'It might take more than one cup to sober you up.' Hannah made her way back into the kitchen, where she reignited the kettle into full boil. 'Fancy another before you go?'

'Aye, please,' said John, as he slurped away at the bitter coffee. 'It tastes great.'

'I'm surprised you can taste anything at all, after what you drank last night,' quipped Hannah. Her face fell again into one of discourse. 'I'm still not happy with you.'

'Look—' John leant towards her for kiss, unwittingly allowing for his towel to fall away from him. 'It won't happen again.'

'You're not going to see your grandparents like that, are you?' Hannah's smile rose, her eyes fixating on John's shrivelling privates. 'You'll give the neighbours a shock, for one thing.'

'It's cold, you know?' replied John, as he looked down to his retreating manhood with a certain level of shame. 'I'll go and get dressed...'

'Yes, please.' Hannah smirked as she tightened John's towel around his waist, so that it wouldn't come loose again. 'There are some clothes out ready for you. Don't take ages. Lucy's waited long enough.'

'Mammy!' interjected Lucy, proceeding to tug at her mother's cardigan with a dire sense of urgency. 'I'm a good girl, aren't I?'

'Sometimes – yes,' said Hannah, whimsically, her frown now turning to a bemused expression. 'Why ask? What have you done now?'

'It's just: Eliza is a good girl, but Daddy won't let me play with her.' Lucy lowered her head, hiding it behind her long, golden hair, knowing instantly from Hannah's responding glare that she had said something to upset her. 'Lucy is a good—'

'Having imaginary friends is fine, Lucy. I used to have one, and I bet Daddy did.' Hannah spoke in a deepened voice, her 'authoritive ' tone. 'But this *Eliza* mustn't be a good girl, if she is a witch.' Hannah clasped her hands against her mouth. 'I've said too much,' she whispered to herself, held in remorse.

'Hold on a sec!' John sprinted back downstairs, half-dressed, and in an angered state. 'Did *you* say something about *Eliza*, and her being a *witch*?' It was John's turn to glare inquisitively. 'I'm sure that's what I heard you say, Han.'

'You heard wrong.' Hannah flicked her hair from one side to the other - a peculiar though common symbol for John to make his retreat. 'Go and get dressed, before Lucy starts kicking off.' She laughed nervously in a futile attempt to distract her husband's attention. However, John easily saw through Hannah's façade. 'And stop eavesdropping.'

'Okay, what you say...' John rose his arms up in submission, thankfully not losing the towel around his waist this time. He was already in Hannah's 'Bad Books', so the last thing he wanted was to add anything else onto this ever-growing list. 'Are you ready, Lucy? Let's go and see Granny and Grandpa!'

'Yay!' screeched the girl. Lucy's frustration had dwindled, replaced by an intense feeling of excitement. 'I love them *so* much! I love you and Mammy *so* much!' she cheered, whilst clapping her hands.

'We love you, too,' replied Hannah and John, in perfect unison with each another. The small family huddled together, regardless of their haunted surroundings, and stayed that way for at least a minute in total harmony. It was only after a knock came from the kitchen door that this passionate embrace ceased.

'I wonder who it is?' enquired Hannah, with shifting eyes. Her first thought was that it could Barbara, of whom she had borrowed some clothes from a few days prior. 'It's probably Mam...'

'I'll get the door, Han,' implored John, smirking with a sly wink. 'Can you help Lucy to get her shoes on?'

'You can't go to the door dressed like THAT!' snorted Hannah, looking to the thin towel around John's midriff. 'If it's Mam, you'll give her a friggin' heart attack!'

'Fair point.' John hurried upstairs, laughing all the way to himself. 'I won't be a minute.'

Hannah ushered Lucy into the living and then made for the kitchen door. Outside stood a petite and elderly-looking woman – certainly not Barbara, from what Hannah could make out. The door was clouded over by a thick layer of condensation, and the lingering fog surrounding Skipton Road didn't help either in deciphering who this stranger was.

'I'm coming. I won't be a moment!' Hannah fumbled through her set of keys to find the correct one. As she finally opened the door, a noticeable sigh of relief left from her – it was Pat, her and John's 'nicer' neighbour. 'Hiya. Sorry it took so long... I couldn't find the right key.'

'Hello, dearie. It's not a problem.' Pat replied with a patient and welcoming smile. She was enclosed within an oversized puffer jacket – it was cold, but this was something else to look at. 'I haven't seen you nor John for a while now. I just wanted to check in on you to see if everything is okay. I hope you don't mind?' A dry outburst of laughter left from her shrivelled lips. 'I'm not being *nosey*, by any means.'

'Of course not. It's very kind of you,' said Hannah, politely, though she also pondered as to what the real reasons were behind Pat's intrusive call. 'John's been doing a lot of overtime recently, and I've been around my mam's helping her out. Lucy's obviously been at school. That's why you haven't seen much of us.'

'You don't need to justify yourself to me, pettle,' quirked Pat, whilst moving herself inside awkwardly. It was difficult to see what her body language was doing underneath the several layers of plastic which smothered her. 'How are you all settling in?'

'Great. We're settling in great.' Hannah responded in a sharp tone, something which Pat instantly picked up on. 'Honestly, we're fine and dandy.'

'I see.' Pat's eyebrows lifted, infused with suspicion. 'I presume you mean that yourself and Lucy are fine?' Her eyes widened. 'John, on the other hand, is a man. I'm more concerned about him.'

"Yes, John is a man. What does that have to do with anything?' asked Hannah, ominously. 'If you came a few seconds earlier, you would have seen that for yourself.'

'Pardon?' Pat's face flushed, the heat from it instantly beaming against Hannah's. 'What was that you said, pet?'

"'Nothing. John's... okay.' Hannah turned her head towards the passageway. She could hear John singing along to 'The Pogues' upstairs, so the coast was clear to gossip. 'To be honest, Pat, he *has* been acting different since we moved here. I'm getting a little worried about him.'

'Oh, dearie,' Pat sighed, as she rubbed at Hannah's arms sympathetically. '*She* has always had such an effect on the men of this household, always has, always will.' She shuddered and then, for some strange reason, performed a crucifix gesture across her chest. 'Evil, wicked creature... she is. I've lived here for over twenty years, and this house has been haunted all that time.' Hannah pleaded ignorance with her responding facial expression, but inside, and to her utter dismay, she truly knew of what evil Pat was referring to.

'Who are you talking about?' Hannah checked the passageway again, then exhaled a lengthy breath of relief at John's lacking presence. 'What do you mean?'

'Skipton Road is a lovely place to live - don't get me wrong.' Pat rubbed at Hannah's arms again, this time in a reassuring manner. 'But we who've lived here the longest know of the witch that haunts this place... and has done for countless years.' Pat inspected the steamy bathroom window from outside, hoping that John was still contained there. 'Sid, the pisshead who lives next to you...' Hannah couldn't help but chuckle at Pat's use of a curse word, as it seemed so wrong. 'He told me about her. He's a piss-kick, you know?'

'Psychic?' chuckled Hannah, apprehensively. 'Is *that* what you mean?'

'Yes! Yes, a Psychic.' Pat frowned slightly in embarrassment. 'He calls her "*The Red Ribbon Witch*". He's completely obsessed with her, too.' Hannah felt herself becoming overwhelmed by shock, almost fainting at this statement from Pat. 'Oh, my dear. Are you alright?'

'Yeah. Cheers for that, Pat,' groaned Hannah, whilst trying not to vomit from her risen fear. 'The Red Ribbon Witch?'

'Shhh! Don't let Sid hear you say that!' Pat frantically tapped a finger across her mouth to emphasize this point. 'He's like a fly around shit when you mention *her* in front of him.' She leant in closer to Hannah now. 'Word has it, that the last tenant was driven barmy by her... he became totally catatonic in the end – a loony!'

'That's terrible. That's just what I need to hear.' Hannah initiated her 'Mother's Glare'. 'John hasn't gone completely mental yet, but thanks for asking, though.'

'No, my dear,' whimpered Pat. 'You're taking this all the wrong way. I'm just trying to warn you, to keep a close eye on your husband – for both your sakes... not to mention the bairn's.' Hannah slipped her fingertips across her keys again, now more familiar with which one locked the kitchen door.

'Thanks for checking on us, Pat. See ya later,' said Hannah, clearly suggesting to her neighbour that their company was no longer welcome.

'Don't be mad at me!' retorted Pat, in shock. 'I'm trying to help you!'

'Bye.' Hannah slammed the door clean against Pat's face, but this cruelty didn't seem to bother her in the slightest. 'The cheeky cow... coming around here, telling me that my husband's going mental. Who does she think she is?'

'Hannah? What the Hell's going on down there?' yelled John, from the bathroom upstairs. 'Christ, I thought you were gonna take the hinges off there!'

'It was just Pat from next-door,' replied Hannah, her voice weakened somewhat from anger and dread. 'She just came around to see how we're doing.' A couple of silent moments passed. 'I said that we're okay.'

'You didn't tell her about the weird things going on, did you?' asked John, with a hint of reluctance in his tone. 'She'll think we've lost the plot.'

She already does, thought Hannah. 'Nah, I told her we're fine, and that we're settling in. I pretty much told her to do one.'

'That's a bit harsh, isn't it? She's knocking on eighty, Han. You shouldn't have sent her off like that.'

'She's a nosey old cow, so I told her to sling it.' Hannah began to tap at the stairwell, loud enough for John to hear. 'Are you going to stay up there all day? Lucy's waiting for you.'

'I'm ready now.' In actuality, John was struggling to stretch a pair of skinny jeans over his knees. The penetrating hangover wasn't much help either. 'It's always a rush with you. My Grandad's not going anywhere, is he?'

'Your gran was expecting you half an hour ago, John.' Hannah took this moment to slip Lucy's shoes and coat on, a miniscule though successful distraction away from Pat's concerning words. 'You take longer than me and you haven't got any hair! Hurry up!'

'I'm here, I'm here.' John gasped as he entered the stale air of his living room, such was the impact of his whiskey-laced bloodstream. 'I'm knackered!' He looked to the clock upon his living room wall. 'I don't think we'll be long at Gran's... it'll be lunchtime soon.'

'You need to spend time with your grandparents, John. I know it's hard for you, but...' Hannah rubbed wearily at her eyes, then reached down across the sofa for her Kindle. 'Grandpa Murray doesn't sound too good.'

'Is Grandpa poorly?' asked Lucy in a cautious whisper, her expression both sad and inquisitive. '"Will he be a star in the sky soon... like my Grandpa Richie?' Hannah kept her fingertips upon her eyes. It had been ten years, yet she still hadn't gotten over the loss of her beloved grandfather. 'No, darling. Grandpa Murray is very poorly but he hasn't died.'

'Dying isn't bad, Mammy,' said Lucy, in a jovial and unexpected manner. 'Eliza told me—'

'Lucy,' growled Hannah, her eyes glaring once again. 'We've told you not to mention your imaginary friend anymore. Be a *good* girl.'

'Eliza *is* real! She's not dead! She's not a star in the sky!' Lucy repeated this a few times until John appeared. 'Daddy! Eliza *is* real!' she continued, much to Hannah's further dismay. John shrugged towards their daughter in agreement with her. 'See, Mammy?'

'Don't drag the bairn into this, John,' seethed Hannah, while the kindle in her hands began to tremble erratically. 'You're not helping.'

'What do you want me to say?' John shrugged his shoulders again, though with more arrogance in their movement now. 'I've seen her in the nightmares I keep having. Doesn't *that* say something?'

'Yeah, it means that Pat is right about you!' Hannah rubbed an opened palm aggressively across her scalp, tearing at it in frustration. 'Just... go and see your grandparents.'

'Calm down, Han. What did Pat say about me?' John edged towards Hannah with a pathetic and whiny look on his face. 'Look, I'm sorry...'

'Aye. You keep saying,' said Hannah with an emotionless stare. 'Never mind what Pat said. Send my love to Gran and Grandpa.'

'I will.' John silently slipped on his trainers, not daring to kiss his beloved wife goodbye – he'd already done too much damage. Right now, John could have killed for another shot of scotch whiskey, his nerves wreaking further havoc across his entire body. 'There's a good girl, Lucy. Let's go.'

'Okay, Daddy.'

As John assisted Lucy into the kitchen, he noticed a sheet of paper that had fallen and then slid beneath the table. He picked it up and instantly froze with dread.

'What's this meant to be?' he asked to Lucy. 'Did you draw this?'

'It's Belly-Bob,' replied Lucy in an innocent tone. 'I can't remember drawing it. Put it in the bin, Daddy.'

'Aye. I think that's a good idea,' said John ominously, as he threw the etching into the bin without further thought. What Lucy had drawn was a series of swirling black lines that interconnected to form, what look to be, the head of a demonic-looking ram. Two horns were noticeably present upon the creature's forehead, adding to John's fearful response. 'Do Daddy a favour please, Lucy: don't ever draw anything like that again.'

'I won't, Daddy,' whimpered Lucy. 'Belly-Bob is scary, anyway. I don't want to draw him again.'

Lucy held onto her father's hand tightly along the short journey to their grandparents' house. On leaving Skipton Road, the permeating fog seemed to lift, though only ever-so slightly. Grandpa Murray's garden - once so proudly adorned with various flowers and vegetables -now looked so bare, with only a single yellow rose bush surviving the impact of his debilitating dementia.

'Here we are,' stated John, as he smirked towards his excitable daughter. 'Remember to give Granny and Grandpa a big hug when you see them.'

'I will!' replied Lucy. 'I love giving them big hugs!'

'I do, too.' John hesitated with his initial steps into Grandpa Murray's home. A raw sensation of dread and bitterness entered his entire being like a sickening disease. He knew that what lay inside would only add to his growing depression. 'This is so hard. Poor Grandad. Poor Gran.'

'Hello, my gorgeous girl!' rejoiced Grandma Marie, on seeing Lucy's innocent smile. 'We've missed you, sweetheart.' Lucy hugged into her great-grandmother without any question, though she looked to Grandpa Murray with a perplexed and startled expression. 'Grandpa's not too well, flower. He's very sleepy today.'

'Hi, Gran,' interjected John, almost formal in his pronouncement. 'We've missed you. I hope you're alright?' Marie waved her hands dismissively against John, an obvious gesture to diminish his guilt. 'How are things going?'

'As good as can be.' Marie instantly turned sideways towards Grandpa Murray, who continued to lay lifeless in his nursing bed. 'Your grandad has another chest infection – a really bad one this time. I don't know what to do.'

'Hi, Grandad,' whispered John softly, in aim of his grandfather's presence. Grandpa Murray was once as stocky and well-built as John, though now he looked so weak and frail, so helpless. He had lost most of his muscle mass, not to mention his dignity through aging and dementia. Due to Grandpa Murray's recent outbursts of aggression, he had also accumulated a mass of facial hair from not tolerating a single shave, and it looked so wrong. John couldn't bear seeing his once proud grandfather like this – he couldn't accept it at all. 'It's John, your grandson. I've brought Lucy along to see you.' Not even a faint murmur left from Grandpa Murray's lips, his dementia now seemingly reaching its final stage. 'Grandad?'

'Doctor Kain has prescribed some 'anti-piss-appy' drugs,' said Marie, solemnly. 'God knows what they're for...'

'Anticipatory drugs, Gran?' John quickly wiped the smirk off his face from finding his grandmother's mistake humorous, realising just how cruel he had become. A by-product of Sabina's influence, perhaps? 'Sorry, Gran. I'm not taking to mickey out of you...'

'I really don't know what to do, John.' Marie just came out with this, leaving him little time to react. 'Doctor Kain said that it's up to me when the nurses should give Grandpa his morphine. I don't want to finish him off!'

'Gran,' John sighed, sympathetically. 'You're not Harold Shipman. The morphine is there for when Grandad is in any pain. Is he in any?' To be fair on Grandma Marie, it was difficult to tell. '*That's* what it's for - not euthanasia.'

'I'm not too sure, John.' Marie shook her head, portraying to John just how helpless she felt. 'The last thing I want is for your Grandpa to suffer. I can't believe that it's come to this.; John reached an arm around his grandmother, supporting her both physically and emotionally. 'Oh, John. I don't want to lose him.'

'You're doing everything possible to make Grandpa comfortable, and that's all that matters now.' John struggled to hold back his pressing tears, as Grandpa Murray meant so much to him. 'If you think - for even one second - that Grandpa is in any pain, phone the District Nurses, okay?'

'I will,' whispered Marie, her gentle voice now sounding frailer than ever before. 'My beautiful husband. He's never hurt anyone. He's done nothing but help others throughout his life and *this* is the treatment our 'Good Lord' bestows on him. It makes me sick to the bone!' John nodded back in agreement. 'I don't see why he should be punished like this.'

Grandpa Murray's proclaimed spiritual stature mirrored his own, in John's opinion: he'd never hurt a soul, yet here he was being hounded by a witch and a demon - and for what? For being a man, for being a 'Son of God'.

'It *is* wrong, Gran. But...' John stumbled over his words. He began this statement held in certainty that he could offer some much-needed reassurance to his grandmother but didn't know how to finish it. 'Life isn't fair – in fact, it's crap at times. But there's always a light in the darkness, even when it doesn't feel that way.' He looked over to Lucy, who at this point had sat herself in front of Grandma Marie's TV set to watch an episode of *Peppa Pig*. 'Lucy is my light in the dark. She keeps me going.'

'She's ours, too,' said Marie, with a proud smirk. 'Watching the bairn grow and seeing how happy you and Hannah are... that's what helps me.' John bit at his lip, not wishing to grant Grandma Marie the painful truth. 'You all keep me going. You help me to keep on fighting to make Grandpa's life better.'

'You're doing an amazing job, Gran,' interjected John, as he tightened his hold around Grandma Marie. 'I'm only a few minutes away if you ever need me. I'll always be there for you.'

'You've got enough to worry about, John, with the move an all.' Marie sighed, burdened with a wrongful sense of guilt herself. 'Don't you be getting yourself stressed. Life's too short.'

'I know, Gran.' In reluctance, John looked again to Grandpa Murray. 'I'm reminded of that often enough at work. Dementia is the cruellest illness; it robs you of everything.'

'How long does Grandpa have?' Marie's piercing stare into John's eyes haunted him more than even Sabina's. How could he answer this, and honestly? 'Just... be frank with me. Does he have long?'

'It's hard to say, Gran.' John scrubbed away at his shaven scalp with both hands, somehow finding this to soothe his awkward and reserved response. 'Dementia's different with each person. It could be days... could be weeks.'

'No!' Marie planted her hands firmly against her tremoring lips. 'Don't say it'll be *weeks*! Hasn't he suffered enough?' *Maybe not in Sabina's eyes*, contemplated John. Without even being near Skipton Road, the Red Ribbon Witch still held an overwhelming force upon his senses – his very soul.

'Seriously, Gran,' groaned John, despite straining not to. 'There isn't a single person on Earth who could give you that answer. Like I've said, all that matters is making Grandad as comfortable and pain-free as possible, which I know - you above all others - can do.'

'You're such a good boy, John.' Marie tugged at his face endearingly, just as she did when he was a child. 'I wish there were more people in this world like you.' *This again?* John's guilty conscience was reaching its boiling point.

'I'm no angel, Gran,' chortled John, his immediate thoughts turning back to Sabina's scornful comments. 'You do what you think is right. You know Grandad best.'

'Granny?' piped up Lucy, after managing to tear away her attention from the TV screen. 'Is my grandpa going to be star?' John frantically waved his hands towards Lucy in hoping to silence her. 'My friend Eliza said that he will be soon.'

'Gracious!' Marie gasped in shock. 'Who is this Eliza?'

'She's an imaginary friend, Gran,' interjected John, as quickly as he could. 'Don't take any notice...'

'Daddy!' whined Lucy, scowling at him. 'You've seen her, so stop lying! Lying is *very* naughty!'

'The bairn's right, John,' remarked Marie, with a sly wink. 'Don't be making Lucy out to be a liar. I believe her.'

'Lucy, we've talked about this...' John tried to stay calm – it was difficult. 'Don't talk about Eliza, please. She's just make-believe. I'm *not* going to tell you again.'

'I'd love to hear more about your *friend*,' implored Marie to Lucy. 'I used to have an imaginary friend when I was a little girl. There's no harm in having imaginary—'

'Eliza is real!' screamed Lucy, with tears now forming in her eyes, her face becoming more scarlet in colour by the second. 'Eliza is a good witch. She wants to help us.'

'ENOUGH!' John not only startled himself with this declaration but Marie and Lucy also with this sudden outburst. 'No more talk about Eliza... and that's FINAL, Lucy.'

'Now, John,' said Marie, with a judgemental frown. 'There's no need to talk to the bairn in that way. I'm surprised in you.'

'Yes... there is,' replied John, his heart now filled with an unnatural air of malice. 'We don't talk about Eliza – ever! She's a big secret, isn't she, Lucy?' He stared upon the child, somehow sharing in Sabina's disdain towards those who had brought harm to her daughter. Their connection was undoubtedly growing stronger. 'Lucy...'

'I guess so?' Lucy shuffled herself back towards the TV screen. 'Eliza's a good witch,' she mumbled under her breath. 'She's an angel.'

'What was that?' hissed John.

Marie instantly yearned to put a stop to her grandson's erratic behaviour. She stood herself between John and Lucy in a protective stance, with her hands held up against both of them.

'I've told her plenty of times, Gran,' implored John. 'It's not on.'

'I don't care, young man.' Marie widened her sapphire eyes against John's own. 'She's only a bairn - behave yourself!' John recoiled at being talked to in this way by his grandmother. The last time Marie had scolded John so was when he hit a frisbee across Katherine's six-year old face, knocking out her two front teeth as a result. It was as painful to bear now as it was back then – twenty years ago. 'Are you listening to me, bonny-lad? Our Lucy is a good bairn and doesn't deserve to be talked to like that... not even from her daddy.'

'Sorry, Gran,' grumbled John, ashamedly, his facial cheeks pulsating like a hamster hoarding their measly portions. 'We'll have to set off again soon, anyway.' He glanced across to Lucy's seated position, stricken with remorse. 'Howay, Lucy. You've got homework to do.' He spoke so gently now, as not to stir Grandpa

Murray from his slumber. 'Come and say goodbye to Granny and Grandpa Murray.'

'I love you, Granny!' Lucy threw herself against her great-grandmother with some considerable force, with arms opened wide and grinning with a hint of pity towards her. 'Don't be sad about Grandpa.' John's daughter stared past him with a loving gaze, aiming her sight solely upon Grandpa Murray's shivering torso. 'The angels will look after my Grandpa... Eliza told me so.'

'Lucy!' snarled John, the veins on his neck throbbing as if about to burst. 'What did Mammy say to you before we left? We don't talk about... your friend.'

'Really, John?' frowned Marie, with her piercing eyes on full display. 'Stop over-reacting. Let the bairn believe what she wants. I mean, what possible harm can come from it?" Marie then fleeted her sight across Grandpa Murray's frail body, with tears now forming. 'I think it's a lovely thought... God's angels watching over him. It's what your Grandad deserves.'

'It's a nice thought, Gran,' said John, his voice tremoring with melancholy. He wanted to believe this 'so-called' truth, though all he had encountered recently were demons and their sub-ordinates. God. Where was God at? Where were the divine powers that be, the Holy Trinity, to counter this persisting terror that John and his family struggled to endure? 'It's a nice notion, but—'

'Eesh, John.' Marie broke into a faint burst of laughter, removing her previous sorrow. 'Can you remember how you and your grandad would always sit on that same bench in Whitby – the one by those whale bones, staring out at the ocean for hours on end? I remember it like it was only yesterday. You haven't changed much.' John gulped in response, his way of hiding the festering emotions that now built up inside of him. 'You were always so happy together. We all were... back then.'

'I'll never forget it, Gran,' said John, pausing only to take in a single, drawn-out breath. He wanted those memories to remain joyful, not shrouded in resentment by more recent events. 'I loved sitting on that bench with Grandad, especially when he'd give me some of those lemon sherbet sweets. He used to hide them in his pocket from you, didn't he?' Marie giggled, given she'd forgotten this. 'He'd always slip you one on the way home though, wouldn't he?'

'Aye. The cheeky begger!' Marie then scrubbed away playfully at Grandpa Murray's knees; they were his only defining feature now, being that they stood out prominently within the several layers of bedding sheets that kept his thin body warm. 'He kept them just for you. The pair of you were always so... inseparable.'

'Still are,' affirmed John. He wrapped an arm across his grandmother's shoulders in the same way his grandfather would have once to alleviate her distress. 'Nothing can change that - not even dementia.' He stared into his grandmother's glistening eyes, emphasizing the latter part to her. 'You'd have thought that in this day and age there would be a cure by now. It's disgraceful.'

'It is, but maybe one day they'll find a cure.' Marie leant into John, sobbing slightly as she made eye contact with him. 'I wish Grandpa could have seen our Lucy grow up.'

'Grandad's still here.' John could scarcely speak now and was in desperate need of intoxication. 'He's still with us... in a way.'

'No, he isn't. The man I fell in love with...' Marie looked again towards Grandpa Murray with love still in her eyes, despite their current hardship. 'What kind of life is this for him? I don't know how you do this for a living.'

'Work's different,' said John, shrugging his shoulders. 'I care about the people I look after, just not in the same way I do with Grandad. It's not the same.'

'Am *I* doing a good job?' Marie slowly turned her gaze back into John's eyes. As they met, an understanding of pity and resentment resonated between them. 'I try my best to look after him. It's not always easy. In fact, it's getting harder each day.'

186

'It goes with saying that you're doing an amazing job, Gran.' John found himself patting at his grandfather's knees in the same way as Grandma Marie now – a strange though settling gesture. 'You're the best carer Grandad could ever have. Don't doubt yourself – not even for a moment.'

'He's not a bad man,' repeated Marie, as she started to sob again. She tried to muffle her voice from Lucy's attention, but it was too late. 'Why should he suffer like this?'

'It's shit.' John strained to inhale now, let alone speak. 'But that's life. All we can do is cope with it the best way we can, and you're amazing at it. Honestly, Gran.'

'I'm glad you think so.' Marie focused her attention back on Lucy, who was still happily lost in a world of her own. 'I've got to stay strong for the bairn's sake, at least.' She wheezed in exhaustion. 'I've got to be strong for all our family.'

'Lucy's too young to understand.' John could remember sitting in the same position before his grandparents' TV set, just as Lucy was, so naïve to all the horrors playing out around them. 'Ignorance is bliss, is what they say.'

'Your grandad would have doted on her, just as he did with you and Katherine.' Marie shook her head in both disbelief and frustration. 'Maybe he will get better?' she smiled, albeit with a hint of desperation. 'Maybe he'll surprise us all one day and just *spring* out of his bed, like nothing is wrong?' John couldn't take anymore. His emotional reserves were now fully drained, and the harrowing sensation of guilt was swiftly kicking in.

'Grandad's wincing a bit there, Gran. When can he have some more pain relief?' John scoured along a set of drawers that were nestled beside Grandpa Murray's bed. Many items covered its surface: wet wipes, barrier creams, clean incontinence pads, some glycerine mouth swabs, and a small bottle of Paracetamol suspension.

187

'In about an hour, John.' Marie pulled aside the bed sheets to reveal Grandpa Murray's PEG tube. It seemed like a good idea at first, when Grandpa's health was far better, for the surgeons in Darlington hospital to instil the plastic device. The PEG tube rested on Grandpa Murray's chest, rocking up and down slowly in unison with his laboured breathing. John's family had fed so much hope into this contraption, praying that it would resolve Grandpa's failing health. Now, it had become a hindrance - a means of stretching out his torment. 'I'll make sure he gets it. The doctor didn't prescribe any antibiotics this time,' said Marie, scowling, almost snapping her words as she spoke the latter. 'He'll never get better, will he?'

'They haven't prescribed anymore antibiotics?' replied John, trying to act surprised. 'The thing is, Gran... if Grandad keeps on taking antibiotics, won't that just prolong his suffering? I think that's what the doctors are trying to avoid.'

'I know,' sighed Marie, exhaling with a horrid sound of defeat. 'I just don't want to accept it. I can't.'

'Come on, Lucy. It's time to go.' John pecked at his grandmother's face with a subtle kiss, then wrapped his coat around himself to make for a swift exit. He couldn't bear seeing his once out-going grandmother succumb to an existence of sadness like this. Though it pained him, he just had to leave. 'I'll call you, Gran. Take care.' He planted another kiss on Marie's face, making sure this one lasted a little longer. 'Love you, Gran.'

'Are you not going to say goodbye to your Grandad?' Marie's expression turned sourer, shifting to a look of horror. 'You said that he can still hear us, even if he can't talk.'

'I did, didn't I?' John leant over his grandfather to rub at his shoulders (their previous way of bidding one another farewell – before the dementia kicked in). 'Just you rest, Grandad. Don't get up to any mischief. You've been through worse...' The words came out before John had any time to consider their ill-placement. *Been through worse?* Even death itself wasn't as cruel as this; it would have been far quicker and more dignified. "Bye, Grandad. See you again soon.'

'Love you, Granny!' gleamed Lucy, as she wrapped her arms around Marie's waist. 'Love you, Grandpa Murray.' She blew a kiss towards him and then waited patiently for Grandpa to return the same gesture. After a few seconds of silence, and having no response from her grandfather, Lucy kissed Marie goodbye and then clasped onto John's hands. 'BYE!' she squealed at Grandpa Murray. 'Be a good boy for Granny.'

'Aww, petal.' Marie finally smiled, bringing a great sense of relief to John. 'Grandpa is *always* a good boy. You be a good girl for Mammy and Daddy – do as you're told.'

'I will,' assured Lucy, with a bashful smirk. 'Come on, Daddy. Let's go and see Mammy now.; John obliged without question.

As John and Lucy waved farewell to Grandma Murray, a single, yellow rosebud fell from Grandpa Murray's prized rosebush. The delicate flower head landed directly before John's muddy trainers – a stark contrast in beauty – and appeared to have several red dots strewn along its petals.

'That's weird...' John retrieved the small flower, admiring its serenity and connection to his grandfather's days of better health. 'I'll be keeping you.' He tucked it inside one of his large coat pockets, hoping that the thick leather wouldn't crush it along the way back to Skipton Road. 'A nice, little keepsake. Isn't it, Lucy?'

However, it would not be Lucy who would respond to John. The cruel and snarling voice of the nameless demon again entered his thoughts:

'Even the Gardens of Babylon fell.'

'Not now, Sabina...' countered John, furiously. 'Leave me alone.'

'I am not Sabina.'

'Then, *who* are you?' John's internal monologue with the demonic presence grew steadily fouler with each passing word. 'I want to know what I'm dealing with.'

'I am death and decay. I am scorn. I am corruption incarnate. I am malice, and I am vengeance. I am your bringer of death, John Davidson.'

'There's a long que, mate,' quipped John, trying to shun off the threatening beast. 'Go and haunt someone else. I'm not in the mood for your games.'

'Daddy?' Lucy tugged at the pocket where John had placed his grandfather's yellow rose. 'I have something for you. I think you need it.' John's eyes flickered erratically, barely able to respond to Lucy's desperate tone. 'Please, Daddy. I want you to have this.' She reached into her own coat pocket, retrieving from it a thin and red line of crimson silk. 'Eliza helped me make this for you.'

'What?' John snapped out his spiritual trance. 'Don't be silly, Lucy. How could that help me in any way?' He brushed aside the fragile cloth and carried on walking ahead, still transfixed on the demon's words within his head. 'Let's go home. I think it's gonna rain.'

'Eliza's ribbon will stop Belly-Bob hurting you, Daddy,' said Lucy in a voice well beyond her innocent years. 'Eliza said that you *must* wear it!' She stamped her feet stubbornly, then sprinted ahead to stand in front of her father's trance-like presence. 'Wear it, Daddy!' she commanded.

'A gift from a witch, is it? That's the last thing I need, darling.' John's voice continued to hold an undertone of malignance and hatred, a sign that the darker forces of this world were now having their desired effect upon him. 'I don't want it, Lucy. I don't need it.' John marched on at a faster in his pace, cursing to himself. 'Anything that's remotely connected to Sabina can't be good... not even Eliza.'

Skipton Road's fog seeped over the main road that separated it from Grandpa Murray's street. Despite it being midday, not even the sun seemed to penetrate the fog's dense and foreboding wave. A distant chorus of crows cackling echoed within the freezing mist, their sound as haunting as Sabina's own vicious laughter.

'Why won't you wear my ribbon, Daddy?' asked Lucy, pleading for her father to reconsider his stance. 'I made it for you... Eliza just helped make the magic.'

'No, Lucy.' John remained lost in-between the physical and spiritual realm, his speech hoarse and disturbed. 'I just want to go home. I need to be with your mammy.' He froze on the spot, seemingly reawakened from his possession and guilt-ridden over the way he had just addressed his precious, little girl. "Lucy, I'm so sorry. I didn't mean to talk to you like that. Daddy's not well.'

'I know,' emphasized Lucy. 'It's Belly-Bob. He wants to make you into a bad man. He wants Sabina to be happy.'

'Please don't mention her name, Lucy. It gives me the creeps.' John wiped at his clammy skin with tremoring fingers, then a horrific realisation crept in. 'They *want* to justify their torture. They *want* me to be a 'sinner'. Those evil...' Both John and Lucy froze again on the spot where they stood, as a tall, skinny figure walked towards them through the fog. It was hard to make out their features at first, given the sun was directly behind them.

'He's a bad man, Daddy,' whispered Lucy into John's back, where she now hid from view. 'He loves the nasty woman, too. He's says bad things.'

'John-boy?' A piercing and distinct Yorkshire accent coursed into John's tender ears from the figure. 'Is that you, pal?'

'Sid?' John's muscles tensed, reacting with his increasing anxiety. 'I've got the bairn with me, so watch your language.'

'Hello, Lucy,' cackled Sid, as he leant down to greet her. His grin was truly perverse to behold, though now lacked its usual aroma of pungent alcohol. He was dressed in a navy-blue suit, with a cheesy bowtie included. No wonder it had been so difficult for John to initially distinguish him. 'What's that you've got there... in yer hands?'

'It's not yours!' snarled Lucy, defensively, as she peeped around her father's waist for a split-second to address the imposing stranger. How could Sid have known about the ribbon held within her palms? 'Leave my daddy alone.'

'Lucy!' interjected John, sharply. It hadn't yet occurred to him how strange it was that Sid knew about the secretive ribbon in Lucy's hands, a foolish error. 'Sorry, Sid. She's been *very* naughty today. Haven't you, Lucy?'

'Ah...' Sid's grin widened, wreaking with sadistic pleasure. 'Do *you* know what happens to naughty girls, Lucy?'

'They get 'trapped', don't they?' replied the child, in truth already knowing the answer. 'Like... Eliza's mammy?'

'Oh, yes,' said Sid, his tone one of warning. '*Exactly* like her... like Sabina - exactly like the *Red Ribbon Witch*. You know all about her, don't you?'

'Sid...' muttered John, reservedly. 'Don't talk about *that* around the bairn.'

'That? Sabina, ya mean?' Sid growled in both anger and shock. 'Why *not* talk about Sabina, John-Boy? Are you afraid of her?' Sid's body began to aggressively flinch, particularly his clenching fists. 'Your Lucy is a 'sensitive' - like you. It's not a bad thing.'

'What do you mean by that?' John restrained his impulse to punch Sid square in the nose, for what good would it possibly serve anyway, other than for him to lose his job in care? 'Lucy's a good girl—'

'Aye. Lucy *is* a good girl.' Sid granted a knowing glance to Lucy, and then back to John. 'She's a white witch – a pure soul. I can smell it on her.' He now focused solely on the cowering child. 'Lucy has been taught in the ancient ways of Sabina's lineage. She is truly blessed.'

'That's enough, Sid!' John couldn't help himself now. He was struggling to contain his urge to strike Sid clean-out. 'You keep your witchcraft to yourself, and don't bring my little girl into this. It's a load of shit!' John wrapped his arms protectively around Lucy, then carried on towards Skipton Road in silence.

'She's already made a bond with the *Red Ribbon Witch*, haven't ya?' Sid revealed his decaying teeth to Lucy, his manner now bolder and more stubborn. 'You *know* how the magic works, *don't ya*, sweetheart?'

'Leave us alone, Sid, unless you want a fight.' John's hatred against his neighbour intensified ten-fold. 'Keep away from my daughter. I mean it, Sid!'

'Oh, John-Boy,' cackled Sid, now dismissively. He noticed John's clenched fists, yet this didn't deter him. 'What's the offence? Lucy is a white witch - there's no doubt about it. I can sense it in her aura: the purity; the sanctity; the impulse to stop Sabina from fulfilling her vengeance. We can't be having that, though...'

'I warned you!' John sprinted back and then nestled his forehead against Sid's. The two shared in a moment of utter aggression and fear, though it fleeted by as quickly as it had arisen. 'Stay away from her!'

'Those incantations you made, Lucy,' whispered Sid to the fearful child. 'They're not strong enough – not even close. You can't hide from Sabina. She's waiting for you. The angrier you become, John, the stronger she does. You're only making things worse for yourself—'

'ENOUGH!' John went to lash out against Sid, though he was immediately halted by Lucy's calming touch against his raised arm. 'Lucy?'

'Don't hurt him, Daddy,' pleaded the child, her voice no longer meek and filled with dread. 'Don't make Sabina or Belly-Bob angry.'

'Why?' asked John in beleaguerment. 'Why shouldn't I, Lucy? They've ruined our life. They've made your mam hate me.' Sid began to walk away at this point, laughing with a muffled grunt, satisfied by John's obvious torment.

'No, but they want her to, Daddy,' responded Lucy, in a vacant and trance-like daze. 'But don't let them. Eliza wants to help us.'

'Does she?' interjected Sid, almost enraged in his response. 'Eliza wishes to help you... defeat Sabina?'

'Yes!' screamed Lucy, stamping her feet. 'She won't let them hurt my daddy and mammy!'

'For now, my darling... for now,' taunted Sid, his eyes cold and mouth foaming. 'Ya can't keep them at bay forever, John-Boy. I can help ya. Only *I* can help ya. Don't be a daft bastard. Don't let yerself become another victim.'

'No thanks, Sid.' John had managed to calm himself; it wasn't worth the effort to entice his neighbour's fury any further. 'Howay, Lucy. We're going home now. Sid doesn't know what he's talking about. Just ignore him.'

'Aye. You ignore me, John-Boy,' cackled Sid, wildly, spluttering on a wave of tobacco-laden phlegm. 'Just you keep telling yourself that all will be well... you'll see. You'll be begging for my help soon enough.'

'Goodbye, Sid,' said John, somewhat more reserved in his mannerism now. He hated confrontation. 'Arsehole...'

'He's a bad man, Daddy. He loves Sabina,' implored Lucy, as she leant in harder against her father's side. 'I don't like him. Eliza doesn't like him.'

'Neither do I, babe,' agreed John, equally as concerned. 'Forget him. Sid's crazy.'

'Veneficus est tenebris.'

'A *Dark Wizard*?' John scratched at his head, perplexed by the demon's sudden intrusion. It also didn't make any sense to him as to how the demon's words could now be understood. Could it be more foul play or trickery from being held under Sabina's will? John was too exhausted now to care. 'I wonder how your mammy is? I can't wait to see her.' As John held onto his daughter's hands, he turned around once more to look upon Sid. 'What's with the suit? It looks so wrong on him.'

'Job interview!' shouted Sid, now seeming to hold no ill-intent against John, despite the feud they had. 'I'm on my way up, John-Boy! Life couldn't be better!'

'What a creep,' mumbled John to himself. 'Howay, Lucy. I bet Mammy is looking forward to seeing us, too.'

CHAPTER NINE

When John and Hannah started dating one another, the first place they visited together as an "official" couple was Whitby – a small fishing town located on the North Yorkshire coast, and where Bram Stoker found his inspiration for *Dracula*. Both John and his wife held a passionate love for Whitby because it was where they first kissed, where they first held hands. It was an ideal place for them to forget about the dire torment their family now suffered under Sabina's curse, or so they hoped.

'We're going to the seaside!' sang Lucy, excitedly, whilst dancing around her father in their kitchen. She didn't even have her shoes on yet, though was already aiming herself towards the door to leave. 'Can we go now, Daddy?'

'Soon, sweetheart,' assured John. He was excited himself about visiting the place he and Hannah adored so much, though not on the same intense level as Lucy. 'Mammy's just getting her makeup on. She won't be long.' He rolled his eyes towards the staircase with a humorous squint. 'Isn't that right, Han?'

'I Won't be a minute! Nearly finished!' Hannah proceeded to chunter away to herself as she combed through her tattered, mousey hair within the reflection of the bathroom mirror. 'John can talk – he's always late.'

'Do you... love him?'

The comb in Hannah's palm froze, still locked within her drying hair. This phantom voice seemed to be coming from the mirror in front of her - but how? She didn't recognise it at all. Thankfully, Hannah had not yet experienced the demon of which John spoke of, only the witch and her maternal side. 'Who said that?' she asked fearfully, whilst looking directly at her own eyes in the cloudy reflection.

'I am Sa—'

'Hannah! Are you coming or not?' screeched John, with a playful hint of impatience. 'The bairn's going mad down here. You look gorgeous, anyway. Don't worry about your hair.'

'Men always wish to control us...'

'Sabina? John... isn't like that.'

'Our bodies... are their possession.'

'He loves me.'

'Wearing a golden ring means NOTHING!'

'I love him, too. Leave us alone... witch.'

'As you wish. You will speak with me once more, then all shall be revealed.'

'S-Sabina?'

'Did you say something, Han?' asked John, in a trembling voice. It was a question he wasn't too keen on asking, especially after his own experience with spooks in the bathroom. 'What are you doing up there? Is everything okay?' He took a couple of steps up the stairwell but quickly halted, sensing that a darker presence lay close by.

'He doesn't care about you. He doesn't care about anyone.'

'Yeah, babe. I'm coming down now.' Hannah took in a deep breath to calm herself, looked into the mirror's reflection once more, and then left - though she still felt as if she was being watched by something. 'You're not real. Neither of you are.'

'Mummy! We're going to be late!' bleated Lucy. By now the child had managed to slip on her flip flops and sunshades – far more prepared than her parents. 'I want to build sandcastles with Daddy, and eat ice cream, and go swimming, and—'

'I'm comi—' Suddenly, Hannah fell faint and lost her footing on the second step. 'John!' She tumbled down the narrow staircase with little decorum, landing hard against a bookshelf at the bottom of it.

'Han?' John sprinted over, already panting from anxiety, and then leant down to comfort his aching wife. 'What happened?'

'I came over all funny. I'm okay, though.' The first action Hannah took was to check her stomach, albeit discreetly, where inside a being no larger than a tangerine now grew. 'I'm... fine.' She gasped in relief. 'It's just my arse that hurts.'

'Would you like me to rub it better?' chortled John. He snorted like a pig at least twice, which did manage to make Hannah smile. 'I don't mind... honestly.'

'I'll pass on that offer, thanks.' Hannah righted herself, again checking her lower abdomen for any tenderness, and still out of view from John. 'It felt like I was... pushed"'

'Did it?' John glared up the stairwell slowly, imagining the Red Ribbon Witch to be stood upon its final step. 'The evil bitch! They needn't start playing games like that!'

'Don't start, John,' muttered Hannah, as she nestled herself into his chest. 'I love you. I want for us to have a lovely day – not one mention of these spooks you and Lucy keep seeing.'

'Oh, I thought you were going to bollock me for a second there.' John rubbed away at Hannah's lower back, given he didn't know what else to do. This kind act brought some ease to Hannah's present discomfort and vanquished any lingering poison which the demon had tried to instil in her mind against him. 'We're going to have lots of fun today. Trust me. And I think we deserve it.'

'Mammy! Daddy!' screeched Lucy, now from outside. 'Hurry!'

'We won't be long, sweetheart!' replied John, gleefully. 'Have you been for a wee yet, Lucy?'

'No.' Lucy chuntered, then quickly ran back inside towards the downstairs toilet. 'Sorry, Daddy.'

'Hold on, John.' Hannah's eyes widened, her physical pain seemingly gone and now replaced by a far worse concern. 'Those tablets you're on... can you still drive safely with them? Don't they have a sedating effect?'

'Aye,' sneered John, dismissively. He continued to despise the fact that he needed to rely on such drugs to live a 'sane' life. Alcohol and nicotine, on the other hand, were perfectly acceptable to him. 'Mirtazapine doesn't knock you out, y'know. Plus, I didn't have much to drink last night.' Hannah returned a fierce glare in response. 'I only had the one whiskey.'

'You're not meant to drink at all,' she snarled, whilst shaking her head like a disgruntled infant. 'What happens if you fall asleep at the wheel? Did you think of that?'

'I'm fine, Han,' implored John, pitifully. 'I wouldn't put you and Lucy in harm's way, man.' In the corner of his eye, John caught a book that was almost about to fall from its dishevelled shelf. 'Woah!' John leant forwards to correct the book's position – it was his bible. 'That's... weird.'

'What's weird?' questioned Hannah. 'Now what?'

'I put this bible away in my wardrobe upstairs. Did you put it back down here?'

'No,' said Hannah, her eyes widening. 'No, I didn't.'

'Seriously? That's so weird.'

'Aye. You keep saying, John.'

'How did it end up back down here, then?'

'I don't know!'

'Sabina...'

'Don't start with that nonsense again, John.'

'Sordes!'

'Did you... just say something, John?' The colour in Hannah's face instantly whitened. 'I'm sure I heard—'

'No. But whoever put this bible back there apparently thinks that it's "filth".' John's complexion was drastically different in comparison to Hannah's now: red, swollen and the veins coursing through it protruding like they were about to burst at any given moment. His anger now lay at an all-time high against the taunting spirits. Hannah didn't reply to John's strange remark - what could she say? Instead, both parents turned silently towards the downstairs toilet, anticipating their daughter's appearance. Finally, the sound of water flushing and creaking of the door handle broke what awkward tension lingered.

'What have you been doing in there, young lady?' questioned Hannah, though John just stared on ahead vacantly, not caring at all. 'You certainly took your time.'

'I was washing my hands, Mammy,' stated Lucy, in a sassy tone. 'See?'

'You've got to be kidding me?' John gasped in dismay - and he had a good right to. Lucy had not only washed her hands, but she had also flooded the entire bathroom. 'That's *naughty*, Lucy.' John pointed a wavering finger towards his daughter, whilst trying not to laugh on realising her innocent mistake. 'You left the plug in,' he groaned, wearily. 'I'll sort it out when we get back.'

'We can't just leave it like *that*!' Hannah ran into the kitchen for a few tea towels; thereafter, strewing them across the small bathroom floor. 'That'll do for now. It could've been worse.'

'Wey aye! Let's go!' John clapped his hands together ecstatically. 'If we don't set off now, we'll never get a parking space in Whitby. Let's mosey, you two!' He ushered his family into the kitchen but immediately recoiled from the pungent smell of death that existed within it. 'How can you not smell *that*, Han?'

'I *can* smell something, John – you've farted, haven't you?' she giggled, though nervously. In truth, Hannah *could* smell the horrific aroma, but didn't want to entice Sabina's attention – unlike John. 'Dirty git.'

'I haven't dropped one, Han. You'd be the first to know!' sniggered John. 'Are we going to Whitby or what?'

Lucy ran outside first, just managing to hold onto one of her prized dollies which would hopefully help settle her usual car sickness. The morning fog was starting to lift from Skipton Road, much to John's satisfaction.

'Thank God for that! Fog's a nightmare to drive in.' John quickly reached into his back pocket. 'I've got the car keys. We're all set to go.'

'Not taking any of your cigarettes?' enquired Hannah, with one eyebrow raised. 'I *know* that you're still smoking, John.'

'Only the odd-one, Han – just now and then.' John attempted to use the same puppy dog eyes Lucy would to win over his wife's affection – it didn't work. 'I've had a lot of stress to deal with recently. The odd cigarette isn't going to kill me.'

'You've looked after a people with lung cancer in the care home, haven't you?' Hannah rose both eyebrows now.

'Aye.' Guilt swiftly filtered through John's conscience like an aggressive form of cancer itself. 'Most were smoking sixty-a-day. There's a difference.'

'You're still feeding those shitty chemicals into your body, John. Just quit. Do it for Lucy's sake, if not for mine,' she pleaded, clearly begging for her husband's submission. 'Can you imagine walking her down the aisle when she's older, leaning on a walking stick, and puffing from an oxygen tank?'

'I've never thought *that* far ahead, to be honest.' John cracked his head from side-to-side, then from his other back pocket retrieved a half-empty carton of cigarettes, which he then held out anxiously before Hannah. 'Here. Take them.' Without hesitation, he dropped the carton into her waiting hands. 'Throw them in the bin for me.'

'No.' Hannah smiled lovingly to her husband, both satisfied at getting one over on him and also by feeling proud at his devotion to both herself and Lucy. 'They're yours - *you* throw them away.'

'Fine. I will.' John initially felt some grief as he looked over the cigarette packet lain in his hand now. For a painful moment he admired its sheen finish, the faint smell of dried tobacco leaves from inside, and then imagined that this must have been how Bilbo felt when parting with his beloved ring in Tolkien's masterpiece. 'There. Bye-bye!' John crumpled the pristine packet into a small bundle and then threw it over his left shoulder. 'They're gone. No more lung cancer. Hello cravings.'

'Oi!' bellowed an elderly voice from next door. John had only gone and thrown the decimated contents of his cigarette carton into Pat's garden. 'Ya cheeky beggar! You're not using my garden as a bloody waste disposal!'

'Sorry, Pat,' whimpered John, in hoping for a sympathetic reply from his "nicer" neighbour. 'I didn't mean to throw them into your garden - honest.' He leant over the fence to personalise his apology and was soon astounded to see how Pat's garden looked more like the Botanical Gardens in Durham, than anything else.
'Nice garden.'

'Yes, and I'd like to keep it that way.' Pat looked down at the crumbled cigarettes, their contents now floating off into the passing breeze. 'I'm glad to see that your stopping such a filthy habit, but don't you make Skipton Road into a pig sty. It's a lovely estate, despite what others on the town may think.'

'Aye, it's lovely,' said John, as genuinely as possible.

'I am sorry about that, Pat. I'll clean the mess up,' interjected Hannah, her whitened cheeks now red again from embarrassment. 'John's so laxy-dazy.'

'All men are,' laughed Pat, sounding more like a sea-lion suffering with heartburn than human. 'I'm so happy to be alone – no men to worry about or care for. After my Gerald died, a few years ago now, that's how it's been - and *that's* how it's staying.'

'Oh, I'm sorry to hear you lost your husband,' mumbled John, in his continuing state of shame. 'How did he pass away?'

'He died, lovie. Just say it like that,' snapped Pat. 'He went loopy and then died. It has happened to a lot of men along this street.' She looked over towards Sid's house and grunted. 'I'm surprised that Sid hasn't gone doo-lally yet. Mind, he *is* a pisshead... so he's not far off.'

Sid's harmless...' John stopped himself mid-sentence. Why on earth did he feel the need to defend such a lowlife? 'And he's a complete tool,' he added, laughing awkwardly.

'Now that's a more accurate term for him,' said Pat, smirking, whilst quickly sealing her lips to prevent her false teeth from falling out. 'His mother was lovely, but you never get two the same, do you?'

'Sid's mother died recently, didn't she?' asked John with some reservation. He knew it was unprofessional to discuss work outside in the open, but his curiosity had taken over. 'I used to look after her at the home where I work.'

'Did you? Oh, Jean. Poor, poor, Jeanie. I always felt so sorry for her,' wallowed Pat. 'She doted on her boy - now look at him! He makes me sick to my stomach, does Sid.'

'I can hear yers talkin' about me... ya set of twats.' Sid slowly rose his head over John's adjoining fence, like a funnel-web spider emerging from its nest. 'No hard feelings, John-Boy?' He winked playfully to John, although how sincere this gesture was could have been open to any interpretation. 'No ill-feelings? Yer a sound fella - I like ya. I fuckin' respect ya.'

'Cheers, Sid.' John gave a thumbs-up sign to him, though he really wanted to raise his middle finger instead. Pat herself beat him to this. 'All water under the bridge. I don't hold grudges, me.'

'What are you both on about?' questioned Hannah, her whole-body shaking with dread. She wasn't one for confrontation like John, either. 'Have you both fallen out over something?'

'Nah, we're alright,' assured John in dismissal. The cold sweat forming on his brow, however, spoke otherwise. 'We're off to Whitby today. We'd better go now, before the traffic gets bad.'

'Whitby!' cackled Sid, in a similar way to how hyenas do once they find their latest carcass to desecrate. 'Watch out for *Dracula*!' He proceeded to mimic a typical Hollywood vampire: bared fangs (which he had a few of), gangly fingers and a transient stare to match. 'You better watch out for the spooks, ha-ha!' Lucy slowly turned around to face Sid, then rose her own middle finger against him.

'Lucy!' gasped Hannah and John in unison. Pat couldn't help but laugh at the child's unexpected response. 'That's so naughty!'

'I'm not doing it,' said Lucy, her voice distant and more formal than usual. 'Eliza asked to me to do it.'

'And on that note, we're off.' John grabbed his daughter by the waist and then bundled her out of the garden, before Sid had any chance to counter this 'message' from Eliza. 'Take care, Pat. See you around, Sid.'

'Take care, dearies. Enjoy yourselves.' Pat pressed on with her garden duties, diverting any eye contact away from Sid who carried on glaring towards her with an utter look of disdain. 'Have a wonderful day at the seaside!'

'Eliza said that Gerald is very happy now!' shouted Lucy over to Pat, despite John's attempt to muffle her mouth with his thick leather coat. 'He doesn't miss your stews, by the way.'

'Gracious!' Pat's mouth fell open, both shocked and enlightened by Lucy's revelation. 'Well, you tell Eliza, to tell my Gerald, that when *I* get up there... that's all he'll be eating!' Lucy chortled into her father's coat, unwittingly soaking it with a trail of thin saliva.

'Enough with *Eliza*, Lucy. Please, sweetheart,' demanded John, through a harsh whisper into his daughter's ears.

'People will think that you're poorly, Lucy.' Hannah gently stroked at her daughter's hair as they walked towards their car. It was her way of saying that she did understand Lucy's 'gift', but that it also scared her. 'There's no harm in having imaginary friends... just keep them to yourself, okay?'

'Okay.' Lucy nodded back to her mother in obedience. 'Eliza's a good girl. *She* won't make me poorly.'

'That's fine. I'm glad to hear that,' said Hannah, also keeping an eye on John's own reaction. He kept quiet which was unusual for him, though this didn't last long. 'Isn't that right, Daddy?'

'Yep! That's right.' John was desperate to turn the conversation over onto something else - anything. 'We should make it to Whitby by midday, which means... Fish & Chips!' He grinned, with a knowing look to Lucy. 'I'm already starving! Fish & Chips are your favourite, aren't they, Lucy? If you behave yourself, you can have some ice cream, too.'

'Yay!' rejoiced the child. 'I want *pink* ice cream!'

'We'll see. No more talk of Eliza though. Understood?' John paused his steps, waiting for Lucy's agreement. 'Do *you* understand what I'm saying, missy?'

'Yes, Daddy. I understand.' Without John's awareness, Lucy reached into her coat pocket and started to play with a thin red ribbon hidden from within it. 'Eliza said that she can't go with us. She has to stay here.'

'She can watch the house for us, can't she?' Hannah scrubbed harder at her daughter's scalp, though not too hard. 'I bet she'd love to visit the seaside with us, but we're not going to talk about her anymore are we, sweetheart?'

'*Hannah*,' growled John under his breath. 'You're not exactly helping.'

'Eliza can't leave, Mammy.' Lucy snapped her head sideways to face Hannah. 'Belly-Bob won't let her. If he's alive, she has to stay here.'

'Right! How about some music?' John fired up his car's ignition and then twizzled the radio's volume switch onto full. 'How about some 'Stone Roses' or 'The Cranberries' to lighten things up?'

'The Cranberries, please.' Hannah couldn't have said this any faster if she'd tried to. 'I can't stand that other crap. It's so boring.'

'*Crap*?' emphasized John, with a drawn look of disappointment. 'There's nothing wrong with 'The Stone Roses'. Your taste in music is what's wrong.' He slipped the Cranberries CD into the dock like an obedient lapdog, smiling to Hannah as he did so. 'Whitby, here we come!'

'Mammy!' Lucy suddenly screeched, almost writhing herself free from her car seat. 'I saw... her.'

'Who?' asked Hannah, held deep with reservation. She turned around, first looking to ensure Lucy hadn't removed her seatbelt, then up towards her tremoring daughter. 'What's the matter, darling? Who did you see?'

'*She* was standing at my window – and still is!' Lucy frantically pointed a finger back towards their house, towards her bedroom window. John lowered his head in cowardice to the opposite direction, while Hannah inspected each windowpane for any signs of an intruder. '*She's* there!'

'I can't see anyone, sweetheart,' assured Hannah. Truthfully, she did want to witness some strange presence, if it could only verify her daughter's incessant claim. 'There's nobody there, Lucy. Calm down, for goodness sake. We're going to have a nice and relaxing day today. No more spooky nonsense.'

For a second or two, John pretended to exhale a thick plume of tobacco smoke, and then breath in the fumes from his Irish whiskey bottle, as a means of calming his fragile nerves. He performed this ridiculous routine to counter his fear in looking back towards Skipton Road, his 'beloved' homestead. Somehow, he knew that Sabina was there, and soon enough Lucy's claim was proven right. There – standing at the window of his daughter's bedroom - John could plainly see a young woman's outline; she was wearing in a white dress, her hair long and brunette in colour, and her eyes sunken back within their pitted sockets. 'S-Sabina!' John shook his head in disbelief. 'No...'

'I *told* you!' Lucy began to sob. Not even her mother's loving smile could appease the child's torment now. '*She's* watching us!'

'She can bloody-well stay there, can't she?' John slammed a foot against his accelerator and then, after an unwanted wheel-spin, sped off out of Skipton Road's cul-de-sac. 'Sod Sabina! If Eliza's stuck in our house, then so is Sabina. In a few hours we'll be well away from them both, and that suits me fine.'

'Don't be so nasty about Eliza, Daddy,' Lucy whined, with a level of maturity that easily outmatched John's. 'They're not stuck in our house... it's just where Eliza's mammy was killed.'

'John? JOHN!' Hannah addressed her husband with a set of terrified gasps, almost hyperventilating. 'What... did Lucy just say?'

'Nothing. She said... nothing.' John increased the bass on his radio, forcing it into its clipping territory. 'She's just a bairn, Han.

She said nothing. We're going to Whitby, and we're going to have a great day - alright?' This was a pathetic attempt made by John, if any, to calm Hannah's increasing nerves. Hannah quickly took to her Kindle, in place of speaking any more to John (or Lucy for that matter). The story Hannah was currently reading involved a woman who had fallen in love with a werewolf. It had a tedious plotline though it helped to pass the time. 'That Kindle may as well be attached to your arm,' chuckled John, his smile forced and bitter. 'Still, if it keeps you happy, it's money well spent.'

'It does make me happy – yeah,' said Hannah, herself already lost within the fantastical world lain out before her. 'You have your booze... I have my Kindle.'

John and his family soon left Newton Escomb and County Durham. The journey into Middlesbrough proved torturous: red traffic lights strew most of the way, and then there was a steep incline into the North Yorkshire moors – something which John always dreaded with each visit.

'I hope the car can make it up this hill.' John took in an anxious breath and then forced his gearstick into first. 'Nightmare, man!' John's car gradually crawled up the winding embankment. Several cars behind him tooted their horns, only adding to his arisen fury. 'Howay! Give me a chance! I'm going as fast as I can... set of impatient arseholes.' John moved a hand to wind his window down but stopped after Hannah tapped away at his inner thigh. 'What are you doing that for?'

'What are *you* doing?' she scorned. 'Keep both hands on the steering wheel. Never-mind what the other cars are doing.' Hannah began to hyperventilate. 'Have you seen the drop beside us? I don't fancy a trip down there.'

'Fair point. I'll try to stay calm.' John leant into his steering wheel, willing for his car to make it to the summit without overheating or stalling. 'Come on – make it!'

'Keep your foot down... stay in a low gear,' commanded Hannah. From her side-mirror, she noticed that Lucy had fallen asleep - an impressive feat, given her father's boisterous ranting. 'Aww, Lucy's fallen asleep, John. She'll miss all the pretty views.'

'She'll miss them anyway, if I can't get to the top of this bloody hill!' humoured John, still with a hint of anxiety in his voice. 'We're nearly there! Almost!'

John's car spluttered to a slow and steady pace on reaching the hillside's summit. Behind it lay the industrial landscape of Middlesbrough, and in front were the ancient moors of North Yorkshire. Hannah signalled for John to pull over into a nearby car park. She was desperate to alleviate her bladder, as well as to take in some fresh air and look over the serene landscape.

'I need a minute, John,' said Hannah, rubbing at her stomach. 'Pull over here, hun.'

'I'm ready for a break, too. My head's proper battered after that ordeal.' John pulled in beside a rusty, mud-soaked Land Rover. An elderly couple waved from inside it to him, oblivious to the torture which he and his wife had just endured. 'Hi.' spoke John silently as he waved back to them. 'I bet they had no bother making it up that hill in a car like theirs. It'd been quicker just to walk it.'

'Give it a rest, babe,' implored Hannah. Her back was still aching from the fall encountered earlier on, although her main concern now was in the pain building up around her expanding womb. 'I need some fresh air,' she said, as a wave of vomit crept its way up into her mouth.

'Okay, hun. Don't wander too far.' John yearned for a cigarette, but it thankfully passed after a moment or two. He looked down to his phone as way of distraction, initially surprised by the fact he had a signal, and then jumped up and down excitedly. 'Nice one!'

'What's that?' asked Hannah, genuinely curious as to what John was so happy about. 'What are you smiling like that for?'

'I contacted my old history teacher on Facebook, and he's replied. I didn't think he would.' John scoured the message meticulously, his smile growing wider by the second. 'He's agreed to meet up with me for a coffee tomorrow. I've asked him about Newton Escomb's ancient history. Looking on Google's been a waste of time.'

'Why?' Hannah scowled, whilst holding onto her throbbing stomach more firmly. 'What's there to know?'

'I'm gonna ask whether he knows anything about any witches or old settlements that used to exist around where Skipton Road is. Maybe he can shed some light on Sabina?'

'For goodness sake, John,' groaned Hannah, wearily. So much for having a day away from their haunting tormentor, she thought. 'He'll think you've gone mad.'

'Mr. Clarence knows his stuff. He's the best person to speak to about these things,' implored John. 'I just want to prove that I'm not going mental, and I think he's the guy to help me.'

'You're not mental, John... just stressed.' Hannah fought against revealing to her husband the harrowing visions of which she herself had experienced. Now was not the right time, in her eyes. 'It's a load of rubbish. Our house isn't haunted...'

'What about Lucy, then?' quipped John, in an arrogant tone. '*She's* not stressed, is she? Explain that.'

'I thought today was meant to be fun? You're making it into the total opposite.' Hannah slowly rubbed again along her stomach; the cramps were worsening now. 'I wish you'd just forget about it all. I'm fed up of you and Lucy going on about witches and demons... it's weird.'

'So, Lucy and I are... weird?' John swallowed heavily, looking across the moors like a lost lamb. 'Is that what you really think?'

'No - ARGH!' Hannah could no longer hide the peculiar twinges inflicting her abdomen, and it wasn't long before John himself

210

noticed these erratic movements. 'There's something I need to tell you, John. I was going to wait—'

'You're pregnant, aren't you?' John smiled, though admittedly in apprehension. Hannah rubbed at the site her womb in the very same manner when she was pregnant with Lucy. 'I am right?'

'Yes,' whispered Hannah in response. She wanted to embrace this good news as joyfully as her husband, but the situation with Sabina and John's deteriorating mental health made this too difficult to achieve. 'Are you... happy?'

'Of course, I am!' John leaped across the boggy marshland towards his despairing wife. 'Why wouldn't I be? Lucy will be so happy!'

'I don't want to tell her yet... it's too soon.' Hannah fleeted her sight across to where Lucy slept in the car. 'I think I'm about ten weeks. I've already had some morning sickness... you just haven't noticed.'

'I thought something was wrong, but I didn't want to bother you.' John removed his leather jacket to wrap it around Hannah, hoping that some warmth from his body remained in it to comfort her. 'Don't ever hide anything from me. If you need to talk – talk. I'm always here for you, even if I've lost the plot a bit recently.' Hannah lifted her head, laughing. 'What?'

'It's nothing, John.' What Hannah wanted to say was how John didn't really sell himself well. *You can talk to me, but I'm cuckoo -* very reassuring. 'Can we set off now? I want to get to Whitby before I feel sick again.

'You can keep my coat on if you like... if your cold?' said John, his voice resounding like a needy child. 'It's meant to rain later on. You should have brought your winter coat, babe.'

'I'll be okay. Hold on a sec...' Hannah peered across the long shards of dry grass and moss surrounding them, admiring the sun as it shone its golden rays over the natural landscape. 'It's nice and peaceful here, isn't it?'

'It stinks of sheep shit,' chortled John, as he sat himself back into the driver's seat. 'I'm sure there's a few viper snakes about, an' all.'

'You always have to go and ruin things,' grumbled Hannah, as she herself sat back inside the car. 'I meant that the scenery is nice – it's beautiful. I've never really noticed it, before because we normally drive through so fast.'

'Aye. I know what you mean.' John's expression looked dreadful, somehow disturbed. 'It reminds me of the marshlands - the ones in my nightmares: the grass, the boggy soil, the disgusting smells. We just need a witch to randomly pop up now...'

'What's that favourite saying of yours?' said Hannah, her question evidently rhetorical. 'You know: *Where there is light, there is always darkness. Where there is darkness, there is always light.*'

'Yeah. So, what?' John nodded his head slightly with a roll of his eyes in perplexment. 'It's easy to say, though, isn't it?' John reignited his car's engine and then tapped gently at the accelerator, ensuring that Lucy wouldn't be woken up. 'It's not far to Whitby now. We should be there in about twenty minutes.'

'Thank God.'

The midday sun seeped through a set of dark and dense rainclouds above, as John and his family made it to Whitby's western cliff. Despite the crowds, John was lucky enough to find a parking space which lay along the cliff's edge, facing out towards the North Sea's horizon. Hannah stepped out the car first. She breathed in the surrounding salty sea air and warmly welcomed its fresh haze.

'That's better.' Hannah panted, her limbs stiff, her thoughts now a cocktail of mixed and raw emotions. 'It's just how I remember it. I love it here.'

'It wasn't *that* long ago when we were last here, Han,' said John dismissively. He hadn't meant to come across as being callous –

212

but he did. 'Maybe a couple of years or so, I reckon. The seagulls are bigger now, aren't they?' At that precise moment, John ducked behind his car door to hide away from a passing gull which was about the size of a French Bulldog, or at least that's how he saw it. 'Bloody *Shite-Hawks* - they're everywhere!'

'What?' giggled Hannah, with a confused sideways glance to John. 'What did you call them?'

'*Shite-Hawks*,' replied John, also laughing. 'Well, it's all seagulls do – that, and they steal your chips.'

'That's why I married you, John.' Hannah sniggered like a pubescent schoolgirl as she hugged into him. 'You're always full of surprises.' She opened the door where Lucy sat as if disarming a bomb, attempting to not awaken the sleeping child. Lucy looked so peaceful and carefree. 'Lucy,' whispered Hannah, into her daughter's ear. 'Lucy, sweetheart. We're at the seaside now. Wake up, darling.'

'The...seaside!' Lucy awoke with an ecstatic jolt and clap of her hands. 'Are we *really* at the seaside, Mammy?'

'Yes!' exclaimed John. His own excitement, however, instantly left from him as a seagull flying over decided to deposit a parting gift upon his left arm. 'Great. What a welcome, that is.'

'Daddy's a poo-poo monster!' sang Lucy, again clapping her small hands together. She then quickly hid behind Hannah, who herself continued to laugh at John's misfortune. 'Ha-ha-ha-haa-ha!'

'Oh, Aye... it's very funny. I look like a right scruff now.' John brushed at the white sludge mark with his other arm, making matters only worse. 'For Frigg'*s* sake. I can't go walking around Whitby like this...'

'Here, John.' Hannah broke her laughter for a moment to retrieve some wet wipes out of Lucy's carry bag. 'Try these. See if they'll clean up that mess.' She handed a small bundle of wipes over to John, still smirking at his misfortune.

'Thanks, hun.' John wiped his coat clean, then proceeded to pounce around his wife and child to avoid any further gull-attacks. 'Sod off! I swear, these bloody seagulls are out to get me!'

'Behave yourself,' scoffed Hannah. 'I don't know about you two, but I'm hungry now. Do you still fancy some Fish & Chips, Lucy?'

'Yes, *please*!' Lucy ran on ahead. Her small figure looked so minute in comparison to the monstrous whalebone archway, which for many years had stood looking over Whitby's harbour as its heavenly gateway.

'It's great to see her happy again,' comment John to Hannah, in a grieving tone. 'She reminds me of when I was little – of being here with Gran and Grandpa Murray.'

'Lucy *is* happy, John. You've been so down about things, that's why you don't see it... like I do.' Hannah wrapped her small fingers around John's plumper digits, caressing them gently. 'Don't let things get on top of you. You're on those tablets now... they'll make you feel better, won't they?'

'Nah, the Mirtazapine just numbs me. It hasn't solved anything at all,' replied John, with a dejected frown. 'It's not the answer I'm after, Han. I've been thinking about, you know, maybe hiring a Medium to come to our house.'

'Really? I thought you didn't believe in all that "bollocks", Mr. Sceptic?' jested Hannah, as she moved in closer to rest her head against John's broad shoulders. 'I've heard some bad stories about people hiring Mediums to perform cleansings. It can make things worse.'

'Name one!' snapped John, his frustration growing as steadily as the afternoon tide. 'Go on...'

'Well, Donnie's mam - Charlotte. Didn't she hire one a few years ago?'

'Aye, when they lived on Skipton Road. I can see where you're going with this.' John froze. He'd said too much. 'That was *years* ago, though.'

'Wait – where did he live?' Hannah lifted her head away from John, burdened with shock and surprise. 'I didn't know that Donnie used to live on the same street as us. You kept that quiet.'

'He lived a few doors down from us.' John's response was calm, though inside he was shaking like a dog emptying its guts. 'The ghost they had was a tall man that used to walk past open doorways and slam doors... apparently. The Medium Charlotte hired ran out saying that there was a darker spirit – something ancient.'

'Oh, God.' Hannah's voice muffled into a rippling rattle of frantic grunts. 'That's awful. Poor Charlotte. No wonder they moved out so fast.'

'They were only there for a few months. Donnie can barely remember it. I think he was only about six years old when it all kicked off - Shit!' John halted his and Hannah's progress again, reaching down into his back pocket to collect his phone. 'I was meant to be meeting up with Donnie and Ryan sometime this week. I forgot to text them back...' He planted a solid palm against his forehead, much to Hannah's amusement. 'I'm always letting people down.'

'No, you're not. Leave it for now, hun. Enjoy your day out with me and Lucy.' In truth, it hurt Hannah's feelings how John seemed to care more about disappointing his friends, rather than herself and their daughter. Now wasn't the time to correct him on this, seeing as there was always room later in the day. 'It's our special trip out - no phones or talking anymore about ghosties. Agreed?' she emphasised this point with a forceful nudge into his side. 'I want us all to relax.'

'Agreed.' John pulled Hannah into himself tighter, clenching onto the love which still burned between them, regardless of Sabina's cancerous effect. 'Love you.'

'Love you, too.' Hannah's smile widened greater than it ever had over the past few weeks. 'You're not a bad bloke really, John.'

'Infidel.'

'Are you alright?' Hannah scoured John's sudden change in expression. He was holding onto his forehead, whether it was in pain from him previously striking it or otherwise couldn't be yet deciphered. 'Do you have a headache? You look awful.'

'I've just got a bit of a migraine... probably from being hungry.' This was a blatant lie, but John didn't wish to explain how he had just heard a demon speak to him, especially after promising Hannah that they wouldn't talk anymore about their ghostly encounters. 'Lucy! Wait for Mammy and Daddy!' A great diversion, though this didn't fool Hannah as intended. 'Quick, Han - before she runs off!'

The enticing aroma of vinegar and warm grease rose along the whole promenade. It wasn't long before John and his family came across the first 'Chippy'. The restaurant's décor was black and white, and boasted a queue at least twenty-foot long which stretched for at least ten yards from a small set of stairs before its entranceway.

'Balls to that,' despaired John. His stomach tore away at itself now like a maelstrom, clouding his judgement somewhat. 'God, I'm so hungry – but not *that* much. There must be another Chippy close by, one without a queue like that.' Lucy again led the way, her light blonde hair just visible through the dense crowds. 'Lucy! Don't run off!' Panic immediately set in. Both John and Hannah sprinted through the crowds, knocking many strangers to their knees in want of reaching their precious daughter. 'Lucy! Stop!'

'Daddy!' screamed the child. It was difficult to tell whether she was excited or frightened. 'Mammy!'

'I'm coming, babe – don't move!' screamed John, his voice breaking with panic. 'We're coming!' All surrounding noises and movements moulded into one agonizing blur to John and Hannah.

All they could see - all they sensed - was their daughter's presence, their light in the darkness. 'Wait where you are!'

'Look!' Lucy was staring vacantly upon a Gothic-themed shop's display window. 'Look, Daddy.'

'You, missy, are in *so* much trouble!' John clenched onto his daughter's soft skin, yearning to never let go of it. 'Don't *ever* run off like that again – you hear me?'

'Look, Daddy.' With fear evident in her eyes, Lucy pointed towards a small figurine, itself nestled within a wave of multi-coloured candles and steampunk paraphernalia. 'It's... Belly-Bob.' John merely pretended to not hear this. 'The *Goat-Man*.'

'Don't you *ever* run off like that, Lucy - ever!' scorned Hannah, as she wrapped her arms protectively around the catatonic child. 'Why did you run away from us?'

'Belly-Bob,' replied Lucy, as if lost in a trance. 'That's... him. He talked to me. He told me to come here.'

'He is one ugly bastard,' commented John to Hannah, utilizing the corner of his mouth. The crude-looking figurine appeared to represent an emaciated man, cross-legged with a goat's head in place of their own. 'I think I've seen this before,' he gulped. 'We're talking years ago... in some of my nightmares.'

'Belly-Bob's *is* real!' Lucy wailed. 'I *told* you, Daddy!'

'Now, hold on.' John rose his palms into the air defensively. 'How about we go inside and ask the shopkeeper what the figurine is called? I'm not having any more arguments today.'

'Seriously, John?' griped Hannah, with her head shaking slowly from side-to-side. 'This shop doesn't seem to be very suitable for a young bairn. There's weird dolls, clothes and tarot cards... no way is our Lucy going in there.'

'Wey aye,' blared John, as stubborn as ever. 'We'll settle this – now.' Without Hannah's consent, he pushed open the shop's doorway. A pungent waft of burning incense and melted candlewax instantly struck at John's nostrils, flaring them into an erratic spasm. 'Bloody Hell - that's strong!'

'Good Afternoon, peeps!' declared the shop's clerk, with a jovial Cornish accent. John felt an instant fondness towards the endearing chap, being that he reminded him of Sam-Wise Gamgee from Peter Jackson's *Lord of the Rings* movies. Lucy thought that he was a pirate, which thankfully helped to relinquish the imposing surroundings. 'Are you just browsing?'

'Actually, I have a question for *you*, my good sir,' said John, amidst chuckling apprehensively. 'That manky figurine you have in the front window—' The shop clerk was noticeably offended by this remark. Does it have a name?" 'He pointed directly to the disturbing doll. 'If you could tell me, I'd really appreciate it.'

'That-there figurine is called *Baphomet*,' explained the clerk, proudly. 'Many-a Knights Templar were burned at the stake... all accused of worshipping that deity.'

'See, it's *not* Belly-Bob,' smirked John, with a feigned smile towards Lucy. 'There's nothing to worry about.'

'Mind you,' interjected the clerk, his face morphing with a melodramatic quality. 'More ancient cultures referred to him by other names. Hmm, just you let me think - 'Baal' was one. The other I believe, was 'Beelzebub'. He is a supposed symbol of knowledge and vengeance... and is made from the finest pewter.'

'Belly-Bob!' screamed Lucy, as if her life was being immediately threatened. 'Belly-Bob!' The clerk gave an awkward smile in response to the child, then prayed for John's wallet to open. 'I want Eliza. Help me, Eliza!'

'Jesus,' whispered John. He was fearful, though also strangely satisfied at finally placing the last pieces of Lucy's jigsaw together. 'Belly-Bob is... Beelzebub. It makes sense now.'

'You wantin' to buy that-there figurine or what, pal?' The clerk looked to John with a frantic smile. Business was obviously poor. 'It's yours for fifty pounds. A fantastic bargain, if I dare say so.'

'No, thanks,' replied Hannah, her tone sharp and final. 'Thanks for your help, though. Let's go, John. I don't like it in here.'

'Can I not interest you in one of our Ouija boards? They're half price, and for today only!' gleamed the clerk, quite desperately. 'I'll even throw in the figurine!'

'Well...' John pondered for a moment if this would be a good idea or not. Surely, business couldn't be that bad for the friendly shop keeper? 'It's a great offer, just—'

'No! Don't you dare buy that horrible thing, John!' Hannah stamped a foot beside John's, emphasising her growing frustration with him plainly. 'I'm hungry – we're all hungry. Let's get something to eat, instead of wasting money on stupid dolls...'

'The offer's only on for today, pal. Sixty quid for the board and figurine.' The clerk's face was starting to redden, perfectly in line with his auburn dreadlocks. 'You won't get a chance like this again.'

'Sold!' John reached down for his wallet. It somehow felt heavier in his hands now as he lifted it. 'Call it fifty?'

'Oh, you - haggler!' laughed the clerk, though it was apparent that they weren't pleased with John's bartering skills. 'It's sold! Fifty quid. Thank you very much.'

'You... utter arsehole,' seethed Hannah under her breath, as she clenched onto Lucy's arms, and then left with her before John had any time to react. 'I can't believe you did that.'

'Oh, dear.' John stared at his reflection in the Ouija board; it appeared so drawn and haggard, much like how his soul now felt. 'I don't think my wife's all-too happy.'

'It's a steal, my friend,' assured the clerk. 'There's just one thing you need to know: make sure that you bless the circle and then close it at the end of a session – otherwise, who knows what could appear. Also, if I were you, I'd store the figurine anywhere but your bedroom. It's had a few previous owners, and that's the warning that came with it.'

'Cheers, mate.' John clasped the Ouija board and figurine under his left arm, finding that they were heavier than expected. 'Some weight in these, like.'

'They're made from the highest quality material – well worth the price,' chuntered the clerk, somewhat hinting for John to leave. 'Have a nice day.'

'Han?' John.' exhaled wearily, his conscience riddled with impulsive guilt. 'Please don't be mad at me

'*Don't be mad*?' Hannah glared back to her husband tenaciously. 'One minute, you want rid of the ghosts - now you want to talk with them!'

'It's not like that, babe.' John reached out a wanting hand to his wife, his face littered with an expression of pity. 'I just want some answers, that's all.'

'I can't believe you went ahead an bought them, especially after I told you not to.'

'Hannah...' John quickened his pace to match his wife's. Being overweight was now his greatest burden. 'Wait up!'

'Lucy and I are hungry, so *we're* going for some food.' Hannah wanted to sprint as far away as feasible from John, but this was cut short by the raising bridge lain before her now. 'That's all we need.'

'I'm only after some answers, Han,' said John, pleadingly. Aren't you?'

'You got one, didn't you? Belly-Bob is an 'ancient demon' called *Beelzebub* or *Baal* or whatever the Hell that Cornish fella told you. I'm sick of all this haunting nonsense.'

'Belly-Bob *is* real, Mammy,' whispered Lucy to her, intimately. She was trying to ignore her parent's ongoing argument, as it was so unusual for them to act this way. 'I told you.'

'I don't want to hear anything else about Belly-Bob or Beelzebub anymore – okay?' Hannah started to sob angrily, pained by her husband's betrayal. 'I can't take much more of this crap.'

'I'm sorry if I've upset you,' said John, throwing himself into submission over his foolish actions. He loved Hannah more than life itself, even more so than finding out the answers he so greatly desired. 'I'm sorry. What else can I say?'

Hannah looked down towards her feet. She was wearing the same shoes worn when John and herself first came to Whitby - a pleasant though sombre reminder. 'Apology accepted. But I don't want to hear anything else today about demons and witches – you got it?'

'Yeah.' John held out his hand again; thankfully Hannah accepted it this time. 'I wonder where the nearest chip shop is? My stomach's killing me.' Hannah didn't reply, but merely kept her eyes fixated upon her sand-laden shoes.

The next Fish & Chip shop John and his family came to appeared more run-down in comparison with the last one – yet still, the aroma of freshly fried fish and vinegar satisfied their grown need of hunger. John and Lucy consumed the entirety of their greasy meal; whereas, Hannah didn't take a single bite. Her mind lay elsewhere, on the demon which dwelled within the safety of her own home - of Sabina and the torment which she and her child had endured almost half-a-century ago.

'Aren't you hungry?' questioned John to Hannah, both bashfully and in a genuine show of concern. 'Have you got morning sickness again?'

'No. It's not that...' Hannah played with the battered fish lying on her plate, pretending that at any given moment it would spring back into life to surprise her. 'I've lost my appetite.'

'There's ten quid wasted,' snorted John, though he soon changed his negative tone. 'You still need to eat Hannah. Think of the baby.'

'A baby!' rejoiced Lucy, her pale-blue eyes opening wide in amazement. Instantly, Hannah looked to her husband with the greatest level of scorn. 'Is there a baby in Mammy's tummy?'

'*Maybe*, sweetheart,' replied Hannah, with shrugging shoulders. 'I'm not sure yet. I need to see a doctor to make sure.' She looked again to John, her eyes glistening with fury at his unwitting reveal. 'Thanks, John. So much for keeping it a secret.'

'I want a baby sister!' demanded Lucy, fleeting her vision between both John and Hannah now. 'I want a baby Lucy!'

'You do realise that we wouldn't be able to call the baby Lucy – Lucy,' explained John, with a sympathetic nod. 'That'd be really confusing for Mammy and I. You'll need to think of a different name.'

'I like Sophia - like the little princess on TV.' Lucy leant over the table towards her parents, willing her enthusiasm on them. 'My baby sister will be called Sophia.'

'We'll think about it, sweetheart.' Hannah rubbed at her face, hiding the tears which now formed in her eyes. 'Nice one, John.'

'Sorry, Han.' John discreetly reached down for his phone again. He then instigated a text message to his mother, asking if she could look after Lucy that night so that he and Hannah could have an evening to themselves. 'Mam's just text me.'

'Has she?' Hannah continued to play with her food, sliding the oily fish around like a hockey puck. 'What's Toyah said?'

'She's offered to watch our Lucy tonight – to give us a night off.' John smiled back to Hannah like a hopeful child. 'It'll be nice, just you and me... like old times.'

'I'm not sure.' Hannah gradually formed a smile, much to John and Lucy's shared relief. 'It's been a while since we've been on a "Date Night". Do you have any plans for us, then?'

'I'll drop Lucy off when we go back home. We can just have a chillout session, maybe?' Hannah rolled her eyes back in disappointment. 'If you're not eating your meal, we may as well set off now.' John ushered for Lucy to put her coat back on, instigating Hannah's own similar response.

'It's such a shame that the tide is in,' sighed Hannah. 'I was hoping to let Lucy play on the beach before we go.'

'Aww! I want to build a sandcastle, Mammy,' whimpered Lucy, herself showing a great deal of disappointment in her eyes. 'It's not fair!'

'The tide's in, sweetheart,' said John, remorsefully. The usual feeling of guilt immediately swept back in. 'We'll come again next week when Daddy's off work, alright?' He scrubbed at Lucy's hair playfully, despite her flailing arms telling him not to. 'The weather might be better then as well. It's too windy now. You'll get sand in your eyes.'

John carefully lifted Lucy onto his shoulders to make the journey back up Whitby's west cliff easier for her, whilst Hannah dawdled on slowly from behind. On reaching the whalebone archway, John paused for a second to take in one last look over Whitby's infamous shoreline and decimated Abbey.

'I need a sit-down, Lucy.' John planted his daughter upon a worn, wooden bench that looked over the harbour, just beside Captain Cook's monument. 'Grandpa Murray and I used to sit here, on this very same bench... for hours on end.' John soon became lost in his own bittersweet reminiscence. 'Grandpa would give me his secret sweeties and tell me silly jokes here. I haven't got either any on me.'

'Grandpa can't do anything now, can he?' asked Lucy, sensing her father's sadness in his poignant expression. 'It makes me sad.'

'Yeah. Me, too.' John held onto Lucy's hands, finding a much-needed warmth from them. 'He wasn't always poorly, though. He was a very funny and kind man. He would have loved sitting here with me and you.' John breathed in a deep and salty breath. The view, which he and his Grandpa both admired so dearly, had scarcely changed. 'I miss sitting here with him. I miss our little chats.'

'Eliza said that Grandpa won't hurt for much longer,' Lucy said this so frankly that it was almost believable to John. 'She said that angels, like her, will look after him. They're helping Granny, too.'

'That's a nice thought, Lucy.' John pretended to sniffle his nose as if suffering from a cold, hiding his grief from Lucy, albeit in a futile way. 'I Love you, sweetheart, even when you come out with some funny things.' He nudged gently into her side. 'I love you to the moon and back.'

'You're so funny, Daddy.' Lucy hugged herself into John's lap, giving Hannah enough time to catch up with them. 'Hi, Mammy!'

'I'm ready to go, John.' Hannah wrapped her arms tightly around herself, shivering from each passing breeze. 'Let's go home. It's freezing out here, and I'm starting to feel sick again.'

'We've still got some time left on the parking meter,' said John, woefully and with a pleading expression. 'Can we not sit here for a little while longer?' Hannah looked out towards the cold North Sea; it was starting to lose its shimmering blue light, replaced with a darkened and dingy grey colour that seemingly forewarned of an incoming storm.

'I think it's going to rain, John.' Hannah rubbed a fingertip along his right facial cheek. 'Thanks for the day out. It's been... eventful.'

'Let's go then, Lucy.' John tapped at his daughter's closet knee. 'You're staying at Grandma's tonight. Won't that be fun?'

'Yay!' squealed the child. 'We'll make cookies, and dance, and sing together, and—'

'Not all at once, I hope,' humoured John, almost losing his grip upon the Ouija board and figurine. 'To be honest, Han, I think... you're right'' Hannah stared back in surprise. 'Ha-ha. I mean, it's going to get dark soon, so we'd better go now – like you said.'

'Tantum... Tenebris.'

224

'Can you not leave us alone - not even for one day?' responded John in his thoughts, answering the demon's taunt. 'I'm ready to talk. You better be ready for me.'

'Ego... DOMINUS!'

CHAPTER TEN

Toyah eagerly awaited her granddaughter and son 's arrival, slurping away at several cups of tea throughout the duration to pass time. John had promised his mother that he'd be at her house for six o'clock; however, it was now closer to seven. John being so late was a greater pity than he would come to realise. His sister, Katherine, and nephew, Andrew, had held on for as long as possible to see there their elusive relative. Their wait had become tedious, therefore they moved to leave. It was so rude and typical of John to let them down in such a way.

'He's taking the mick, Mam,' scowled Katherine to Toyah, as she buttoned up Andrew's winter coat. 'Tell John, when he arrives, that he's a selfish knob.'

'John's probably stuck in traffic, Kath,' implored Toyah, anxious herself at her son's lacking presence. 'I hope that his car hasn't broke down...' She peered through her kitchen blinds, outside. 'He's never this late.'

'There's nothing wrong with his car,' interjected Sean, from the living room. 'He gets his punctuality from you.'

'I'm not in the mood for jokes,' muttered Toyah in response. 'John has a lot on his mind... with the move an all. He won't be much longer - you'll see.' She couldn't even persuade herself. 'My John is a good boy.'

'He moved ages ago, Mam,' simpered Katherine, whilst stroking away her son's wavy blonde hair to comfort him. 'Poor Andrew wanted to see his uncle. John has a lot to answer for.'

'*Katherine...*'

'We're going, Mam.' Katherine knelt herself to correctly place Andrew's shoes upon his feet, all the while trying not to let her anger fester and display itself fully. 'I love him - we both do - but

John needs to be there for us more. He says that he'd do anything for us, yet he can't even turn up on time. See you later, love you.'

'Kath!' Toyah motioned her eyes across Andrew's sorrowful face. 'John *does* care about you and Andrew. Don't ever think he doesn't.' She paused momentarily, unsure as to whether mentioning John's depression could ease his sister's present scorn. 'I'm going to tell you something that Hannah told me, and you mustn't mention a word of it to John,' she said, strongly emphasising this point with her mother's glare. 'Promise me.'

'I promise. What is it?' asked Katherine, who at this point had already made her move to leave. 'Is he in trouble?'

'No. It's—' Toyah exhaled a sharpened breath, reflecting on Hannah's confession in both doubt and apprehension. 'His house is haunted, apparently. Hannah thinks that's why John is behaving so differently, and why he's become so angry all the time.'

'She's talking a load of crap, Mam.' Katherine swiped the kitchen door open, then froze her steps. Outside - in the cold rain and blistering wind - stood John with Lucy in his arms. 'John?'

'Aye. Sorry we're late.' John smiled on seeing his young nephew, though the gesture was sadly not mirrored by Andrew. 'Hello, my mate. Have you been a good boy for Mammy?'

"He's tired - I'm tired. We're going home, Bro,' snapped Katherine, with a deadly precision. 'You're late... as usual. What excuse is it this time?' she asked, shrugging her shoulders.

'Hannah felt sick on the way back. I had to pull over,' explained John in a defensive manner. The muscles contracting in his face, displaying his instant anger against Katherine, only made matters worse. 'She had some car sickness. Please don't start with me, Kath.'

'I'm starting nothing! When you give a time – stick to it. We're leaving. Come on, Andrew.' Katherine brushed past John, not even granting a farewell glance to him. 'Text me when you're free.'

'Bloody Hell, Mam. What's her problem?' John looked to Toyah with the most-innocent expression he could muster. 'It's not *my* fault Hannah felt sick.'

'Don't worry about it, Son.' Toyah leant out her arms, willing for John to place Lucy into them. 'How long has the bairn been asleep?' Katherine then left with Andrew, without uttering another word. John immediately succumbed to his guilt, promising himself that he would make it up to his sister and nephew, somehow.

'She's only just nodded off. Thanks again for watching her.' John smiled to his mother affectionately. 'It's been ages since me and Hannah had a night to ourselves. We need it.'

'Well, you enjoy it and don't worry about Lucy. I've been looking forward to our little sleepover.' As Toyah nestled Lucy's into against her bosom she was immediately reminded of when John was the same age: so innocent, so perfect and unspoiled by life's corrupting influences. 'Shhh, sweetheart. There's a good girl. Grandma's here.'

'You don't mind taking Lucy to school in the morning, do you, Mam?' John swayed to-and-froe, from side-to-side, now feeling the drenching rain seep down the back of his neck. 'We really appreciate you looking after her.'

'That's not a problem, Son.' Toyah smiled down at her granddaughter, and then back towards her troubled son. 'Go on, before you get a cold. Send my love to Hannah.'

'Thanks, Mam. You're a saint!' shouted John on making a hasty retreat to his car, which he had thankfully parked nearby. The rain beat off John's windscreen like a rampant percussionist, the rattling noise of striking water droplets overshadowing the rock music still playing inside. 'I've managed to annoy Katherine – again,' he said to an impatient-looking Hannah.

'You did say to her that you'd be at your mam's house over an hour ago. I'm not surprised she's angry,' replied Hannah, herself still inflicted with the increasing need to vomit at any given second. 'You shouldn't let people down like that... especially family.'

'Don't *you* start. I've already been put on a guilt trip from Katherine and Mam.' John revved at his engine; a compulsive habit he had now made normal. 'Fancy some pizza tonight?'

'No, thanks. I don't think my stomach could handle it.' Hannah clasped onto her mouth with both hands. The thought of greasy cheese and over-cooked pepperoni began to hinder her ability to keep this nausea at bay. 'Can we just go home and chill with a movie?'

'Sure, you're the boss.' John drove as slowly as possible along the short journey back to Skipton Road, more so when the street's fog reached him. 'This fog is relentless!'

'Keep driving,' commanded Hannah, her mouth just about to burst with an array of oily vomit. 'Seriously, John, Get us home – quick! I'm going to be sick!'

After parking his car, John shot out to assist Hannah. He felt deeply ashamed at not realising just how ill his wife's pregnancy was making her. In his politest and most gentile manner, he opened Hannah's door with a held-out hand, willing to assist her, desperate to prove his worth.

'Oh, who's a gentleman all of a sudden?' giggled Hannah, her face reddening with embarrassment on John's behalf. 'How very kind. I'm not used to this.' She accepted John's kind gesture, though at the same time wanted to plant a firm fist against the extremities which had wrought her present state of incapacity. 'This is so unexpected. I could get used to you being my slave,' she said in a mocking accent, similar to those heard on 'Downton Abbey'. 'Lead the way, servant-boy.'

'Cheeky bitch,' humoured John, now feeling embarrassed himself. 'You moan when I don't help, then you rip the shit out of me when I do!'

'Take me to my quarters, Butler,' cackled Hannah, in-between the odd gurgling noise that steadily rose from her stomach. 'Or else I shall find some skivvy work for you!'

'The damned cheek!' bleated John. He then slammed Hannah's door shut, proceeding to point at their humble abode. 'Howay-in, before you *catch a cold, Ma'am.*'

'John-Boy!' Sid was leaning out precariously from his bedroom window, and it was difficult to tell if he was drunk or sober. 'Did ya bring some ice cream back for me?'

'No, mate. You're asking a bit much of me there.' John sank his eyes deep into their sockets, wrenching at having to be civil with his nuisance neighbour. 'Having a quiet night in tonight, are you?' he shouted, unwittingly deafening Hannah stood beside him. 'Sorry, Han.'

'Night in for me too, John-Boy!' smirked Sid. He appeared to be half-sober, given his semi-ability to fuse a sentence together. 'I've got my vodka, got my fags, and got my right hand - all's well!'

'There's an image I didn't want,' mumbled Hannah, retching. 'Stop talking to him, John. The thought of him jacking off is making me even more sick.'

'Goodnight, Sid. Behave yourself!' John paced forwards, clenching onto Hannah with every ounce of his will to drag her steps in line with his. 'Come on, babe, before you're sick again.'

'I hear you've had some good news?' Sid flared his eyes inquisitively, though no sparkle resonated within them. 'You gonna tell me the big news or what?' John looked to Hannah as she did the same to him. What on earth was Sid talking about? 'A little bird tells me that you're having a baby?'

'How the fu—' John's mouth instantly fell with shock. 'Who told you?'

'A little birdie did.' Sid started to laugh, and then coughed from the pungent rollie-cigarette fumes which now plumed before his face. 'It's a big... secret.'

'I tell you what—' John snapped Hannah's grasp away and made towards Sid's garden fence, burning inside with a renewed sense of fury, fear and hatred. 'Come down for a sec, Sid. We need to talk.'

'No, John!' Hannah reached out for him, but this desire soon passed. She fumbled through her purse, finding her own set of keys, and then left him to confront their neighbour over - what she believed was - nothing more than a coincidental comment. 'I'm going inside.'

'Alright, Johnny?' cackled Sid, as he towered himself over John's smaller stature. 'So, *now* you want to talk.'

'Aye, I do.' John's response was forcibly calm, his voice soothing if only to deter any possible fight. 'Which *little birdie* told you? I only found out myself today.'

'You know who, John-boy.' Sid drew in a thick wave of tobacco smoke, only to then casually blow it back against John's flinching face. '*She* told me.'

'Sabina?' John couldn't believe that he was even acknowledging the witch as if she was an actual, real person. 'You're twisting my melons, Sid. Don't take the piss. Who told you?'

'I'm a fuckin' medium, and I know what I'm talkin' about!' Sid went to blow another wave of smoke in John's face, but John managed to counteract this by removing the cigarette clean from his mouth, placing it thereafter within his own. 'Ya cheeky twat. That's *my* baccy!'

'I need this more than you do.' John inhaled a welcomed wave of carcinogenic fumes; their calming effect was immediate, though it left him feeling even more guilty. 'Sabina – the evil, fucking witch that's plaguing my family - told you that Hannah is pregnant?'

'I'd appreciate it if you wouldn't talk about Sabina like that, John.' For the first time, Sid sounded serious to John when speaking to him. 'Show her the respect she deserves.'

'You're barmy, you are.' John took in another draw. The tobacco was obviously counterfeit as it left a raw, burning sensation across his entire air passageway. 'You need help.'

'I don't need help, John - you do!' Sid wrapped his skeletal fingers around John's throat, almost choking him. Again, John was reminded of Tolkien's masterpiece, where Frodo strangled Gollum in the same manner – desperate and full of malice. 'I've offered you help but - being the selfish cunt you are, *you* won't take it.'

'Get out of my face – NOW!' John easily overpowered Sid's alcohol-riddled muscles, tearing his hands away from him without any exertion. If you know what's go for you, you'll leave me and my family alone.' Sid merely shook his head from side-to-side despairingly in response. No reflex to strike back at John even entered his thoughts. 'You hear?'

'Suit yourself, John-boy. Don't say I didn't try to help ya.' Sid stumbled to stand upright, all the while slowly moving away from his surprisingly aggressive neighbour. 'Sabina will haunt your family forever, and I hope - I really, fuckin' do - that you'll be her next trophy.' Sid's breathing crackled on each step taken as he gradually slithered his way back into the pit from whence he came. 'Nighty-Night, John. Don't let the demons bite...'

'I'm not scared of them.' John slammed Sid's gate shut, yearning for it to fall away from its rusty hinges, although this sadly wasn't the case. All those hours wasted in the gym seemed to be personified in this sporadic moment. 'You make me sick! It's you that should be getting haunted – not us!' roared John, not caring in any way what his other, more civilised, neighbours would think of this random outburst. 'Pisshead! Waster! Leave my family alone – or else!' With that, John retrieved the Ouija board and ghastly figurine of Baphomet from his car, then made for his back home.

'Goodnight, John. *She's* waiting for you... in the marshes.' Sid calmly waved from the safety of his bedroom window now towards John's deranged figure outside. He hadn't expected such a violent reaction, though knew in satisfaction that this could only mean Sabina's vengeance was reaching its ultimate climax. 'They're *both* waiting for you...' He worded this clearly enough for John to decipher. 'You're gonna pay for your sins!'

'What were you and Sid shouting about outside?" asked Hannah, as she cowered behind her Kindle's screen. Moments prior to this, John had burst through the kitchen door, almost breaking its window against the nearby worktop, and nearly dropped the Ouija board and figurine from his shaking hands. He looked even more dishevelled now than usual. 'I was getting scared, you know. I thought that Sid was going to hurt you.'

'Really?' tutted John, laughing in dismissal. He sat himself down beside Hannah, before throwing their Ouija board beside them. He had left the demonic figurine of Baphomet in his kitchen, having spent enough time in its foul presence. 'If he'd fart, he'd blow himself over. There's nothing on him, Han. He couldn't hurt a fly, could Sid.' John stretched out his chest, battering it like King Kong to display his sense of masculinity. 'I'd soon sort him out – no problem.'

'What's gotten into you? You've never been one for fighting.' Hannah's voice trembled in unison with the rest of her body as she spoke. 'Aren't those tablets you're on meant to calm you down?'

'I'll be honest, Han... I forgot to take them last night,' said John, shuddering from guilt and disdain. 'I won't forget tonight, though. Anyway, we're meant to be having a chillout session, just me and you. That should help me to relax.' John dared to look upon Hannah's face and then into her glistening eyes, hoping to rid the tension rising between them. 'What do you fancy doing? Should we have a look down the Tin Donkey?'

'I'm not going to the pub, John. It's hardly romantic.' Hannah lifted her Kindle again to bar John's incessant gaze. 'I just want to watch some TV with you, if that's okay?'

'Sure. I'm pretty worn out from the sea air – I could do with a night-in,' replied John, submissively. 'It's "Ghost Night" on the reality TV channel. Why don't we watch some *Ghost Adventures* and *Most Haunted* to help pass the time?'

'I'd like that.' Hannah briefly lowered her Kindle. The sight of John's solemn expression was still something she hadn't got used to - and didn't want to. Over all the years she had known her husband, Hannah had barely seen him frown, let alone lower himself to the same standard as Sid. Moving to Skipton Road had certainly left its negative impact on them all. 'You never know, one day they might make a program about this house? Wouldn't that be something?'

'I doubt it. Who'd care about a manky old house like ours?' John nestled himself into Hannah's thigh with his face, seeking her warmth and loving touch. As the TV set came on, *Most Haunted* screened first. 'Hannah...'

'What?'

'*Mary loves Dick*!' John laughed at his remark like a demented swine; whereas, Hannah could only manage a faint chuckle in response. 'These sorts of shows are so staged.'

'I don't think they are. You would say that, being a sceptic,' countered Hannah. 'You can't tell me that you're still sceptical now, not after all the weird things that have happened to us recently. It *must* be real.'

'There's a big difference, Han,' assured John. 'Here we go: one hour of watching some lass screech whenever there's a little noise nearby. I'd rather watch a program about antiques.'

'If you don't want to watch it, then put something else on – it was *your* suggestion, anyway.' Hannah responded in dreary tone, her interest in this so-called "Date Night" now dwindling fast. 'Watch your stupid news channels instead. I'm really not that fussed,' she implored, with a mocking smirk. 'If you're going to whinge all the way through... there's not much point, is there?'

'It's too much fun watching them all scream over stupid things,' sniggered John. 'We'll stick to the spooky programs, I think.'

'That suits me.' Hannah returned to her vampire stories for the remainder of *Most Haunted*. Her attention only moved back to the TV set when *Ghost Adventures* came on, as she had a soft spot for the Lead Investigator, Zak Bagans. 'This is more like it.'

'Too right. At least these lads don't scream like a bunch of little school-girls when something makes a noise.' John tapped at his remote's volume setting, raising it. 'These are real ghost hunters. I actually respect what they do.'

'Whatever.' Yawning, Hannah ran her sight between her Kindle and TV set. The vampire she was reading about seemed so alike to the Lead Investigator from *Ghost Adventures*: dark haired, muscular and utterly fearless... unlike John. 'Tell me when something exciting happens.' The familiar sound of snoring began to rise from her husband's throat, adding to Hannah's disappointment. John had fallen asleep, exhausted from his confrontation with Sid and the sedation now sweeping through his system. 'Wow,' groaned Hannah, sarcastically. 'What an exciting Date Night we're having. I may as well have gone to bed.'

John had slipped into total unconsciousness. Within his dream, he awoke to find himself sat, cross-legged, inside a small, wooden shack, which looked to be medieval in origin. The distinct smell of sage and wildflowers trickled through his nostrils, their strong scents invoking and somehow calming him. A small fire also flickered away in the corner of John's eye and hung above it was a crude-looking cauldron, which released even more enticing aromas into the surrounding atmosphere.

'What is this place?' John motioned to stand but couldn't. An invisible presence was holding him down. 'Shit!' It felt as if John's wrists were also bound together by some unseen force. He writhed against these unseen restraints with all his might, though the more he struggled, the tighter this cruel grasp became. 'Sabina!' he roared. 'Let me go!'

'Mama?' The sound of a young girl entered John's mind. He turned to face its whereabouts, though again couldn't move. 'Why are you shunning my help?' asked girl, sorrowfully, her voice eerily sounding so much like Lucy's. 'I can channel my powers through your daughter, and I have no will to cause any harm.'

'You don't talk funny like Sabina, but I still can't trust you.' John shook his head violently, wishing to rid the witch's influence over him. 'I've had enough of witches and demons...'

'I am *not* Sabina, and I am most-certainly not a demon,' implored the girl. 'My mother is lost in both time and virtue. However, you must not pity her – that is how she creates a bond.' John felt a soothing sensation instantly course over his body now, then the peculiar feeling of tiny fingers trickling along his right forearm. 'My mother's fate is sealed. She cannot be saved... unlike you.'

'You're not Eliza. This is just some new trick you're trying to pull one me, Sabina – isn't it?!' John scorned, his calm manner now falling into pure hatred. 'Leave my family alone! I don't know what it is you want—'

'I am Eliza, John, and my time spent with you is precious... and short,' she implored. 'Baal is coming. He is my mother's master and a far greater threat to you than she could ever be.' Eliza seemed truly frightened, though somehow rational despite this, particularly as she spoke the demon's name. 'Baal's strength is growing beyond a point where I can intervene, and you're not helping with these aggressive thoughts and actions of yours. Remember - above all else - that you are blessed with love. Focus on the light, John: your wife and Lucy.'

'Eliza?' John slowly accepted the truth, despite his pressing doubts. 'How can a daughter of Sabina be good?'

'I am *not* her. My heart is pure - not clouded by vengeance nor malice,' replied the child, in a reflective tone. 'My mother was not always wicked. Where light exists so too does darkness. Where darkness exists, so too does light. Blood can protect, but blood can also cause harm. My mother often spoke those words to me, though her path only led to evil. No light shines upon her now,' continued Eliza, tearfully. 'I was too late to stop her.'

'Sabina... was once a good witch?' John couldn't believe that he was even asking this question. How could the woman who had tormented him for so many weeks now have any salvageable qualities? He also questioned again to himself as to why Eliza did not speak in the same Olde English as her mother did. However, there would be little point, he felt, in divulging this curiosity. 'I saw what she did to that monk, how she made a pact with the devil. I'm sorry, Eliza, but your mother is nothing but pure evil... and I hate her for what she's done to my family. I can't get her out of my head!'

'Blood bound to cloth invokes me. Blood bound to cloth can protect - yes. Blood bound to cloth can keep your enemies at bay. Once connected, never can a bond be broken.'

'Sabina? Eliza – help me!' John's heart rate paced faster. The witch's growling voice had somehow rendered Eliza's gracious presence, their own rancid words now taking a vicious hold over John's rational thoughts. 'No! Eliza – come back! Oh, God!'

'There is no God, Yahweh, Jehovah - only Lucifer and Baal!'

John clenched his eyelids shut. He reasoned that this was a dream – a truly horrific nightmare, but it still felt so real. The pleasant aromas quickly faded, only to be replaced by the stench of rotten decay and distilled swamp water. John was now back in Newton Escomb's medieval marshes, Sabina's final resting place.

'Whatever it is you want to show me – do it!' commanded John. 'Do your worst to me, Sabina. I'm already at my lowest point – I can't sink any lower.'

'Have you? I think not. You have not fallen enough to endure my suffering, John Davidson. For your sins, you shall suffer!'

John's eye suddenly started to burn, as if dowsed with boiling acid. Against all his might, he managed to open them. A yellowish fog glimmered faintly from the setting sun which then gradually dispersed, leaving a haunting scene and one which John would never forget.

There - knelt in the darkening marshes and bound by rope - was Sabina. Her white dress was torn and defiled by the murky marsh water, her red ribbon still gleaming in the dim sunlight around her waist. Towering over Sabina were several large, monk-like figures, all chanting in Latin. Across the near-distance, John could make out some local villagers who had come to watch this harrowing scene take place; some of which notably wore similar ribbons to what Sabina herself adorned.

'Accursed wench! Thy Witch of Satan!' bellowed one of the monks in authority over Sabina's helpless body. 'Thou hast committed murder! Thou art a sinner! Thy punishment shalt be righteous in God's gracious eyes and pure spirit!'

Some of the onlookers cheered, driven by bloodlust. However, a handful of female witnesses scarcely set their eyes on Sabina, somehow revealing to John a hidden feeling of guilt over her circumstances.

'My soul is innocent! Where for art thou Heavenly Father to protect me?' Sabina lowered her head permissively, resting it upon her exposed chest. She had spoken at first in a grovelling voice, though this rapidly developed into her darker, malicious tone. 'Thou art murderers! Thou art sinners – rapists – thieves... DEMONS! Yahweh hast curst thee all!'

'Heed not this witch's words, for they art venom!' implored another monk towards the baiting crowd, with fear clearly present within their eyes. 'Pater noster, habitator caeli!'

'What in the hell is going on here?' John gulped apprehensively. For reasons still unbeknown to himself, he felt a strange pity towards Sabina. It was proving difficult for him to watch her struggle under this wicked tribunal, to see the look of horror in her fair expression. 'What are they doing to her?'

Just then, a terrifying burst of thunder scattered across the heavens above Sabina, unleashing a demonic voice from within their harrowing chorus:

'Thy will be done! I shalt not forsake thee, Sabina!'

'Ego Sabina!' howled the witch, contorting her body like an enraged animal. She wrenched at her mud-soaked dress and looked to her red ribbon solemnly, seeing that it now somehow tightened around her waist, burning it. 'Ego sum Rubrum Uitta Pythonissam! I curse thee all!' she roared, then lowered her head again as if in defeat. 'Thy Heavenly Father hast forsaken me – he hast forsaken all who bear witness this treachery. My master, Baal, hast not forsaken me. My vengeance shalt be cast upon all mankind,' she said, whimpering, whilst looking to those in the crowd who adorned red ribbons like herself. 'Thou art Daughters of Judas – traitors! A sister to thee I became, but dost that mean nought? I shalt enact revenge upon my daughter's death – upon all and thy bloodlines!'

'In Terris sicut est in Caelis!' chanted the monks in unison, their unified chorus resounding with an element of malice and lacking sanctity. 'Sanctus Spiritus!'

'It's the Lord's prayer, I think.' John wiped at his face wearily. He then considered whether this was nothing more than an act of trickery on Sabina's behalf, or if it was in fact a true representation of what had taken place. 'What a bunch of animals. No one – not even Sabina – deserves this kind of treatmeant!'

'Amen.'

'I curse thee all! Hallowed be thy vengeance!' Sabina screeched at the top of her lungs, aiming her ferocity solely against those stood watching over this barbaric torture. Every vein in her body pulsated like a throbbing, albeit diseased, heart. 'All men shalt suffer and BURN!'

'Enough with this witch's ramblings! Sabina de Lockewood...' The monk speaking faltered over his next few words, fearing that one day they may too come back to haunt him, whether it be in this life or the next. 'Thy corrupted soul shalt be cleansed, Witch! Sanctus Spiritus! Nisi nos... Amen.'

'Leave her alone!' cried out John, though his words fell silent in the tumultuous breeze and thunderstrokes. 'Leave her alone, you evil monsters!'

Within the fearful crowd, Sabina's devout followers now cast their physical bond with the witch towards her – their ribbons – allowing them to fall onto the filthy earth beneath their feet. The sound of rippling thunder cascaded louder across the blood-red sky, followed by a deluge of rain that beat off the ground like a firing machine gun.

'Thou hast defiled my child! Thou shalt pay in agony!' Sabina spat at each of the monks, ensuring her aim was true on all attempts made. 'I summon thee, Lord of Despair and Vengeance! Come to my aid! I summon thee... Baal.'

At that moment the soggy marshland rumbled as if struck by an earthquake, and the heavens above burst into an array of terrifying lightning strikes. John eagerly watched as the crowd dispersed into a frenzied riot; their howls and screams scorching away painfully at his tender ear lobes. Then, from within the midst, rose a dark mass – a shadow – a monstrous demon. The monks began to panic amongst themselves and then, without any warning, one lunged forward to plunge Sabina into her shallow grave, where the rain waters now rose. Sabina spluttered and floundered in the muddy water, desperate for air. Her last breaths echoed across John's conscience, riddling him with guilt and agony, as he shared in the witch's last moments of torment.

'Sabina!' screamed John. He felt an irrational urge to save her, yet also yearned to enjoy the witch's final moments – just as she willed the same on him. 'Drown... you, fucking bitch! I *want* to see this! I *want* to see you hurt! You've torn my family apart!'

'You don't mean that.' Lucy's voice spoke again to John, relinquishing his anger in an instant. 'You wouldn't hurt anyone, John. You're not a bad man. There is another way...'

'You will burn as all men shall, John Davidson!'

John awoke, gasping with panic, his body soaked in cold sweat and the taste of pungent swamp water still clinging to his throat – but how? He rose his head to see if Hannah had fallen asleep – she hadn't. John then released a lengthy sigh of relief which took Hannah by surprise, as she had become totally engrossed in her vampire novel.

'Jesus! You made me jump, John!' scolded Hannah, as she peered over her Kindle towards John. 'Have you had another nightmare?'

'Sort of... yeah,' replied John, with a confused expression. 'What time is it?'

'It's two-thirty in the morning. Shit!' Hannah raised her eyebrows in disbelief; she genuinely hadn't realised what time it

241

was, prior to John asking. 'We'd better get to bed. It's a good job that your mam is taking Lucy to school tomorrow.'

'Do you fancy a quick go on the Ouija board?' John stared at Hannah in eagerly waiting for her response. 'Howay, just a little try.'

'I'm tired, hun. I just want to get some sleep.' Hannah forced out a yawn and was thankful that this had the same desired effect on John. 'Come to bed with me. Don't sleep on the sofa again.'

'We can always have a go tomorrow, maybe?' John yawned again himself, but the thought of sleeping was now something which he fought hard against. 'I'm meeting up with Mr. Clarence in the morning for coffee – remember?'

'Won't it be weird, you know, spending time with your old history teacher?' asked Hannah, finding the notion to be utterly ridiculous. 'I couldn't do it. I hated my history teacher – he was such a boring, old git.'

'Nah, he's a sound bloke, is Mr. Clarence.' John switched off the TV and then slumped back into the sofa like a wet sandbag. 'I hope he can shed some light on Sabina. Otherwise, I might need to book myself into a mental unit.'

'Just be careful. I don't think it's a good idea to be looking into this "Sabina" - who knows what you might conjure up?' Hannah herself stood up, straightened her pyjamas, and then made for the hallway. John eventually followed suit. 'Don't come across as being 'mental' to him. I don't want for us to be the talk of the town.'

'I am not mental, Han. I just want answers,' said John, in a frustrated tone. 'He'll prove what we know already - that Skipton Road is haunted.'

'Whatever. I'm going to sleep.' Hannah left John to his own devices.

'What's that noise?' John leant an ear into kitchen, certain that some disembodied, demonic voices were coming from the grotesque figurine. 'No, it can't be... Baal?' Without hesitation, John collected the figurine and proceeded to store it within a walk-in cupboard on the upper passageway, where it would remain for some time afterwards, out of sight and mind.

John and Hannah bundled themselves into bed, soon latching onto one another for both a sense of warmth and comfort.

'Goodnight, John.'

'Goodnight... love you.' John pecked at Hannah's cheek - then recoiled. A slithering shadow crept along the adjoining wall, catching his attention and increasing his heart rate. 'What's that?' He sprung out of bed again, now in direct aim of his bedroom's light switch. 'Is that... writing? Is there something written on the wall?'

'For goodness sake, John. Please, get back into bed.' Hannah slowly moved her gaze to where John now aimed a pointed finger. Etched along the wall were three, distinctive scratch marks, despite it being recently coated in a new layer of paint. 'You're taking the piss, aren't you? Did you do that? Is this... some sick joke?'

'I didn't do it, Han - I swear!' countered John, his sight still firmly fixated against the demonic slashes. 'Why would I scratch a wall that I've only just painted – seriously? It doesn't make any sense.'

'To prove a point, maybe? To make me believe in the rubbish you and Lucy keeping talking about? You're a stubborn git at times.' Hannah looked to him with a fierce essence of scorn, her patience now fully gone. 'Get into bed! You can sort it out tomorrow.'

'There are three scratches. John threw himself against the bedroom door, lost in an increasing maelstrom of anxiety and dread. 'Isn't that the sign of a demonic entity, you know, like what they say in *Ghost Adventures*? It's a mockery of the Holy Trinity.'

'It's a sign that you should come to bed and stop being so paranoid, John.' Hannah wrapped the bedsheets around herself,

243

pretending that they held some invisible power against the evil which now obviously lurked within their bedroom. 'Come to bed, babe. I'm cold.'

'Okay.' John lay cautiously lay himself upon the bed beside Hannah, praying in silence that whatever loitered in their bedroom's shadowy corners would go away. 'Leave us alone, Sabina,' he whispered, pleadingly. 'You're not welcome here—'

'John!' snapped Hannah. 'Don't say her name. You'll just provoke whatever's here.'

'I never thought of that,' said John, as he nudged his body into Hannah's. 'Here... where's the cat? I haven't seen Sox all night.'

'She's been sleeping in Lucy's room. There's something wrong with her, John.' Hannah moved aside a strand of hair that had fallen precisely into her mouth, unwittingly flicking it across John's face. 'Seamus is taking her back tomorrow. I've already spoken to Katelyn about it.'

'I thought Sox drove your sister crazy?' chuntered John. 'I'll miss her, in a weird way. It's been nice having a pet around the house again. Plus, witches don't like black cats.'

'She keeps poopin' all over the house, John,' sniggered Hannah in response. 'And it's starting to freak me out how she'll whine at things that aren't there... like we've got enough to deal with.'

'Animals are more sensitive to things than we are.' John slid Hannah's hair away from his face, placing it gently alongside her narrow shoulder blades. 'I bet that Sox can see Sabina as well.'

'John. What did I say?' Even without looking at Hannah, John could tell that she was glaring at him. 'Don't say that name anymore – got it?'

'Aye. G'night, babe.' John rolled over to form his body into a foetal position. Hannah missed her husband's warm touch, though his sweaty odour made this parting somewhat easier to deal with.

***

The morning after, John woke up feeling greatly refreshed and not scared at all, nor tormented by any further nightmarish visions. Hannah had already taken herself downstairs; this was made evident by the 'Disturbed' music being played, and at an incredibly loud volume.

'Hannah?' shouted John from the stairwell. 'Can you make me a cup of coffee, please? I Won't be long.' His bladder was about to burst, though the thought of Sabina possibly speaking to him through the bathroom mirror again played against this natural urge. John ran downstairs, almost losing his footing. After relieving himself in the downstairs toilet, he walked into the kitchen where Hannah now stood waiting for him, and with a look of suspicion on her face.

'Did you use the Ouija board last night, at any point?' she asked, shaking her head from side-to-side. 'The friggin' thing has moved.'

'No!' gasped John, genuinely in shock. 'I went to bed at the same time you did. I've been nowhere near it.' He peered around the corner, looking to where he had last left the spiritual device. It had indeed moved, but only slightly. 'I might have knocked it by accident when I was going to bed?'

'Right. Then why was that bible of yours placed on top of it?' asked Hannah, fearfully. 'I can't remember you moving *that*.'

'No. I haven't touched the bible, either. Was it open?' John peered around the corner again, finding that Hannah had replaced the bible in its previous position upon their bookshelf. 'No way?'

'yep, and it was open on the bit about Jesus being crucified.' Hannah's anger and suspicion instantly rose 'If you're trying to scare me, you can sod off. It's *not* funny.'

'I swear I haven't touched it!' pleaded John. 'I haven't touched the bible *or* Ouija board. It's Sabina,' he whispered under his breath. Hannah merely rolled her eyes back in response. 'Seriously, Han. I wouldn't do something like that to you –

especially with you being pregnant.' He leant into kiss her but was swiftly jilted. 'Do you really think I'd play games like that with you?'

'You need to get dressed. We both do.' Hannah pointed towards the kitchen's clock. 'You're meeting up with Mr. Clarence in an hour or so, and Seamus is coming to collect Sox.'

'Alright. I'll go and get ready.' John reached across for the mug of scorching black coffee which Hannah had made for him, consuming it in one sitting, regardless of the fact this burned away at his gullet. 'That's better. I needed a good caffeine kick,' he said, licking at his lips, trying not to show the burning discomfort across them. 'Thanks, hun. I wonder what Mr. Clarence is going to say?'

'Let me know if anything is said – not that I really want to know.' Hannah slurped at her own mug of sugary coffee, though hers was far cooler than John's and less painful to consume. 'Only tell me the interesting parts.'

'I will,' assured John, whilst downing the last few drops of his bitter espresso. He needed a shave but didn't particularly care about this, not even in slightest. All that mattered now was finding out the truth regarding Sabina's true history, about Newton Escomb's shameful past. 'I'll take a pen and some paper. I don't want to miss a thing.'

'With your short-term memory, that's probably a good idea,' Hannah humoured. 'Don't forget that Lucy is coming home at about five o'clock tonight. Try to be back by then.'

'No worries. I won't make any sly trips to the pub...' John turned around to face the kitchen's clock, then slapped a palm firmly against his forehead. 'I've only got ten minutes. Give my regards to Seamus when you see him.'

'I will. Love you, and don't take ages.' Hannah planted a subtle kiss upon John's greasy face. He showered less now, a resulting mixture of both his worsening depression and Sabina's sordid influence. Hannah hated seeing her once-proud husband in this dilapidated state and knew that if things didn't change soon, some drastic measures would have to be taken – with or without meds. 'Don't be late... you normally are with things.' She planted one, final kiss on John's lips. He then left without further word, something which Hannah didn't seem to mind.

John stepped away from his gate, whilst peering through Skipton Road's thick fog that now lay ahead along the path into town. He hadn't walked far before a familiar voice shouted over to him from behind – it was his brother-in-law, Seamus.

'Alright, John? How's tricks?' asked Seamus, as he stepped in front of John to block his path. 'How are things going with the new house? It's been a while since we last had a catchup.' John sauntered across the muddy path towards Seamus, trying not show his anxious expression. 'You look like shit, mate,' commented Seamus, laughing awkwardly. He looked up and down John's body; it was thinner than the last time they had met, and the smell of stale whiskey burned at his senses. 'Have you lost weight?'

'Aye, just a bit around the waist and chin,' replied John, equally as awkward in his response. He opened his coat to show Seamus a bony rib cage, and several stretch marks that lay along the stomach line. 'Healthy living, Seamus-Lad. That's how I've managed to get this figure.'

'Bollocks,' grunted Seamus in dismissal. 'I can smell the whiskey on you. You've been drinking more of that an'all, haven't you, John-boy?' He looked to John with a discerning frown now. 'That's not healthy living, John; that's a one-way ticket to an early grave, mate.'

'The past few weeks have been pretty stressful.' John left it at that. He didn't think for one second that Seamus would understand his haunting ordeal, or Sabina's crippling influence over him.

'You've got Hannah and Lucy to think about, John.' Seamus planted a finger firmly against John's wasting chest muscles. 'You've got to be strong for them. Don't be so... soft. I'm saying this for your own good, pal.' Without warning, Seamus wrapped his arms around John - a gesture welcomed by him. 'You're a sound lad. Don't let life get on top of you.'

'I won't, mate.' John winced - though not because of Seamus' lecture, but because he could smell some fresh cigarette smoke on him. His past nicotine urges again reared their ugly heads. 'You need to take care of yourself. The whole family is starting to get worried about you.'

'I will, mate. Promise.' John's need for nicotine outmatched any other unwanted emotions now coursing through him. He pondered whether to ask Seamus for a cigarette or not, though knew that this act of betrayal would only torment him more in the long run. 'I've got to go into town, mate. Hannah's waiting for you with Sox, in the kitchen.'

'Catch up soon, yeah?' Seamus turned to light a cigarette, tormenting John's urges even more. 'Do you fancy one before you go? You haven't stopped yet, have you?'

'No thanks, mate. I've finally managed to quit,' whined John, inside grieving over this lost opportunity. 'I'm gonna be late. Catch you later, Seamus. We'll have a look in the Tin Donkey sometime soon.'

'Aye. Take care, John,' were Seamus' parting words to him. The dense wave of fog gradually managed to clear, once John walked over the bridge separating Skipton Road from Newton Escomb's town centre. He looked down into the thin stream below, imaging that Lucy's wish - whatever it was - had come true from her gifted penny.

'Maybe I should have made a wish like you, Lucy?' John despaired. His gaunt reflection in the flowing water quickly spurred him on to meet up with Mr. Clarence. 'Magic - what a crock of horse shit!"

'John.'

248

'Leave me alone, Sabina.'

'Your family and friends... hate you.'

'Shut up, Sabina! I don't want to hear it.'

'Your wife... no longer loves you.'

'FUCK OFF!'

'Your child... is no longer safe in your arms.'

John froze on the spot where he stood. The tremors from his anxiety inflicted his body now like never before, rendering it useless to take even another step forward – not without shedding a few, reluctant tears first.

'I shall wait for you in the marshes. I am Sabina. I am the Red Ribbon Witch. You are doomed to suffer – to die alone, John.'

In town, when John finally made it there, the coffee shop was already packed to its full capacity. He looked around the faces passing by, recognising some, but none seemed to acknowledge him. The sound of strangers talking and laughing somehow angered him, although this wouldn't usually cause any upset. Sabina's corruption and torment were reaching an unbearable finale, at least in John's eyes.

'My goodness! Is that you, John Davidson?' chuckled a frail-sounding voice from behind – Mr. Clarence. 'By gosh, you haven't changed much!'

249

'Hi, Jack. Neither have you.' John coughed awkwardly; it was so strange for him to refer to his old history teacher in such an informal manner. 'Sorry, I mean... Mr. Clarence.'

'Don't be silly. You can call me what you like,' assured Mr. Clarence. Unlike John he had certainly changed through age: his brown beard was now white, and he had lost a considerable amount of weight and muscle density. 'It's not everyday that I have an ex-pupil message me about history. I'm so very chuffed about this meeting!'

'I'm glad to hear that, Jack.' John reached out a tremoring hand to shake it with Mr. Clarence's. 'I appreciate your time. I can imagine you're very busy—'

'It's my pleasure, John. Shall we go inside for a coffee now?' Mr. Clarence snapped his hand away from John's to point it in the coffee shop's direction. 'It's bloody freezing out here. A coffee would do us some good, hey?' John obliged, though groaned as he looked at how long the queue inside was. 'There's a good lad. Go on, you lead the way.'

John then paid for his and Mr. Clarence's coffee, only after a tense stalemate between themselves as to who should 'cough up the dough'. As they sat themselves down at a nearby table, John and Mr. Clarence then gave a glancing look at the other customers bustling around them - one in particular stood out most, John's old neighbour – Janice.

'John - is that you?' Janice had the same-old, happy glint in her eyes, as she stared back in awe to her former neighbour. 'Why haven't you called me like you said you would?' John wiped at his face in a weary fashion, again riddled with guilt.

'Sorry, Jan.' John nodded apologetically to Mr. Clarence, then stood to greet his old friend. 'The past few weeks have been pretty mad. I haven't had a minute to spare – which I know isn't much of an excuse.'

'That's no excuse,' implied Janice, with a pitiful expression. 'I've missed you and Hannah – especially your Lucy. What happened to the house-warming party you promised me?'

'We knocked that on the head,' replied John, in a mumbling voice. 'There's been so much going on at work and that...'

'Don't be daft!' Janice wrapped an arm around John, whilst balancing a coffee in the other. 'I understand. Call me when you're free for a catch up and a fag – okay?'

'Aye. Will do.' John patted at Janice's shoulders sympathetically and then turned again towards Mr. Clarence. 'I'll message you, Jan. I'm just with Mr. Clarence here... he's a busy bloke.' Janice took the hint.

'Okay, hun. See you around.' Janice reached for her coat, sensing that her presence was no longer welcome. 'Take care and send my love to the girls.' She glanced down at Mr. Clarence. 'Sorry for bothering you.'

'She's a nice lady – very pleasant,' commented Mr. Clarence, in his "teacher" voice: straight to the point and monotonous in tone. 'Now then, what is it you want to know about Newton Escomb's history, my friend?' John nervously fumbled with his fingers, then after a few more slurps of coffee looked to Mr. Clarence like a lost child.

'I'd appreciate it if you could tell me about Newton Escomb's ancient history.' John had wanted to mention Sabina – to get her out of the way, but something seemed to stop him from doing so. 'You know, its bygone past... the stuff most people don't talk about.'

'History *is* the past, young lad,' sneered Mr. Clarence, as he glanced at John over his thin spectacles. 'Well, there was the ammunition factory which was used during the Second World War – that's the site our present town was built around. Haven't you heard of the *Escomb Angels*? They were very brave women who worked there and in very dangerous conditions, I must say.'

251

'I know about that. I meant its *ancient* history,' said John in correction, bashfully. 'Maybe I should have been more specific.'

'Ancient history?' Mr. Clarence frowned; his expression confused, yet strangely intrigued. 'There aren't many records for Newton Escomb before the late 1950's, other than the farms and marshlands that once occupied it. What *is* it that you want to know? You've gained my curiosity.'

'Erm...' John froze again in hesitation. He pretended to sip away at his coffee, whilst contemplating the next line of discussion. 'What was here before, like, in medieval times?'

'Oh, my! That *is* going far back!' exclaimed Mr. Clarence in astonishment. It was evident to John that he hadn't prepared to look so far afield. 'In a nutshell, Newton Escomb was once nothing more than boggy marshlands. It had the odd Saxon settlement, but that's about it. The industrial town it has become, which we are constituents of now, didn't come into fruition until about the late 1950's... as I've already stated.'

John wasn't satisfied. He needed to know more. 'Were there any main settlements, like with a church?' He closed his eyes and then rolled them back in embarrassment. Here he was, sat with his old history teacher, talking like an absolute moron. 'I'm interested to know if there are any stories as well, regarding them.'

'Well, I think there is one...' Mr. Clarence took his turn at sipping away in a feigning manner. He now looked at John with a frightful expression. 'There is this *one* story, but it's way too far-fetched to be real – that is, it's not on any written records, just merely handed down through word-of-mouth over the years. I don't believe it, I might add.'

'What is it?' John leant across the table in anticipation, almost knocking his coffee over, yearning for this information more than anything else. 'I'd love to know, even if it's a load of nonsense.'

'It's not a pleasant story,' added Mr. Clarence, grimacing. 'Apparently - and your talking many hundreds of years ago now -

there was a settlement here in Newton Escomb. The people that lived there were incredibly poor – impoverished beyond our modern measures and understanding. Most of the inhabitants suffered from starvation or from the lasting effects of civil war. Most, I might add, were women and children, with only a group of holy men being placed in charge of their welfare.' John's jaw dropped instantly. This was too much of a coincidence not to be real.

'Do you know anything else about this story?" questioned John, his eyes widening more now in anticipation. 'I'd really appreciate it if you could tell me everything you know about this.'

'Well, the tale goes that these *holy men* used to exploit the vulnerable women – and girls, I dread to say. Prostitution was an easy way to make wealth for these holy men, even if it meant adding onto the agony those poor women and children already suffered.' John gasped again, then quickly slurped at his coffee to distract Mr. Clarence away from this action. 'One day, a young woman had her daughter cruelly taken from her. As an act of revenge, she made a pact with other women in the village to put a stop to these holy men and their foul antics.' Mr. Clarence rose his coffee mug to drink from it, though John's eager expression made him continue and with a faster pace. 'Rumour has it, that this woman was a *powerful* witch, and one who had made a pact with an even stronger demon. She created a clandestine group, which members wore a red piece of cloth to symbolise their bond to this witch – with their own spilled blood, apparently.'

'Red ribbons?' asked John, after releasing a few nervous breaths. 'Was she called the *Red Ribbon Witch*?' Mr. Clarence shook his head in dismissal and found that he now wanted to leave this subject, given John's peculiar remark. 'Was she called... Sabina?'

'Nobody knows for sure, John.' Mr. Clarence gave out a sporadic burst of laughter, clearly bemused. 'This is nothing but folklore – old wives' tales. It's open to interpretation,' said Mr. Clarence, now in a frustrated tone. 'The witch and her followers would entice the holy men into their bedrooms on the promise of some heated action – one by one - then poison them with Belladonna or 'Deadly Nightshade' as other folk might call it,' he whispered, in a precarious voice. 'Unfortunately, the leader of this group was caught and then made to be an example of—'

'How?' interjected John, over his shaking coffee mug. 'What happened to her?'

'The holy men gathered all the women of this settlement together and made them watch a *truly* horrific scene... allegedly. What they did, John, was take this group's leader and made her bear witness as they raped and then strangled her daughter – in broad daylight. Afterwards, they then took this 'supposed' witch into the marshes where they drowned her in a shallow grave filled with water. It's an awful story, simply awful. They left her there to rot, or that's what I've come to establish about this tale. I can't imagine it to be true, however. It' sounds like a load of rubbish to me – unbelievable.'

'Really? So, they did do that to her. That's barbaric!' bleated John, in trying to act shocked at this revelation. 'That's pure evil!'

'Yes, John,' sighed Mr. Clarence, now showing some fatigue in divulging into this story any further. 'It is also said that the witch placed a curse on those wicked men, her followers' bloodlines, and – refutably, a stone church which once stood within the heart of this community that collapsed on that very same day. In my honest and humble opinion... it's a load of codswallop. I mean, witches and demons aren't real, are they?' he laughed, nervously. 'I wouldn't take much notice, John. It's such an unbelievable story.'

John sat silently for a minute or so, imagining Sabina and Eliza's last painful moments together. Despite his hatred towards the Red Ribbon Witch, he couldn't help but feel sorry for her and for her murdered child. Mr. Clarence briskly finished off his coffee, then looked down to his Rolex watch. What should have been a pleasant and enlightening discussion had soon turned sour.

'I must be going, John. Duty calls,' said Mr. Clarence, shunting his chair away from the table. 'I'm meeting with someone else in half-an-hour.' The way in which he said this was suspicious, though John was too lost in his dwelling thoughts to care. 'Take care of yourself, John. It's been lovely to see you again. All the best.' Mr. Clarence left then with an incredibly fast pace – especially given his age.

'Thanks, Jack,' responded John, vacantly, and without even looking to him. 'I really appreciate your help. You've helped to open my eyes.' John gradually made the journey back to Skipton Road, all the while playing over what Mr. Clarence had shared with him. Was it true that Sabina died in such a sadistic way, and had her daughter succumbed to such a horrific and agonizing demise? John unwillingly compared them to both Hannah and Lucy, and then - against all his might - he shed a single tear on behalf of the witch who had recently taken over his life.

'I understand now, Sabina,' simpered John, as he entered Skipton Road's haunting fog. 'I understand... why you hate men. Those monks were evil, but I'm not one of them. I'm not a murderer or rapist. Please, just leave me and my family alone. We've done nothing wrong.'

'Your words mean nothing!'

'You don't scare me. I'll find a way to stop you,' countered John against Sabina's ethereal voice, as bravely as he could. Sabina's influence was clearly at its strongest now. 'I'm ready for you *and* your master. I'll take you both on! You won't get away with torturing my family like you have done. You're dead! You can't hurt me! Get out of my head! I can't take much more of this!' John

255

fell into an instant panic. What was he thinking to challenge such powerful and demonic entities?

'I'm waiting for you, John Davidson... in the marshes.'

CHAPTER ELEVEN

The scene that welcomed John on his return home from meeting with Mr Clarence was nothing short of chaotic. As he entered his kitchen, the first thing to take John by surprise - other than the pungent smell of rotten flesh - was a pool of amber liquid which had several shards of broken glass strewn across it.

'*Hannah*!' called out John, sounding similar to a needy toddler, as he carefully manoeuvred himself around the razor-sharp obstacles. 'What's happened in here? It's like a bomb's gone off!' There was no immediate reply from her, which made him panic more. 'What the hell?' On top of the fridge where his treasured and half-empty bottle of scotch whisky once lay, John now found the space to be empty. 'You're having a laugh?!'

'Thank God you're back, John.' Hannah peeped her head into the kitchen from the lower passageway, anxiously. All the colour in her face had drained away, even her twinkling eyes had seemed to dim. 'Be careful where you step—'

'Did *you* do this?' John pointed down at the broken whiskey bottle with a look of bitterness and fury. 'That cost me forty quid. Bloody Hell...'

'I didn't smash it,' emphasized Hannah, in a meek and vulnerable voice. However, her strong personality and resolve soon returned. 'I was having a pee when it happened. There was this *almighty* crash... after I heard a growl. The bottle fell off the fridge on its own, John.'

'A growl?' John rubbed at his sore eyes. They were starting to burn from the strong alcohol fumes, or that's what he told himself, anyway. Inside the feeling of being watched quickly crept into John's mind, into his very soul. 'When *did* this happen?'

'About five minutes ago.' Hannah could feel herself getting angrier by the second towards John. How dare he accuse her, and how dare he talk to her like this. 'It's a blessing, really. You're drinking too much, John. People are starting to notice.'

'Are they?' John's breathing paced faster in unison with his growing resentment. 'You mean... Seamus?'

'Not just Seamus – *Everyone*.' Hannah went to lunge forward, but the thought of her bare feet coming into contact with the tiny shards of brittle glass deterred her from doing so. 'We're all worried about you, babe,' she said, softly. 'What happened to the care-free, loveable lad I fell in love with? Where's he gone?'

'There's nothing wrong with me, Han. Why do keep saying that?' John suddenly stopped in his tracks. A burning pain coursed over his forehead, down into his chest, and then into the pit of his stomach. 'I'm fine. There's nothing wrong with me.' A cold line of sweat began to pour from his forehead. As it ran down onto his lips, the sour taste of salt and anxiety riddled him into feeling both nauseous and fearful. 'Why won't people just leave me alone?'

'We won't stop nagging because we *care* about you!' Hannah could clearly see just how distressed John was becoming. There were so many things she wanted to say to him, to clear her own conscience, though now that level of effort just seemed futile. 'I'll clean this mess up. How did your meeting go, anyway?'

'It was a waste of time,' snapped John. His disappointment was in fact aimed more at Mr. Clarence than Hannah, but it didn't come across this way. 'He just told me what I already know.'

'Which is?' Hannah leant forward, genuinely interested as to what John's ex-history teacher had to offer. 'Tell me. I know I've been funny with you about the ghosts, but I'd rather you get this offer your chest, than to hold onto it.' John exhaled heavily before committing to his explanation.

'He said that "supposedly" Sabina was a witch – a good one that turned bad. She did so because her daughter - like many of the other girls and women in their settlement - was forced into prostitution and then murdered. Sabina herself became a murderer,

258

and then got killed for it. End of story.' John shook his head to show just how disappointed he was with Mr. Clarence's lecture. 'The thing is, Han, I already know all that stuff... because I've seen it all in my nightmares. I didn't want to say anything to you—'

'I have, too,' uttered Hannah, as she tilted her face downward. The relief this apparent confession wrought was indescribable to her; it was like having a weight lifted off her entire body. 'I'm sorry for not being honest with you, John. I should have said something sooner.' She had expected a furious response from her husband; however, the total opposite occurred.

'I knew it. I... knew it,' responded John, himself relieved by Hannah's admittance. 'There's something in this house, Han, and we're the focus of their malice and need for revenge. Sabina's daughter was raped and murdered right before her very eyes.'

'SILENTIUM!'

'Did you say something, John?' Hannah's eyes widened, fearfully. 'Oh, my God! It was her – Sabina!' Everything turned into a blur now. Hannah knew that she was about to faint. She tried hard to fight this, but all her strength had been somehow torn from her. 'John!'

'DOMINUS!'

'Hannah!' John luckily caught his wife during her collapse. Hannah lay in his arms for ten minutes, lifeless and cold, then slowly started to regain her composure. 'Bloody Hell, Hannah. You had me worried sick, there. Is your stomach okay? The baby...'

'I saw *her*!' Hannah looked to him, frantically. 'I saw Sabina, John!' Tears steadily began to well in her eyes. 'Why us? WHY US?!'

259

'We've done nothing wrong, Han. And I *will* find a way to put a stop to this haunting.' John glared into the living room where their Ouija board lay. 'Tonight, when Lucy goes to sleep, we're going to use that board. We'll contact Sabina and sort this shit out – once and for all.'

'No, John, that's a bad idea,' implored Hannah, still barely able to muster her words through sheer panic. 'It's too dangerous. We might make things worse.'

''How the *fuck* can things get any worse than they are already?! We don't have a choice, Han.' John aided Hannah to her feet, then escorted her into the living room. Utter shock and dread coursed through them on entering. Along the back wall, behind their sofa, were three new slash marks. The scratches were too big for human hands; they were more beast-like, such as a bear or lions.

'Not again!' John gawked at the suspicious vandalism in total anger. 'This is getting beyond a joke.'

'I'm scared, John. I don't want to be here anymore.' Hannah rested her head against John's shoulders, though found no warmth in them. 'I think we should move again.'

'Hell no!' declared John, with an air of stubborn resolve. 'I'm not letting some dead hag scare us into moving home. Besides, what if she follows us? You know, like the "attachments" you hear about on *Ghost Adventures*.' A freezing draft suddenly flowed across Hannah and John's bodies, and they could swear that a sadistic laughter was also being carried along with it. 'Shit.'

'What are we going to do? Who is going to believe us when we say that our house is haunted?' asked Hannah, despairingly, as she tightened her grip around John's waist. 'They'll think we've gone mad!' Another breeze flew by, although this time it was even colder than the last. 'Stop it – whoever you are!'

'This haunting ends - tonight!' John fuelled his words with melancholy and malice, aiming them directly at the three demonic slash marks. 'I'll make sure they know that they're not welcome here. I'll put a stop to this!'

'I'm still not sure about using that board,' mumbled Hannah in torment. 'We're playing with fire, John. This won't end well.'

'Et in flammis... Infernos.'

'We're already living in Hell!' countered John against Sabina's disembodied voice, unsettling Hannah even more and mostly by the fact he somehow could now understand Latin. 'Right. I'm on the back shift today, Han.' He turned around to nestle her gently into his side. 'Why don't you and Lucy spend the afternoon at your mam's, away from here?' Hannah slowly nodded back in agreement. 'You know, to be on the safe side.'

'I think I will.' Hannah wiped at her face, removing what tears remained. John shot into the master bedroom, where he had already lain out his uniform for the shift ahead.

'Try to take things easy at work, hun!' shouted Hannah, from the downstairs passageway. She motioned her eyes back and forth between the kitchen and living room, sensing something was still there and watching her. 'Don't say anything about what's going on.'

'Oh, aye! That would go down well with my colleagues, wouldn't it?' sneered John, as he struggled to close the worn zipper on his uniform. 'I'd end up getting sectioned, man! Sod that for a laugh!' He returned down the stairs as fast as he had gone up them. Hannah hadn't moved an inch. 'I'll walk with you to your mam's, babe. The fresh air might do us some good?'

'Yeah, maybe?' Hannah moved at half the speed John accomplished, in getting herself ready. She still felt a little faint; however, on leaving Skipton Road this quickly passed. 'I feel a bit better now.'

'Good,' said John, with a half-formed smile. 'You had me worried back there. If it happens again, please go and see a doctor... or call me.' Hannah firmly clasped her mouth shut, in not wanting to discuss this embarrassing matter any further. 'Now that you're pregnant, you've got to be careful – especially for the bairn's sake. We can't take any risks.'

'I know. I'm not stupid, John.' Hannah tore her hand away from him and then the two carried on walking apart from one another – yet again. 'I wish you wouldn't talk to me like a kid.'

'Look, I'm sorry—' John reached out for her but recoiled in terror; his wife's features had dramatically changed: Her short brown hair was now long, filthy and tattered. Her skin - which was usually tanned - now looked grey, bruised and ghastly. Even Hannah's walk was different; she dragged her feet along the tarmacked pathway like a zombie. 'Hannah?' John reasoned that it was perhaps the fog playing tricks on his tired eyes, for there seemed to be no other rational explanation. 'Wait!'

To John's dismay, Sabina's growling voice responded in place of Hannah's:

'I am waiting for you in the marshes... in your NIGHTMARES!'

John envisioned Hannah turning around to face him, though it was not his wife that would appear – no, it was Sabina. The witch stared upon her latest victim in utter satisfaction, glaring into John's weakened soul with her black and empty eye sockets. It was evident that Sabina found great joy at having forced John into his lowest point. She formed an evil smirk and then, with a blood-curdling cackle, held out both arms towards him, welcoming him in.

'Hannah?' John tried to shout but couldn't. It felt like a set of bony fingers were now being wrapped around his throat, strangling it from consuming any breath. 'No!' Sabina reacted by teasing her fingers across her breasts, then down along her stomach to land upon her empty womb.

'Thou art powerless to resist me, John Davidson,' taunted the witch in a distant whisper, although her voice reached John without fail. 'Thou shalt suffer, otherwise. Thou shalt forever linger in despair. Thou shalt bow before me and my master. A lonely existence awaits thee!' The only action John could manage - in attempt to counter Sabina's cruelty - was to kneel himself into a prayer-like position, lowly and pathetic. 'Ha! Thou art no man. Thou art meeker than any mouse!' she cackled.

'If I'm not a man, then why don't you just fuck off and leave me alone?' John finally mustered some strength to physically retaliate. 'You hear me?!'

'I shalt enchant thine ears and heart, John Davidson,' growled Sabina, her voice as sharp and painful on the ears as any gunshot would be. 'Sayeth those foul words again - vanquish my solemn presence!'

'FUCK-OFF!' John's throat seared from the ferocity of his command to Sabina. A blinding, red light suddenly burst in his eyes, and then as he opened them John was met with a new level of hatred – Hannah.

'Did you just tell me to fuck off!' snarled Hannah, as she turned to face her husband. 'Who do you think you're talking to?'

'I thought – I was certain you were...' John wanted to answer truthfully; he yearned for nothing more than this, if it could explain his random outburst. However, his stuttering took precedence. Hannah had been tormented enough by Sabina, and this mindset only forced John into a reluctant silence. 'I'm so sorry.'

'And, so you should be.' Hannah carried on with her Journey, not caring at all that John kept himself at an apparent safe distance behind. 'Those tablets are useless!' she hollered. 'You need to see your doctor again, John – and soon.'

'Yeah. That's what I need... more drugs to me.'

'I mean it!'

'I will! Jesus, Hannah!' John continued to cautiously traipse along, still only few yards behind Hannah, whilst contemplating Sabina's threatening words and how he could possibly end her curse. A painful migraine quickly set in - just what he needed before his six-hour shift. 'You won't get away with this, Sabina. You're not going to break my family apart, and you're not going to break me!' John emptied his mind for a few peaceful moments, anticipating Sabina's callous response. Only the sound of Hannah's heavy footsteps echoed within Skipton Road's fog, however. 'You're turning her against me.'

'Thou art mistaken, John.'

'No, I'm not!' John tried to calm himself; he was only a couple of minutes away from reaching the care home and the last thing he wanted was to go in angry. His manager, Sally, would surely notice. 'Ever since we've moved here, you've tortured us – driven us apart. Some *mother* you are.'

'Dare not speak so foul of me, John Davidson!'

'Go on, get angry at me – I want you to!' John instantly regretted confronting Sabina in this way; he didn't even know if it was *her* that was talking, after all. 'I'm not scared of you *or* Baal, Beelzebub - whatever the hell that goat-headed freak is called. I'm ready to take you on!"

'Fool! Our vengeance shalt fall hardest upon thee...'

Before leaving John's company, Hannah slowed down to grant him a parting kiss, albeit through an unwilling urge to break the ice between them. She looked at her doting husband, at his gaunt face, his protruding ribcage - which recently started to show through his thick uniform – and despaired. Hannah had never felt so depressed and helpless.

'Have a good afternoon, babe. Don't work too hard.' Hannah leant in to offer some show of affection, but still a bitterness at how John spoke to her only a few minutes earlier continued to dissuade her. 'I'll see you tonight.'

'I love you, Han.' John surprised Hannah by wrapping his emaciated arms around her. All resentment between both seemed to dwindle, and for a moment the two seemed as in love as they had ever been. 'I love you so much. I'm sorry.'

'It's okay,' uttered Hannah, through a set of anxious gasps. 'We'll get through this together, like we always do.' She didn't want to leave go of John, not now, not ever. Regardless of this desire, the smell of roast dinner wafting in from John's workplace instigated him to move away, before he would be late to clock in. 'Bye, hun.'

'See you tonight, Han.' John smiled back to her, forcibly. 'And don't forget that we'll need to settle Lucy down quick, so that we can crack on with the Ouija board.' Hannah shook her head in dismissal, a gesture John foolishly failed to notice. 'I'll put an end to Sabina... no matter what it costs.'

***

"You're cutting it close again, John,' groaned his manager, Sally, from her office chair. 'That's the third time you've nearly been late in the past week or so.'

'It won't happen again, Sally. Sorry.' John nervously fumbled through his uniform's deep pockets. Finding his fob-in key shouldn't have been this hard, though his tremors weren't helping. 'Hannah wasn't feeling well. I was just making sure that she was alright...'

'She seemed fine to me a minute ago.' Sally rose an eyebrow to John and then towards her window; a universal signal that his game was up. 'I saw you kissing each other outside,' she added, in a disappointed tone. 'My office *does* have a window, you know.'

'Hannah's feeling better now, but she didn't ten minutes ago.' John hadn't seen this side of Sally; she was so full of frustration and anger, emotions rarely seen – especially against him. 'I promise it won't happen again.'

'You're not well yourself, are you, John?' questioned Sally, her tone now more empathetic towards him. 'We're getting a little worried about you, if I'm going to be honest.'

'I'm fine. There's no need to worry.' John lowered his sight towards the ground, like a schoolboy being punished by their headmistress.

'I've known you for six years, so don't think I haven't noticed your weight loss, or how down you've seemed over the last few weeks.' Sally swivelled her chair around, then stood herself to face John in person. 'I wouldn't usually pry into this, but are you having problems at home? You can talk to me, John.'

'No, Sally. Hannah and I are okay. There's nothing wrong.'

'Are you sure? You can tell me. Maybe I can offer you some help or advice?'

'NO!' John froze, fearing that the next thing Sally would be offering him would be his P45. 'Sorry. I didn't get much sleep last night. I'm a little out of sorts.' Thankfully, Sally held no grudge with John over his outburst, only pity. She thought back to the young, twenty-two-year-old who had started his job so carefree and full of promise. And then she faced a harsh reality. The man now stood in front of her, looking so lost and beat-down, was a total shadow of his former self. Sally was left with little other option but to intervene.

'I think you should take some time off work, John,' suggested Sally.' Spend some time with your family... and relax. Perhaps that will help make you feel better?'

'Really?' asked John, somewhat surprised by this offer, given he had already used up most of his annual leave with moving to Skipton Road. 'That's so kind of you, Sally. That'd be great.'

'It's the least I can do,' assured Sally, as she brushed a hand over John's left shoulder. 'Work today, then take the rest of this week off. I'd rather you do that, than do something which will result in further action being taken. That's the last thing I want.'

'Thanks. Thank you, so much.' John didn't know if he wanted to laugh or cry. A week off would give him the chance to organise moving home again – if necessary. 'I'll be back to normal in no-time. I promise.'

'I certainly hope so,' mumbled Sally under her breath, with a forlorn expression. 'You're good at your job. It'd be a shame for you to jeopardise it.'

'I won't let you down.' John proudly walked down the hallway which led into the ground floor lounge area, sighing with relief. As he entered, the nightmare scenario of Skipton Road quickly left from him; his passion to care for others - who themselves were so vulnerable - instantly took over. 'Good Afternoon, everyone.' He managed to form a smile towards the residents within his care, though his colleagues easily saw right through it. 'How are things going, Zanna?' he asked to his fellow carer, who just looked back to him with a vacant stare. 'What's up?'

'You look terrible, John. Not had much sleep, again?' Zanna folded her arms, as if standing in judgement over him. 'Has Sally seen you?'

'That's a 'yes' to all three,' chuntered John, trying not to show his displeasure. 'Thanks for the warm welcome, Zan.' He tried to remain civil, yet it was difficult. 'You had a busy day, so far?'

'Aye,' snapped Zanna, 'and it doesn't help with you turning up late.'

'I'm *not* late.' John's frustration swiftly grew. 'I clocked in with two minutes to spare.'

'Good for you. Do you want a medal?'

'Oh, *great*. This shift's going to be fantastic.' John moved away from Zanna before saying something which he'd regret. A sea of frail, smiling faces looked up to him as he walked by each resident, whilst greeting them. Some of the residents in John's care had been *Escomb Angels* – workers in the ammunition factory - and he had a soft-spot for one in particular – Eva.

'Hello, John,' said Eva, endearingly, in a meek and breaking voice. Despite being ninety-six years old, she wasn't doing too bad. 'It's nice to see you. How is your little baby doing?'

'It's lovely to see you too, Eva. Lucy is almost five years old now. Doesn't time fly?' he asked, smiling back sincerely. 'How is the pain in your back doing?'

'My back's fine, dear, it's my arse that's bloody killing me.' Eva shifted her small rump along the pressure-relief cushion she sat on, grimacing and shaking her head. 'This wretched thing doesn't help - it's making my bottom all sweaty and crinkly.'

'I'll find you a different one,' sniggered John, in unison with Eva. 'We can't have you suffering like that, can we?'

'Wey, I've been through worse.' Eva reached down to pick up a small photo album from beside her chair. 'Look at this, John.' In it were several photographs of herself and many others who had worked at the ammunition plant during World War Two. So many happy faces, despite the horrors of war going on around them. 'I remember when this town wasn't so big, when it was just marshlands...'

'I bet.' John's thoughts reluctantly turned back to the harrowing scenes encountered within his nightmares: Sabina, the putrid marshes, the recurring sense of agony and death. 'Can you tell me a little about that time, if you don't mind? Please, Eva. I love our chats.' He almost sounded like a beggar, yearning for what scraps could be offered. 'I'd really appreciate it.'

'What's to say? It was a bloody shit-hole!' cackled Eva, in a high pitch voice. 'Everywhere you looked there were smelly bogs and muddy ditches. The only good thing, which I used to love doing as a youngster, was to go blackberry picking near the old woods. You don't get fresh blackberries like those nowadays!' she divulged, almost falling asleep. 'There used to be a big pile of stones that my friends and I would play hide-and-seek in, but the council shifted them during the seventies to make way for new houses.'

'A big pile of stones?' enquired John, his curiosity steadily rising. 'Where was that at?'

'Oh, now let me think...' Eva tapped an arthritic finger across her chin, then stared up blankly towards the ceiling. 'Bugger me, I can't remember. Just... wait a minute. It'll come back to me. Ah! I remember now! I think they named the new estate *Skipton Road*, though I could be mistaken.' Eva twisted her body to face a portly gentleman seated further along. 'Harold used to live there. Ask him, dear.'

'Thanks, Eva. I'll find you a comfier cushion in a second, okay?' John smiled back politely to her, then stepped across towards Harold. 'Good Afternoon, Harold. How are you today?'

'Hello, sonny!' Harold grinned in response, almost knocking off his thick spectacles. 'I'm fine and dandy. How are you?'

'I'm good, thanks.' John's smile unwittingly shifted again to an expression of dread and intrigue. 'I just have a little question to ask, if you don't mind?'

'If it's about my piles, they're gone. Thank Christ,' chuckled Harold, to several grunts in response from his fellow residents. 'Go on then, what is it?'

'I'm just wondering if you can remember a big pile of stones where Skipton Close was built?' John knelt himself on one knee to match his and Harold's height. 'I know that it seems like a daft question to ask...'

'Not at all, my boy,' assured Harold, his own expression now filled with fear. 'You're on about the *cursed stones*, aren't you?'

'I'm not actually sure, Harold.' John lowered his eyes, as not to appear rude and disrespectful in staring. 'I'd appreciate it if you could tell me more about them.'

'Bloody Hell! You're not asking much, are you?' chuckled Harold, again, though with an awkward smirk this time. 'I've got Alzheimer's for Pete's sake. I can't remember what I had for lunch, let alone anything else.'

'Just tell the boy what he wants to know you daft, old sod!' commanded Eva, with a crippled finger aimed straight against Harold. 'Don't be stupid.'

'I will woman! God, it's like being back at home with the wife, replied Harold, his face now reddening. 'I don't know, John,' he sighed. 'Am I to be straddled with that wily, old bird as company for the rest of my days?'

'Eva. Harold. Please try and be civil to one another,' pleaded John, gently. The trio attempted not to laugh, but it was futile.

'Anyway, bonny-lad,' Harold continued. 'Like I was saying, there were these huge stones, and you're going years back now. Me and my friends would dare one another to touch them. It was said that if you did, a terrifying witch would haunt you – forever!' The room burst into a chorus of laughter, with John being the only person left silent in contemplation. 'The marshes in Newton Escomb used to be a perfect hiding place for witches, with all the fog and that. It's even said that there was a witch's coven, and that they would pray on hapless men - silly beggars with no common sense - who would dare to enter their domain. My dad used to say that those stones were once an old church that collapsed... nobody knows for sure.' Harold eagerly waved his fingers in John's face to highlight the spookiness of this story. John laughed back faintly, though inside all he wanted to do was scream.

'Thanks for your help, Harold. Would you like me to get you anything?' John stood himself upright, looking down at Harold's empty teacup. 'Would you like another cuppa?'

'I daren't, lad.' Harold waved his arms in a frantic and dismissing manner. 'Those bloody water tablets you lot give out make me piss for Great Britain!'

'I'm sorry about that, but you *do* need them for your swollen legs,' explained John, before turning to walk away, still dwelling on the haunted visions of Newton Escomb and Sabina.

'You take them next time, sonny!' stated Harold, to a rapturous applause from a few other residents nearby. 'I don't know, kids these days...' he tutted. 'You can't make it up.'

The remainder of John's shift soon passed by, and thankfully without any issues. It wasn't long before he was clocking out, and the morbid vision of Newton Escomb's marshlands resurfaced in his mind. 'Just you wait, Sabina. I'm going to sort this out tonight. Just me... and you. I'm not scared.'

'So brave and fearless. So... pathetic.'

'I'm not scared of some dead psychopath.' Again, John hesitated on being so bold against the Red Ribbon Witch. She had managed to render him completely into a pitiful shadow, one which lingered only in guilt and melancholy. Was it truly worth the risk? 'If you've got something to say, tonight will be your chance.' There was no response from the demonic voice this time. 'Who's scared now?'

Skipton Road's fog soon crept into John's lungs. Home was near but so, too, was Sabina. For the first time in his life, John considered running away from it all, though that would mean leaving behind the only light in his life – Hannah and Lucy. It

271

wasn't worth considering. How would he cope? What would he do, should Sabina and her demon follow him? All hope was seeming to fade in John's eyes.

'Hi, John,' said Hannah, forebodingly, as she opened the kitchen door for him. 'How was work?'

'It was canny,' replied John, in a surprisingly joyful tone. 'I found out some more things about Newton Escomb's marshlands...'

'I don't want to know.' Hannah was about to kiss John, though instead walked away from him after this revelation. 'Whatever it is that you've been told, I'd rather not know. There's been some more random bumps, and another set of scratch marks have appeared on the living room wall. I can't take it.' John silently nodded back in acknowledgment. Deep down, he was praying that Hannah wouldn't back out of their decision to use the Ouija board. Many questions needed answering. His own hatred needed venting, and this seemed the only way possible now.

'Is Lucy asleep?' asked John, peering up the dark stairwell. 'I can't hear her.'

'She fell asleep about half-an-hour ago, but it took some doing.' Hannah bit at her bottom lip, anxiously. It was obvious to John that she was trying to halt herself from saying whatever troubled her.

'What?'

'The scratch marks... there's more upstairs, too.' Hannah tried to bite at her lip again, though John's pitiful look stopped her from doing so. 'And one of our family portraits has been smashed, the new one we had taken before moving here.'

'No,' said John, sorrowfully. 'I love that picture. Lucy looks so happy in it.' John wiped at his eyes, trying not to weep. 'For God's sake! What have we done to deserve this? I don't understand!'

'Shhh! You'll wake up our Lucy,' implored Hannah, in a desperate-sounding whisper. 'I've been thinking...'

'Thinking...what?' John wiped at his eyes again. It was becoming difficult to stop the tears from welling up.

'I think you're right about using the board. Things are only getting worse, aren't they? We need answer.' Hannah slowly lifted her sight to look upon the device situated nearby. She hated it. But, like John, it seemed the only answer they had in ending Sabina's reign of terror. 'Maybe the ghosts are just trying to communicate with us? What if we've been taking things out of context?' She shook her head in dismay, still fearful of what the possible repercussions could be. 'I can't believe I'm saying this, but maybe Sabina just wants our help?'

'No, Han,' stated John, his anxiety now growing beyond any control. 'She wants to tear us apart... and nearly has. She's pure evil.' A single tear ran down his face, leaving an imperfect trail in its wake. Hannah removed it with a gentle swipe of her fingertips, then rubbed sympathetically at John's temple. 'We've suffered enough. Fuck listening to her!' John's foreign temper rose again, his expression now looking more like the demonic version of Sabina. 'Let's get this over with.'

'Wait!' Hannah clenched onto her husband, but his strength and resentment were too strong. He moved towards the board with a manic smile, regardless of her reservations, and carefree of the consequences. 'Don't go rushing in. We need to do a blessing first.'

'Like *that's* going to help us?' sneered John, as he reached down to collect the board from its resting place on their dining table. 'What happened when I read from my bible?' Hannah stared back in dread, the answer to this still haunting her. 'Sabina and her demon just laughed at me! They turned me into a helpless worm that could barely move!' He opened the case that protected the board and was instantly reminded of the movie 'Jumanji' during, although this wasn't anywhere near as enjoyable to witness.

'What exactly are hoping to achieve from doing this?' asked Hannah, reservedly.

'We're going to face them head-on - just like they do with us in our nightmares,' said John, with some flicker of hope in his eyes.

'I want to do a blessing,' pleaded Hannah. She then quietly ran back into the passageway, returning with John's bible held within her sweaty palms. 'Let me read something out of this first. It'll make me feel more comfortable.'

'Fine. Whatever makes you feel more relaxed,' said John, wearily. 'But you'll be just wasting your time. This *isn't* a movie - things don't work like that in real life.' He ran his tremoring fingers over each of the letters upon the Ouija board. The device itself looked so tacky and cheap, despite it feeling heavy. In truth, John didn't believe that anything would come through; he was only going ahead with this decision to satiate his illogical urges, his need to get one over on Sabina. 'Maybe try one of the Psalms?'

This would be the first time Hannah had ever looked inside a bible; it wasn't something she had considered doing before, being that she was mostly a spiritualist by nature and in no way religious. Hannah carefully flicked through the bible's wafer-thin pages, choosing to land upon the Gospel of Luke, only because she liked the name.

'Right!' Hannah inhaled a deep and nervous breath, her hands trembling as severely as John's now. 'This seems fitting: "Behold, I give unto you power to tread on serpents and scorpions, and over all the power of the enemy: and nothing shall by any means hurt you".'

A deep and unholy voice responded:

'NIHIL! EGO DOMINUS!'

'Shit!' Hannah looked to John in panic, knowing that he too had heard the demonic growl nearby. 'What was that?'

274

'*They don't like you reading from the Holy Bible!*' sang John, to the tune of 'Ring-a-Ring of Roses', and in a taunting and husky voice. He was already losing control, his dwindling sanity, and they hadn't even started the séance session yet. Hannah now reached her breaking point with this all.

'Neither do I,' she replied, sternly. 'I'm not using that Ouija thing, John – it's too dangerous!' Hannah slammed the bible shut, and the feeling that they were no longer alone immediately crept in. Suddenly, an instant wave of negative energy flowed against them like having a cannon fired directly into their stomachs. 'I want that board out of this house!' commanded Hannah, her voice breaking through fear and hatred. 'If that doesn't go - *you* do!' John merely ignored Hannah's plea. He walked into the kitchen and then came back with a sadistic smile and empty whiskey glass held in his hands. 'Don't-you-dare!'

'We need answers!' implored John. The light in his eyes had all but gone now. 'I need answers...'

'You're so selfish, John.' Hannah began to sob, though John still seemed ignorant towards her pressing torment. 'If you won't throw it away – I will!' John slammed his whiskey glass firmly upon the Ouija board's centre in defiance. 'What are you doing?!'

'How can you not understand?' asked John, recoiling bitterly. His obsession with Sabina had taken full control over any other need. Hannah wasn't scared of confronting the witch anymore, instead she now feared how long her marriage to John would last. 'You wouldn't understand though, would you? It's *me* that Sabina's latched onto. All she wants is for me to lose the plot, for you to hate me, and for us to leave this house. I'm not letting that happen!' John paused in his lecture - he had to, as Hannah glared down towards the board behind them with a grave expression. 'What now?'

'Look!' Hannah wretched, as if she was about to vomit. 'I told you, John. I told you that this was a bad idea!' The whiskey glass had moved on its own, landing precisely over the word "Yes".

"Oh, so you *do* want those things to happen!' roared John, aiming his words against every corner of the living room. 'You can't break us, Sabina! I won't let you!'

'Please, John, throw the board away!' wailed Hannah. However, her despair quickly turned into anger. John wrapped an open palm across the whiskey glass and then slid it along to leave a single, resting fingertip that lingered there like a perched vulture. 'Are you for real?!'

'I know you're waiting for me... in the marshes,' whispered John, his voice distant and monotonous. 'I call upon thee, Sabina, the *Red Ribbon Witch...*'

'You... arsehole!' Hannah turned to leave but was halted in her tracks by a frantic-looking Lucy. The child had hurtled down the stairs, screaming wildly, begging for her mother's attention. 'What are you doing out of bed, sweetheart?' asked Hannah in a soft tone, trying not to display her melancholy. 'It's past your bedtime.'

'Stop it, Mammy!' screamed the child, as she threw herself into Hannah's waiting arms. 'Stop talking to Belly-Bob! Eliza said that you are!'

'We're not, darling.' Hannah held onto Lucy, both in fright and to protect her from whatever lurked within the moving shadows. 'John,' she said, in a defiant tone. 'Look at what you're doing to us. It's *you* that doesn't understand and doesn't care about your own family!'

'I see you...'

'Sabina...' John continued to chant the witch's name in a trance-like state, his eyes rolling back to reveal their whites. He was deafened to all surrounding sounds, only his heartbeat and the distant cackle of Sabina's laughter existed now. 'I'm ready for you... to cleanse me.'

'Daddy - NO!' begged Lucy, her command swiftly followed with a fearsome shriek. 'It's Belly-Bob, not Eliza's mammy!' Hannah clenched onto Lucy tighter.

'Stop it!' ordered Hannah, fiercely. 'For God's sake, John! STOP!'

'Once connected, never can a bond be broken...' John's voice sounded so different now; it was malicious and - in an unnerving way - perverse. 'Sabina. I know you're near...'

The whiskey glass moved again by itself, this time landing upon the number zero. Both Hannah and Lucy screamed in unison, though John saw this move as a symbol of Sabina's infinite power and eternal lust for revenge. The Red Ribbon Witch had finally taken complete control over her latest victim. What remained of John's persona - his carefree nature, his love towards Hannah and Lucy - seemed to vanish in this truly horrific moment.

'Daddy! Listen to me!' howled Lucy, but it was no use. She turned to look up at her mother, who herself was riddled with overwhelming emotions. 'Where's Eliza, Mammy? I can't see her anymore!'

'This needs to stop, John!' Hannah unwittingly ignored Lucy's question, her sole focus now being on snapping John out of Sabina's sadistic possession. 'Can't you hear us? What are you doing?'

'Ego peccator. Impius sum,' chanted John, sounding more like the demon in his dreams with every word spoken. 'Sabina.'

'Enough!' Hannah lunged at the Ouija board in attempt to knock John's whiskey glass away from him, but an invisible force proceeded to hold her at bay. 'I'm burning this thing!' she screamed. 'What has that witch done to you? Talk to me, John!'

'You mean, what WILL she do?'

'It's Belly-Bob!' despaired Lucy, clasping onto her father's side. 'Don't hurt my daddy! Where are you, Eliza?'

"Ego peccator. Impius sum. Ego peccator. Impius sum.' John repeated these words over and over, despite Hannah striking at every one of his limbs with an impassioned ferocity in attempt to silence him. She was more than desperate to end this disturbing scene, though there seemed to be no end in sight. 'Tu Sabina. Ego... John. Ego... Deus. Ego... Dominus.'

As John proceeded to confess his sins in Latin, each lightbulb instantaneously burst within the living room. A ghastly cackle and cough then entered the space between Hannah and John, thus fermenting Sabina's ethereal presence. Meanwhile, Lucy knelt herself as if in prayer and was chanting some unknown Latin verses, but they didn't seem malignant in any way – at least not to Hannah.

'Lucy, what are you saying?' Hannah nestled her hands under the child's chin, supporting her weakening neck muscles with every ounce of strength left. Lucy was as lost as John within a spiritual trance of her own, and poor Hannah had no control over either. 'Lucy! Speak to me! What am I going to do?'

'Et non lucem.'

'There is no light,' declared John, his speech riddled with the demon's own satanic voice. 'Only darkness and death exist... in the marshes.'

'Stay away from us, Sabina!' commanded Hannah, her voice defiant and powerful. She couldn't see John in the darkened room, though could feel and hear his breaths moving closer towards her. 'Stay away from my little girl, Witch!'

Without warning, Lucy fell lifelessly against her mother's legs. Hannah shook at her child's limp body, yearning to awaken Lucy from this paranormal experience, though all she could muster was a faint sigh. Hannah herself soon felt a peculiar, cold shock trickle throughout her veins. Within a matter of seconds, she too fainted into a pitted world of darkness and sorrow, whilst her husband remained blissfully unaware.

'Ego Baal! Ego Dominus! Ego Deus!'

John carried on with his demonic blessing, for the desire to see Sabina in person again vanquished any other thought or impulse now. He imagined the witch standing there, within the murky marshes, alone and vulnerable in a sea of hellish flames. He too would soon fall under Sabina's accursed spell. In the forgotten marshlands of Newton Escomb, the Red Ribbon Witch waited patiently for her prey to arrive. Her wait was now over.

CHAPTER TWELVE

Across the moonlit and misty distance, John could hear a murder of crows bustle away as if frightened – *but by what or whom?* he pondered. He found himself back in the ancient marshlands of Newton Escomb, his recurring realm of torment. A festering smell of foist and death lingered within the air, adding to the foreboding sense which now rose in John as steadily as his racing heartbeat.

'Where are you, Sabina?' questioned John, his anger and impatience held against her growing even more. 'I know that you're here... somewhere. What vision do you want to show me now?'

A melancholic, feminine voice swept through the stale air in response to John – Sabina:

'I am a mother. I am the Red Ribbon Witch. I am forsaken. I am cursed. I am retribution – vengeance. I am... Sabina.'

John reluctantly twisted his body to meet with the source of this voice; however, the witch remained to be unseen. The evening sky above suddenly burst into a deafening chorus of thunder and lightning strikes, with a shower of acid-like rain following suit that terrified John to his core. The rainwater burned at his skin, but he didn't care as anyone else would have. John's thoughts focused on his wife and child, his helplessness and deepening depression, and the need to put a stop to Sabina's reign of malice.

'I am John!' He declared boldly in defiance, aiming his sight against where the witch's voice appeared to be coming from. 'I am a husband! I am a father! I am *not* scared of you...Sabina. Show yourself, coward!'

The sporadic flashes of lightning eerily revealed a solemn figure that now stood themselves directly opposite John, and within the heart of this boggy marshland. The Red Ribbon Witch had emerged from her eternal prison – Hell. Sabina cackled in delight at how far she had driven John into madness, just as she had so desired.

'Thou art brave,' commented Sabina, in a callous tone. 'Thou art foolish to call me a coward. I shalt make thee regret those words.'

'Shut your fucking mouth, Witch!' roared John through parched and tremoring lips. 'Didn't you hear me? I'm not scared of you. You can't hurt me!' He began to laugh manically as if in reflection of Sabina herself, lost in comprehension to his present and dire surroundings. 'What are you? What *are* you? You're dead - that's what you are! An evil woman like you should *never* have been a mother!' Though Sabina had pitted eye sockets, it was clear to John that his words made her weep – a surprising revelation, even to him. 'So, you do have feelings...'

'Thy wife and child worship thee?' questioned the witch, her voice now sounding more masculine than John's, layered with cruelty and malignant. 'Art thou innocent? Art thou a perfect father?'

'Hannah and Lucy love me, and I love them. I've never said that I'm perfect!' implored John, although who it was that he was attempting to convince, between himself and the witch, remained unclear 'I'd do anything for them, but I certainly wouldn't sell my soul to the devil... like you did.'

'I had no choice, John. My vengeance was wrought from a greater power - a demon eternal, yes. But he is no devil. My master saved me,' said Sabina with a knowing smirk. 'He is my protector, and never lies far away from me.'

'Baal?!' sneered John viciously. 'I've tried my best to make a better life for Hannah and Lucy. I'm not a monster, and I would never ask for help from the likes of Baal... not like you.'

'John?' Hannah's familiar voice and presence suddenly met with him, standing only feet away. 'Where are we?'

'Hannah?!' John gasped in shock as he glanced sideways to meet with his wife's fearful glare. 'What are *you* doing here?'

'How would *I* know?' she snapped. Hannah didn't look John in the eye, instead she searched around them for any sign of Lucy. 'We're back in Sabina's marshlands...aren't we?' Sabina cackled again in ecstasy, taking Hannah by surprise. 'Shit! It's *her*, John. I knew that Ouija board was a bad idea!'

A darker, beast-like voice soared through the air, aiming itself against John and Hannah:

'PECCATORUM!'

'My master longs for thy suffering,' said Sabina, smirking in relief. 'Baal!'

'Oh, God,' whispered Hannah to John. 'What are we going to do? They're stronger than us.'

'Fuck them. Like you said, there's two of us now. It's a fair fight!' John leered towards Sabina, showing no love nor empathy to Hannah as he should have. 'Summon your master! Summon Baal! I *dare* you! I am flesh and blood. Baal is nothing but a fantasy of yours – WITCH!' It would soon be proven to John that he would long regret saying this statement. 'You don't exist, and you can't hurt us!'

Baal held no hesitation in addressing John's taunt:

'SUM DOLOR! CRUCIOR! EGO... BAAL!'

The scarlet thunderclouds above burst into a rapture of endless clashes, perfectly in line with Sabina's ferocious smile. Underneath both Hannah and John, the marshland now shifted like an awakening serpent; its shards of brittle grass convulsed; its water flowed somehow unnaturally to unveil a slithering and ancient malignance.

282

'Baal hast heard my call,' announced Sabina gleefully, her fervent cackle now displaying what insanity lay within. 'Thy sinful ways shalt be cleansed, John Davidson. Baal will see to it!'

John and Hannah were given no time to react. The coursing water suddenly burst into a line of searing flames, separating the Red Ribbon Witch from her victims, as well as themselves.

'That was a cheap move!' screamed John bravely. However, his true fear was no longer hidden from view. 'You're not going to ruin our lives – not anymore! I'm putting a stop to this!'

A reverberating, guttural growl then came from within the risen flames

'I am pain, suffering, torment. I am malice pure, fallen from the heavens. I am the Lord of Vengeance and Judgement – YOUR judgement, John Davidson. I am... Baal!'

After a momentary burst of laughter from Sabina. the tall, dark outline of a humanoid figure emerged from within the amber flames. This monstrous creature stood at least ten-feet tall. Its legs were dark and hairy, just like a Tarantula's. Its torso was strangely furry, white, and similar to that of an emaciated though muscular man. The demon's arms were long and wiry, with talons that stretched out far from their skeletal hands. It's right hand, for reasons unbeknown to John, was evidently painted in fresh blood. The most-peculiar feature this demonic beast boasted, was that of its head that looked to be of an ageing ram, their eyes looking alien - large and black in colour, as dark as polished obsidian.

'Long have I watched over you, John. Now, finally, you shall be cleansed – purged of your sins!'

'A treasured trophy, shalt thou wretched corpse become, John,' interjected Sabina as she looked to him, and then to Baal. 'Thou art foolish to challenge my master!'

'Oh, aye?'" John snarled. 'I'll take both you on! I've had enough of your haunting!'

'No prayer can save you. God does not exist here!'

John motioned to counter the demon's taunt, though at this moment an agonizing surge of negative energy coursed through every cell in his body - putting an immediate stop to his impassioned attempt. Baal held out its red hand towards John, whilst contorting its fingers to form a telekinetic clasp around the helpless victim's throat.

'You would declare yourself innocent like God's only son, lowly sinner? God's child, Yeshua, bore mankind's cruelty for his innocence and so shall you... in the same manner.'

Hannah froze in dread, unable to muster even the faintest noise from her mouth. All she could do was watch on powerlessly as a series of thorny vines emerged from the marshes which then wrapped around John's entire body. The vines then slithered up his torso, focusing their thorns upon his forehead to form a painful crown around it with them. This was obviously a disgraceful re-enactment of Christ's passion - a harrowing symbol to John that he did not have the control which he wrongly thought he had.

'Get off me!' John squealed like a pig being gutted alive, his screams of terror only adding to Baal and Sabina's enjoyment. He could feel each metallic thorn pierce into his flesh, each one as painful as the last. 'No! Why are you doing this to me?'

The thorny vines then provided Baal with a horrific cage to entrap John's body in. John proceed to writhe upon the ground like a bird trapped within their cruel, man-made housings – screaming within his own sadistic cage. Baal leant down to clasp upon a vine that lay within the murky waters, then dragged John's shaking body through the marshes with it towards their evil presence.

'Leave him alone!' pleaded Hannah, weeping, looking to her oppressors with a fatigued expression. Hannah then focused all her attention on the Red Ribbon Witch. The surrounding flames highlighted the witch's deathly features, especially her lack of human compassion. 'Please, Sabina – I'm begging you - leave my husband alone. He doesn't deserve to be treated like this. No one does.'

'All men shalt suffer my sacred punishment! None shalt be spared!' responded the witch, her manner bitter and heartless. 'Thou shalt reap thy sown seeds, John.' Sabina hastily turned away from Hannah in wanting to witness John's long-awaited torture. 'My will is done.'

'He's my husband. Yes, he *can* be selfish at times, but I *still* love him!' despaired Hannah. She held out her arms like a desperate beggar, shunning her pride to salvage John's diminishing life. 'Have mercy on him. Our daughter will be heartbroken if anything happens to John. From a mother to a mother, Sabina, please take mercy on him – for Lucy's sake.' Sabina continued to watch on, regardless of Hannah's sincerity, for the summoned demon was about to enact her vengeance – a scene not to be missed. 'I hate you, Sabina! I HATE YOU!'

'Thou would not be the first,' simpered the witch, lulling her head. 'My will *must* be done. My curse *must* be enacted!'

Baal lifted John's constricted body into the choking air with ease. The demon then glared upon its cowering victim, showing no pity nor sign of ending this evil punishment at all. Baal's final judgement, its weeks of taunting, now came into full fruition.

'A crown of thorns for a noble king. Thirty-nine lashes to inflict thee! Suffer, John! SUFFER!!'

The iron-like thorns encasing John's body cruelly slithered around his flesh again, mimicking the brutal lashes of which Jesus Christ allegedly received. They tore away at his muscle fibres, also ripping the fatty tissue away to ultimately reveal some of his bones beneath, and with a barbaric precision. Sabina cackled ecstatically. Baal growled sadistically. Hannah screamed out in utter horror and anguish. John howled in agony against a pain he had not yet ever felt throughout his short existence.

'Your life is spent. Your life is worthless. No love to encounter, nor dwell on. No sorrow upon your death shall be felt. Now... feel the Fires of HELL!'

With a harrowing cry, Baal dangled John's body before its beastly eyes, using them to stare upon him with the utmost of malice. The demon then callously swung John's crippled body around, adding even more agony, to linger him above the flames that heightened beside them. Instantly, a gut-wrenching scream left from John's struggling lungs, his lower half now sizzling like a steak above the intense flames.

'NO!' pleaded John with all his might. It was a sound that most in their lifetime would be fortunate enough not to experience. Hannah, on the other hand, had no choice. 'NO!!'

'Let him go!' commanded Hannah frantically. She managed to remain strong in her resolve for John's sake, turning to Sabina with a look of pure fury. 'He doesn't deserve this! I know those monks hurt your daughter, but this is wrong! You can't justify this!'

'Thou art forsaken and blinded by false love,' sighed Sabina after releasing an orgasmic groan. She was still too enticed by John's increasing agony to pay too much attention to Hannah. 'Love only leads to despair. Innocence only leads to corruption. Life only leads... to death. Light only leads... to darkness.'

'You're wrong.' Hannah shook her head dismissively. She was too strong for Sabrina to break. 'He is someone's child. Would *you* wish the same pain on your own, on Eliza?' Sabina's smirk instantly turned into a hateful frown. 'No, you wouldn't. What would Eliza—'

'MY CHILD WAS RAPED! MURDERED!' wailed Sabina, echoing the grief still dwelling inside to overpower the thunder above, whilst clenching on to where her empty womb lay. 'My child is dead.' Sabina sounded as if she was weeping, though no tears left from her empty sockets. 'My precious child...'

'Why have you brought me here, into this nightmare - to bear witness over John's suffering? You're sick!' Hannah could barely hold herself back from lunging against the arrogant witch. 'You're so wrong about him! You're wrong about everything!' Hannah paused momentarily in attempt to deafen herself from John's shrieking cries with her hands. 'Eliza *isn't* dead, Sabina.' The witch's attention immediately turned back from John towards Hannah. 'She has been teaching our little girl some spells, the sort that would really mess you up!'

'Thou art fouler than any demon, Hannah Davidson!' responded Sabina in a heightened level of hatred. 'Thy words are nought but false! Thou speaketh no truth.'

'Eliza is a good witch – like *you* used to be!' scorned Hannah to the stricken wench. 'She is *not* dead. Her spirit lives on...'

'Silence!' the witch howled. 'End this cruel torment! Speaketh not of my fallen daughter!'

As Hannah and the witch fought with their words, Baal gradually lowered John further into the intense wave of flames, looking across to Sabina all the while in want of her keen affection and appreciation. John gasped out louder in anguish, though his breaths were beginning to fail, the thin air in his body almost completely

287

spent on this unprecedented exertion. He was slowly dipping in and out of consciousness. How could this possibly be a dream or nightmare? It felt so real. He could feel the flesh melting away from his bones and smell his roasting tissue. Death was surely near?

A dazzling, white light suddenly broke through the permeating fog. The piercing hue blinded all but Hannah, who herself looked upon it in relief and awe. Two small, angelic figures appeared; their auras still clad in this heavenly array of light. They were a welcomed balance to the darkness of Newton Escomb's ancient marshland, to Sabina's sordid existence. They were also a threat that neither the Red Ribbon Witch nor Baal had anticipated.

'Lux in tenebris!'

For a moment, Hannah thought that this sweet voice was Lucy speaking. The figure sounded so child-like, so innocent and pure.

'Vincere bolem!'

'Mammy!' shrieked Lucy as she left the serene light to stand by her mother's side. 'Eliza has come to help my daddy!' gleamed the child, looking back to angelic light with a hopeful smile. Hannah merely gasped in response. It was clear to see, within the divine wave of light, a second child – one equal in appearance to Sabina: the same white dress; the same red ribbon around her waist; the same long and wavy, brunette hair. Their only distinguishing feature being a set of deep brown eyes and shorter stature. 'Eliza is an angel! She is a *good* girl! I told you, Mammy!'

'Lux in tenebris! Vincere bolem!'

Baal unleashed a harrowing cry, infused with its own infliction in response to Eliza's appearance. The demon had no option but to remove its victim from their relentless flames, if only to face this new adversary head-on. Eliza stepped forward, holding out a single hand that she aimed against her mother's bane, reciting her Latin verses as taught by Sabina herself.

A battle between good and evil thus began:

'Deus est mortus!'

'Lux in tenebris! Vincere bolem!'

'Deus est mortus!'

'Lux in tenebris! Vincere bolem!'

Baal and Eliza intensified their countering spells, their ancient chants which most in this world have long forgotten. Sabina turned her back to Eliza, choosing to blindly look upon the marshlands of which she had called home for so long instead of her child. She couldn't believe that it was Eliza. She didn't want to believe that it was her fallen child. Death had taken her so many long years ago. In truth, it was guilt and shame that forced Sabina into not looking upon her only child, that and her overwhelming grief.

From Baal now came a wave of thick, black smoke, though it only seemed to reflect against Eliza's shielding light. Both adversaries rose their voices in attempt to overpower the other. Hannah wrapped Lucy tenderly against her bosom, the need to save her husband now far out-weighed by the desire to maternally protect their only child; a sad and reflective mirror-image of how Sabina herself reacted.

'Is she really Eliza?' asked Hannah to Lucy, her hope rekindling. 'Is that little girl...your imaginary friend?'

'Yes! Eliza came from Heaven to help Daddy!' responded Lucy, though her smile rapidly faded upon looking upon Baal's hate-filled glare again. '*She* isn't scared of Belly-Bob!'

'DEUS EST MORTUS!'

'God is *not* dead!' declared Eliza, her stance proud and voice passionate. 'You have no dominion over me! You have no power over this man's soul!' Sabina's child was strong, seemingly powerful enough to counter the demon's ancient evil. Eliza would be Hannah's last hope in saving her husband, for who else could save them now?

'Ego sum... DEUS!'

'*You* are not God. You are nothing! You are dust from the depths of Hell, and I shall cleanse *you*!' Eliza moved forwards, her bare feet landing perfectly upon the marshlands water like Jesus Christ himself. 'I will release him from your incarceration!' She rose her other arm towards John. At first it felt like the thorny vines shifted away, possessed solely by Eliza's own supernatural powers, but Baal continued to keep control over them. 'You have no dominion here! Lux in tenebris!'

'EGO SUM DEUS!'

Sabina screamed and then turned around in response now. It had been hundreds of years since she had last seen her daughter, since she had last heard her gentle voice. Eliza looked in no way different: her beauty unchanged by time nor through the disgusting ordeals she had endured.

'Even your daughter thinks that you're a monster,' commented Hannah, whilst looking across to the Red Ribbon Witch with all the anger she could muster. 'Your own daughter hates you.'

'Eliza?' She gasped as spoke, her voice breaking from the conflict festering inside. 'Thy wicked fate hast cursed my mind! Thou art dead!'

Baal unleashed another blood-curling roar, which the demon quickly followed with a greater wave of thick and choking smoke, aiming it viciously against Eliza's scrawny throat. Sabina's daughter fought hard against this demonic attack, but the smoke started to form stronger around her throat, paralysing her to the spot.

Eliza's angelic voice then resounded throughout the nightmare landscape, again to be met with Baal's foul tongue:

'Vita in morte! Vita in morte!'

'Morte in vitam!'

'What kind of mother *are* you?' asked Hannah to Sabina in disbelief, her judgement over the witch impassioned and just. 'Don't you care about Eliza – your own daughter?!' Sabina, for the first time during these nightmarish ordeals, remained silent. 'You... monster! You'd let that demon harm Eliza without a fight, without a single care?!'

'Baal is my master,' countered Sabina, despondently. 'Baal is my vengeance. Baal is my saviour.' Another set of harrowing cries left from John as the demon plunged him once again into the roaring flames. 'My vengeance is...' whimpered Sabina.

'You're not a mother! No mother would ever let their child be treat this way!' screamed Hannah, her emotions now driven solely by empathy towards Eliza. 'I'd *never* let my daughter suffer like this!'

'Baal... my master... my... master.' Sabina's satanic appearance began to morph back and forth again between her fair and demonic form. Hannah knew that there was still some good inside of this cold-hearted witch, but how she could exploit this was an unanswerable burden. 'Baal...' Sabina tearfully faced away from her daughter's plight once more. She tried to convince herself that it wasn't in fact Eliza, that this was just some trick being played on her. 'My child is dead. Her soul art lost to me.'

The dark clouds above once again released a deafening wave of thunder and scarlet lightning strikes. For a moment it seemed that Baal had submitted itself to Eliza's positive influence, though sadly this would not last. The monstrous demon summoned what smoke it could from the nearby flames, aiming more against Eliza's whole body. Baal then used its inhuman might to lift the poor child at least thirty feet into the air and without any exertion.

'Pati sum vobis!" PATI SUM VOBIS!'

Cackling wildly, Baal proceeded to swing Eliza through the air by her throat with its telepathic powers like a doll held under the control of some sadistic puppet master. The angelic witch continued with her Latin verses, defiant to the last ounce of strength against this most-evil of foes, though she now greatly struggled to enact her will upon it.

'Mammy!' cried Lucy, clasping frantically onto her. 'Help Eliza! You need to help her!'

'I don't know how to, sweetheart,' despaired Hannah, her own hold upon Lucy tightening. 'There's nothing we can do.'

'Lux in tenebris! Lux in... tenebris!'

'I can't believe you'd just stand there and watch your own daughter being tortured like this!' roared Hannah to Sabina. The

Red Ribbon Witch held her head down and then played with her bony fingers like a fearful child herself. 'Coward! You *deserve* to rot in Hell!'

'Lux...Lux - Mama! MAMA!'

Eliza howled, her piercing cries as haunting as the wicked demon itself. She violently kicked her legs through the ash-filled air, wrapping her small fingers around the choking smoke, praying that she could somehow remove it. Hannah couldn't speak. She was totally lost for words at how heartless Sabina appeared. How could Sabina let her own daughter suffer like this? Eliza changed from being defiant and hopeful into a helpless, innocent victim. Lucy now stepped in to aid her friend, brave and bold.

'Lux in tenis!' screamed Lucy to Baal. She tapped away at her head, dismayed over not being able to recite the Latin phrases correctly 'Lux in...tenbis.' She then bravely held out a wavering hand against the towering demon, just as Eliza had. 'Lux in TEBBIS!'

Baal bore no patience to be playing such games with Lucy:

'SILENTIUM!!'

'I can't remember what Eliza said! I can't remember the words, mammy!' wailed Lucy, on fleeing from the demon's view to stand behind her mother. 'It's no good! Belly-Bob's too nasty! I don't like him! He's horrible!'

'Oh, sweetheart,' whispered Hannah sympathetically. She then forced herself and Lucy to kneel in the sodden marshes, for they were too emotionally exhausted to stand any longer. 'We'll be okay. I won't let them hurt you, Lucy.'

'I'm scared, Mammy,' Lucy sobbed, now riddled with fear. 'I want to go home. I want my daddy to come home!'

'I do, too.' With a judgemental scowl, Hannah tilted her head around to look upon Sabina's shadowy figure. 'You evil bitch. That is *your* child being strangled by *your* demon! Do something!'

Silently and with her head still bowed, Sabina stepped forth into this gruesome scene, towards her master and child. She looked upon John's writhing body and listened to his tortured screams, finding that they now wrought no joy in her as they had before. The witch then reluctantly observed her own daughter, Eliza, squirming in mid-air, still fighting to free herself from Baal's smoky noose. Sabina had never felt so conflicted.

'Help her! For God's sake!' implored Hannah. She rested her forehead against Lucy's, just as Sabina did with Eliza before their abduction hundreds of years ago. The witch tried to dismiss this comparison, but it was proving too hard. 'I won't let them hurt you, Lucy. I won't let them take you away. I'm here, baby. Mammy's here...'

Somewhere within Sabina's diseased heart she rediscovered those painful memories, those last terrifying moments spent with her daughter: Eliza's kidnapping, her defilement and barbaric death at the hands of those evil monks - they all flooded back.

'MAMA! MAMA!!'

'My child,' whimpered Sabina, as she clasped her hands firmly against her ears to shield them from Eliza's distressing cries. 'Thou art dead. Thou art lost to thy possession. This is but falsehood.'

'MAMA!!'

'Ego Omnipotem!'

'I won't let them take you,' repeated Hannah, though her words brought no reassurance to Lucy. The child was fixated on her father's twisting body, the flames that swept over him, his screams. There was nothing that could numb this pain Lucy now felt. 'I won't let them hurt you, darling. I won't let them take you!'

Suddenly, Sabina shuddered from an emotion that she had long but forgotten – love. The witch glared at Baal and then to Eliza, and then back to the wicked demon. Sabina reluctantly toyed her fingers around the red ribbon upon her waist, her own form of incarceration, and with a deafening roar tore it asunder.

'NO!' roared the witch to Baal. Sabina's red ribbon then flew up into the ash-filled air, floating gradually towards John. 'Thou foulest spawn of Satan shalt not harm my child! Lux in tenebris! Vincere bolem!' Sabina held a tremoring hand out against the beast, just as Eliza and Lucy had. As she spoke the divine, Latin words, Sabina's features began to appear fairer again, as did her voice. 'Lux in tenebris! VINCERE BOLEM!!'

Baal gave out a haunting shriek as if all the festering air in its lungs had been abruptly removed. Sabina's torn ribbon coursed faster through air now, eventually landing within the flames beneath John. A burst of intense, scarlet fire then proceeded, which immediately drew back into the demon's flailing body – fully igniting its sordid flesh.

'DEUS TUUS EGO SUM! SABINA!'

'Thou art no longer a master to me. Though art no God. I am no slave to thee,' stammered Sabina, her entire body wrenching in unison with Baal's own pain. 'My child...' The witch eagerly moved forwards whilst reaching out for Eliza, as the angelic child slowly returned to the boggy earth beneath and thankfully unharmed.

Without warning, though it was welcomed by all, Baal burst into an array of crimson embers, ultimately releasing John from its grasp to fall into a lifeless heap – releasing him from the searing bonds that tore into his flesh and bones. Where John landed the damp grass instantly became scorched, and the surrounding water unleashed a wave of putrid steam. His pain at this moment - wholly indescribable.

'John!' cried Hannah as she and Lucy ran over to him, briefly fleeting by Eliza who continued to watch on over them. 'What has that thing done to you? Oh, God! This can't be happening?'

John's body had been burned and slashed beyond any recognition. What flesh remained was charred and torn, his limbs unnaturally contorted, his breaths faint and dwindling, with only a small area around his eyes seemingly left unharmed. The look of fear and agony still lingered within John's pale, blue eyes, despite the fact his ordeal was now over, and it was a sight Hannah could barely bring herself to look at.

'Daddy?' Lucy held out a hand over John's face, compelled to offer him any comfort she could with her gentle touch. However, the heat radiating from his scorched skin prevented her from doing so. 'My poor daddy...' wept the child.

'What has that monster done to you?' Unlike Lucy, Hannah fought against the searing heat to place a hand upon her husband's cremated flesh. 'Don't leave us, John. Please, don't go. Don't leave me.'

Meanwhile, Sabina trudged through the murky marshlands towards Eliza's position, not once looking to the Davidsons and their current plight.

'Daughter?' Sabina had fully returned to her fairer form now, though a malevolent aura continued to shroud the witch's entire body. 'Eliza?' Sabina reached out a yearning hand to her child, but Eliza merely stood still, only looking back to her mother with a pitying expression. 'My child – come to me! Embrace thy mother!' As Sabina took another step forward one of her legs sank into the marshland's freezing waters. She tried to force it out but couldn't.

As if encased in concrete, Sabina – no matter how much she tried – could not remove her trapped leg. 'Eliza!'

'I cannot aid thee, Mother,' said Eliza reluctantly. 'Thou art beyond saving.'

'Eliza!' Instantly, Sabina sunk further into the black, tar-like, water - despite all her might and will to reach her fallen child. The witch no longer cared for vengeance, for to physically hold onto Eliza again meant more to her than anything else. 'No! Help me, my child – save me!' pleaded Sabina; however, Eliza merely seemed to ignore her mother's desperation and presence now. 'Dost no love for me exist in thy heart? Art thou so filled with hatred against me, Eliza?' Sabina was now waist-deep in the viscous marsh. The thick mud and cold waters crushed the very air from Sabina's ribcage, filling her now with more anger and sorrow. 'My daughter. My precious... Eliza. For thee I shalt mourn over a thousand lifetimes. For thee—'

Through the distilled waters slowly emerged several corpse-like hands that pulled at Sabina's dress, dragging her further into her awaiting damnation. The witch used her razor-sharp fingernails to strike at the hands, though this only enticed more to emerge from the dark depths.

'Eliza!' screamed Sabina, desperate and driven by her innate love towards the child. 'Must thee forsake thy mother? Help me! Save thy mother from the clutches of demons!'

In her peripheral vision, Hannah noticed Sabina's present struggle, her anguish, and justified punishment. A maelstrom of emotions then flowed through Hannah, thereafter. Although she detested the witch, it was still hard to watch a mother and daughter being drawn apart by unseen forces. Nevertheless, after what cruelty Sabina's demon offered to her husband, Hannah soon rediscovered her disdain and firm resolve against the Red Ribbon Witch.

'What did you expect?' asked Hannah through gritted teeth, as she stared into Sabina's auburn eyes. Despite there being a poor field of vision, she could clearly see the witch's misery and remorse in them. 'You sold your soul to Satan. Rot in Hell... where you belong.'

'Eliza – please!' wailed Sabina as she desperately stretched out her remaining arm towards the child. 'Eliza!!' The demonic hands surrounding Sabina then dragged her deeper into her watery grave. 'NO!!'

With a haunting roar, Sabina's face eerily changed back to that of her malignant state: her eyes sunk back into their sockets, her skin fell deathly pale, her mouth foamed with a black substance. In knowing that she would never again hold onto her beloved daughter, Sabina's last desire was to inflict as much agony as possible on John – on the man who had wrought about this cruel fate – and she did so:

'SECARE!'

A deep, slashing wound instantly tore across John's throat as if it had been cut by a thick blade, and what breath remained in him then quickly escaped from the open wound. Sabina finally plunged into her horrific resting place, satisfied that her last incantation had managed to pull through. Eliza watched on in horror, shedding but a single tear in remorse, in wake of her mother's sordid fate.

'John!' screamed Hannah, whilst she and Lucy pressed their hands firmly against John's haemorrhaging windpipe. It was no use. 'No! Don't die! You can't die!'

John didn't feel any pain, that he had already spent. A calming warmth instead flowed through his body now, which increased once Eliza stood above him; her hands held out as if blessing him.

'Non senties dolore. Amoris sentire. Amoris sentire...'

298

John was certain that he was still conscious, but the sound of roaring flames and his family's cries no longer entered his ears. As he gradually awoke, he found himself sat upon his favourite bench in Whitby, overlooking the North Sea. The sun was starting to rise over the distance, and even a flock of monstrous seagulls flew overhead.

'How is this possible? Am I... dead?' John looked down and was shocked to find his body was no longer burned nor scarred – it was, in fact, completely unharmed. 'What's going on?' Suddenly, he felt a firm but gentle hand rustle across his shaven scalp.

'Hello, bonny-lad.'

'It can't be?' asked John as a powerful surge of joy and relief flowed across his renewed body. Without even needing to look, he swiftly recognised to whom the gentle voice and hand belonged to. 'Grandad? Is that... you?'

John's grandfather slowly sauntered around the bench to stand before him. Surprisingly, Grandpa Murray appeared younger, with his hair looking more blonde than white, his face plump and red – just as John remembered him to be during childhood.

'I'm dreaming,' said John dismissively. 'You haven't walked or talked for months.'

'How are you doing, Son?' asked Grandpa Murray, whilst casually seating himself beside John. After a momentary pause, he reached into one of his trouser pockets to retrieve a small, paper bag. 'Lemon sherbets. They're still you're favourite, aren't?' smiled John's grandfather. 'Go on and take a handful. I know you want to.'

'Thanks,' stuttered John as he reached into the bag, still held in disbelief. 'This can't be real? Is it real, Grandad?' He took a single sweet from the bag, savouring its familiar scent. On placing the hard piece of candy into his mouth John shuddered with joy – it tasted just as he remembered it! 'Nice. And, yes, they are still my favourite.' John's eyebrows rose in ecstasy, then the peculiar sensation of wanting to cry set in. 'It's so great to hear your voice again, Grandad. I almost forgot what you sounded like.

Grandpa Murray chuckled in response.

'Don't be so daft, John,' commented Grandpa Murray with a sly wink. 'I haven't gone yet, you know.'

'It's been so long since you last spoke to me,' John sniffled, as discreetly as he could. 'I miss you,' he whispered.

'Yes. I miss our little talks as well.' Grandpa Murray scrubbed away at John's scalp again. 'I'm glad that you got rid of that stupid mohawk hairstyle. You never suited it.'

'Oh, thanks very much,' sniggered John with an embarrassed smirk. He looked out again towards the serene ocean waves, their shimmering light somehow reflecting now upon Grandpa Murray's blue eyes. 'Lucy is doing well at nursery. She's growing up so fast.'

'I bet she is - clever lass,' commented Grandpa Murray with a widened smile. 'She's just like her dad. Mind you, at least she gets her good looks from Hannah,' he added, chuckling.

'I'm very proud of Lucy, Grandad. She keeps me going.' John reached into the bag for another sweet, and it tasted just as good as the previous one. 'Hannah's alright, too, but we've had a bad time recently.'

'Aye. That witch caused you some bother, didn't she?'

'How... how do you know about that?' questioned John, his expression both perplexed and saddened. 'You've been stuck in bed all this time.'

'AA little bird told me... and she'll be here soon,' explained Grandpa Murray in a jovial then woeful tone. 'I'm proud of who you've become, John. Always have been, always will be.'

'I don't see why,' interjected John. 'I'm hardly the best father or husband. I should have treated Hannah and Lucy better. I've taken them both for granted. I guess... it's too late to make up for things now.'

'Everyone makes mistakes,' said Grandpa Murray sympathetically. 'I've told you that plenty of times. When you sink to your lowest point, you're more open to make better changes in your life. You've got to take the good with the bad.' Grandpa Murray patted at John's knee, his way of showing him affection. He used to do this when John felt down or scared – even in later adulthood. 'Here, never mind looking so glum. Your ordeal's over now – lookahead and move on.' Grandpa Murray's smile widened even more, revealing his natural teeth in place of the empty mouth which now presently resided in real life. 'How about one of my jokes to cheer you up?'

'Erm...' John had heard all his grandfather's cheesy jokes before, but he did miss them and especially during more recent times. 'Go on then, Grandad. Make me laugh. Nothing dirty, though.'

'A group of German soldiers walk into a village, and the only thing there is this pig...' John rolled his eyes and tried to remember that his grandfather's generation did have a different, albeit less politically correct, sense of humour. 'Anyhow, one of these soldiers goes up to this pig and says, "Vair are all zee people?" The pig responds in a snorting voice, "I don't know." Another soldier turns up and says to the pig, "Tell us vair all ze people are. You know, Vee do have vays of making you *pork*!' Grandpa Murray immediately burst into a fit of laughter, whilst John stayed silent - at first. Soon enough, John smiled and laughed back in unison with his grandfather, both chortling away like naughty schoolboys. 'It's a good'un, isn't it?'

'Bloody Hell, Grandad.' John's voice rippled with an awkward sense of pleasure. 'You'd never get away with saying that one now.'

'Aye. Times have changed. We have changed, and change isn't always a bad thing.' Grandpa Murray's merry expression fell once again. 'We all have to move on at some point, John.'

'But... I don't want you to,' whimpered John in response with his head resting against his chest. 'I don't want you to move on. I'm not ready—'

'I've lived my life,' replied Grandpa Murray, and in a tone that would quickly dismiss his grandson's grief. 'I've seen my bairns grow old, and you and your sister become adults. I even had the chance to meet little Andrew and Lucy. I'm happy.' He winked to John playfully. 'It's your turn now. Stop with your boozing and focus on making your family happy – then *you* will be. It's not rocket science.'

'I know. I know, Grandad. I will make those changes.; John's voice rose out from his melancholy and now sounded positive for the first time in many months. 'I won't let you down. I won't let them down.'

A young girl's voice suddenly resounded alongside the passing breeze:

'You don't have long.'

John turned from Grandpa Murray to look back across the sweeping, sea waves. Eliza now stood upon the cliff's edge; her body still surrounded by a brilliant-white light. Sabina's daughter glanced between John and his grandfather, smiling gladly to both, as if relieved to see them sat together in this way.

'What are you doing here, Eliza?' John questioned somewhat anxiously. 'Was it *you* that healed me – that brought me here?'

'Your time spent with one another... is running out.'

'You heard the girl, John.' Grandpa Murray suddenly looked older and frailer, exactly as how John now recognised him to be. 'Be a good lad and send my love to everyone – especially your Gran.'

'No...' John moved his head slowly from side-to-side, interchanging his look between Grandpa Murray and Eliza. 'I don't want you to go. You can't go.'

'Henry...'

Eliza held out one her small hands, yearning for Grandpa Murray to clasp onto it. He did so, against John's reluctance, only after scrubbing away at his grandson's head once last time.

'Be at peace, John Davidson. Linger not in the past. Love your wife and child. Do not fall back into the darkness.'

'Don't go!' pleaded John as he attempted to latch onto his grandfather's arm in restraint. *'Please!'*

'Goodbye, bonny-lad. Don't get up to any mischief.' Grandpa Murray smiled and winked again to John as he stood himself up. A stronger burst of light then rose from the sun which fed through them all, and then it vanished to awaken John back into reality.

'Grandad?!'' John jolted upright, finding his skin to be again saturated with cold sweat. He was also somehow lain upon the living room's floor, exactly where he and his family had passed out the previous night. 'It was all a dream. It wasn't real.' John shot into the passageway, peering into his kitchen for any sign of life. 'The kettle's been boiled. Hannah?!' There was no reply. 'Lucy?!'

'Daddy! We're upstairs!'' Lucy's tone was laced with dread. 'Come up! Quick!'' John obeyed his daughter's request without question. As he entered his and Hannah's bedroom an even more surprising scene met with him. 'What are you doing, Hannah?'

'What does it look like I'm doing? I'm packing our things, John,' said Hannah as she busily folded a pile of John's clothes into their holiday suitcase. 'I can't anymore.'

'Are you... throwing me out? Are you leaving me?' John choked on his words. For so long now he had only focused on Sabina when, if truth be told, he should have been devoting his time on Hannah and Lucy. In this dire moment, John's whole world began to collapse around him. The very thought of his wife and child leaving him was more haunting than the Red Ribbon Witch herself. 'I'm sorry, Han. I'm sorry for everything. I'll do anything I can to make things right,' he uttered, held deep in remorse. 'Please don't leave me. I love you and Lucy more than anything.'

'I'm not leaving you!' emphasized Hannah with a dismissive shrug, breaking her husband's emotional paralysis. 'We're *all* leaving - today. I've arranged with my mam and yours to stay at their houses until we can find a new house.' She glanced again at John, sensing his dread. 'I can't stay here - not for even one more night.'

John scrubbed away at his scalp, lost for words, though secretly he welcomed Hannah's revelation.

'You... want to move?' John wrapped his arms around Lucy, her gentle skin and scent instantly calming him. 'To be honest, I've already been looking for somewhere else. There's a house close to your mam's in Hawkesdale Place. I arrange for a viewing in a few days or so.'

'That's fine. Anywhere will do. Anywhere... but here.' Hannah zipped the suitcase shut, just about managing to contain its contents. 'It's not safe for us to stay here, John.'

'Why?'

'You *know* why,' hinted Hannah with a confused expression. She didn't need to speak another word on the subject for John to understand this decision of hers. 'My dad's coming in half-an-hour to collect us, so get showered. The sooner I can get out this house, the better.'

'Aww! But I won't see Eliza anymore if we move,' whined Lucy, as she leant herself into John's side. 'I'll miss her *so* much.'

'Listen to me, young lady,' retorted Hannah as gently as she could. 'From now on we'll never speak about Eliza or her mammy again. Is that understood?'

'Aye,' agreed John, like a bashful child.

'Yes, Mammy,' mumbled Lucy, in unison with her father's submission. 'I'll be a good girl.'

'I seriously can't wait to leave this place.' Precisely as Hannah had instructed, within twenty minutes or so, Ivan arrived with Barbara. They had left their car's engine on in anticipation of a rush to escape Skipton Road would certainly follow.

'Alright, John?' gleamed Ivan to him, hinting at some apprehension in his voice. 'I thought you said that this was a nice estate. It mustn't be, if Hannah wants to move so quick.'

'It's not that, mate,' replied John, politely. 'The neighbours are spot-on, it's just—'

'There's a house closer to you we've come across, Dad,' interjected Hannah. 'And it's closer to Lucy's school. That's why we're moving.'

'Okay. Seems like a good reason to me,' assured Ivan, raising both palms in defence. It goes without saying that he was taken aback by Hannah's sharp response. 'I'll give you a hand to move some of the smaller things. There should be enough room in our boot to carry a few boxes, I reckon.'

'Don't worry, Dad. John can get Dennis to collect whatever's left. I want to leave... and now.' Hannah softly wept as she lifted Lucy up into her arms, and then brushed past John towards Barbara's people-carrier. 'Let's go, John.'

'I can't believe that we're leaving,' sighed John to Barbara. 'I wanted to make this "our home", to make a fresh start for us all.'

'You've done nothing wrong, pet,' said Barbara in assurance, whilst hugging into John to offer him some much-needed comfort. 'There's still plenty of time for that. Things don't always go to plan in life; that's what makes it interesting.'

Before locking his kitchen door for the last time, John grimaced in confusion - there wasn't a smell of death anymore, and the haunting sensation that had recently tormented him and his family seemed to have lifted away.

'Goodbye... Sabina.' John slowly turned the key into its locking position, finding it painful to do so – but why? The Red Ribbon Witch was no-more. Surely, Sabina could not taunt him forever?

'Not *another* one,' whined Pat to John. She was stood with her arms over John's fence, glaring over towards her absconding neighbours with a judgemental stare. 'At least you're getting out before you go cuckoo!' she laughed, though no-one else present saw the funny side of this. 'Take care, dearies. Hopefully, things will turn out alright for you now.'

'Cheers, Pat. See you later.' John immediately turned to look at Sid's adjoining fence and then exhaled a deep sigh of relief at the fact he wasn't there. 'Fuck you, Sid. I won't be missing you.'

'I can see why you want to move now,' chuckled Ivan to Hannah. 'With neighbours like that, I couldn't blame you.'

'There's far worse, Dad.' Hannah looked up herself towards Sid's house and like John was thankful at his apparent absence. 'Come on, Lucy. There's a good girl. We're staying at Nanna's house for a few days.'

'It's okay, Mammy,' said Lucy, almost joyful in her composure. 'Eliza isn't here anymore. She can sleep now.'

As Barbara pulled her car out of Skipton Road, John felt a strange feeling of grief and sadness at leaving. This peculiar urge soon passed, however, along with the hatred he had grown from spending so much time there.

306

'Are you okay, hun?' asked Hannah to John, whilst the two held one another's trembling hands. 'We'll be alright.'

'Yeah.' John looked to his wife in the way he did when they first met. 'I feel better already. I Love you.'

'I love you, too.'

The proceeding week, which should have been a relaxing time off work for John, proved to be a chaotic nightmare. Hannah took the lead this time in contacting their new landlord, thankfully removing this heavy burden from John. In fairness, he was still attempting to recover from the haunting experience at Skipton Road, from Sabina's possession over him.

'Dad's going to shift the rest of our stuff today,' said John to Hannah over Barbara's breakfast table. It was their second week at her house, and neither had suffered any further encounters with the witch, nor her demon. 'We should be able to move into Hawkesdale tomorrow... fingers crossed.'

'Thank God,' Hannah replied wearily. 'I can't bear another night with Lucy not sleeping.' She leant over to whisper into John's ears, 'She's still talking about *Eliza*.'

'That's not a bad thing, Han,' assured John. He then looked across to his daughter, who herself was gorging on an oversized bowl of sugary cereal. 'As long as she's happy - as long as you're happy - then so am I.'

With an anxious expression, Hannah held onto John's hands and asked him, 'What did you do with the Ouija board and that horrible figurine? Don't tell me you've gotten them hidden somewhere.'

'No. I burned the Ouija board and threw that figurine of Baal into the stream that runs alongside Skipton Road,' assured John. 'You've got nothing to worry about. I'll buy anything like that again.'

'Morning, campers!' bellowed Ivan in an energetic voice. 'Are you going to have a house-warming this time round, John?'

'Too right!' John's enthusiasm also spread into Hannah's more-reserved thoughts. 'It'd be a good way to catch up with folks.'

'Good lad!' rejoiced Ivan. He then leant down to kiss Lucy upon her brow. 'Are you excited about seeing your new bedroom, Lucy?'

'Yes, Grandad!' gleamed the child. 'I wish my friend Eliza could come, but she can't.' Hannah gestured towards her daughter to end this conversation promptly. It was a wasted effort. 'She's happy now. She's waiting for Grandpa.' Ivan looked over his bi-focals to fixate on John and Hannah with a beleaguered stare. 'He won't be poorly anymore... where Eliza sleeps.'

'That's no-more sugary cereal for you then, young missy!' chortled Ivan to Lucy, somewhat anxiously. He could see how distressed Hannah had become, so chose not to divulge more into this subject. 'You'd better get your things packed again, Han, if you're going to be moving in tomorrow.'

'It's sorted, Dad.' Hannah shoved aside her plate of buttered toast, feeling full now and in more ways than one. 'Thanks again for helping us out.'

'No worries.'

The move went ahead without a single issue, despite the short length of time in which it was organised. Dennis wasn't too happy about having to shift John's belongings without him and struggled to understand why his son chose to stay away from Skipton Road. To be fair on Dennis, he wasn't given a decent explanation, although once he caught a glimpse of Sid it all began to make sense.

***

On the evening of John and his family's first day at Hawkesdale Place, most of their relatives and friends turned up to celebrate alongside them. It would be a joyous occasion, though one that would quickly turn sorrowful. As John laughed with Donnie and Ryan his mother, Toyah, approached him. She was trembling, weeping, with her phone still clenched tightly within her hands.

'John, sweetheart,' stammered Toyah to her son. 'Grandpa Murray's passed away. Your uncle has just phoned me...' She threw herself into John's waiting arms. He should have felt sad, but he didn't, not even in the slightest. Why should he have been sorrowful? Eliza's vision proved to be of great comfort to him during this moment, as it vanquished any resentment or expected melancholy. John knew that his grandfather was being well cared for. 'I can't believe it, John. I can't believe my dad has died.'

'It's okay, Mam,' whispered John into his mother's left ear, as he solemnly embraced her. 'Grandad's not suffering now. Was Grandma with him?'

'Yes,' sniffled Toyah, barely able to form a basic syllable. Her flowing tears immediately drew the attention of Hannah and the rest of their family over. 'Your Grandma and Aunty Margo were with him. They were singing his favourite song, *What A Wonderful World*, before he stopped breathing.' Toyah now began to sob uncontrollably. It was understandable given her great loss.

'Oh, John,' said Hannah, looking over in sympathy to both himself and Toyah. 'Poor Grandad.' She sprinted over and then, with John and Toyah, they embraced one another. 'I'm so sorry. He was such a kind man.'

'It's okay, Hannah. John is right.' Toyah formed a faint smile, aimed solely against her son. 'My dad's not suffering anymore. You look so much like him, John, when he was younger.'

'He'll always be with us,' assured John. 'Grandad will be looking down on us all – right now. He wouldn't be best-pleased in seeing you cry, Mam.' He gently rubbed at Hannah's back and she responded in the same, loving way. 'We'd better go and see Gran... and Grandad. Sorry, folks,' said John to his fellow guests standing by in observation. 'The party's over. Thanks for coming.'

John supported his mother and stepfather in any way he could as they stepped into Grandpa Murray's silent home. Grandma Murray was sat beside her husband, still rubbing at his arthritic hands affectionately, lost in a painful grief that was beyond description. One-by-One, John and his relatives sat beside their beloved father-figure, each sharing with him their final and solemn farewells.

'Love you, Grandad. Rest in peace.' John slowly leant down over his grandfather's rigid body to place a gentle kiss upon his cold forehead. In all honesty, there wasn't much left for John to say, not after Eliza's gifted meeting between them. 'I know you're at rest, Grandad. You're not in any pain now. Don't get up to any mischief – wherever you are.' And with that - after giving Grandma Murray and Toyah an extended hug - John left, not shedding a single tear.

Hannah and Lucy waited patiently in their new kitchen, fearful of what state John would be in on his return. Would he be sad? Would he be angry? Would he have snuck off to the Tin Donkey pub and come home drunk? As John entered his home, Hannah and Lucy immediately sprinted over to him. The three stood there for a few minutes, not saying a word nor moving an inch away from one another.

'How's Grandma coping?' asked Hannah nervously, whilst hugging into John with all her strength. 'Poor Marie. I can't imagine what she's going through.'

'Gran will be alright,' replied John in a surprisingly calm tone. 'I'm exhausted. It's an early night for me, I think.'

'Yeah. That's sounds like a good idea.' Hannah softly nudged Lucy away from her grasp, directing the child towards their living room. 'It'll do you some good to have some alone time, you know, to think things over.' John shook his head against this notion. It would be the total opposite of what he now desired. 'What? You want us to come to bed as well with you?'

'If you don't mind, Han?' John held out a steady palm for Hannah to hold onto. 'It'd be nice just to have a chillout session –

310

like we used to.' Hannah flickered her eyelashes, trying not to break from her strong composure. She had so far managed to avoid crying. 'I'll put some tunes on my phone. I want this first night in our new house to be relaxing.' Hannah nodded back enthusiastically and then called out for Lucy to join both herself and John in walking upstairs. 'Bedtime, Lucy!' bellowed John enthusiastically. 'We're going for a lie-down – listen to some music together.' The child soon returned to her parents, displaying a keen smile herself. 'There's my girl. Let's go and have a nice lie down.'

John's new home had no foul smells within it, no dark bricks outside (they were a pleasant, golden-brown colour), no random scratch marks, and no apparent signs of any haunting – it was perfect. Together, John and his small family lay upon his bed, directly beside one another. They stared at the pristine-white ceiling, sensing no malignant presence, only a reignited love and sense of security between them.

'Have you thought of any names, yet?' questioned Hannah to John with a satisfied smirk, whilst glancing down towards her expanding womb. 'I can't wait to tell everyone about the scan results. In hindsight, maybe we should have told them at the start of our party?' she wallowed.

'No. It'll be a nice surprise – especially for Mam and Grandma,' John insisted, while stroking at his wife's tender abdomen. He could feel the odd kick inside it which made his smile widen even more. 'What about "Poppy" or "Sophia".'

'Sophia!' interjected Lucy, who herself started to rub at her mother's budging belly. 'Baby Sophia! My baby sister!'

'Well, that's us told!' chuckled John. 'It's settled then. Hello, Sophia,' he whispered tenderly, to Hannah's motioning stomach. 'We can't *wait* to meet you, sweetheart.'

'I like it,' said Hannah in agreement. 'Sophia Marie Davidson.' She then carefully reached over for John's phone. 'Can we listen to some 'Disturbed'? I like the new song they've brought out, that 'Simon and Garfunkel' cover: *Sound of Silence.*'

'Nah, sneered John with a playful wink. 'I want you to listen to another one first. It's called *Walls* by the 'Kings of Leon'. It's just come out. The words pretty much sum up all the chaos we've been through recently. See what you think.' John gently removed the phone from Hannah's possession, then filtered through its YouTube app to land upon this new favourite track of his. The starting chords instantly set Lucy off into a deep sleep. Hannah and John gradually followed suit, both dozing off into their own unearthly realms.

'Love you, Han,' whispered John, displaying all the love he held for her within a single breath. '*You're* the light in my darkness.'

'Love you too, babe,' Hannah replied bashfully, now finding the love which she and John had lost at Skipton suddenly reignite itself. 'I think the worst is over for us now.'

'Aye,' replied John in a confident voice. '*This* is our home now. No more witches or demons - no more booze or cigarettes – just us.'

John and his family never encountered the Red Ribbon Witch or the ancient marshlands of Newton Escomb in their nightmares again. They had finally achieved their 'new' start in life and, with baby Sophia, they looked ahead to the future, no longer dwelling on their haunted past. Baal, on the other hand, had one last message to share with John before parting ways with him:

'Once connected, never can a bond be broken!'

EPILOGUE

It was three o'clock in the morning and all of Skipton Road's occupants were fast asleep – all but one. Sid left from his home in a drunken stupor, covered from head-to-toe in his own urine and faeces, his foul stench made even worse by the dense fog that swept around him. Nestled within a trembling fist, Sid held a torn carrier bag full of black candles, and in the other hand a half-empty bottle of over-proof vodka (which he gulped down profusely).

'Bastards!' howled Sid into the stale night air. 'Where am I gonna get the fuckin' rent money from now? Selfish Bastards!' Sid stumbled precariously into the garden next door, almost falling over a passing black cat. 'Fuck off, ya flea-bitten, little twat! Go on... FUCK OFF!'

John's old home looked vacant from the outside, though Sid - being a so-called psychic - keenly sensed that there remained a powerful presence within. He approached the door, licking at blistered lips hungrily, and closed his eyes.

'I'm comin', Sabina. Just you fuckin' wait for me! I'll never let ya down!' Sid managed to somehow place his vodka bottle down upon the concrete path below without shattering it. Then, after holding back a rising flow of self-induced vomit, he reached into a back pocket where his landlord's copy-key lay. Sid smirked to himself sadistically. 'You're not leaving me - not ever! Ya hear? NEVER!'

Inside the abandoned home, its kitchen space was now totally bare and not even a single aroma lingered, apart from Sid's pungent body odour. John had hastily painted over all the demon's scratch marks before he left to ensure no lasting evidence would exist. John's act of cleaning merely enraged Sid even more.

'I'm sorry, Sabina!' wailed Sid, whilst shaking his head towards the cold surface of the floor. 'What have they done to you? This wasn't meant to happen!'

Despite his inebriation, Sid managed to gather his senses: an important task lay ahead of him. 'I know you're down there – somewhere. I wish I could hold ya. I fuckin' love ya, Sabina!' Sid then carefully laid out his black candles to form them into a perfect circle around him, also placing a single red ribbon amongst them at their centre, and then he revealed a toothless smile.

'I said to ya that I'd make things right, didn't I?' gasped Sid, remorsefully, like an addict fighting their urges. 'I said that I'd enact your revenge, and *I'm* not a man that breaks a promise!'

As a cold wave of air swept over him, Sid carefully lit each candle with his cigarette lighter; the burning circle formed perfectly over where Sabina's body had been laid to rest hundreds of years prior. Sid then knelt himself as if in prayer, with his arms held out to either side of him.

'I summon thee, *Witch of The Marshlands*!' he declared ecstatically. 'I summon thee, *Scarlet Angel of Vengeance*!' Sid's voice rose like the thunderous plains witnessed in Sabina's visions, as did the flames upon each candle. 'I summon thee, *Lord of Deception - Lord of Malice*! I summon thee, Baal! I summon thy gracious presences! SABINA! BAAL! RISE!'

Suddenly, Sid felt a cold breath run down the back of his neck - just as all the black candles sporadically extinguished. He could sense someone or something lurking directly from behind him now. In this moment, Sid froze in a cocktail of fear and servitude. His incantation had worked... yet again.

'Ego Sabina... Ego sum Rubrum Uitta Pythonissam!'

The End

Thank you for reading this second edition of my debut horror novel. I would greatly appreciate it if you could leave an honest review on Amazon and/or Goodreads.

Also...

I would be more than happy to answer any questions that you may have on my email, Facebook and/or Twitter addresses.

With kind regards,
Andrew John Bell (a.k.a. John Davidson)

BOOKS AVAILABLE AND UPCOMING

*** Literary Fiction ***

One Day of Lucidity

An honest and moving account of caring for someone at the end of their life.

Isabella Cunningham awakens to find herself being cared for by unfamiliar people, in an unfamiliar setting, and with little knowledge of how this has come to be. She can no longer talk or move, and to her further dismay is confined within a nursing bed. Unable to fully express herself, Isabella's only means of solace lie in her love for classical music, her enduring sense of humour, a passionate determination to be reunited with her loved ones - particularly her husband - and to discover what ailments now forge their cruel hold. Through a series of peculiar events and moving flashbacks, Isabella gradually learns of what is inflicting her body and mind, her true age, and why her family appear to be so distant at times - all during this one day of lucidity.

The reader is placed into Isabella's vulnerable position - to look through her eyes - to see and feel what she is going through. The author has written this novel to highlight some common provisions and experiences relating to cancer, dementia and palliative care, in the hope of addressing the stigma that still surrounds them. There are many people like Isabella in our world... this book is dedicated to each of them and their caregivers.

An ideal read for fans of Lisa Genova and Wendy Mitchell which is available now on Amazon Kindle and Paperback.

The Skipton Haunting:
Curse of the Red Ribbon Witch

Two years have passed since the events seen in *Tale of the Red Ribbon Witch*.

As a result of accepting a promotion at work, Christopher Joyce had no option but to relocate his family from London to Newton Escomb in County Durham, where he would be a Safety Officer at the local chemicals factory. Due to the cheap rent and ideal location, Christopher set his heart on moving into a house situated along Skipton Road, despite holding no knowledge of its sordid past.

Almost instantly, Christopher and his family sensed that they were not alone within their new dwelling. Through a series of harrowing nightmares and unexplainable occurrences, the Joyce family soon came to learn of two demonic presences – Sabina, the Red Ribbon Witch, and an ancient demon – Baal. Christopher's wife, Amy, gradually bore the brunt of Sabina's malice, with the witch slowly taking over her body and soul after preying on her weaknesses. Unable to watch his wife and children suffer any longer, Christopher set in motion a turn of events that would forever change their family, and also their belief in the supernatural.

(Anticipated release date on Amazon Kindle/Paperback: September 2019)

ABOUT THE AUTHOR

Andrew John Bell was born and raised in Newton Aycliffe, County Durham, England, UK. He is a full-time Senior Care Assistant that specialises in caring for people who suffer from Alzheimer's disease (along with other mental and physical health illnesses), a keen musician and (now) an avid believer in the supernatural.

Writing is Andrew's form of escape and is a passion which he hopes to continue throughout his upcoming fantasy and horror books. This novel *is* based on an actual 'haunting' experience that Andrew and his family once faced. They now live happily at a new address, having not seen the 'Red Ribbon Witch' since leaving their previous home, although the memories of that horrendous time still linger on to this day.

www.ingramcontent.com/pod-product-compliance
Lightning Source LLC
Chambersburg PA
CBHW020910200626
46814CB00001BA/264